Regrowth

NORTHWESTERN WORLD CLASSICS

Northwestern World Classics brings readers
the world's greatest literature. The series features
essential new editions of well-known works,
lesser-known books that merit reconsideration,
and lost classics of fiction, drama, and poetry.
Insightful commentary and compelling new translations
help readers discover the joy of outstanding writing
from all regions of the world.

Der Nister

Regrowth

*Seven Tales of Jewish Life Before,
During, and After Nazi Occupation*

Translated from the Yiddish by Erik Butler

Northwestern University Press ✦ *Evanston, Illinois*

Northwestern University Press
www.nupress.northwestern.edu

English translation copyright © 2011 by Northwestern University Press.
Published 2011. Yiddish edition originally published as *Vidervuks* (Moscow: Sovietski Pisatel, 1969). All rights reserved.

Printed in the United States of America

10 9 8 7 6 5 4 3 2 1

Library of Congress Cataloging-in-Publication Data

Nister, 1884–1950.
    [Vidervuks. English]
    Regrowth : seven tales of Jewish life before, during, and after
Nazi occupation / Der Nister; translated from the Yiddish by Erik
Butler.
      p. cm. — (Northwestern world classics)
    "Yiddish edition originally published as Vidervuks in 1969."
    ISBN-13: 978-0-8101-2736-4 (pbk. : alk. paper)
    ISBN-10: 0-8101-2736-9 (pbk. : alk. paper)
    1. Nister, 1884–1950. 2. Nister, 1884–1950—Translations into
English. I. Title. II. Series: Northwestern world classics.
PJ5129.K27V513 2011
839.133—dc22

                                      2011000502

My thanks, first of all, to Henry Hollander of San Francisco. Some years ago, he made this project possible by selling me the Yiddish original of the work here translated; this acquisition was my introduction to Der Nister. I am also grateful to Jeremy Dauber and the Institute for Israel and Jewish Studies at Columbia University, as well as to Marina Rustow and the Tam Institute for Jewish Studies at Emory University for the opportunity to deliver talks about my research on this singular author. Marian Broida, Elena Glazov-Corrigan, and Juliette Stapanian-Apkarian patiently answered my questions about Hebrew and Russian expressions. Valuable feedback on matters of English style was provided by Jackie Abrams, Elizabeth Bishop, Adam Rosenthal, and Andy Shoenig. I also appreciate the interest that Dan Friedman, Shawn-Marie Garrett, Sander Gilman, and Caroline Manesse have shown for the project. Henry Carrigan, Jenny Gavacs, and Anne Gendler at Northwestern University Press helped this book see print. As always, my heartfelt gratitude goes to my family, especially my mother. Kimberly Jannarone deserves the greatest praise for reading everything, urging me to share Der Nister's works with a broader audience, and, finally, being the best companion anyone could desire.

The stories presented in this volume offer considerable difficulty to the translator. Der Nister's *Vidervuks* moves between unmannered folk culture and high modernist artifice. While written in Yiddish, the tales include words and phrases in Hebrew, German, and Slavic languages. I have made an effort to preserve Der Nister's style and syntax as much as possible. Occasionally, a foreign word is used in order to preserve the tone of the source text; section divisions (which can be idio-syncratic) are retained as well. Explanatory notes have been kept to a minimum, for enhanced readability. Anyone drawn to the subtleties of Der Nister's art should consult the original, whose richness exceeds anything a translation can provide.

Regrowth

Meylekh Magnus

(Pages of a Biography)

1

"What? When was that?!"

It was approximately the sixth or seventh year[*] when Meylekh Magnus (as people still called him then) became a regular at Feygele's. Even though her cheeks had a sickly red to them (because her lungs weren't right, she often joked), Feygele had many suitors, many followers, many admirers. . . . She would ask: "Well, what do you think? How long do I still have to gad about? How many more brides will I rob of their fiancés?" Even though they always found her in her special, girlish room, perched on the soft ottoman with her feet drawn up beneath her, her dress pulled over her knees, and always wrapped in a soft shawl, because she was chilly—despite all that, the gentlemen callers were much, much more numerous at her place than at those of other ladies. Why was that? Because something looked out at them from the black, cleverly arranged locks over her short-haired, boyish forehead—something that gave her the appeal of both sexes at once. And when she nimbly, in a catlike manner, cast one of her glamours—even just a

[*]That is, 1906 or 1907.

glance—at her admirers, a cooling and cooking in their hearts would start. Moreover, she had a smooth little tongue, which extracted one pearl of wisdom after another, one joke after the next, so that she was never outshone by anyone. . . .

"Oh, oh," her admirers quietly thought in great amazement. With enamored sighs, they sought to be close to her.

That's what it was like to desire someone. . . . And now, to-day, who should show up other than the same lucky soul who, until now, had never once crossed her doorway? The one who, as might be thought, also had had no reason to come: he was a bookworm who kept far away from women, out of bashfulness; all the comrades in the Karlikow party, to which he belonged, made jokes about him. They did so as one jokes about an old maid, even though, for all that, he wasn't old at all yet. On the contrary, he was young and in the prime of youth: he was always modestly dressed, he always had his hair precisely parted, and he was always so smooth-shaven that one might have even thought he had nothing to shave.

Yes, he was a little odd—an eccentric who stuck to the periphery in all the company he kept, except for the group in which he was a party member. He performed editorial work for them, correcting and improving items in the daily press—and more serious print matters, too, for they had enlisted him as someone with great knowledge in many different fields.

Except for those duties, he kept away even from those nearest to him—to the extent that nobody even knew where he lived, how he lived, or with whom he was friends.

They only knew that he was very musical, and that he could, without a sound, sing entire operas, as if he had the score lying before his eyes. Moreover, it was known that he performed concerts for himself alone—for nobody—as he stood at the window or, at other times, facing the wall. Strange!

And even stranger: as decently and as courteously as he acted toward those who were in his camp, he did just the opposite with people on another side. He did so even with people he had only just met, who had made the slightest turn in a direction other than his—by belonging, let us say, to another Karlikow party (when, fundamentally, there wasn't such a big difference between his group and theirs at all).

For example, people talked about how, once, in the fifth year,* one night he had had to provide shelter to a comrade involved in a conspiracy—a man who, only a little while back, had drifted over from his party to another. When that individual stayed with him in his little room—the one with a single, tiny table, a little bench, and a bed—and the time came to go to sleep, he let the man, his former comrade, have the bed. He sat awake the whole night, not wishing to argue or be his neighbor even in sleep—and he also didn't exchange a single word with him before bedtime, because of his dislike and incomprehension of the man.

Yes, as resolutely sectarian as he had proved with men, then, it was understandable that he would hold distant from relationships with women, now. People found it only natural, and they ascribed it to his dry character—about which, from time to time, they permitted themselves a little joke, but nothing more.

Everyone made peace with his reserve, and they didn't press him, try to change him, or impose ways that were different from the ones he had been given. He was accepted as he was, and they respected him for his conscientiousness and great knowledge, which he displayed in fulfilling his duties and obligations to the party.

But then again, on holidays, at comradely get-togethers— when people let go and the group brought in the last of the liquor—you could also see how he warmed up and joined in

*A year of widespread civil unrest in the Russian Empire following decades of populist initiatives. The resulting reforms did not satisfy revolutionary ambitions and led both to governmental backlash and heightened activism (in smaller groups).

the celebration. They brought him one cup after the other: "Drink, drink up, Meylekh!" Then, when he had grown somewhat heated—when color appeared in his always-pale face, his gray eyes began to shine, and his permanently closed mouth started to speak more freely—then no one could resist his performance of the "hit song" he kept ready for such times. It was a song of the people, "My Mikhelke." On such occasions, he would sing out with great enthusiasm and display his trained voice.

"My Mikhelke, my Mikhelke, who lives on the long street . . . ," it went. Then, festively, he would stand up on his chair. When the song reached the refrain—"He gives me, he gives me a little whistle"—then he showed his skill with his lips, teaching the group, which had joined in, the measure and the rhythm: how to whistle softly and in the most musical manner.

And then . . . having finished his "hit song"—being done with "My Mikhelke"—he became an outsider again, with tightly closed, thin lips and a newly pale face (despite the alcohol he had consumed, which, for a time—before the singing and during the song—had warmed him up). And for the whole evening afterward—when everybody else had found a partner to pass time with in secret company—then, he, Meylekh, would stay somewhere, in a corner, without a companion, alone, and in the dark (whether he felt sorry for himself or not, it was impossible to tell).

And then, all of a sudden, there he was: Meylekh at Feygele's—the girl young men from here and elsewhere were always visiting. They received a warm welcome from her parents—and also, especially, from her. Sitting at her place in her room, shivering on the ottoman, she felt like someone whom all the passing, youthful feet were incapable of avoiding. Whether visitors had serious intentions or not, they had to stop in and see her.

She was well known in party circles as a compassionate daughter of the well-to-do. They demanded nothing more from her—or from her parents, who, although they didn't participate in the "movement," also didn't lock the door on people whose credit wasn't too good with the political powers of the time (or with those who served them—the police and gendarmerie, who kept a careful watch).

By the way, they—the parents—did so, first, for the sake of their little daughter, who wanted it, because it provided her with an impish, girlish joy. And, second, they also did so because of their moral, liberal principles. They knew that their house, as the dwelling of people who earned quite well, stood above suspicion, and that it therefore provided protection to those who were, in fact, themselves suspicious—the kind that should be observed more closely (if, after all, they had somehow managed to gain entry into a house like that).

Yes, all that is true, but how, then, does Meylekh wind up at Feygele's?

Here's how:

It was already after Year Five, after the Revolution had gone down the drain—after many Karlikow parties were through and members had run off; after the masses had withdrawn support, their hopes disappointed. The riverbed stayed so dry, afterward, that there was no longer even a sign it had existed. It was after the greatest part of the intellectual participants and activists in the movement (who, meanwhile, had few enduring ties with the masses—even if, apparently, they had enjoyed their favor in the time of revolution) now no longer had anything more to do among the people. And so they returned to their fathers' professions, where they had come from—the one to trade and finance, as an employee in a countinghouse or bank, and another to his studies, which he had broken off when the movement swept him along.

There, then, was someone like Meylekh Magnus—a rider struck from the saddle. Not having anywhere to go—because his earlier party occupation had become void—now, he was forced to do *something* against the emptiness that followed the excitement, even if it meant something like running after a young lady. . . .

Whether he displayed any initiative of his own when once— one evening—he went into Feygele's room there . . . or maybe it wasn't his own idea, and a friend or acquaintance dragged him along (another thing that would have been utterly impossible beforehand). One way or the other, when it happened— that is, when Meylekh entered Feygele's room there—he surprised even himself—and certainly Feygele, too. She had heard much about him—both in general terms (that he was a very serious person) and in particular (that he possessed great knowledge). For all that, he still was known for being so disconnected and distant from women that he was the subject of everyone's conversation, and people talked about him as a singular exception. But now it had happened—to her, Feygele, her alone. She was certainly flattered by the visit. It surprised her, and she considered herself an exception, too—that is, she thought even a man like Meylekh wasn't beyond her womanly charm: he, too, wanted to enter her doorway—or didn't—he *had to*. . . .

Thus, Feygele already knew about him, about Meylekh. The very fact that he was spotted in this cozy, feminine environment—where the walls were hung with carpets, and the girl herself sat on an ottoman, lighted by a lamp under a rosy-reddish shade on a nearby table . . . This fact—that he had been sighted where he never had been seen before—this, already, said something about him. So it was understandable that his face started to change from pale to red and his mouth stayed closed around his firmly sealed lips. But then it opened! Hoarsely, he let out a low, limping sound (an uneven one, like a boy whose voice is cracking or someone who hasn't cleared his throat well).

He felt frightfully lost the whole first evening. If she, Feygele, had not known who was sitting before her—afterward, after his departure, having heard what he had said to her (and hadn't said—just half muttered, half mumbled)—she might have made fun of him or, in her clever way, even tarred and feathered him altogether.

But she didn't do that. She saw that his air of being lost and his half-mute mumbling were not the result of ignorance or because he didn't have anything to say in general. No, it was just because she, as a woman, had made such a strong impression on him—a man who was not used to women. This had made him alternately dumb and the opposite: so that he talked too much and beside the point. . . .

And it was off. . . . Already after the first visit at Feygele's, Meylekh was caught, as they say, both in one way—and in the other, too. If he stayed away from women—it was far. But as soon as he had made the first step, suddenly he knew no way to stop. He felt bound—unable to tear himself away. And, as much as he had previously been capable of giving his sectarian fervor and devotion over to party activities—to the same extent, now, he transferred his zeal to another area, as if he saw nothing more in the universe than her, Feygele—there on her ottoman, always wrapped in a shawl, because she was sickly and it was a little cold.

He became a constant visitor at her place. . . . Whether he said anything at all when he sat before Feygele or not—if he was silent—it's all the same. He never tore his eyes away from her. He was like a worshipper before an idol; his gazes were directed toward her in silent, respectful amazement. Soon, one thought, he would open his mouth and utter a prayer.

Feygele did not push him away. On the contrary: she preferred his visits to those of the others, and she observed ceremony much more closely when he was there. When he sat before her, she wouldn't allow herself any frivolous or loose behavior (as she did with the others). Quite the opposite: she established a kind of respectful boundary, and she didn't dare exit or step out of it—not when he quietly said something into her ear, and even when he just sat there, silently enamored and wrapped up in his thoughts.

All her previous interaction with this stranger—about whom *they,* during his initial visits, had even laughed, because they did not consider him a real competitor. . . . Now, with regret, they came to the conclusion that their own efforts and great familiarity with Feygele had remained without success. The opposite had occurred. For the very reason why, according to them, Meylekh had had no chance with her—now, by some misunderstanding or because of a womanly caprice, he had been chosen. Finally—one fine day—she would say to him what all the others, already for a long time now, had been waiting to hear in vain. Yes, she was his. . . .

That's how it was. Her suitors saw it, and her parents did, too. The latter certainly did not object, for they saw in him, in Meylekh there, a very odd but very, very enamored party—a man with a strong, clean past, who would certainly keep their one and only, spoiled little daughter honorably and protect her (as is the characteristic of a man like that when he falls head over heels and gives himself over to love that can look no other way). That's how it was. A word on her part, or a wave on his, and the open declaration of their engagement would happen. In fact, people already thought they could sense its imminent proclamation. It was clear that one morning, they would find both of them, Meylekh and Feygele, sitting together hand in hand, united as bride and groom.

But then, suddenly, something occurred that disturbed the couple's union.

It happened one evening, when Meylekh had come to Feygele on a bridegroom's visit. He already felt secure that he was coming to his rightful place, so to speak (because, the next morning, all the outsiders would leave them alone, to pronounce the final word). But then and there it happened that, along with Meylekh, another one of Feygele's acquaintances made his way in. The latter was a former activist in the socialist movement. However, after the fifth year—after the revolutionary wave had drained off—he, too, had been in a state of decline. It seems that out of disappointment and despair he was keeping to the side, inactive. Yet as a person with strong social convictions, he felt that he was living without air, and he tumbled over into the so-called anarchist party—which, truly, was not really a party all but rather a scattered, demoralized gang that still had the party phraseology (in appearance, anyway) and was concerned with the "loose ends" of party business. In fact, they were already acting more for their own benefit—for their stray, wayward bellies and pockets.

He was a young man from the ranks of the "Homels" or the "Białystoks"—at that time, the last remaining nests where people like that still lingered. Previously, he had been a successful agitator and propagandist, with the necessary skills and abilities. Also, besides that, he was a sly fox, a clever fellow. He was the kind who, if he hadn't slipped and fallen, would have been a smash in all kinds of society (and especially among women, whom he liked a great deal—and they liked him, finding both masculine charm and wisdom in him, as well as everything else they value).

He arrived drunk and brazen, with the broad dissoluteness of a stray anarchist who knew that, as he sat there and seemed to spend his time the same as everyone else, he was already a candidate for arrest, which had to occur eventually. The police were on the hunt for him, following him step by step. Soon, they would grab him and lead him off to where he "belonged"; after a quick "trial" and a little time in the death chamber, he would be married to the noose. It's possible that the police would do it, but it was also possible that they wouldn't—because he wouldn't allow them to. He would resist, as was the commandment for anarchists. Seeing himself surrounded and without hope of getting out and giving his pursuers the slip, he would shoot himself with a bullet from his own "piece" (which people like him carried constantly—he even kept his under the pillow at night).

He came in, as if to his own house, a little drunk. When he entered Feygele's room and found Meylekh there—at his rightful, bridegroom's place, right next to Feygele—he knew, it seems, what the couple would soon do. It gave him quite a start. Once, he, too—perhaps—had had serious intentions and a lover's interest in this very woman. It was only because of his complete devotion to social issues—which had laid hold of everyone and entangled and consumed them—that he had put matters off until later, until a more appropriate time. But now he saw that he had been passed by. Another had taken his place.

Yes, when he went in and saw the closeness of the couple, in quiet and jealous respect, he stayed seated for a while. . . . But he soon gained hold of himself. It wasn't fitting for somebody like him to give in and allow himself to be dominated by his own weakness—not when it concerned something that his people revered so highly, something no government, no society, and no private party had any right to make laws about: free will and individual choice.

Then, all of a sudden—arrogantly and with feigned and affected sincerity—he cast off the cowardice that, for a moment, had gotten the better of him. He took a look at Feygele, who sat, as always, lighted by a rosy-red lamp on her ottoman (although now, this time, she also had Meylekh at her side).

Wanting to show that he stood above his competitor (whose presence it was not easy for him to accept), the man spoke:

"Feygele, have some refreshments brought in for your guest. I want to drink to you—and also to him." Not nobly—with barely contained jealousy—he made a gesture at Meylekh, whom Feygele had so close by her side. "Best wishes"—if it couldn't be otherwise.

He mumbled drunkenly, meaning both to wish them well and also, at the same time, to make an ironic comment about the couple sitting so cozily on the ottoman, so far removed from the danger-filled world he faced. He was embarking on a risky mission—or, the other way around, peril approached him, even now. He would lose his head if even a hair were out of place.

"Have drinks brought in, Feygele," he said, repeating his request.

Feygele, of course, didn't respond negatively or refuse what he had asked for. And whether she thought what he was saying was only drunken talk, or whether she knew that it wasn't straightforward—that his words expressed the regrets of someone who found himself deprived of what he could have obtained—and maybe she, too, for her part, missed him. . . . It's all the same. She wanted to oblige him. Being well disposed and now having another man at her side—the one who would soon be hers—she wanted the third party to participate in the good cheer, too.

She called for what he had requested. And soon, on her little table, there appeared both drink and appropriate food to eat (which was never wanting in her daddy's wealthy house).

The man did not wait. He started to pour the alcohol right away. Having already filled his glass—on the occasion of the great celebration and as an accompaniment to the drink that stood before them—he produced a pistol from his pocket, his "piece" (from which he, and all his people, never separated). Half seriously and half jokingly, he said it was a toast to good luck for Feygele, and he performed the gesture with a festive salute.

"Don't be afraid," he said. Seeing how the couple seated across from him began to exchange glances, he added: "Don't worry: it's empty, unloaded." He only wanted it as a witness; for people like him, it was a companion in all of life's situations.

"*L'chaim*, to life!" he cried, raising the glass in his left hand. Forgetting his promise to leave the gun on the table, as a witness, he took the weapon up in his right. And when he rose from the bench—in order, now, to pronounce the proper words of blessing and, afterward, to drink to the health of those seated before him—then, the couple, Meylekh and Feygele, saw that he was not to be trusted. They had been fools to think that he, who was obviously drunk, was still in a half-sober state. And soon, when he got up and continued what he had begun, they were more firmly convinced of their error.

"*L'chaim*, to life!" He went on: "To you, Feygele, with whom I maybe once had a chance—and maybe not, but certainly not now—because who am I and what am I thinking—that you would ever consider someone like me at all, much less want to join your life with mine? Well, marry another, and may you be happy. And as a sign that I bear no ill will toward you and what your heart has decided—that I have not resolved to oppose or object to your choice—here's the gun, which I'm placing here. It's empty and there for your honor and happiness."

Thereby, in drunken innocence, he directed the gun toward Feygele. . . . And before she or Meylekh could act on the bad feeling they had and turn his hand away—or even say a word to stop him (that he shouldn't make jokes and play the clown)—before they could do that, as Feygele was standing up from her seat in order to keep him, somehow, from his drunken fun—then, soon, she had to set herself back down again, for she had been struck by a bullet that he, unknowingly, had fired, after all. . . .

Feygele didn't make a sound. She just remained still, quiet—her little head cast down; she didn't utter a single sob. There wasn't even a trace of blood dripping from her.

A misfortune! Such a misfortune! He certainly didn't mean it, he certainly didn't want to, this person; even if it were possible—if one allows that he might have been jealous—but what does it matter if he meant to or not? Feygele was no more.

We pass over what a calamity the event was for her parents. We omit how much the culprit—the individual himself—after he had performed the deed, left the house in a wretched state. He was certainly sober now, with nowhere to show his face and guilt-ridden gaze. But we must say how the matter affected Meylekh. The whole time, he could be seen sitting in a side room, thunderstruck, while Feygele lay there. He held his head in both hands, and his face was so distorted that it seemed he had buried himself alive.

That's how it was. Later, people learned that he had settled in a non-Jewish street, a boarder in a non-Jewish poorhouse. He ate only bread and water, as if he were in prison, and he permitted himself no pleasures. He even went so far that he wouldn't wear leather shoes—only wooden ones of some kind. He knocked and creaked about in them, going to the well to fetch water for his non-Jewish landlady, who gave him lodging because he did housework for her—a kind utterly unsuited to him.

He also neglected his appearance for a time—he, whom everyone had always seen with a clean-shaven face until now (so much so that you might even think he had nothing to shave).

He went so far in his unkemptness that the agents of the czar—who, after the fifth year, during the reaction, started to seek out parties still in hiding (the last of those who had been strongly active in the movement, who were to be dealt with according to police regulations)—they, the secret police, when they finally reached the dwelling of Meylekh (whose name stood in their files) and wanted to take care of him, too, as they had done with others of his kind (that is, provide him with "free board" and a "room with a view")—they, the agents, when they saw him so deformed, so deteriorated, and wearing wooden shoes—a kind of servant for his non-Jewish landlady (for whom he, Meylekh, carried water and performed all the other housework)—they, the agents, when they met up with him in that condition and attire, dismissed him with a wave of the hand. They considered him a demented lunatic who could do no harm at all. "He'll take care of himself," they said—that man there with the wild, overgrown beard and the clunky wooden shoes. . . .

✦

After a time, when the wounds from what had happened with Feygele had closed, after he had passed some time as a recluse, with wooden shoes, bread, and water—as if he were in prison—all of a sudden, the desire seized him to return to his studies, which he—like everyone else—had interrupted when the movement was on the rise. And in the very same getup he was wearing, he went off, there and then, to Kronstadt, where a university was located—a well-known one, where many future scholars received their training.

He arrived with nothing at all, with empty hands, without luggage, without a satchel—maybe a couple of books and a bit of linen on his legs. He settled in a poor worker's district, in lodgings he didn't have to pay for except by giving lessons to a mob of the landlord's children (who didn't attend school).

He certainly could have turned for support to societies that promoted Jewish culture, which operated on the donations provided by rich men, benefactors—as so many other students with inadequate resources did. But he didn't. Maybe he didn't want to resort to accepting handouts, or maybe out of shyness—because he didn't wish to come into contact with people to whom he had grown unaccustomed, not having had any interaction with them.

Whatever the case, he managed like this: He obtained a dwelling, as mentioned, and he was a tutor, thanks to his diploma (with good marks) from the *Gymnasium,* which he had finished long ago; that freed him from his lack of funds. Now, in order to get a cheap midday meal in the student cafeteria, do his laundry, and occasionally get a shoe repaired, he had an announcement printed in a newspaper—like all the other students who, lacking means, shared his situation. It was written in the standard fashion: so-and-so—such and such student philologist—gives lessons in foreign languages for a small price. And, in bold print, he added words at the end of the advertisement: "Distance no object." (This indicated that no matter how far away a pupil might live, it wouldn't prevent the tutor from coming to him on foot—he didn't have enough for transportation.)

And so Meylekh Magnus—an outsider, whom no one noticed—quietly went through the university curriculum in even less time than the five years normally required, because his abilities enabled him to complete two courses at once. And so, quietly, he obtained his diploma—finally. It made him no richer than he had been before it landed in his hands—and no richer than when he first arrived seeking to earn it. On the day he received the degree—complete with professors' signatures and university seals—he walked down the busy street of the capital with the intention of celebrating—if not, as is customary, with other graduates, then by himself—with a meal and alcohol (which, until now, he had denied himself). Yet his situation was so utterly unimproved that when the desire seized him and he intended to act—to make his way down the street, to a restaurant of one kind or another. . . . Then, abruptly, he stopped and, wondering, put a hand in his pocket to see whether what was there would allow him to do as he wished—whether such a luxury was possible. When he realized that it wasn't, he just stood there, ashamed, his desires unsatisfied, in the middle of the street.

But then it so happened—as Meylekh stood there empty-handed in silent shame—that, suddenly, he caught sight of an acquaintance from his political days—a rich playboy who, every now and then, used to finance party activities.

Boris Grosbaytl, he was called—a real landowner, a broad-shouldered man, with a contented, smooth face and a broad, flowing, bushy beard. He would always toy with his beard absentmindedly, pretending not to care, as if it weren't his at all. In fact, however, he cared a great deal—it seemed every hair had it own special place.

That beard there, by the way, had helped him, in Year Five, to obtain legitimate status. That is, being, as he was, the son of a rich Jewish landholder somewhere in the northwestern parts, he possessed, besides wealth, such a broad, bushy beard that no one even dared imagine he was sympathetic to the antigovernmental movement—much less think that he supported it materially. That's one thing the beard helped him out with. Second, it served him as claws serve the wild turkey and the comb serves the cock—to be noticed by women (among whom he was already a big hit) as a handsome man and, moreover, as a rich one. He had a mighty hand and a great landowner's manners, but that was not enough for him: he wanted even more—and especially, as much as possible, to look good in a manly way.

That there was Boris, who often made trips to the capital, both for the purpose of taking care of his aged father's business—which he stood to inherit soon—and also for the sake of carefree carousing. Now, he was overjoyed to see Meylekh, an old acquaintance from "those days." Not asking his friend whether he wanted to or not, he immediately took him under the arm and went off with him to an opulent restaurant—the kind that someone like Meylekh had never even had the courage to peer into. Even now, swept along by Boris, it seemed he lacked the strength to step across the entryway in his poor commoner's shoes.

They went in and took a seat. Soon, their table was attended to—with that sugary, fawning manneredness that waiters display when they go by appearances and consider themselves in the presence of a well-to-do individual.

Boris, greatly cheered by the meeting, displayed his generosity. He wished to help out a former friend, whom everyone used to esteem so highly. He, too—Boris, his host—knew all about him (and especially the story with Feygele—and how, afterward, he had acted like an ancient hermit . . .).

He proceeded in a genteel manner, asking the waiter for the most varied delicacies of metropolitan restaurant fare. As a regular visitor, he was a great connoisseur. Also, he ordered liquor. As the establishment's finest offerings animated him and Meylekh, the pleasantly unusual restaurant ambience loosened the latter's tongue. He confided in Boris that, before he happened to meet him, he had already been thinking of doing this very thing—that is, of going to a restaurant—because today was a special one: the day he finished his studies and obtained a diploma.

"Really?! Why on earth are you so quiet, then?" asked Boris. Warmed a little by the liquor, he was taken by the happy news from Meylekh, seated across from him there—the poor guy, a student who had just graduated, whose pale cheeks now glowed from the food and alcohol (which he, having lived within his limited means, hadn't had before his eyes, much less tasted for so long).

"Really?! What are you so quiet for? Today's your day!" Now, right away, Meylekh should pack his bags and travel with him, Boris, to his country estate for the summer—and in winter, they would go to his town house. Both here and there was plenty of room, and he would see to it he was provided with everything he needed. After all, he knew him—Meylekh knew Boris. Just as Boris honorably supported party matters, he also esteemed learning. "It would provide me," Grosbaytl added in good humor—a great pleasure if, to all his other deeds of benefaction, should now come that of being able to serve, as is prescribed, a man of the Talmud, a scholar—for whom he (and he was not the biggest ignoramus himself) had no small respect.

He said this candidly, as someone who really has an appreciation for parties worthy of support. Also, he spoke as the kind of person who, besides that, has the charitable ambition of seeing how, in certain respects, scholarly individuals should find themselves dependent on his generosity (which he offered as a friend, of course).

Meylekh allowed himself to be talked into it. He had already practically agreed to Boris's suggestion in its entirety. First, because the offer had truly been made with candor. Second, because he felt a pull homeward, into the Pale of Settlement*—and, moreover, a pull away from the metropolis, where, for all his years of study, he had felt alienated, as if he were only a guest for a while. He was drawn to the home of his youth, which he had spent surrounded by party comrades and, more generally, living among the masses. There, he had felt both free and attached; from their sap—which was always dear to him—he had drawn his nourishment.

He was drawn there no less—it should be said—than was Boris Grosbaytl, the wealthy son of a wealthy landowner in the northwestern parts, now seated opposite. Boris, with his lordly beard (whose every hair was arranged just so)—despite his capacious, lordly possessions (which would have allowed him to reside in the metropolis year-round)—always felt drawn

*Territory where permanent Jewish residence was allowed, in 1791, by Catherine the Great; the Pale extended along the German–Austrian border from the Baltic south to the Ukraine, including Poland and western Russia.

to those simple villages. Notwithstanding his money, somehow they ignited a folksy spark in him, which made him feel, a little bit, that he belonged to the masses, among whom he had originated—unlike others of his rank and income, who had grown estranged from them. And earlier, that folksy spark there had made him align himself with—and support, in a regal manner—various party activities during the time of immobility and reaction. In any event, he kept the desire in his breast to take somebody like Meylekh under his wealthy wing. He meant to draw him close and make him a participant in the so-called cultural renaissance that a certain portion of Jewish intellectuals now—after Year Five—intended to build after turning their backs on politics in general and rising again, spiritually. . . . In the latter camp stood Boris, too. He assumed the role of a sympathetic patron—ready, as much as possible, to finance the renewal.

Well, in a word—since it seemed that Meylekh, at his core, also belonged to that class of culture-spreading intelligentsia and shared its political roots—the suggestion made by Boris, who was seated across from him, came made to order and at exactly the right time. He agreed to it. Right there, at the table—as they sat in the restaurant—their match was happily sealed.

A little later, Meylekh could already be seen on Boris's estate—a constant guest who was always well provided for, just like an indigent relative at a rich man's home.

He wanted for nothing at all. The estate possessed forests and fields and orchards and gardens, and also stables for workhorses and carriage horses—and also dogs for hunting. Boris pursued this activity in hearty fellowship with his lordly neighbors, chasing game. Once, he even caught a little bear, which he took in to raise. He led it around on a chain. He would appear with it before Meylekh—while the latter was in the middle of his work—and interrupt him.

Making a joke, Boris said: "You see? It's a 'she.'" He was raising her as a mate for his friend (if he would oblige him and agree to engagement and marriage in the proper Jewish manner, as God had intended).

Yes, Meylekh wanted for nothing at all. He had the fullest freedom to do as he wished, and he had at hand all the means of assistance that he needed—such as, first of all, a well-stocked library (which Boris, the landholder, had gladly established even there, in that far-removed, rural setting). Moreover, he still had the possibility to write for (and receive) the most recent publications—whatever had appeared in the various fields that interested him, whether domestically or abroad. Boris—his patron, the benefactor who wished him only the best—never stinted with money. And, by the way, it should be mentioned here—to Boris's credit—that the only payment he got in return was that, from time to time, he could come to Meylekh's rooms in order to "do a little Torah," so to speak—that is, ask and inquire about the most recent activities in the field that Meylekh was studying. Meylekh—sitting by himself and always busy—was in the position to devote himself entirely to learning. Boris, as a busy businessman—and, in addition to that, a playboy—had no time to get things directly from the source, even as an amateur, so he gladly received them secondhand from Meylekh.

And here, too, incidentally, a weakness of Boris's should be mentioned. Besides his business interests and those of a playboy, he also had other ones—modern ones, not at all like those who held his rank and position. . . .

Now, after the fifth year, he still maintained conspiratorial connections with individuals in the underground—people from the party he previously had supported and financed. For instance, he would maintain someone hidden somewhere as an ordinary office worker. Even now, from time to time, he would provide a loan under the table, according to holy writ—that is, with no intention of ever getting it back, knowing that the borrower had it very rough under the circumstances (someone whose face and body had deteriorated because he didn't even have the simple means to survive).

He also had the vice of bringing whole groups from the underground down there to his estate, quietly, whose members he would put up and provide for. He talked with them until the early hours, asking how things were going for the movement—if an upswing was to be noticed. He wanted to make them forget temporary setbacks and arouse the hope that the cause was not lost: soon they would be called upon, again, to perform the activities they so desired—once the great awakening had occurred. . . .

Then he would throw a ball, which would remind them of former, comradely get-togethers. There was food and drink, and candles burned in the lamps and candelabras that decorated the great table in the lordly and capacious hall. And after the gang had arrived, people would grow warm and heated from the wines and punch—for some time now, they hadn't enjoyed anything decent. Then, Boris would summon Meylekh and demand—in order that the celebration be complete (and the illusion of previous gatherings whole)—that he whip out his "hit song," "My Mikhelke." Now, too, Meylekh sang with a full voice, with inebriated enthusiasm and musical discipline—measure and rhythm—and he directed the whole crowd sitting at the table, demanding that they accompany him.

But then, the lord within the breast of the host heated up, the playboy inside awakened, and Boris showed his other side. On the sly, he would give an order to a servant attending the table to bring in his ward, his little bear. Unexpectedly—before the crowd—he would let it climb up onto the table. His ward—with its clumsy little head and its young, awkward joints—would stroll around over the table in an ungainly fashion and, without any discretion, take care of the vessels, bottles, lights, and surfaces that had been so neatly arranged.

"Look!" Boris, heated by the liquor, would then exclaim. He turned to the throng sitting at the table, the people the bear had surprised. "Look and see, you experts. It's a 'she.'" Wouldn't she want—when she was all grown up—to be the fiancée of our Meylekh? The latter had assumed a stubborn position—holding out, against everyone's better judgment, that there were monasteries for Jews (when everybody knew there weren't).

The stunt with the bear and the business of marrying it to Meylekh were, of course, no more than friendly fun—whether he played the joke on him when he was alone, or if he took the liberty of doing so in public, in company. Both times—in both cases—Meylekh would just sink his eyes out of self-consciousness. He wouldn't feel offended—God forbid!—because it was his friend who was doing it. He knew the sincere, almost brotherly relationship between his patron, Boris, and himself.

Yes, it was fun. But what nobody knew was that Boris there—Meylekh's benefactor—had gotten something into his head—a kind of melancholy, it seems, because he didn't want to see Meylekh withdrawn like that and still a bachelor. Apparently, he considered it his obligation, one way or the other, to marry him off.

To say it was just the whim of a rich playboy—something he did for a pining ascetic he wanted to pull over among the living and make like the others. . . . That's not possible. No, more than anything, his purposes were serious, for he saw how Meylekh's temples—because of his preoccupation with scholarly matters—were becoming more and more fallen, his cheeks paler, and his lips thinner. And there—on his lips—dried-out little scales often appeared—as on someone who, in a lifetime of long fasting, has not moistened them.

Boris really loved him and was devoted to him. In addition to what he did as a patron for Meylekh—subsidizing him for his professional, scholarly benefit—he also wanted to see him live a little as a human being, in a family environment, as was proper: he wanted to drag him out of the loneliness in which he had been hiding (without consideration or a thought for what Boris, his sponsor, had long been urging him to do).

Boris took him along wherever he could—wherever Meylekh would let him. He thrust him into the company of women—without success. For a long time, it didn't work. Whomever he had him meet, to whomever he introduced him—the way it happens between men and women—it just didn't work. Until, finally, it did. Then, things seemed to be on the right course.

It happened when Meylekh was already so far along in his research that he had become quite well known not only in Jewish academic circles but also abroad—among non-Jews, too—for example, among famous Germanists, who struck, as it happened, on the Yiddish language as a branch of their primary field of study. They learned about this Meylekh, who was occupied mainly with researching Yiddish and possessed great knowledge and erudition. Whenever, one way or the other—under the right circumstances—they needed information, they would come for his assistance.

By then, he had already corresponded with many famous philologists in Vienna, Berlin, and Budapest. He had already held lectures, and scholars from his home region knew him well, even though he kept far away from the urban center, where they usually spent their time. They always sent him their works before publication—for consultation and to obtain advice—or after publication, as a present, in order to make his acquaintance.

It happened that his sponsor, the aforementioned Boris—in a presumptuous manner and with amateur opinions—was already boasting as if Meylekh owed his success to *him*. He understood what prominence Meylekh would achieve in Jewish linguistics—and he knew, also, that his name had already passed beyond properly Jewish borders and reached the great scholars of other peoples and lands.

Then, he started to talk about him with everyone he met and whoever was around—in keeping with his estimation, understanding, and liking for such matters. To men, he boasted about his intellectual "client" (so to speak) as if he were a precious jewel. And, of course, he also did so, with special intentions, in his encounters with young, unmarried women—those he knew were still free, whose hearts had not yet been taken by others.

Then he cast an eye on a girl—a distant relative—named Bloymke. She was a happy girl, and a clever one. But she had a slight fault: she was a little too happy, a little too clever—a girl with two smart curls down her cheeks, a little too forward and direct. She frequently had a song on her lips about somewhat ambiguous love affairs, which she had learned from Yiddish operettas. She had a weakness for them and would go as soon as one showed up in town.

> If you want pleasure
> And a woman for that—
> Take a wife, take a wife. . . .

With her singing, she commanded the men in the room—or maybe they were taken by her overall appearance. It was nothing bad, but also nothing noble—just that whoever was grabbed by her impish singing found that he sympathized with the sincerity in her voice. If nothing else—with her smart curls, little nose, and playful eyes—she certainly made an impression.

She was clever in a commanding way, but practical, too. She was the mistress of a household with no mother in it. She, the oldest, was supposed to take care of the younger children—and, also, of her father, who provided for them all.

The father was an honorably silent Jew—a son of the Torah—whose livelihood was travel, and his passion—cards. He could play the game for so long, with such quiet determination, that he would stay up all night and through the early morning;

then, not rising from the table, he would continue for another whole day, into the night.

He was a Jew who, without knowing a word of Russian, had dealings and conducted business mainly in the area of the Don Cossacks—whose territory lay outside the Pale of Settlement, where Jews were not supposed to set foot. (And whoever did, in any event, needed to know Russian to approach a Cossack.)

He—didn't. He was a manager for some foreign, German firm, which delivered agricultural machines for cash and on credit. The company provided him with some kind of elaborate document that allowed him to go where one wasn't permitted (and spare talking, which he couldn't do anyway). A German, they said. A Jewish word was enough—the rest could be done by hand. . . .

He would go away for a while, collect new orders, and remind merchants buying on credit of their obligations when they happened to miss payments. Then he would come back home with the money he had earned traveling, so that he could spend his time in peace and comfort with what he liked most and hadn't been able to do on the road—cards.

At home, he would squander much more than his earnings permitted. When the money had run out, they would start to take the clothing for pawn (to the butcher's, the wood and coal dealer's, and so on).

Then, his practical little daughter Bloymke would appear on the stage. She managed the household affairs and knew how to talk to people—how to persuade those who had come to serve notice that the debt of Mr. So-and-So (meaning Bloymke's father) had already reached heights that could not be exceeded. . . .

Then, with no alternative, Mr. Bloymke's-Father would tear himself away from his passionate occupation—cards—and go off again where he didn't need to talk, where he struck upon his further sustenance by waves and gestures alone.

Then, after her father had gone off, his daughter Bloymke would remain without the slightest means of maintaining the household. She was forced to cheat with her little mouth—to persuade the creditors knocking down the doors that, God forbid, they wouldn't be debtors anymore: as soon as her father came back from his travels, they would receive everything coming to them—all the money due, plus interest.

Then, she was mistress of the house and the children's provider again. And she was also the mistress of her own person—her body and soul—which she nourished with visits from young men. They greatly desired to see her, and she, for her part—with the cards lying before her in this way—granted it to them. Sometimes by day, sometimes in the evening—and also late at night—she would sit in their lap. But just that. After a day's work, after she had taken care of the children and put them to bed, she would indulge in a little flirting—sometimes with a couplet from a cabaret song, and sometimes without. It didn't hurt anyone. God forbid!

Once she did that, by the way, when her father was at home. As he sat busy with his company of cardplayers in one room, she, at the same time, was with her group in the other room, and then in a third. Yes, that was a weakness of hers: to sit on a young man's lap, to be very close to him. But at the same time, she would stretch a hand out to his face—to discourage and prevent him, should he want anything more than just to have her on his knee.

That Bloymke there—when the father had come back from one of his trips—was paid a visit by Boris. He was a distant but very desirable relation, whose presence was wholly welcome. His visits were sought on account of his person alone—the very fact that he was in the house made the relatives stand at attention—and also he was an exceedingly wealthy man, one whose presence one ought to welcome. They were glad to see him, because often—in difficult times—they could approach him for a small, temporary loan. He, the wealthy Boris, would just let it slip from his mind and forget about it—and they, the family members who had borrowed from him, apparently didn't think about it afterward, either.

"Well, Bloymke?"

"Well, Boris?"

They greeted each other politely but with great emotion, too—as was the loving and cheerful way they shared. He, a handsome man, displayed a courteous generosity even to older women he didn't know; he did the same, now, to this young girl (who, moreover, was a relation). Well, and she, Bloymke, when she saw him before her—both a relation and, as mentioned, a handsome fellow—definitely felt a tug inside. Coquettishly, she wished to find his favor.

So, why did they have the honor to receive such a distinguished guest? Bloymke soon asked—after Boris had taken a seat at the table across from the honorably silent father and opposite to her (who, with him in front of her, couldn't stop turning and preening like a bird).

"What's that—*why?*" For country cooking, for no reason, out of pride, he answered. Despite his wealth and means to indulge in various luxuries, Boris—he was among family, and it didn't stand far from his tastes to do so—tended, now and then, to enjoy simple, peasant meals, which he would eat with particular gusto (to the point of even letting a tiny crumb fall on his beard).

It was a homey conversation—a free and familiar one. Boris spoke with the father, to whom he had come to ask some questions, as one does—and ought to do. And often, in the course of speaking to him, Boris's eyes would wander over to the daughter. He also had something to ask of her today:

"So, you're all ready to get married now, Bloymke?" he asked jokingly.

"Sure . . . gladly. . . ." If he had anyone decent to propose, she joked back—half to herself and half openly (with ashamed glances toward her father). She continued: "Yes, but where do you find someone like that?"

Well, what about—let us say—somebody like Boris? Would he be all right?

"Sure," she replied, looking at Boris a little more evenly and with evident pleasure.

Okay, then, how about someone better than him?

But was there any such person? She asked in a tone as if she didn't believe it possible.

In short, participating in the conversation and eating the Jewish delicacies he had been offered for refreshment, Boris found a way to present to Bloymke (who listened with great interest) and to her father—Meylekh Magnus, the kind of gentleman and scholar one could be proud of.

"At any rate, Bloymke, should you be interested," he added in conclusion—she would thank him when she met him. And in no time at all, people would be drinking to the engagement. After the wedding—he added humorously, in the manner of a matchmaker—if there was a bris, he would be the godfather. And, if not—if it was a girl—that would be Bloymke's good luck. He would put off being the godfather for later. . . .

Well, the same thing he had undertaken with Bloymke—on the bride's side—he afterward had to do with the second party, with Meylekh: persuade him that he should, at some point, pay a visit to his cousin's house. And, half jokingly and half in earnest, he suggested to Meylekh that he go have a look and see. He wasn't forcing him to buy a cat in a bag, God forbid!

He finally managed to bring the couple together. It was difficult for him to trick Meylekh out of the house and steer his steps toward what he wasn't used to because, previously, an unlucky blow had struck him when he tried to follow the path of everyone else. Meylekh resisted with tooth and nail, protested that he wasn't going to, and always came up with some new excuse—saying that, at the moment, he was busy with this or that, he was right in the middle of it, he had to finish. . . .

But finally, somehow, he let Boris persuade him. He submitted, and he found the time to go there, to her house, and even set foot inside.

Just imagine: it was no small matter for him. . . . Imagine: the first time things were so bad that his tongue failed him entirely—he didn't know where to begin and where to stop—from lack of habit and because he felt utterly lost.

But then she came to his aid. Bloymke was practical enough to see right away who she was dealing with; she wouldn't be able to count on his initiative, and she would have to make the first move.

She already knew how to do it, even though she had never had anything to do with someone like him before. Now she had him in front of her—a pale man with closed, thin lips and dry, thirsty scales on them (as if he were someone who, in a lifetime of long fasting, had had nothing to drink).

It flattered her that someone like him—someone who stood above her in the exalted enterprise of learning—had come to her. Even if he hadn't been free but had done so under constraint—now he was in her power alone. It was just some kind of bachelor's demeanor, really—a mournful, unexpressed one. And even if he had no words, nor even a glance to express what he meant, still, she thought—in time and later on—everything would work out: she would see to it that he got the right look and even say what she wanted. . . .

First, she wanted to "try him out," as they say: see who he was, what plans he had, and what she, Bloymke—a cheerful girl with locks and curls (and also songs in couplets)—could get from him that she might use to make him over into what her gay tastes demanded.

She finally managed to do it. At first, he had been a party dragged into her house by force. Afterward, both habit and also, it seems, something else drew him there, and he started to visit the house on his own, without the least coaxing from Boris. Bloymke's little smile just called and invited him every time. She would wear it when he arrived at the door—and afterward, when she accompanied him as he said good-bye and went away—there it was, like a "Farewell!" and a request for a second visit—and still more after that.

She had already made him over to suit her, and she knew how to approach him, how to open his closed mouth, and even call forth a smile from him—from this man who was so busy with things that were above her.

Seeing what his character was—that it came from having been shut off and unaccustomed to dealing with women like her—Bloymke was at first forced to yield a little, too, and she had to act as he did, with a little distance. But from time to time, she made sure that, one way or another, he would feel her close to him after all—by means of an (apparently) unintentional touch; this, she noticed, made his head turn, and a stream of strange pleasure flooded his heart and brains.

She quickly noticed that she already had the upper hand and dominion over him, for whenever it came time to leave, he was unable to do so, and he remained glued to his seat, incapable of standing up.

And yet she saw that from the moment of his arrival until he departed and took leave—the whole time—he kept his gaze so attached to her that he couldn't hear or see what was happening around him, or even once laugh. Ultimately, she would have to wake him up, as if from sleep, and say: come on, stop looking at me like that. . . .

Because, indeed, he couldn't do so at all, as we've heard. If someone like that becomes infatuated by what has been blocked by various obstacles until now—if someone like that falls for somebody like Bloymke (with her jet-black curls and cleverly practical gaze)—he can't just look somewhere else or tear himself away. His enamored state went straight to his head.

Things were moving along. They continued until his patron and benefactor, Boris, noticed that another color was beginning to show in Meylekh's face—not the pining one, the one he had displayed until now. His suffering, constantly captivated looks started to glint with something else. Seeing this, Boris lit up with inner joy, and he smiled into his lordly, bushy beard.

Yes, it was like that all right. Late—very late—at night, that same Boris there would encounter Meylekh (who until then had remained perpetually at home) as he returned from somewhere. Jokingly and half in sign language—with a gesture—he would ask:

"Well? Back from there? Her place?"

"Hmm," Meylekh would mutter. Then he would turn and promptly go to his room—as if he didn't wish to desecrate his mouth with cheap fun or ordinary talk, after he had come from there, from her—from that lofty and secret glory, which today, it seemed, had touched him with a hand and, through this hand alone, had let him feel the whole of its womanly essence. . . .

Yes, it had already gone pretty far between them, and on the proper course. . . . Only there, all of a sudden, Amor, the highly capricious god of love, got involved. This occurred, to Meylekh's misfortune, in the form of a director of some provincial enterprise—a combination circus and zoo, whose attendant devil had brought him to the city.

He was a young-looking person—similar to an actor who always plays lovers' roles, with a fine ring on the second-to-last finger of his right hand and a cape. In addition to that, he was clean-shaven—that is, not just the beard, but the mustache, too, in the style of the day. And all of that together—the handsome figure, the cape, the keenly shaved upper lip, and the ring on the second-to-last finger of his right hand—all that made quite an impression on certain kinds of ladies and young women.

Among them was Bloymke, who—just between us—was also capable of losing her head (which wasn't too clever to begin with) over operetta actors; whenever she saw one on stage, in her enthusiasm, she thought that no bird more beautiful or heavenly existed in all the world.

But that doesn't mean she was really capable of losing her head entirely, and silliness isn't strong enough for true love—and certainly not *now* (as had occurred earlier, with the actors).

It so happened that the director became her neighbor. It happened because the half-circus, half-zoo business was, quite simply put, faring poorly. The ticket window was hardly stormed by what clientele remained. Expecting a good turnout and profitable returns, the director had taken up residence in a more-or-less decent hotel, but afterward, when Shlemiel became his cashier and the street urchins started peering in the window to ridicule him and call out names—then, the director, because of his shabby finances, had to drop below his respectable station, move out of the hotel, and take up residence with a private party (with the excuse that, allegedly, he didn't like hotels and felt best in a private home).

It so happened that he found accommodations in the same house, practically under the same roof, as our Bloymke.

It turned out he was Jewish—a guest for Jewish midday meals, dinner, and supper, all of which the mistress of the house gave him on credit. She hoped to receive payment before a certain date, together with the rent money (which, he assured her, he would pay).

Soon he had become a little more familiar with the landlady. She, for her part, would visit Bloymke in her parlor, as one neighbor does another—once to borrow something, and another time to tell her some big news about the lodger (about his person or distinguished wardrobe—the cape, the pressed white shirt, and the shiny boots that befit a director).

Moreover, the opposite also occurred. Bloymke would go over to the landlady's, either to borrow something or with another intention—to steal a glance at the boarder (who, coincidentally, would happen to walk out in his fine robe of aristocratic tailoring).

It further happened that the director—when he passed the courtyard, the open window, or the open door at Bloymke's—would hear her sing. She had just happened to start singing at that moment, as was her way. "If you want pleasure / and a woman for that. . . ." Or maybe she sang it with a certain intention, knowing that he would pass by just then. One way or the other, she got to know him, and afterward she, Bloymke, became a rather frequent visitor in the half-empty circus, which already had Shlemiel for a cashier. (Street urchins would needle him and yell into his window, and at other times they would replace the letters on the sign with a bad word. . . .)

She became a visitor, without paying—with all the privileges and a right to the best seats—since she was a very close friend of the director's. He, after collecting the meager receipts, would accompany her home, because, after all, he lived right next door to her.

In a word, little Bloymke, with the jet-black locks, with her curls turned in toward her face, pleased the director pretty well. And he pleased her, too, it should be added. He, the handsomely proportioned individual—with a cape and the gait of a provincial duke aware of his worth—also knew his power to capture weak-hearted ladies and young women: first, simply through his noble bearing, and then, also, by means of his self-assured approach (whose success he never doubted, as he had had extensive experience on the hunt and knew that the god of love himself would keep him from falling).

Their love was no joking matter at all. While he, the director, maintained a steady approach—not hurrying or rushing at all—she, our Bloymke, was all ablaze—and not as she had been so many times before now, when she had sat on a bachelor's lap (with a hand extended toward his face, to keep him away and prevent what he wanted from her).

Now—but then no, not now—she was a bit lost and, on the whole, under the power of this handsome individual—the one with the ring on the finger of his right hand—who, moreover, was so smoothly shaven and without a mustache, even—upon whom, moreover, an odor from the circus and zoo still lingered, which stimulated her (as did the whole artistic profession, which she now knew intimately).

She was so taken, as her affection grew, that she almost lost sight of her previous admirer and visitor—Meylekh, whose love had already reached very great heights. He saw nothing but her; unawares, he had even begun to neglect his scholarly activities, to show them less devotion. Often, he would catch himself—as he sat before a book that once had engaged him fully (to the point that he forgot about everything and couldn't stop reading)—now, he turned his eyes away and thought about what had nothing to do with books—about her. . . .

Naturally, Meylekh didn't stop his visits. Despite the fact that recently he hadn't found her at home when he arrived in the evening (as he always did). Sometimes, he asked where she had gone—the day before yesterday, on this, that, or another night. She replied that she had gone to the circus, which she loved doing; and she invited him, Meylekh, too—half coldly and distractedly.

He had no desire to accept the invitation. He considered circus entertainment a waste in general, and, more particularly, he had no desire to attend it as often as she did—his Bloymke, who burned with such passion. Finally, she renounced the project of converting him, Meylekh. She didn't even realize— although he had noticed—that recently, her eyes were not her own at all. It was as if she were dreaming, carried away. Often, when Meylekh turned to her about something or the other, his question would remain on her lips. Mutely confused, she just repeated the words, not knowing what to respond.

Well, the outcome was lamentable—woeful for all parties. It was sorrowful for Bloymke, who had been ensnared by innocent frivolity in vain—for nothing at all. It was sorrowful for her father, who lost her—a child, his eldest one, the mistress of his house and the caretaker of his children—and he never even knew where her bones finally wound up. (As for every father in a case like that, the shame and grief were intolerable.) It was also woeful for Boris. Afterward—just as soon as he had found out about what had happened—he could no longer look Meylekh in the eye and avoided him; he wouldn't meet with him and, like a real criminal, steered clear of chance encounters in the doorway. Well, and it was certainly woeful for Meylekh. There and then he abandoned his association with people and the idea of merging with another half (to which he had been drawn in such a youthfully sincere way). There and then . . . suddenly: crash!

Shlemiel the cashier, for a decent spell, sat day and night in the ticket window. Very few visitors offered him a hand holding money. Very few people went in his general direction. They didn't display the slightest interest in the circus, whether because of their financial situation or because there was nothing to see. . . .

Of course, this had bad consequences for the performers, the tightrope walkers, the actors, as well as the simple technical workers—who started to crawl away in the middle of the season, breaking their contracts and abandoning their positions because there was no way for them to receive their wages.

It even had bad consequences for the director. Even though he always, as the head of the enterprise, was the first to dip into the cashbox—now that it was empty, he, too, was materially embarrassed, and he, too, was often forced to hide his handsome face from creditors.

Under the table, he had to sell the wardrobe he kept in his suitcases, in order, somehow, to cover the debts he owed the landlady where he kept board and ate Jewish meals.

In a word, it came to bankruptcy. He, the good-looking director—with the cape and the fine ring on the second-to-last finger of his right hand—had to go.

He did so. He took off one night—left at full tilt, as they say. He didn't say good-bye to anyone, so that no one would know where his traces had vanished. And, a few days after his disappearance, one could see how, of the whole circus enterprise, there remained nothing more than buildings standing empty, with boards for walls and canvas for a roof. There was also a little monkey—an orphan, a hungry little thing, which no one fed anymore. Moreover, it was consumptive and sickly; it could already hardly move, even when someone drew too close. You could see the little monkey dangling by its claws, as if on a scale, at the still-open door of the circus entrance. It begged miserably with an outstretched hand and accepted everything it was given (whether for eating or amusement); when no one gave it anything, it picked the fleas from its fur.

There also remained a camel with two humps—one this way, the other that. It had a round, collapsed belly—hardly even enough to make a drum out of—and no one, even the knacker, would approach it. That camel stood the whole day long at the edge of a river not far from the circus. Not having anything to eat, it was lost in desert thoughts. Pondering its lostness, neither kneeling nor holding itself up on its flat feet, it just chewed and digested the air and nothing else.

Yes, the director went away, dodging his employees, the people under contract with him, and staff. He also skipped out on his landlady, whom he owed the most money, which he was unable to pay. (He left her a pair of empty suitcases with a few dirty things inside.) But for all that, he really acted in a cowardly way with our poor Bloymke, whom he had enchanted to the point that she didn't ask and didn't even want to know where he was taking her in the middle of the night—without any luggage at all, except for what she managed to grab in haste, not even having had the time to say good-bye or kiss the sleeping children (whom she had raised and whose mother she had been).

She was so blinded that she even forgot her very own father, not asking herself how he—the quietly honorable Jew, well-read in holy books, who, just then, was off traveling—would take the news of her running off with somebody whose origin and destination were unknown: with her, his eldest daughter, that party disappeared, without leaving an address to find him.

It is understood, of course, that she had forgotten Meylekh entirely—the man who, for her sake, had renounced his professional activities and given himself over to her magic alone. She didn't appreciate his sacrifice. A romantically blinded girl, she abandoned his foundering, overburdened ship to flit off and take a frivolous love jaunt with a man who, as it later turned out (after long searching and inquiries), seduced her on the way from Hamburg to Buenos Aires. It ended as such trips often do: halfway along, the sea—a quiet or a stormy one—would hear the frightened cries of girls imprisoned in the desolate element, like Bloymke.

Then, the First World War erupted. One of the results was the formation of the state of Poland, which included the city where Meylekh Magnus lived.

Later on, in the same city—which had a venerable tradition of Jewish culture—a scientific institute was founded. It had various divisions for teaching different disciplines. As the leader and head of one of its divisions—the department of linguistics—Meylekh Magnus, whom everybody in the field recognized, was given a chair. His name elicited great respect even among foreigners and nonspecialists, and in particular among the most promising students—degree candidates who studied under his supervision and poured water on his hands, who served him as students do a teacher they respect so much that they do not even permit themselves to sit down in his presence (if he demands it of them).

Meylekh Magnus, a solitary man, did not direct his department as other chairmen do, from afar—that is, coming in only at certain hours. Instead, he was given a private residence there, which was attended to by the servants of the institute, because he had no one else to take care of him.

They saw him so greatly committed—and overcommitted—to his work that they thought he could see and hear nothing else. It was as if he perpetually had cotton in his ears and some covering pulled over his head—like a man constantly in shame.

Only his servants (who also helped outside the institute) came into contact with him. Only they knew about his lonesome habit of walking around in his study. He did so whenever he had free time—sometimes, just at one wall, back and forth; at other times, elsewhere in the study; still other times, he walked around all four walls, often changing the path of his march from one to the other.

He had another habit the servants noticed: when he was left alone, he would also talk—sometimes in a voice that others could hear, and sometimes only with himself for an audience.

That and nothing else. His only other contact with people outside the institute occurred when, from time to time, he permitted himself to go to a concert. He had a subscription and his regular seat, and he would spend the whole evening sitting with his eyes closed, his head turned to the side, straining his ears to make out the tiniest sound—the slightest note of the whole orchestra or a single soloist. And if, God forbid, someone missed a note or didn't play it properly, he would distort his entire face in pain. After he had listened and gone home—also now, as in his youth—he could be seen with his face turned toward the window or the wall, repeating what he had heard at the concert. Coming to those passages where the conductor or a player had made a mistake—also now, standing at the wall or a window—he would grimace out of dissatisfaction at the musician's error.

Well, and then—when people were already absolutely sure that he, Meylekh Magnus, would never give up his obsessive behavior, and that, on the contrary, he would only sink deeper—then, suddenly, he changed: he left his isolation behind and got married without anyone's help—indeed, without even being in love.

"How's that?"

Like this: He was devoted up over his head to scholarship—so much so that neither day nor night were his own, and he had no possibility of freeing himself even for a minute from his all-consuming labors. He, who stood at such distance from everyone else (especially now, after his difficult experience, the doubly sad failure in matters of love), now—behold a wonder. Without anyone's help at all—without the assistance of Boris, for example (who previously had aided him and prepared a smooth road to Bloymke)—now, he struck upon a woman. He found both the time and the uninhibited speech to make a proposal. And she, the woman, for her part, received his words gladly, without the slightest surprise—as if she had long anticipated them.

Indeed, she was already older—a widow, or someone who had divorced her husband. She didn't have curls and jet-black locks to make him tremble and lose his tongue in her presence (as had happened before, with the other one). She was simply a solid person—even if her gaze was already a little extinguished and lacked that dazzling artistry of younger women; in exchange, she had enough sense to know who was seated before her, who was making the proposal, and how to value him.

It's a reasonable guess that she was an old acquaintance of his—either from somewhere in his hometown of younger days, or from a little later—someone from his former party circles in the city where he now found himself. Once, presumably, she had come by chance, on a visit, and cast a pitying, maternally loyal gaze upon him, seeing him there in his dwelling all by himself—in his dusty study full of books. And that gaze had served him, Meylekh Magnus, as a sure sign that the person now looking upon him in his loneliness—if she were to draw closer—would be able to alleviate much that he endured and bring into the house what had been missing until now—womanly cheer. . . .

So, back and forth it went, and still again. And after one or two more of her visits, he found the words to propose, feeling that no difficulty would present itself from her side, and that he had struck upon someone who would not reject him for anything at all.

That's how it went. In the first few days he was already convinced that he was not fooling himself and had made no mistake by proposing—even though he had done so with some delay, as he was pushing forty.

Anyway, what happened, happened. But now a happier day was shining on him than before—as if the sun had risen earlier and set later. His few free hours were spent in a much better way: he was spared the solitary walks in his study—and also the conversations with himself (as had always occurred before, when no one was in the house, and he couldn't control himself in his loneliness).

And more and more, his life became complete. After he had grown closer to her and more familiar with her, they married. In a few months, in a conversation between man and wife, she confided to him that she was "expecting."

A whole band of musicians suddenly struck up a song inside him—as on the eve of a great success, which now, despite the delay, had finally happened. That's what people want: a strongly devoted woman who knows the value of a great man, and also a third life in the near future, which will unite the couple still more and bind them together.

He, Meylekh Magnus, at that time of great exaltation, even put his professional activities to the side. As if he had lost the desire for them altogether, he contented himself with the joy that he would soon be a father.

Out of great, dizzying overfullness, he often brought forth entire pieces of joyful music—quietly, for himself—both when he was alone and undisturbed by others and also in the presence of strangers (such as students at the institute, whom he didn't let disturb him—it was as if he didn't notice them at all; for their part, they knew where the music came from and what the reason was).

Truly, then, he ought to have been happiest of all—paid and rewarded, finally, for all that he had had to endure. . . .

But woe. As they say, where it's not right, it's not right, and when it's bad—no matter what opposition and protest one expresses, in a full voice, to all the world—all the declarations that "He lives forever, incomprehensible in His acts of bounty. . . ."

When the time for delivery came, no effort sufficed to birth the child. Whether because it was a firstborn—and moreover a late one—or for another reason, they had to "take out" the child. It was difficult, and, in the end, one life was sacrificed for the other. The mother died, while the child emerged healthy and full of life.

It is understandable that Meylekh Magnus, after what had befallen him once again, should now tell himself for certain: "So much for personal happiness," while still giving great thanks to God that he had been left with a small comfort in this world—his child.

He devoted himself to the baby with all his loyalty—as much as a person like that, one who has not fully lived out his love, can do.

First, a wet nurse was hired when the child needed one. And when it was weaned, of course it didn't remain without supervision. On the contrary: it was as if not just a single pair of eyes—a mother's—were watching but ten pairs, from ten mothers. . . .

So faithfully and attentively did the father provide for the child, surrounding it with every comfort, that the wee thing felt no lack of motherliness at all for the first few years. He, the father, was enough, and he loved the child and acted as two people—a father and a mother.

The child, therefore—as soon as it first saw the light—recognized him, the father, as its nearest and most devoted relation. As soon as it could extend its little hands in welcoming love to the one who deserved this love, the child reached out, in heartfelt recognition, toward the father.

And so, whenever the child woke up, and also when it went to sleep, one could see the father watching. He drew near after work and stood over the little bed in the middle of the day, unable to detach his benevolent, fatherly gaze.

Year after year passed. And then, people saw Meylekh Magnus leading a toddler by its little hand on a walk. Later, it was a larger and more fully grown child, after turning three, four, and so on.

2

Now comes an interruption in the biography of Meylekh Magnus. For ten or fifteen years or more, there is nothing to be told, except that the child, in the course of time, continued to grow—passing from childhood into adolescence, and from adolescence to young manhood. But an extremely important political occurrence should be noted here. Just then, it surfaced and reared its head. Later, when it had emerged in its complete, prescribed dimensions, it brought with it the destruction and ruin of millions of lives—including those of Meylekh Magnus and his son.

It was an event in that well-known western European land, which even now bears the mark of Cain. Everyone had to confront it—even people like Meylekh Magnus (who had given himself over to his scholarly institute wholly and stood so far from politics).

Looking at him from afar, one might have thought that he—the professional submerged entirely in his scholarship—didn't care about anything else. There was room for doubt whether he even knew what was being said and written in the press about the emerging threat, upon which a great portion of the world's fortune depended.

That's how one might think, looking at him from afar. But whoever knew him more closely and had a nearer connection, noticed that, no, the matter concerned him greatly.

People noticed how, in conjunction with the unease that was spreading like a cloud, a couple of wrinkles had appeared on Meylekh Magnus's face—from his forehead to down below his nose. On the whole, he was beginning to look like a quietly assembled army on the eve of a defensive maneuver or an attack.

Because, indeed, Meylekh Magnus was not, in fact, removed from his former political practice, and no moss had grown over the path leading to such activity. Now, when *that* ordained power made it its objective to drag the train of progress back to its point of departure, into the primeval jungle—naturally, one didn't need to be anybody special (that is, an exceptional individual) to stand among those seeking to prevent a retrograde historical movement.

That was true in general. In particular, it was true of Meylekh Magnus, since he belonged to the community of people with whom the foreign power had decided to proceed in a way different than what it foresaw for others (once its hand had reached that far).

And, again, this was especially the case when one added, to the concerns he had as a human being and a Jew, his worry about what was dearest to him personally—his concern for his child. The boy had already pretty much grown up by then, and every time the father read or heard about what was happening (or getting ready to happen) in lands not far from his own, he would take a secret look, with a particularly troubled expression. He did so both with unexpressed sympathy and as if readying the crow that a rooster makes when it sees danger for its young, spreads its wings, and prepares to protect them.

At such times, his face would grow angry not just in the presence of his child but also before strangers. And even when he was alone, by himself, he still looked awake and tense, and he seemed to strain his hearing to the utmost—as if, any minute, a knock on the door would come and someone would enter with a terrible message.

Then, people would hear him bring forth an angry word, a pointed question, or even a heated tirade against those who wanted to minimize the threat and wave it off, saying: "Don't worry! The sky hasn't fallen. It isn't as horrible as it seems— and, anyway, our heads haven't been chopped off here. *They* should know they can't take on the whole world; and, moreover, even what they promise to do with us Jews is nothing more than overblown agitation, which will serve them until they think they control the masses that are following them blindly in their mood for destruction. As soon as they want to govern any land at all, they will have to conduct themselves differently and forget their criminal prattle."

Then Meylekh Magnus—the quiet, withdrawn scholar— would rise up and release a heated tirade that didn't suit his elderly, otherwise tranquil temperament. "So, 'prattle,' you say? True, they can't take on the whole world and conquer it all, but they can certainly inflict great trouble—and especially on us, about whom they have become experts enough, having been sufficiently schooled to think they have a thousand-year, historical right of possession.

"On the contrary," he would continue, "we should remember: if a gang of field robbers in the Middle Ages—one led by a knight named Rindfleisch*—was able to incinerate a whole Jewish community—over a hundred thousand souls—who lived between the Rhine and the Oder—why shouldn't his successor do it again, or something like it? That 'louse-ridden corporal,' as the famous field marshal Wilhelm contemptuously called him. Why can't this pathological cripple do that—with his mania for conquering the world like Napoleon, Charlemagne, or Alexander? His possibilities are bigger and his fantasy is sicker. And he's better armed than those before him—like that medieval thief Rindfleisch."

One would hear these and similar words when Meylekh Magnus spoke in excitement.

Well, it wasn't long. The danger—which had already come to the border—had grown larger in the meanwhile. Also, the forces held in reserve had grown—those that resisted the danger, subsequently. Also, the sons of the present generation grew up—those who, on whatever side they fought—would carry out the conflict to come. They included Meylekh Magnus's son, with whom the scholar could often be seen walking on days of rest—when the son was relieved of school assignments, and the father free from work.

That was when the son was thirteen or fourteen years old, already capable of taking in everything to which his father had

*Literally, "Beef"—perhaps an allusion to the butchery he performed. This was allegedly the name of a German knight responsible for the murder of twenty-one Jews accused of desecrating the host in the Franconian town of Röttingen in 1298; events in Röttingen sparked a wave of pogroms throughout Germany that claimed as many as five thousand Jewish lives.

made him heir (passing it along in an accessible, understandable way, as is appropriate for an adolescent). And the father's authority in the son's eyes reached so far that the boy would turn to him with all the thirsty questions of youth storming in his breast (as is normal for boys at that age).

That was after the thirteen- or fourteen-year-old youth—already for some time now—no longer stood under the supervision of the domestics who had provided for him when he was small. He sought the authority of his father, whose observant eye never left him, who helped him in school assignments, when he needed assistance, and also, besides that, answered all the other questions that torment an intellectually curious boy who is still growing.

The father provided instruction whenever he had a moment to spare, and especially on days of rest—on strolls through the streets, or in the city park. He, the teacher, and his son, the pupil, appeared so close and tightly knit that people thought all the knowledge and learning the father held in his parental well of experience would pass over to the son at his side without a single drop being lost (because of the boy's thirst for knowledge).

An illustration of what has just now been said about the relationship between father and son is left in a photograph:

They stand, one next to the other. The father's hand rests on the son's shoulder, and the son holds his father at the waist. The father's gaze is full of modest, trembling triumph because, despite his ill-starred life, he has finally managed to draw a lucky number: the model boy there at his side—whom it seems he fears fate will take away, after all. In contrast, the boy, holding his father's waist, is full of young, vigorous certainty. He shows the opposite of his father's fear: no, they are here, they will always be together, and no one will take the one away from the other, ever.

✦

And then, the terrible events came—just as a cloud descends, all of a sudden. Like everyone in Poland, Meylekh Magnus was unable to do or learn anything more than anyone else. First, he remained dumbstruck under the blows of hail—stupefied and unprotected. Afterward, he was blasted by the thunderbolt that the cloud threw down. Just think: a mountain had disappeared, along with millions.

In short, after a while, *that* power ruled the Polish lands. Meylekh Magnus and all his people wound up in the infamous ghetto. All his possessions were thrown together, along with his former reputation (which now yielded nothing, despite the fact that the authorities, for the sake of appearances—and in order to fool those who let themselves be fooled—allowed his institute to continue to exist, leaving him in his director's position with all the seeming respect and privileges granted to a man in such an office). He entered the ghetto with what was dearest to him—the sixteen- or seventeen-year-old boy he had raised with such apprehension.

There is no need, now, to mention what happened there. The witnesses who survived and escaped have given us such rich material—both orally and in writing—and we, the present generation, have torn our hair out over it (and later generations, too, will have cause to do the same—if they want to . . .).

Yes, all that is known, and there is no need to spend further words on the matter. But if, indeed, it is necessary to add anything, then it's this: when Meylekh Magnus found himself in the dogcatcher's cage, he immediately seemed to turn mute— as if his tongue had failed him. This was the case not only when he dealt with strangers but even with his own son—his boy, who would soon turn seventeen. He cast his eyes down in shame, as if he felt guilty that he had brought him into the world—and as if he himself had created it and allowed such outrages to occur.

That happened soon after the seventeen-year-old youth had seen, for the first time, how well the authorities succeeded in casting his people down into the dirt and debasing them to the utmost degree. Downcast and broken by what he had seen, he turned to his father—to the authority he had always esteemed so highly, from whom he had always received the right explanations. He asked:

"*Tate*, what's going on? What is happening here? And why us?"

"I don't know, either." The father, who was shaken himself, had nothing more to say. As he spoke, he lowered his eyes in shame—like a person without a clean conscience who turns his gaze away when he has no way to justify himself.

That's how he acted with his own child—and also with others when they turned to him, an older and experienced man, from whom they hoped to receive a word of comfort in their grave trouble.

With no alternative, he left his child alone to try and find sense and meaning in the chaotic events the bitter skies had let fall. And, of course, he also did so with the others—those who felt lost and couldn't see where help might come from.

That's how it was in the beginning. But later, that power (which initially strode from victory to victory, facing only parties much weaker than itself) started to be hit on both fronts. First, there were external, unbowed adversaries in the east, upon whom war had been declared lightheartedly, for *they* thought they would do the same with them as with the ones before—grab them and choke them. Afterward, there were internal opponents, too, everywhere in the hinterlands. Whoever had the slightest love of freedom found like-minded souls and joined with them. As much as the means sufficed, and as many sound heads as sat on sound shoulders—to that extent they sought to get at the invaders by stealth, damage them, tear into them, and rip at them in a way matching their anger and rage (even if it was not healthy).

Later, when they started to hear about the deeds performed by the underground (which was already nearby . . .), then, a glint appeared in Meylekh Magnus's eyes. When, in silence, he heard about what was happening—more and more about the defeats that the invaders had experienced either on the front or at the hands of the underground, which sapped their strength—then, he would often mutter under his breath and angrily agree. And sometimes, he would hold forth:

"Well, sure, what are they thinking—the dogs, the such and suches? That the fight with the enemy would be so easy? They have no idea—they don't know his nature or his character. They're ignorant about his ideals, hidden away at the core of his being, from which he derives his implacable will to resist and willingness for self-sacrifice.

"What are they thinking? That they're just walking around their home, or at the house of others like them—on shiny, paved roads? They don't know that the earth here is sticky and it comes off on your feet. The map alone is death for them. Not just once has it happened to them—and other reckless conquerors. Those who tried thought they would live off the fat of the land—but in the end, they barely escaped with their lives."

One shouldn't understand things in the wrong way and think that this proud talk from Meylekh Magnus came from his inherent heroism, or that it was due to his age (and also, possibly, his character in general). No, it came to him only from his human dignity and desire for self-defense, which found expression in a feeling of wrath that burns in everyone facing this kind of situation: the wish to see the enemy cast down in pieces, when one looks to all sides and seeks salvation (and even in the air . . .).

When he responded in this manner, his declarations were enough for him not to despair entirely. They were also an indication that it was possible to be saved. True, it occurred passively, for he did not know where rescue would come from. However, he also displayed it actively, since he was able to look at all (if a little cautiously and with reserve—just as a child looks for safety, already knowing, it seems, where it will be found).

At that time, Meylekh Magnus also observed that his own child—his boy, who would soon be seventeen years old—faced another menace, one besides the danger threatening him along with everyone else in the ghetto. The youth took this second danger upon himself—although his father, with his afore-mentioned view on certain matters (which the son couldn't know about) had, in certain respects, pushed him to it.

He saw how his son started to be friends and keep secrets—a little too much—with a group of youths he had gotten to know at the beginning of the time in the ghetto, in the vocational school that still existed then, where young men were prepared for the trades (to be a carpenter, a locksmith, and so on). The authorities had left the school in existence only for the sake of fooling people—in order to maintain illusions among those who allowed themselves to be fooled—and especially so that the compliant personnel employed there could keep an eye on the young people attending it (lest they, after falling under others' influence, go down the "wrong" road—one undesirable in the eyes of the authorities, before they could liquidate them . . .).

The father saw how this group from school often assembled at his home in free hours. Half with words, half with gestures, they had something to share with one another, but their conversations were always conducted in a way so that he, the father, couldn't understand what was being discussed, even when he concentrated intently on what they said.

The group had picked the modest corner where he dwelled as their meeting place. They knew that they were safer there than anywhere else from sleuthing, enemy eyes. They weren't mistaken and had made no error: both native and foreign observers—those to whom supervision of the ghetto had been entrusted—knew who lived where; therefore, they were aware he was a more or less reclusive individual, whom the authorities had granted a privileged, separate status; thus, it would take more time before the group's meetings were noticed and attracted suspicion.

The father looked on and, at first, pretended not to know what was happening—as if he saw no reason to disturb them. . . .

But later, he recognized what the half-disguised words and gestures pointed to—a situation in which the authorities would see their interests damaged. It was certain they would make sure the youths were brought to a place where, as he knew, others already, for similar actions, had been hanged both day and night—a warning to everyone else.

Later, when he had convinced himself about what, earlier, he couldn't believe, he started to hesitate. Different thoughts came to him, in confusion.

On the one hand—he thought—why others and not them? Why was he so indulgent when it came to strangers who took action, and why did he content himself with passive sympathy? Why was he so hesitant with regard to his own son? It was, after all, one and the same: if the matter was just and right, then it was just and right for everyone—and if it wasn't, then it wasn't for anybody. In brief: aren't they truly righteous who, seeing that they are condemned to die anyway—that they will perish—at least resolve to do so with honor and depart from the world with fists clenched in vengeance?

That's how he thought, on the one hand. But, on the other hand: who knows? Maybe the boy would manage to survive—him, especially, since he was among those whom the authorities had granted a better lot and a position of privilege. And if so—who knows?—maybe he would have further good luck? And if so, should one stick one's head in the gallows noose before hope is entirely extinguished?

That's how he thought in the cowardice one always faces at a moral crossroads—when it's necessary to decide to go either this way or that.

Then, one day, a person appeared before him: the secretary of the Jewish Council. To all appearances, he was a servant of the authorities. But, for all that, he also served another power—the one that operated in the underground, maintaining connections with the necessary parties (and also in the public sphere). He was twenty-five or twenty-six years old, with an aristocratic appearance and cultivated manners. Nature herself had given him these qualities, but he also, for the sake of certain purposes, cultivated them. Even in the ghetto, people always saw him exceptionally well dressed and clean-shaven, with his hair combed in a part. He was a man of action—one who stemmed from an altogether different sphere than the others driven into the ghetto.

He hailed from a faraway region—one right at the German border. There, he had attended a Polish middle school, and, afterward, high school. He was well assimilated, and in his early youth he had had very little contact with his people. Only later, when the Jewish national-bourgeois movement swept him along and stirred his passion, did he find his way to his own kind—and even a little too much. When he reoriented himself and joined the international movement, he did what someone like that does—but at the same time he didn't break with his people; on the contrary, he continued to operate in their milieu, in order to move things in the proper direction.

And then, when he took up what the Polish government didn't like at all, he had to uproot himself from his hometown and country (where he fit in easily). Receiving a new name, he went off to where Meylekh Magnus lived (having received orders from appropriate instances higher up).

To perform his duty there, he immediately had to orient himself in the foreign environment—that is, get to know the new surroundings, people, and conditions where he found himself. Keeping a distance—so that no one would notice him—and at the same time aware of everything that was happening, he gathered information from those operating underneath him (their leader, sent from central command, according to the party line).

He already knew everything and everyone in the city, from the half-legal professional workers' movement to those one might recruit for action later on. He also knew everyone in the intelligentsia. It was necessary to keep a watch on them, so that whoever was still young could be raised according to the party's principles. And if someone wasn't, it should, in all events, be known what he did and which way his sympathies inclined (should it be necessary at some point to use him one way or the other, they would know how).

And then the war erupted. He—who had come from the faraway Polish territory and was already an illegal even in times of peace—was now illegal twice over: really stuck in a boiling kettle. Here, he was exposed to a double danger—either traitors could find him and hand him over to the authorities, or the authorities themselves, using their own apparatus of detection, could nab him.

But there, his aristocratic appearance, his excellent education in Polish, as well as his familiarity with Jewish matters, all came to his benefit.

And there, thanks to all that—thanks to his impressive exterior, thanks to his knowledgeability (which were necessary for an officeholder), and especially thanks to the fact that he extended, on the sly, a helping hand to whoever needed it—he managed to become the secretary of the Jewish Council. The authorities had no reason not to have confidence in him, because they thought someone like that would not betray them—certainly, he didn't belong to the kind to be suspicious of.

He conducted himself like this: First, he saw to acquiring a good name among those he had to impress (in order to obtain the necessary credit). Later, when he had taken care of that, he used his legal status to do what his conscience demanded. On the sly, he started to organize all the young people he could for resistance—and also older people whose attitude and outlook he trusted. He also knew what kind of person not to mess around with—or, rather, on the contrary, those to keep contented, well fed, clothed, and equipped with papers and protective documents rendering them harmless (because they possessed greater privileges).

And there, among the latter, was someone like Meylekh Magnus. The secretary, in keeping with his second "office," needed to know about him, and, indeed, he did know. Whether he undertook the aforementioned visit on his own initiative, or whether he was especially charged to do so—it's a fact that once he had made his appearance (alleging that he had come with an order from the authorities concerning certain institutions in which they—those in higher positions—took an interest), he pursued a wholly different objective.

And so, as soon as he had taken a seat in Magnus's room—as soon as he found himself seated across from the scholar—and as soon as he had finished the business with the supposed order from the occupying powers (which didn't take him a minute), he immediately went over to the real reason he had come.

He spoke: as he knew the attitude and convictions of his host, Meylekh Magnus, he believed that what he intended to confide in him now would remain between them—"under four eyes."

He had come to him in particular on confidential business, because a danger confronted both him (a party who was officially employed, should anybody learn the truth) and the individual who now had his confidence (lest anyone go and share their meeting with the authorities). With Meylekh Magnus, he knew he could speak frankly.

In short: Meylekh Magnus knew that, besides the present struggle on the front, there was a second fight in the underground being waged by the best sons of the people against the enemy (who had come to destroy everything and everyone); he, Meylekh Magnus, had a son drawn to activities that the authorities had forbidden; and his son wanted to participate, too—though he was still young and inexperienced, it didn't matter, it played no role (on the contrary: in a certain sense, it was more desirable . . .).

He had come, then, to tell him that if he, Meylekh Magnus—who, possibly, didn't know anything about it—were, now that he had found out, opposed to what his son wanted—if he should seek to prevent the latter from participating in what he had taken on voluntarily and in honest, youthful fervor— then, in the secretary's opinion, he would be committing a wrong against himself and his child.

He didn't believe, he continued, that Meylekh Magnus would have anything to object to in the son's activities in general. He knew well enough what kind of situation faced the population that had been chased into the ghetto. He had been able to observe all that had happened until now. He also probably knew and had learned all about the true nature and criminal methods of those into whose hands they had fallen—that if *they* got something into their heads, if *they* decided to do something (and should it be the most violent and inhuman design), they would carry it out thoroughly and stop at nothing; nor would they feel the slightest pang of conscience—no drop of which was to be found at the bottom of their so-called souls.

Knowing all this, he—the secretary of the Jewish Council— was certain that a man like Meylekh Magnus could in no way oppose the activities of the underground. On the contrary, more than others, he must welcome them as one who wishes the best for his people—and also for other peoples and the whole of humanity (which included his son and himself).

True, the secretary didn't deny there was a risk—a great chance of failing and departing from life in a horrible way. But, on the other hand, wasn't laying one's own head on the block terrible enough—and, moreover, shameful? Resistance is dignified, and—whatever the outcome—there is something comforting about it, for both the one who perishes and those who survive him.

"I speak with certainty," he added. The secretary declined to stress the chief issue, which anyone at all could see clearly—and especially someone like his interlocutor, a man like Meylekh Magnus. However, he did want to mention one other thing. Namely: besides the fact that struggle is inherently dignified—even if it is hopeless—here, in this particular case, there were also good prospects that he might save himself and others, too.

"You probably know, Pan Magnus. . . ."* And if he didn't, the secretary told him again: After fighters in the underground proved themselves reliable in action, they were taken—individually or in groups—to more secure locations. There, whole partisan cells were formed—with better weapons and under better military leadership. There, they had possibilities for obtaining more effective means of combat against the enemy. This provided better chances to save one's own life (and also to inflict greater harm on the adversary and destroy him at his very core). That's how it went with everybody—and, ultimately, that's what would happen with his son, too—once, soon, he had completed a certain training. . . . Also, it was not impossible that after a large part of young people had man-

*Pan (literally, "Lord") is the formal mode of address in Polish when speaking to a man. Below, the secretary awkwardly juggles various ways of addressing the story's hero. Besides Pan, he employs the German Herr and Yiddish Khaver; the latter term can mean both "friend" and "comrade," in the Soviet sense of the word.

aged to cross over the ghetto fences, a helping hand would be extended to older people, and they would be drawn over to the cells being formed there. Then—quite possibly—he, too—Meylekh Magnus—would be able to join them.

The secretary didn't need to say the last bit. One could see that when he spoke about him—Meylekh Magnus—and his own rescue, the father's gaze didn't light up with life and animated interest. It did so only when the son's prospects were mentioned (after the boy had proven himself meritorious to those who decide).

The whole time that he listened to the secretary, he was silent, and he didn't respond with a single word. Then, finally, only when the secretary had concluded and he, Meylekh Magnus, saw that the other had nothing more to add—that he had laid everything out and now simply waited for his interlocutor's response—yes or no, he agreed or didn't. . . . Then, Meylekh Magnus, still without saying anything at all, lifted his eyes with a kind of playfully understanding, thankful gaze. He also rose a little from his seat, and, silently—continuing to spare words—he extended a hand: "I agree," it meant.

Later, the secretary was ready to get up and depart. He had nothing more to add, and he had received an outstretched hand signifying assent. But at that very moment—at the entryway of the room where the two were seated—Meylekh Magnus's boy appeared. Whether this occurred by chance or not is difficult to say—or, rather, it isn't. For at the very moment when the boy saw the stranger with his father, and when the stranger saw him—someone looking on, from the side, would have noticed a disguised exchange of glances pass between them (as from one friend to another, who, earlier, had made an agreement about something).

Then, Meylekh Magnus, the father, spotted his son, too—right after the conversation with his guest, after the latter had persuaded him to agree, and he had accepted. Then he rose from his chair and approached his son. At first, it seemed he did so as a father does in general—whenever he sees his dear child and goes over to him. But no, not this time. It did not occur in the normal way. He didn't ask, as usual, "What brings you here?" Now, he asked nothing at all. Instead—quietly and without words—he put his hands on the boy's head as old people sometimes do with children, when they bless them on the eve of Yom Kippur. Holding a hand on his head, it seemed he also whispered something—a little something not to be noticed by the son and also not by the guest (who sat nearby, gazing at the silent picture in rapt interest).

The guest, who had come there on his well-intentioned mission, understood that the father, by means of the quiet approach and silent laying of hands upon the son's head, was confirming what they had agreed on: it was like a seal on what had been signed earlier. . . .

The secretary also understood and sensed, as he looked upon the ceremony taking place, that even if he had not come here on this mission—even if the son himself had just declared to the father that this was how it would be (that he intended to go with those whose path was both a danger and an honor)—even then, the father would not have objected. The same hands he now laid upon his son's head he would have placed upon his child's brow even if the stranger were not there.

He could tell from the barely noticeable smile that appeared on the father's lips after he had performed the gesture. Evidently, when he saw his son, he always acted this way—placing his hands on him out of loving fondness. . . . True, the smile looked as if it came from a condemned man—and it seemed the kind of smile that any ghetto father would bring forth. Still, the guest also discerned a kind of satisfaction—that of a person who has managed to overcome and master himself. . . .

Yes, as much as any ghetto father was still capable of smiling at that time—and especially when he faced the danger of placing, with his very hands and before his own eyes, his child under a knife. Our Meylekh Magnus, after he had given his assent (though he expressed it in an ambivalent manner), still found the courage to bring forth a fearful smile from his lips.

. . . As evidence and as proof, the description should be interrupted here for a moment. To give us a picture of the mouth that smile came from, we have a photograph of Meylekh Magnus and his son.

"A photograph? From that time?"

Yes. There was a photographer who lived in the same ghetto house as Meylekh Magnus. Earlier, his atelier had been located there, and after the arrival of the foreign power it had fallen into ruin. Of all his earlier possessions, nothing remained besides a little camera—a dusty one lying in the corner of a room in disarray. From time to time, the photographer would remember it, and sometimes he would pick it up. Then, he would ask whoever was around to pose for a picture.

"I'll do it for free," he would say—"and pretty well, too." The other party would try to decline, saying, "I don't know— who can think of that now?" "No, no," he would reply, "it will be useful. . . . Later, when we're all free of these pests, people will want to see the way we looked."

And then, the photographer—once, on a day of rest—spotted Meylekh Magnus together with his son. He turned to them with his request: they should be so good and stand before the camera a couple of minutes. Meylekh Magnus could not refuse—it simply didn't occur to him more than to any of the others.

The photographer, one can tell, took pains in making the portrait and arranging things so the man in the picture— whom, it seems, he held in great esteem (since he knew who he was and how he was different from others)—would appear in the best light and, both now and afterward, have a professional work to be proud of.

He succeeded. And there, we have evidence in the picture. All by itself, it seems, it provides a certain representation of everything that happened in that part of the earth formed by eastern and western Europe. Also, it proves just how much the dogs of modern times have exceeded outrages that occurred earlier.

At first glance, it doesn't seem all that powerful. . . . One sees two people in the picture: a dad and his son. The father has not been massacred, nor has the boy. It's just that the father looks like the death of joy in life, like someone coming out from the *other* world. . . . That is Meylekh Magnus. From his youth on, he had the habit of being well-groomed, of having one hair lying straight by the next; and when he grew older, he didn't give up his proper manners. But now, a storm seems to have thrown the hair on his head into disarray—each hair, individually, and also all of them together. One need only look at the picture—just glance at his eyes. His gaze resembles the look of a constant user of hashish when he sobers up and, for a time, remains in his half-pale, fantastic confusion. It looks like the gaze of Ahasver at the moment of his very greatest despair, when he sees himself condemned to the never-ending fate of living and wandering forever—without rest, without respite. . . .[*]

But it is truly terrible to look at the son. He is still young. Externally, he has not yet been so strongly affected by accursed reality. Instead, he has a compassionate gaze, and he is turned toward the man next to him, who rests his hand on his shoulder. Already, it seems, he feels there—not the hand of his living *tate*, who has always been so beloved to him—but the hand of a dead man, one he regards as a stranger, both out of sorrow and fear.

---

*Ahasver, or "The Wandering Jew," is a legendary figure of Christian origin that became popular in the eighteenth and nineteenth centuries. Cursed for mocking Christ, Ahasver cannot live or die but roams the earth eternally.

Well, enough of the picture and Meylekh Magnus's smile then. . . .

Anyway: for as long as the son remained his son, for as long as the father had him before his eyes—every day in the morning, before going to work, and at night, when he came back—this mere pleasure was enough for him (when, in his mute presence, he had someone to eat with and, somehow, also to talk with).

But later, the son, bit by bit, was drawn, more and more, into his all-consuming work for the underground. It demanded everything of him—to the point that he didn't have a single minute to share with his father—even to offer the simple joy of his presence. On evenings that were free of forced labor, he was busy with meetings, in which one always had to talk about what had been done for the cause today, that evening—and also what to do tomorrow and the day after that. Then, when the father no longer had his presence to enjoy in the evening—and also not in the early morning (when the son, even *before* work, would hurry off for some reason). . . . Then, reports of frequent captures in both the city and ghetto started to reach the father's ears—whenever underground agents were caught red-handed carrying something or giving one another what the authorities had forbidden (and also, how dearly these parties had paid for anything that was prohibited). . . .

Then, had one taken a look at Meylekh Magnus—the father of an only son who now had become the partner of the aforementioned agents—one would have had to tell him: better no, it's better not to look; when someone is already committed so deeply and not leading the same life, mere words are not enough. (Even though a simple look at his son, when he took time off and granted his father a whole evening or just a part—somehow, the time he spent together with him, despite everything, gave him comfort.)

It was as if he didn't see his son in a realistic light, because of his love for him. Yet he sensed that at any moment the last thread, on which all that remained to him was hanging, would tear.

✦

Finally, it happened—what he, Meylekh Magnus, the father, had sensed just a while back. He had felt it, but he had not let it enter his thoughts, out of fear.

It occurred when he—the boy—had the task of bringing what the underground needed from him into the ghetto: items he could obtain at work—illicit ones, of course, to be obtained only through great self-sacrifice. Once, he was carrying such contraband hidden under his clothes (guns or something else). When he arrived at the gates of the ghetto, where they searched people returning from the city, they caught him.

There, some mangy demon of destruction was present among the police forces—the kind of person who knew all the sly tricks and cunning works of artistry employed by those who concealed and smuggled what was prohibited. Meylekh Magnus's boy seemed suspicious to this individual.

Right away, he ordered that he step away from the others and come over for inspection. At first, the boy wanted to run off—to hide in the crowd. But when he saw that it wasn't possible to make himself scarce, to escape, then he realized that he had had bad luck—and what that entailed: he was going to get a raw deal. When he tried to run, the other man had a gun ready to prevent him. He called out: "Stop! Halt!" But the boy still didn't listen and stayed his course. The man fired at him: one bullet hit his back, and the second his head. The two shots, it seemed, yielded a single cry: "*Tate!*" He fell—dead, cut down. It was over. . . .

Then, that evening, after the interception—after everyone in the ghetto had heard about it—the father still didn't know, because no one had had the heart to tell him. Then, afterward, when the authorities realized the identity of the individual who had been shot and where he lived, they came to his father's house to investigate, thinking they would find something that would reveal the connection between the party they had stopped and his associates (whose names were written in their black book). During the investigation, no one told the father anything at all. They let him think that his son had been captured alive—that is, that he had been arrested without real evidence, but he was guilty of something, and they had come to obtain further information.

Then, after the investigators had gone, there came to the father the same secretary from the Jewish Council who, a little while back, had appeared for another reason (to talk to him and convince him that his son's underground work was desirable from all points of view—advantageous both for him and everyone else). Now, the same secretary arrived on a second mission: to let him know what had happened—as calmly as possible and in a way that his words would not make the father, Meylekh Magnus, collapse once and for all when he heard them.

Entering, he saw only worry on the father's face. This troubled expression had stayed there when the officials went away and left him aware that a misfortune had befallen his son (although he was uncertain what kind). When the secretary saw the father's worry, at first he wanted to turn around, for he lacked both the courage and the words to tell him the truth.

But soon, he got hold of himself. He gathered his wits, thinking it his duty to tell the father personally—not to allow him to hear it from others.

Still, he stammered at first. Not knowing how to begin—not even sure how to address his interlocutor—he turned to him. "Pan Magnus, Herr Magnus, Khaver Magnus . . ." Finally, he mustered the firmness necessary to conclude what he had started: "One way or the other. . . ."

As difficult as it was for him, he was forced to speak, because what had occurred couldn't be undone. He, Meylekh Magnus, needed to be strong in hearing the news that the worst had befallen his son. . . . He was neither the first nor the last. . . . In any event, he should take comfort that the boy had died while pursuing the noblest duty, and in the noblest way.

Well, what else could he, the secretary, say? He saw that after the father received the news, nothing changed in his general appearance (which was that of a man condemned). He didn't cast himself down to the earth. He didn't strike his head against the wall. He just sank his eyes a little lower than usual—as if he were silently taking in the last bit of what fate had dealt him. After a moment, he lifted his eyes back up to the man who had brought the news. He asked only one question:

"Well, what do you think, Mr. Secretary"—would he be able to see him and attend the burial?

"Yes," the other replied (even though he knew it wouldn't be easy to arrange for someone like that to have family members—or anyone else—attend him on his journey to eternal rest).

Then, the secretary departed. He saw to it that everything was done to fulfill his promise. And for tomorrow, the day after (when permission had been granted to bury the boy properly), the secretary managed to arrange things so that he, the father, could accompany the hearse that took bodies from the ghetto to the Jewish cemetery—allegedly as a member of the burial society, as a gravedigger.

There is no need to say just what happened when the father met his son again. The first stood there as the second was loaded onto the hearse—uncovered and in the same clothing as when the bullets had struck him (because, understandably, under such conditions, one did not do what usually was a matter of obligation to the dead: wash them and clothe them; instead, they were simply buried, as means permitted).

There is no need to say that no one besides the father—even among the nearest relatives—accompanied the body. We should only mention that when it was time for the hearse to depart and the driver—who was already sitting up front—gave the father a wave to sit down next to him (as the Jewish Council had arranged, earlier, when it took care of official matters), he, Meylekh Magnus, appeared as a member of the burial society, as a gravedigger.

When the driver gave him a sign, Meylekh Magnus, for a few minutes, acted as if he had not registered the man's gesture—until the latter yelled out crudely: "Well, come on, what's keeping you, Jew?" Then he seated himself. He did so quietly and in a manner that the driver—who was used to death, and also to those who accompanied dead people (especially in recent times, in the ghetto)—he, the driver, when he looked at the man seated at his side, felt even more uncomfortable than if a corpse had been sitting next to him.

The father was silent as they drove out from the ghetto gates (with the proper authorization, of course). He was also silent the whole time the hearse passed through the city. He didn't look back to see *who* was lying there or *how* he was lying. He didn't look back, and he didn't look forward—it was as if he had shed all his sorrow. Only when they had left the city and started for the cemetery—then, suddenly, the father, the passenger in the front, turned his head to the back of the hearse. And seeing what lay there—an uncovered body in the same clothing that he, the father, always used to see his son in—he turned to the driver and spoke:

"Just a short while, Cousin. . . ." He wanted to go to *him* for a moment. . . . He gestured with a finger toward the body that was being transported—not in a coffin, but in an empty hearse.

Sooner said than done. Before the driver could even speak a word, the other man—more swiftly than his years seemed to permit—had already stepped into the back of the hearse. And what the driver never had seen the livelong day—or any other day—he now saw: the father lying down next to his son, as if he were still alive.

The driver tried to stop the hearse, to go back and wake the passenger from his madness—to dissuade him and bring him back to his seat. But his efforts were in vain. "Talk today, talk tomorrow"—the passenger wouldn't move or listen. Finally, the driver spat and said, "He's out of his mind." Having no alternative, he took a seat and gave the horses a start. After the way to the cemetery was complete (which took as much time as it always did)—finally—he passed through the gate not with one dead man but, as it were, with two at once.

Afterward, it cost the members of the burial society great effort to separate the father from his dead son. They finally succeeded in doing so. Somehow or other, the dead man was given his due. He was even buried in a special grave reserved for him alone—which in those circumstances was an exception (a privilege, it seems, arranged by the Jewish Council, as he had certainly earned it). When the body was brought to the grave—when they lowered it down and started to cover it up—the father stood as if he were made of stone. The whole time, he remained silent. But finally, when the grave was already half filled, he made a leap—with both feet—into the grave that was still half empty. "Bury, bury, Jews," he cried, "it makes no difference." He meant something in particular: he wanted to be the tombstone on his son's grave.

Naturally, they somehow got him out of there, and (with great effort) they led him away.

There and then, already, the lid of a coffin was about to close on him, the father, too—the earth had covered his only son, his only possession in the world. But it did not turn out that way, because what is supposed to happen doesn't always come to pass.

✦

A little later, Meylekh Magnus found himself in a bunker that an experienced man—an agricultural engineer—had made. (He did so with real expertise, for, besides the proper knowledge, he also had all the materials necessary for construction.)

The bunker was a cave within a cave. The first cave began with a descending passage that led under a house on a side street. When one reached the bottom, the wall contained a secret door that, through a corridor and narrow passages, burrowed into a more secure place. It was impossible to see light from there, for a spying soul to hear any voice at all, or the best-trained tracking dog to smell a thing (even with its heightened senses).

The bunker was located close to the city sewer system. From there, it drew no small amount of dampness, stench, and, especially, rats—a flurry of black-haired ones, gray ones, yellow ones, both old and young. They had long snouts and fattened bellies, and it was impossible to get rid of them entirely, or even to chase them away from the food; there was no choice but to get used to them.

But otherwise, in all other respects, the arrangement was exemplary (to the extent that it is possible to speak of an "example").

There, one found two rows of little chambers, one facing the other like monks' cells. The walls, ceilings, and floors were covered in wood. It had been arranged that the whole structure would be provided with light obtained—by contrivance and for no money—from the old city electric station. There were further comforts, such as a kitchen and other domestic appointments.

There, a dwelling place was provided for entire families, as well as individuals. The expenses were covered by our well-known friend Boris Grosbaytl, who now, in the meanwhile, had come to look plenty old and worn—without the well-groomed, bushy, and lordly beard he had had before.

After the Jewish population had been thrown in the ghetto and robbed of its property, Boris still retained quite a bit, which he had managed to preserve from the authorities: money in cash and valuable objects, which took up little room. He had managed to trade for them, in anticipation of having to make deals later, uncertain how long the troubles would last.

Incidentally, our Boris deserves that his story be told in a little more detail.

The same thing happened to him that befell Meylekh Magnus—only he had a girl who was the same age as Magnus's boy. A born beauty, she had already blossomed in her fourteenth-fifteenth year. Full of life and love, she displayed her father's gay nature.

Already then, a buzzing host of young men surrounded her perpetually. Although she was not yet aware what it meant, still it flattered her and brought a playfully rosy color to her cheeks (whose whiteness she had inherited from her father).

She grew up like a young poplar tree, and no one who saw her could tear his eyes away, even if he wanted to.

Even somebody like the perpetually beaten-down and reclusive scholar Meylekh Magnus—with whom her father, Boris, still maintained friendly and patronly ties (often coming to his house as a guest, and, from time to time, receiving him at his own home)—even someone like our Meylekh Magnus, when he laid eyes upon her—despite his gloominess—beheld her as if she were a wonder of nature (a surprise for an old man).

She surprised him especially—and it gave him paternal joy—when, later, he saw her together with his grown son, who was her age. (It seems the two attended the same school.) He saw how the boy was right for her—how he always remained clumsy and speechless when he looked into her eyes in silently smitten amazement. She, on the other hand, was casual and free with him—as familiar and easygoing as if he were her brother.

The couple's relationship quietly pleased the father, Meylekh Magnus. Out of adoration, his son remained mute before her, and she was almost sisterly to him—still without a girl's intentions.

It pleased him that—who knows?—something might develop between the couple there.

Boris, the girl's father—watching from the side—also looked on approvingly. He had nothing against receiving Meylekh Magnus's boy as a match for his daughter—and Meylekh Magnus himself as brother-in-law.

Ultimately, it was possible—should the stars of the parents or the children be in proper alignment. Then it would be, as they say, "the union of learning and wealth"—a delight to both parents and also a great happiness for the young people (whom Meylekh Magnus certainly wanted to enjoy this honor, in keeping with his paternal wish that she bless his son with her treelike blossoming and give him shade).

In the future, it was possible. Some signs were already visible now, from time to time. But apparently, somewhere else, it was written otherwise.

The catastrophe of the war arrived, with all its terrible consequences for everybody—and especially for Jews, among whom Boris and Meylekh Magnus were, of course, no exception. We have already heard what happened to Meylekh Magnus's son. Soon—in a moment—we will learn what befell Boris's daughter.

The father had long-standing business relations not only with the Jewish residents of the city but also with non-Jews. Therefore, when the troubles erupted and the decree was issued that Jews had to leave their established residences and move into the ghetto—then, Boris found a non-Jewish party who took his daughter into protection, allegedly as his own relation and under an assumed name, and he guaranteed her security and well-being on the safe, Aryan side. (For this service, by the way, her father paid well: leaving the ghetto, he gave the benefactor a generous emolument for what they had agreed on.)

Then the authorities issued their infamous decree that those who hid Jews would pay with their heads. No one knows whether Boris's Aryan acquaintance got scared and was forced to deny further support to the daughter, or if evil neighbors did some talking about the good intentions of Boris's friend. Whatever the case, one day Boris's daughter fell among those from whose hands no one emerges whole.

It's a reasonable guess, however, that her Jewish ancestry was not the sole reason for her capture—that it also occurred because of certain acts of sabotage in which she was involved. The girl had contact with the kind of people who pushed her toward it—but whom, it is also possible, she would have sought out anyway.

After all, she was the child of her father, who loved her dearly, pampered her, never denied her anything, and anticipated her every wish. She was raised and taught in a privileged way. Besides regular school, she had special teachers in different areas (such as languages, music, and dance). In her sixteenth-seventeenth year, when the misfortune arrived, she not only possessed a better general education than others of her age (whose parents were less prosperous) but also, besides that, a great respect for her ancestry. As already mentioned, her father himself never broke with tradition, and he brought his child up in the same spirit—that is, firmly connected with her people. . . .

The result was that, when she saw what her father and the whole Jewish community had fallen into—even though she, herself, was an exception and had landed on a more secure shore—the pride in her upbringing that grew within her, as well as her love for her father, meant she could not accept her privileged status. Morally, it weighed on her like a stone.

Yes, her privileged position choked her, and she sought means, in a childish and inexperienced way, to extend a hand to those of her kind, who suffered as if from plague, whom it was forbidden to approach (including her father).

Well, seek and ye shall find. . . . But no, she did not find the means; rather, she herself was found to be a means, for others. . . . That is, she was noticed by certain circles operating on the Aryan side as someone they could exploit for their own clandestine purposes and also as someone with whom it would be easy to do so.

After all, they knew her illegal status. They knew her to be someone whose alleged legality was hanging by a thread: then and there it could tear, because at any point, anyone at all could hand her over. They also knew in what prosperity her father had raised her, and that she had a very, very loving relationship with him. Surely, she regretted that he had been torn away from her like that—and she, from him. And, finally, they knew that she, that beauty there—who, moreover, was so rich and elegant (because her father had left her plenty of fine clothes before parting)—would cause no suspicion among those whose mistrust one should fear. On the contrary, they knew she would be a grand success. Thanks to her arresting appearance, she would always get out of dangerous situations—without looking like that, one wouldn't be able to.

Knowing all that, those in the aforementioned circles gained access to her through a boy her age. He was dispatched to her. He trusted her, and she him—and she let herself be persuaded to do what her heart, her inborn filial love, and her sense of ethnic dignity were inclined to do anyway, even without the influence of another.

She set off down a certain path. She was recruited for illegal work and always received tasks for which she was absolutely perfect. She—such a beauty, and moreover dressed so elegantly—always managed to avoid the dangers that surfaced when she came from theaters, cafés, and clubs—places where someone else, in any other case, wouldn't have gained entry, because it would have been obvious that the individual didn't belong there.

It's not important when, after how much time, how, or on what mission she was caught. It's only important that they, into whose hands she had fallen, thought they had found the right key to unlock the secrets they desired. They saw before them someone who was still a child, from whom they could extract what they needed, whether by "proper" or "improper" means (more, of course, by improper ones).

They tried proper means at first. It didn't work: she had too great a sense of responsibility to her people and too much hatred and bitterness for everyone's oppressors and insulters to betray her own kind. She had sense enough to know that handing others over would be self-betrayal, for they shared a single destiny.

Then she was taken away for interrogation—half naked and without even a shirt (which, because of her delicate upbringing, made her cry both blood and tears). And when that hadn't worked either, they did much worse, and she emerged half insane—no longer capable of anything, not knowing what was happening at all. And then, with a whole company of youths—packed together because of their common cause—they made her a date with the noose.

When her father, Boris, heard what had happened, at first he erupted in cries—mourning in a wholly Jewish manner and walking about in torn garments. He also, it seems, sat in mourning for the traditional seven days. Afterward, he got hold of himself. Nobody knows how—whether he got the idea himself or others gave it to him—but one day he removed what he had hidden away—the things he had brought along into the ghetto. He assessed the gold and precious stones according to their current value, and he waited for the secretary of the Jewish Council where he knew he would pass by. Meeting him face-to-face, he brought up a very confidential matter.

He had something to say to the secretary.

"You, sir, to me?" the other asked Boris in amazement. Nowadays, Boris looked very shabby—because of his poorly groomed beard and, also, his whole outfit (which it wasn't possible, even for somebody like him, to maintain in the ghetto).

"What do you desire?" the secretary asked. Like everyone else, he had always known Boris as a liberal patron and, moreover, a person with a lust for life—someone who, it seemed, never lowered his eyes before anyone, whether in shame or for another reason. He now saw the same man standing before him there: half worn-out, with a lip that trembled before he brought out the words he spoke.

"For one reason or another," Boris said—the secretary certainly knew him or had heard of him. He is so-and-so. He had come to share his plan to place his entire fortune—all he had managed to preserve and bring into the ghetto—in the service of the interests that he, the secretary, also served.

"Do not ask, Mr. Secretary, how I know about your double business—about the public one and the secret one. . . ." Also, he shouldn't be amazed by what he had come to propose, because he, Boris, also had a connection of sorts to the matter. His share in the business was very sad. . . . In case the Herr Secretary wasn't aware, he should know that, a little while back, his child was handed over—together with a group of other young people like her—for an underground act of sabotage. . . . He had a request: the secretary should agree to take what remained of his fortune and do as he saw fit—whatever would be most useful. He had confidence in him. He would just keep a certain sum for himself, to get by—and, also, to build a bunker for some people close to him; he also gave the secretary the right to recommend whomever he considered necessary to bring there.

The secretary, hearing all this, looked at Boris for a while. After all, he knew him—he had to know him—in keeping with the information he had received from higher up, earlier on, before he was sent into the ghetto. And it's also a safe bet that what Boris had told him just now about his child, who had died, was not news for him, as he kept up on all acts of sabotage performed in the ghetto and also outside it, in the city.

Thus, he had no reason at all to doubt the good intentions of Boris, who stood before him now, because he understood very, very well how great his despair must be—and also the desire for vengeance of a man like that, after losing a child in such a horrible way.

He didn't doubt that Boris was in no way to be suspected (if not for the goodwill he now exhibited by offering all the support he could to the cause that his child had followed). True, she had done so without his knowledge and without his consent, but post-factum—after what had happened, had happened—he, the father, was now adding his own signature, so to speak, to his child's honorable deed.

The secretary, therefore, without hesitation, accepted Boris's proposal and did not refuse what the other had presented to him.

It was agreed that now and then they would meet again to talk over—in its entirety or in part—the gift that Boris had offered to make for certain purposes. And they would also discuss the second half of Boris's proposition—to build a bunker, for which the secretary had received the right to recommend some parties whom *he* desired to hide there; he intended to exploit the opportunity for comrades who were in need, both in the short term and the long term, depending on what the situation called for.

He also wanted to provide for some so-called civilians; among them, he included Meylekh Magnus, whom he thought to lodge there. But, it turns out, it wasn't necessary, for Boris, earlier on, had already thought of him and entered his name in his little book—both because he was an old friend from way back and especially now that they shared a single sorrow and one and the same misery united them.

Yes, the idea came to them both at the same time—among the only visitors who came to Meylekh Magnus to sustain him spiritually was Boris, who would console him with his own example, saying that it was no better for him, either, and that certainly it should have and could have been better than this.

"Well, well," Boris would always say after his half-mute, consolatory discourse, when words were no longer enough and Meylekh Magnus remained seated—his thoughts would have stayed scattered anyway, even if his interlocutor had been able to offer more.

Because, indeed, he had been struck by misfortune; he had asked the members of the burial society to permit him to be the tombstone on his son's grave; he had been led to the gate of the cemetery and pointed back toward the city—then, turned to stone, he stood there and couldn't understand what they were saying; they saw that there was nothing to be done with him—he wasn't in the same world as everybody else—and they couldn't leave him in that condition: stunned, not even crawling in the direction he needed to go. Mindful of all that, they decided to take him back in the same hearse that had brought him and his son's body to the cemetery and give him over to the Jewish Council.

From that point on, since then—after they had led him back to the ghetto and, with the help of the secretary of the Jewish Council, returned him to his dwelling—afterward, he was to be found sitting in the corner, staring blankly at all that happened around him in domestic life, which held no concern for him. And he was this way even about things that did concern him—for example, when some of his students would come over, wishing to help him and provide a service of one kind or another, offering him a change of clothes, and so on.

For a time he remained like a corpse, as if his brains had been struck from him.

Once, during that time, the secretary of the Jewish Council also came to console him. Maybe it was because the secretary felt guilty that he had sought to persuade him (and pressed him) not to oppose his son's will but let the boy go down his chosen path; because this path had proved fatal for son and father alike (and the latter had not objected to the son but rather hastened his death by who knows how much). Or maybe it was because the secretary felt a little guilty about Meylekh Magnus, just because—out of compassion and sympathy for a scholar, to whom, now that various *Aktionen* had occurred in the ghetto, nothing remained . . . a person with intellectual roots like him, the secretary, who often, after his difficult and dangerous work (both for the Jewish Council and elsewhere) was drawn to those with whom he could talk, to distract himself a little and forget.

One way or the other: the secretary appeared before him again, supposedly with a command from the authorities concerning the institute (which, already, in the meanwhile, they had plundered, robbed, and disgraced).

He entered Meylekh Magnus's room not long after the meeting with Boris, after the latter had told him how he wished to create a well-protected hiding place for those whom he, Boris, thought it necessary (and he had also given the secretary the right to recommend those whom he considered it desirable to preserve . . .).

When he entered, he encountered Meylekh Magnus—as always in recent times—at leave from his senses. And when, still standing in the doorway, he spotted him, the thought occurred that maybe it would be better to leave him in peace—to put his visit off for another time—or even give up visiting him altogether.

There, sitting in the corner, was Meylekh Magnus—in a complete void, not seeing anything in front of him, not noticing that a person he knew stood at the door.

Finally, the secretary decided not to go away and leave with empty hands. (After all, he had already found the time to come there.) But he had to try to wake up Meylekh Magnus, who was so lost. . . .

"Khaver Magnus"—the secretary suddenly turned to the dumbfounded man with a familiar address. He had no doubt that it was right to speak to him in this way, and he was sure that he was not doing it just for the sake of buying the other man's confidence cheaply—as one might do with a sick person or an idiot. No, he spoke in an upright manner, because, after all, he saw before him a man who, more willingly than unwillingly, had contributed to the cause he held dear. . . .

"Khaver Magnus," he repeated, rousing him again. "It's me, the secretary of the Jewish Council. For some time now, I haven't paid you a visit. Now I've come on some business."

Then the other man looked at him. He extended a hand in greeting, but the greeting was the cold kind that shows the greeter isn't really thinking about the other party—and also, apparently, does not like him much.

"Take a chair." Meylekh Magnus still had a couple of decent words to say to his guest, besides the greeting.

The other took a chair and sat down. Then, immediately, he began to speak:

"I'm extremely busy, otherwise I'd already have come more than once. . . ." He said he was very concerned about the bad news he had received from reliable, official sources, which said that the ghetto there would soon be liquidated—just as many others had already been. Just now, he had barely managed to get away. . . . . And since he was already there, Meylekh Magnus should pardon him if he took the liberty of telling him clearly—without mincing words—what, at another time, he would have presented at greater length. Namely: being a witness of what they had already carried out up to now, and knowing what was planned for later on, he, the secretary, saw how Meylekh Magnus was deeply immersed in his own, personal woe—over his head; it looked to him—pardon—like the sea crying because a passing bird had had a little drink. . . .

God forbid, Meylekh Magnus should not suspect him of heartlessness or think him the kind who wished to keep another from his self-evident right to mourn someone who, naturally, fully deserved to be mourned. But yet: in view of the general calamity—given that the enemy regarded no one as an exception and he was weighed down only by his own despair—the secretary had to compare him with somebody who lamented that the ceiling was falling on his head, while, outside, a flood had already been raging forty days.

May he excuse his bluntness—which he permitted himself only because he wanted to do him a favor and tell the truth as someone detached from sentiments, like a doctor (who thinks of the good in the ill). . . .

He, the secretary, thought that even if one did not consider things in universal and international terms (which, by the way, were certainly suited to someone like Meylekh Magnus) but simply knew that the angel of death, armed with the plague, was now going around with a broom through the thousand-year Jewish settlement and sweeping them away until everything was *judenrein,*[*] and knowing, also, that he, Meylekh Magnus— who until now had enjoyed a privileged position and respect from the authorities—would ultimately have to disappear to a

___

*"Clean of Jews" (German).

disgraceful place, where it would be impossible to mourn even what was dearest to him. . . . Knowing all that, it was a wonder that someone like him—for as long as he still breathed, and as long as he didn't do as others had done in similar cases by "settling his debts" (that is, committing suicide)—it was a wonder that he was not doing the opposite of what he was doing now. That is, it was a wonder he wasn't telling himself that if he was indeed to suffer, then he would suffer for the sake of the truth—and if he didn't throw himself into the struggle (which, perhaps, he was no longer capable of), then, in any case, despite that, still he had the worthy ambition of preserving himself until the day one would see how the immense game for the world—the fight between Ormuzd and Ahriman,* between light and darkness—would end. . . .

No, the secretary said—he wasn't expressing himself clearly or correctly. Meylekh Magnus knew, after all, who he was—he was a man of the party, and for someone like that it wasn't fitting to use the word "game" with other people who knew the enemy's goal full well (that no sacrifice was too dear)—it was an insult, and it sounded like weakness. . . . Among his associates, he would certainly not have spoken like this, but here— before him, Meylekh Magnus, someone not in that group—he granted himself the liberty, if only in the hope of drawing him back to the side of the living, where he, the secretary, desired to see him.

"Because, in the first place"—he felt a little guilty before his interlocutor. And then—as he was an honorable party (even if he wasn't due as much honor as Meylekh Magnus)—he didn't want to see the other so devastated and endlessly removed from life. He wouldn't give the enemy that. The awful fate of those

*Pre-Islamic deities of Persia representing Good and Evil, popularized by the occultist "Madame" Helena Petrovna Blavatsky (1831–91), founder of Theosophy; Ormuzd and Ahriman feature prominently as allegories in fin de siècle literature throughout Europe.

who still survived didn't justify that the best heads on the best shoulders should sink so low, and that personal disaster, however great it may be, govern one in such a cowardly fashion.

He, the secretary, said all this because, as the other knew, a bunker was now being constructed for a certain number of persons; and he saw the possibility that he, Meylekh Magnus, would count among them. Out of fear, however—lest weariness and indifference make Meylekh Magnus give up and renounce the possibility of having a place there—now, he had come to tell him: it would be an injustice—or worse—if such a man did not to wish to save himself (if only to see, one day, the world breathing more freely, once the criminal stench had been cleared away).

Meylekh Magnus was older than he was, and certainly it was not his—the secretary's—place to lecture him. Still, he took the liberty of presenting the matter, so that he might see how he, the secretary—every minute of the day—risked falling into the enemy's hands (whose mercy was not to be wished upon anyone, because what is to be expected from them is well-known). He was, after all, engaged in a tightrope walk, and an abyss gaped below. Still, he adhered to that strict discipline that demands no rest until the end—and also that one exact the same price from the enemy as what has cost you dearly (by which he meant, of course, Meylekh Magnus's loss).

He asked for pardon again: it was certainly not right to set oneself forward as an example and demand from others that they do as you do. But after he had heard about Meylekh Magnus from his people—how he was living in a state of affliction—and after he had now seen for himself that three quarters of what he said was lost to him because of his distraction and immersion in sorrow (which gnawed away at him). . . . Seeing all this, he permitted himself the immodesty of speaking a favorable word about his own person—not, of course, for the sake of boasting, or because he wanted to play a self-important role (which was not at all in keeping with the principles of his kind)—but, instead, he had had the idea that perhaps it would succeed as a final expedient in this utmost case, now that they were standing before the absolute.

Well, then. . . . He had nothing more to add, because that was everything he had to say. Coming here and seeing him in such a downcast state—it seemed impossible that a human being with dignity could submit so fully.

While the secretary seated across from him was saying all this, Meylekh Magnus half listened but half didn't—less yes than no, it seemed. Only when the secretary had ended his last sentence did he raise his eyes and look at him for a moment in silence. Then, he made a bow over the table, where the other man was sitting across from him. And, just as had occurred the first time the secretary had arrived with the mission concerning his son, thus did he now, again, extend a hand to him— mutely and without words but trustingly and as if in complete agreement with what the other, just now, had proposed.

There, a good, trained eye would have noticed, right after the secretary's speech, that a welcome rain seemed to have fallen on Meylekh Magnus's long-parched soil. As great as his dormancy had been up to this point—now, after the other man's speech, all of a sudden and miraculously, there awoke in him understanding, interest, and also a little bit of vital energy (which, for a long while, he had no longer possessed).

This time, the secretary did not go away immediately after his speech. Instead, he stayed for a longer conversation, in which the newly awakened Meylekh Magnus started to ask him particulars about the situation in the ghetto in general—as well as the details about the bunker project the secretary had mentioned. Then, the secretary told him that, actually, the project wasn't his idea but Boris's—Boris, whom everyone knew, and certainly Meylekh Magnus, too, having been his friend for a long time already.

"Oh? Really? It's Boris's idea?" With satisfaction, Meylekh Magnus heard the news that Boris knew about the bunker, too—and he was even the one who initiated the construction. . . .

✦

Well, from then on—until the matter was settled, that is, and they took Meylekh Magnus into the completed bunker (which had been provided with all manner of comforts)—one could see a changed man, like someone whose darkness had been dispelled by light.

He gained a new perspective on himself, and the tongue in his mouth spoke again. And it should be said for clarification that this change did not come about because he had been singled out for privilege and better treatment; rather, it happened because, it turns out, his submersion in sorrow at his son's death had already reached a limit. The secretary's moralizing talk was the last push.

It sometimes happens, after all, that a human being passes from an oppressed condition to its cheery opposite. This seems to occur thanks, let us say, to a fitting word—something another person says at the right moment; but it can even come about for a more insignificant reason—even a swarm of flies buzzing past can make one forget one's condition and serve as a moment of crisis does a sick man.

Yes, it was as if Meylekh Magnus, too, had passed over to the opposite state. True, he was quiet and reserved, but he floated in a kind of energized exaltation all the same. (If a trained eye had taken a look at him then, his state would have been found to be as exaggerated and unnatural as, one might say, the long mourning for his son had been.)

People noticed that even in those very dangerous times—when nighttime attacks were carried out, and the ghetto echoed with all manner of tools people used as alarms, waking one another because of the threat of the police (who came at night, while everyone slept, to drag victims from their beds, because they considered the moment opportune for hunting, and no one would manage to stir from where they were and save themselves)—even then, Meylekh Magnus (nobody knows why) kept somewhat distant, to the side, as if he stood outside the wall containing the general terror, and he would always say to himself, and also to others: well, who knows . . . it's not forever. . . it will pass. . . .

At that time, people noticed how a little song often appeared on his lips. It was something one cannot imagine at all (well, "if you weren't there, you wouldn't know")—that a human being in the ghetto should indulge in any song at all—even if it was muted and he didn't let it pass a hair's breadth beyond his mouth.

But that's not important, it didn't bother anybody—and least of all him. During that time, he ate normally and even more than usual (when there was anything there at all)—not like before, when he had looked away from everything and wouldn't accept any food, because he couldn't get it down his throat.

During that period, he also spent time with neighbors, as is proper. There was just a slight exception to the rule: often, he would get lost in thought for a while, in the middle of speaking, and withdraw from the conversation (as if he hadn't started it—as if, until now, he had not participated and others had conducted it by themselves).

But that doesn't matter either. Nobody noticed, because, first, it didn't occur to anyone at that time to pay attention to others' quirks; and also, second, because of the separation mentioned above, that is: sometimes he got lost in song or withdrew in the middle of a conversation; but it always lasted so little that if one had no particular interest in getting behind it—to find the reasons for his conduct—one paid it no attention, even if one did notice. Especially then—with everything else that was happening—Meylekh Magnus didn't act any more drastically or idiosyncratically than anybody else. On the contrary: now, one could see him in a better and more cheerful mood than before, when mourning had oppressed him, and, for a time, he could not break free.

✦

The time came for him to be brought into the finished bunker. It had long been kept a secret even from close neighbors—and particularly strangers, about whom one had reason to be suspicious. It took some time until they had dug out the double cave and brought the excavated earth to a fitting place (so that no noticeable sign would remain). Apart from the digging, preparations also lasted until the smallest arrangements had been made—until they had covered the walls, the floors, and the ceiling with boards, so that the cave would be more livable.

And in the end—when everything was ready and the underground hideout was already occupied by others, and space remained only for Meylekh Magnus—none other than our Boris, the patron who had subsidized the construction, took on the responsibility of bringing him down into the bunker.

With Meylekh Magnus—an older person who wasn't at all quick when faced with danger—they needed to be especially careful. Already it was no small undertaking for others: when one came to the bottom of the first cellar, it was necessary to shrink down, in order somehow to creep through the winding, narrow tunnel and reach the actual bunker. And with someone like Meylekh Magnus (who was already an aged man without the ability to crawl around) things certainly proved difficult.

It even proved difficult just getting him out of the house. It had to be done at night, before the gates of the ghetto were closed (after which no one was allowed on the streets).

Boris took it upon himself to do all that. Everyone in the ghetto knew him well, so there was no danger. If he should be noticed alone, or together with someone else—even such a distinguished party—no one would hold him, or them, in any suspicion.

He acted properly, to protect himself and the individual he escorted—Meylekh Magnus—whom, every time the secretary had had a conversation with him about those to be lodged in the bunker, he had mentioned in particular and set apart, reserving more for him than the others.

And there Boris led him out of the house, making the excuse to neighbors that, allegedly, he was taking him to his own place for the night—his old friend, with whom he shared a single destiny because the same thing had happened to both their children—so they could spill their hearts out to each other in privacy and alone.

On the street, to strangers, he pretended they were going somewhere on business or back home—at such a late hour, one had to hurry a little, so that no one would stop them.

And then he brought him to the dwelling—separate and protected from prying eyes—where the first cellar was found, through which one passed to the other one—the one deeper down, where the actual hideout was located.

Boris crawled ahead, showing the way to Meylekh Magnus. Boris, with his still half-lordly countenance and broad-shouldered back—which, despite the fact that his time in the ghetto had diminished it, was still sufficiently wide that he could not, without difficulty, make it through what a younger man who was slighter in build could have. . . . But he crawled through. He crept, holding a light in his hand. It was always going out—and even when it burned, for Meylekh Magnus, who was crawling behind, it was practically nonexistent, except as a kind of will-o'-the-wisp (because Boris, who was carrying it in front of him, had no room to turn around and illuminate the way for the man following him).

Somehow they made it through one cellar, and afterward the second, until—the skin of their hands and faces worn raw—they finally reached the opening where it was possible to stand at full height and go in.

They started to make themselves at home. Everyone had, according to the previously devised plan, received a corner. When it came to Meylekh Magnus's quarters, Boris—as on the way down—once again took him under his wing (as one does a helpless child who can do nothing at all by itself and stands waiting for an older person to take care of it).

Then, Meylekh Magnus, according to the previous decision, received the very last chamber in the long row of rooms. It was his alone—with a table made of a few boards fastened to the floor, and a bed made out of boards, too.

They also provided him with light—as they did for everyone—and even with ink and a pen, for they thought that someone like that (who was certainly not inclined to self-interest), should, in any event, be able to busy himself with whatever he could; maybe writing would be a comfort to him in his underground existence.

✦

It will remain unsaid how one "lived" there and spent the time, because that has already been done—and will continue to be done, with more knowledge and more skill—by those who went through that bunker "life" themselves and were fortunate enough to be delivered from it.

In the case of Meylekh Magnus, there's also somebody else—a kind of student of his. He emerged intact and was able to report both at length and in detail about the bunker there—the one we're talking about—in which, besides Meylekh Magnus, there was the aforementioned Boris, as well as the secretary, who finally wound up there because, during a final *Aktion* (when the Jewish Council was being liquidated), all other paths of rescue were blocked to him.

Yes, that pupil there could say a great deal, but that isn't the point. The point here is the little bit of inheritance from his teacher that he managed to save—that is, a bundle of writings by Meylekh Magnus. Sitting there and not having anything else to do (because he was free from other kinds of work), he wrote them—not systematically, and in no proper order, just in fragments—whatever, at a given moment, came to mind to record and commit to paper.

That sole remaining pupil—afterward, at the appropriate time (that is, when the city where the ghetto was located had already been liberated)—went down into the bunker and rummaged around with a light. From a wall, he extracted a white tin box with scattered sheets of paper inside, which he himself had buried there. After great effort, he managed to sort the pages that remained chronologically (to the extent that dates could be determined), and also based on how the contents were connected.

Finally—bringing all that to a close and having already bound the pages in a certain order—he gave them a Latin name: *De profundis*. He was pretty sure that, under one fragment, he had found that his teacher had signed "A Voice from the Depths"—certainly a citation from the well-known passage of the Psalms, which reads, "Out of deep fear I call to you, O Lord." It seemed that in the situation he found himself, there was no better or more fitting name for him.

By the way, that's not how it was at all, because among the various fragments the pupil also found other signatures: for example, at the bottom of one, he found it had been signed "Troglodyte"; under another, "I Am the Man"; under a third: "Woe Is My Name." . . .

And so on, and so on. But the meaning of all the different signatures is one and the same, namely: the caveman. Who knows how many thousands and ten thousands of years one would have to go back to find another human being who has withstood so much suffering and inhumanity.

Meylekh Magnus took up the pen—the pupil notes here, in a short preface to his teacher's writings—not, as one might think, in order to record his beliefs, nor to write anything related to his scholarly activities. Rather, he recorded half-clear, half-unclear experiences that would better suit a professional writer—one whose task is always to balance his spiritual accounts and see their every part neatly arranged, fixed, and given form.

After all, there does occur—and here, the pupil is trying to justify the teacher (as if he needed any justification!)—what is called "sublimation"—that is, the ability to channel feelings and thoughts that beset one at a given moment into entirely different directions: first, in order to distract oneself for a while, and, then, to make one's psychic matter circulate for longer and more thoroughly (which, by the way, is known to be one of the healthiest instincts of self-preservation).

It was also the case here, with his teacher Meylekh Magnus, and the result was the aforementioned bundle of writings—which the pupil, after great difficulty, gathered together and put in the proper order.

1945–1946

Flora

1

I take up my diary:

    Day. . . . Month. . . . Year. . . .

    Dear *tate*, soon it will be a year that you aren't here anymore. You, my pride and my honor, joy of my heart, and the one who brought me up—under whose protective wing I was taken and grew, without a mother, whom I didn't even know. You, the well-known doctor among us here in the Polish-Jewish city and its surroundings—who, more than as a doctor, were known as a community leader with the cleanest hands and purest intentions. You, for whom—I noticed every time you appeared with me in town—children respectfully cleared the way, just as older people did when they crossed your path. You, whose good name and reputation among great and small, it seems, were due mainly to everyone's familiarity with your activities for the synagogue, which you loved and gave all your free time to, with the complete devotion of which you were so very capable.

    You were the father and patron of the Jewish Council, which the Polish state didn't consider a matter it had the responsibility to worry about. And you—and still other nationally minded men like you—saw yourself obliged to administrate the people's budget. Our own teachers, the buildings of our own that they required. . . . There arose the ambition to prove, to whoever needed it, that the Jewish education you worked for would not stand behind, nor remain inferior to, what the state considered its obligation to provide.

This was your idea, and you had the worthy satisfaction of seeing your own children raised together with those of the people, not separated by language or custom—as had occurred formerly, when intellectual do-gooders tended to create institutions of learning they did not consider for their own use—or that of their fellow Jews (because, otherwise, they could not help them at all . . .).

Despite how you provided for me and took care of me from the earliest age on—first with doting maids and then with foreign governesses (so that I would learn other languages)—when the time came for me to go to school, you found, in what you had established, nothing wanting at all—be it the methods of instruction or the provision of external necessities—nothing to make you wonder, even for a brief moment, whether you should perhaps *not* send me, because, evidently, it wasn't right. . . . No, the other way around: I saw how you showed up every time you were invited to the exams; and at the promotion of students from one grade to the next, I saw how you watched the progress that all the children had made over the year—among them me, too—your one and only, dearly beloved daughter.

I especially recall the last time you attended graduation exams, when I had to say good-bye to school, at the ball that was organized in honor of the occasion with dances and amusements. You let me sew a dress—a somewhat longer one than I had worn until now as a schoolgirl—one out of white silk, with a sash from the same material, tied in the back, whose ends fell down to the hem. . . .

Then, when I, your already grown-up daughter—already grown a little too tall, on my long stork legs (as you used to joke when you looked at me)—then, when I—in my dress sewn especially for the festivities—joined my partner at the first note of the music, in the great big hall, as the first in a row of dancers, and I made the first few steps—watching as the crowd of invited parents, along with the teachers and waitstaff, gathered to the side and took in the spectacle of the dance—then, I noticed you, too, hidden in the crowd, as had always been your way, looking at me and trying not to look, as if afraid of bringing bad luck. . . .

Then, when I—accustomed to and trained in dancing—when I went away again, with my first partner—my hand on his back and his . . . on mine—lightly arm in arm and airily arranged above the shiny, polished parquet—touching and not touching, not even feeling anything underfoot. . . . Then, as we carried each other aloft like a breeze, and, when the rules of the dance required it, also from time to time parted for a while, now coming face-to-face and now back-to-back, and then embraced each other again, in order to do what the rules of the dance further required, until the end, when everyone, all the couples, let go in a circle at a dizzying gallop, past the watching crowd that stayed to the side, looking on in pleasure. . . .

And then, when the first round was over and all the dancers went off, exhausted and overheated, for a brief rest, to their parents, who were standing to the side and waiting to encourage and congratulate them—some to wipe, with a loving hand, the sweat from their brow, and others, just to say another kind word—I, your already tallish-grown daughter, met you, modestly withdrawn in the crowd, after my first, dizzying success at the dance—from which I felt no fatigue, but quite the opposite: only thirst and the desire to be called for the next, approaching round. . . .

I saw that I had been a success with everyone who had watched me dance—and also with you—yes, you, who, as if afraid of bad luck, didn't want to look at me. . . . I fell in so close to you, a child to her father—a beloved father—and you, in turn, as was your modest way, didn't permit me anything more, although I saw perfectly well that, holding me at a distance, you desired to hold me close—as I wished to hold you.

Soon, when they came to invite me for the second dance, you let go, not making the slightest indication that you would like to keep me near a little longer.

I went away and danced some more. Thus it went—one after another, as the music grew quiet and others appeared, inviting me to be their partner. And willing parties, to tell the truth, were not lacking that whole evening—even up to the last dance.

And then, when the evening was over, when we went off for home, late—me with my head full of girlish dreams of head-dizzying success—and you, it seems, with the pride of a father and council member, which could be read on your face. . . . Then, when we came home and separated—me to my room, you . . . to yours—when I was left alone before undressing and going to bed—a little depleted by intoxicating reveries and also a little saddened by them—that today was the day I had to part from my carefree youth and take up seriousness, leaving my dearly beloved friends from the school bench and everything connected with them—then, you quietly knocked at my door and called me to you:

"What is it?"

You had something for me. . . .

Wakened unexpectedly from girlish dreams (although I still needed to get undressed), I went to your room, astonished and unknowing—why were you calling me so late, and what, in this manner, had you now to share with me, which, earlier, you hadn't? Then, you went to your desk, opened a drawer—which had always been there, it seems, locked up in your room—and you removed some kind of jewelry box, opened it, and, taking out a ring—an antique, golden ring of fine craftsmanship set with precious stones—handing it to me, you spoke:

"I have saved this for you. . . . It is an heirloom, from my grandmother, and back to times I no longer recall. . . . That is, by the way," you added, "a present your great-great-grandfather received. He was also a doctor, still in the time of Reb Manasseh ben Israel.* Born in Padua, Italy, he emigrated to England and, again, from there—by way of Holland and Germany—to Poland, where he became the personal physician in a royal court. He left behind," you said again, "a name of historical renown with his *Book of Healings*—and, in his family, the memory of a highly ethical human being. He acquired great influence and respect and was richly rewarded. And one of the gifts is this ring, especially commissioned, I was told, from a Jewish goldsmith.

"It is perhaps a little romantic," you said with an embarrassed smile, "but no matter. . . . Take it. Wear it in health and with dignity, as your grandmothers—great-grandmothers back to times I no longer recall—also wore it.

"Thereby," you continued, your voice sounding a little festive, "I betroth you, so to speak, to your past. To the future, child, another man will betroth you."

◆

Day. . . . Month. . . . Year. . . .

Dear *tate*. I want to remember how it happened: after they arrived. After they, in the first days—without any moderation—carried out the first thefts and murders of the Jewish population, which immediately felt devastated, outside the law, and like dogs without a tag, with no protection from the dogcatcher. Soon, a little later, the *Gebietskommissar* showed up in town—a certain von Lemke, who was supposed to govern

*Hebrew name of Manoel Dias Soeiro (1604–57), a Portuguese scholar and rabbi who established the first Hebrew printing press in Amsterdam in 1626.

the surrounding region, which had fallen under his authority, and command it with our city as the center.

As I later had the "honor" to learn, he was already older, over fifty. A creature of the Prussian gentry, with a straight, seemingly flat-planed back—an inheritance of the military discipline from the times of Frederick the Great, or maybe from much earlier—from Barbarossa.* Moreover, a man apparently attended to by many servants. This had given him the opportunity to study and possibly complete an academy, a university—which could be seen by the pale-brown scar on his face: a remnant of sword dueling, as is practiced in their drunken student fraternities.

In a word, both militarily schooled and also "highly educated"—a suitable administrator and regional plenipotentiary. . . .

And then, just as he appeared in town, you, *tate*, were summoned to him immediately, according to information from impure tongues the authorities had found or, earlier still, secretly hidden in the city, for racial purposes—or from people who had foolishly entered into agreement with the authorities (but later became aware what—who—was at stake).

They endorsed you as the man most highly esteemed by the Jewish populace, which had immense confidence in you.

And then, when you appeared before the party who had summoned you, he immediately offered something you certainly would have excused yourself from doing and declined as impure—but your only option was to agree and let your neck be harnessed in a yoke you did not seek.

"As we know, Herr Doktor, according to the information we have received from reliable sources, you are most respected among those of your tribe—a person upon whom both we,

*Frederick I Barbarossa (ca. 1123–90), crowned Holy Roman emperor of the German nation in 1155. "Operation Barbarossa" was the Nazi code name for the invasion of the Soviet Union in 1941.

the authorities, and your people will certainly be able to rely. We have found your candidacy most appropriate—and commission you with leadership in office. We have decided to create an organ to regulate relations between our directorship and your populace—and to select you as a representative, a mediator."

"Me?" you asked. Why you, who were so overburdened with the work of your profession? You wouldn't have the time—or ability—to hold such a position, to which you were not at all accustomed. . . .

"We're not forcing you. We are simply presenting an opportunity. And anyway, Herr Doktor—if it is all right with you to see the command over your people in rather bad, undesirable hands—you have the choice to do as you wish, as you alone decide."

Already the invitation sent to you by a pair of soldiers with the double *S* and certain emblems (skulls and bones) . . . ; your arrival, afterward, in the building, to see the commissar—when you had to go through a guard post, once again, of men armed with guns, and still more guns—men with cold, menacing stares . . . ; then, your arrival before the commissar himself, when he acted as if he didn't notice you, and he let you stand there, hardly answering your salutation (as if he had no mouth). . . ; then, when you mentioned the distinguished people who had been the first to die—with whose death the authorities had established themselves as soon as they entered the city. . . . All this, together, clearly indicated with whom you were dealing, what stood before us, and that no one had anything good to expect—and also that this was indeed an exceptionally important relationship. This, too, put pressure on you, so that you saw yourself forced to accept what was so repulsive to you—knowing that if not you, others would certainly be found, and they would be undesirable parties capable, in a calamity, of deriving advantage only for themselves.

"Good-bye," said the *Gebietskommissar,* quickly taking leave—as coldly as he had "welcomed" you, when he said nothing at all (and soon afterward, when you, already the head of the *Judenrat,* had tried—with a right you thought you now possessed—to say something about the outrages already committed, which had occurred with the arrival of the military, to the disgrace of the Jewish populace, so it was clear that nothing restrained the authorities: anything they wanted to do with us was permitted, and what they had done was just the beginning . . .).

"Good-bye, Herr Doktor. There is no time now to talk about it. . . . By the way, there is a matter not to be avoided, so to speak, and certainly caused by unruly, irresponsible elements. . . ."

I had to see you as you came home from the commissar—after your first visit to him. It was as if you had grown smaller. I had also never seen you so pale, and I could swear that it was the first time I saw your tie not to be well arranged. I don't know whether you left home that way, or if you came back like that: you walked out of there the fully authorized head of the Jewish Council, which later was put to such shame and so greatly maligned that its name should not be mentioned. . . .

And there began something I don't want my mouth to speak or my pen to write, because it is enough that I am a living witness of it: persecution and evil decrees of a measure and kind that no human being, only yesterday, could have conceived them, even in fantasy. (Even if one happened upon the wildest savages, no one would think such things possible.)

And all that, *tate,* you went through—the pain in your hand, which had to sign all the orders, and the pain in your eyes, which saw you stand side by side with the antisemites. . . . I know you certainly meant well—that is, for the better in the worse, knowing that what approached must be inevitable, thinking that how-it-isn't would perhaps show you a way to keep things within certain limits.

Yes, but. . . . When it was still just a matter of the ghetto and a wretchedly herded-together, greatly humiliated existence—misery under restraint and supervision; when it was not yet a matter of slaughter—nor of having to give daughters over to shame—or of bringing them to the point that they offered themselves. . . . When it was still, so to speak, halfway bearable—already then, a few were to be found who publicly (and still more in private) started to mutter about your guilt, seeing in your forced actions, turned against their families, how you only served yourself.

That was then—when things were still, as mentioned, tolerable. But later, when antisemitism poured out and spilled over like a flood, taking the form of certain *Aktionen*—covered by mendacious assurances from the authorities that there would be no more, and what had occurred was called for because of this or that (the blame, allegedly, only of victims, who had to be dealt with like dogs . . .).

At that point, you could not take any more and you told yourself: enough. All pure illusions about being able to check what had been unleashed were squeezed dry, and then, when you were supposed to permit these things and remain in the accursed office to which you were bound: truly, *that* would have been betrayal on a level almost matching those who, in their own interest, were ready to sell their own people.

Then, at that point, coming home from the bureau, you called me to you again, into your room. Looking as if you stood before something even worse than what would soon happen, you spoke to me. "Child. . . ." After that word, you couldn't find another to follow. You stuttered—as if your tongue were impure. Afterward, when you had calmed down a little, you addressed me: "Know that I have decided to resign from my office, regardless of the consequences that will result. Understand, my child. . . ."

"I understand," I said, not knowing exactly what you meant by the word "consequences." "What do you mean, *tate?*"

"I mean that, as far as I know and based on what I can be sure of—having come into closer contact with them and having been able to hear both candid words and disguised ones—I have reason to believe that there is a secret agreement among them—something accepted at the very top—that one way or the other, now or later, they will put an end to us all, down to the last man. . . .

"I must not stay any longer. I must not give anyone hope. . . . I must go away," you said, "and that will mean insubordination. That is how they will interpret it, and the results may be sad, very sad. But I can't do it." And then you made a certain pause. "It may be that you will soon be alone; I know what you have to do. Defend yourself. But I don't see rescue coming anytime soon. I see only one way out: away, out of here, and off to there." Abruptly, you turned your face to the east of our country's border, where it seems you sensed the only possibility for salvation.

"I know," you said quietly, pensively, and confidentially, "according to the reports I have secretly received in my official capacity, that, not far away, in the forests, they are gathering the means of resistance; and whoever has been struck by the usurpers and feels outraged—and is also capable of fighting—goes there.

"I know, also," you continued, "that the path is full of the enemy—both in getting out from the power of the usurpers here and in getting there. But I also know—again, secretly, in my official capacity—that already here, among our people, there are parties in charge of helping those they need on the other side. One has to find them. As for me, the path is already blocked, because I am too old, too conspicuous, and many would suffer on account of me if I failed. But you—consider it, whether you can manage by yourself."

Then, as before, you went to your desk, opened the drawer that had always been under lock and key, and took something out—but this time not to give to me—just something for yourself, for your own use. . . . I could have sworn that I saw you take out some kind of pharmaceutical thing, a kind of drug in a powder—which quickly, without delay (so that I wouldn't be able to see it) you put in your vest pocket. Besides that, you removed something else—a gold knife wrapped in ordinary paper, it seemed.

The whole time you were busy with the items you had taken out, you didn't look me in the eye. Just as you didn't look me in the eye when you indicated where I should go and used words like "struggle" and "resistance"—which had never, it seemed to me, been part of your vocabulary. And it is, by the way, also understandable why: because you, as a weak politician, as someone who sometimes turned—or didn't—to our loose, drunkenly overheated People's Party* (which, it seems, never distinguished itself by anything other than occasionally voting)—you, here, in your own house—employed words like this, which your mouth was not accustomed to speaking, and I wasn't used to hearing from you.

But that is not the important point. The main thing is that—not knowing that I was seeing you for the second-to-last time in my life and yours—I, not appreciating the immense gravity of your statements, didn't understand what was at stake.

I didn't think about the substance you took from the drawer and put in your vest pocket. I assumed it was a powder for headaches—from which, in recent times, holding the office you did—you suffered a great deal (and often complained about).

I also hardly noticed that this time, when you left—before going away—you bent over me and kissed me on the head. I

*Folkspartei, a populist, non-Zionist Jewish party founded after pogroms in 1905. It advocated the preservation of Jewish autonomy; its base was formed by the middle classes, craftsmen, and members of the intelligentsia.

was used to it; it was nothing new. New and uncustomary to me was that when you kissed me, you let your mouth stay a little longer—as if you wanted to forget yourself for a while (even a little longer than one ought to . . .).

Also, I didn't notice how, when you left the room and I accompanied you, you opened the door, went out, and then had to close it a second time. You did so slowly. As if forgetting yourself again, or as if you still had something to tell me (which you didn't know before)—you held the door open a while and looked at me in embarrassment.

I didn't know that you had already decided to go to the *Gebietskommissar* with your heart resolved to hand in your resignation, to step down from the position, and in no case to allow yourself to be persuaded to take it up again—prepared for anything and knowing the consequences that could result.

And truly: no one was present at the conversation between you and the *Gebietskommissar,* but the results made themselves known immediately: right away, a patrol led you off to prison—the place from where, as everyone knows, one doesn't emerge, because either one is eliminated directly, or they do it by other means, sending the condemned to a more distant location—it's all the same.

✦

And then, *tate,* I, your daughter, was left alone on the stage. . . .

I don't know where my ability to act came from—whether from innocence or desperation. I only know that the desire to save you impelled me—you, my one and only.

As soon as the report reached me, right away—not stopping to think what I was doing and what the result would be—I started to write a petition to the *Gebietskommissar,* asking him to receive me. I had a good command of the commissar's language—but *what* I said in my petition and *how* I put my request for an audience, I can't remember. I only know that, miraculously, it didn't take long for it to be communicated that my request had been granted: on such and such a day, at such and such an hour, I could appear before his highly decorated person.

I don't know whether he thought he would obtain through me what, with you, had been denied him—to put you in his service again, in order to cover himself with your authority and reputation as a mask, so he would be able to keep doing what he wanted. I don't know whether he meant it seriously or maybe just wanted to give himself the perverse joy—when the appointed hour came—of seeing how, after the victim, the child of the victim would tremble before him.

Either way—but when the time came to prepare myself to appear before that man, I, so young and inexperienced, already had a feeling that I had no prospects of obtaining anything by means other than myself. . . .

I got dressed in the best and prettiest clothes I could find among the things that had remained in greater quantity for you and me than others. (When they robbed everyone, you, an official, and I, your child, had been spared.)

Unknowingly—even to myself—I didn't neglect to bring your present along: a little something, it seems, to serve as protection. (And also with the underlying idea that I would look good. . . .)

I made my way to the building where the audience was to occur. Just like you, when you had appeared there, I, too, went past the green-uniformed guards with weapons ready and cold, menacing gazes.

I finally went in to him—by myself, to His Majesty—whom I encountered seated at his desk in a corner between two walls, in the half-light of a side window.

As with you, he seemed not to notice me for the first minute. He paid no attention to my humble entry, my opening the door, or my first steps on the carpet (which it swallowed up).

Afterward, however, when he did notice me, after all—when, as if by chance, he lifted his eyes from the work that lay before him—he put a question to me as if to a person coming at an inconvenient time and without permission:

"Who are you, Miss?"

Stuttering, I gave my name—as well as yours, for whose sake I had the honor of addressing him, the Herr Gebietskommissar.

"*Ach so,* the daughter of Herr Chairman of the Jewish Council?"

"*Jawohl,* sir."

"Is there something, then, I can to say to ease your guilt?" he asked. And—like an adult deigning to speak in language comprehensible to a child—he started to explain what was at issue and what an enormous wrong you had committed with respect to the authorities. That is to say: if anyone else had done this, he would have been dealt with without further ado and received his punishment immediately—there, then, and in full. You had been shown great mercy—sitting in prison, you had received time to reconsider and repent your deed.

"That's it, maybe that's really what brought me here—to beseech you, Herr Kommissar"—to permit me to see my father and, as your own child, help you, *tate;* to remind you of the enemy: possibly, you don't know how vast and powerful they are. . . .

Once again—like an adult speaking with a child—he snatched my words up as if I had no mouth. Suddenly, he raised himself, suddenly, from his place of honor—he, the already more than middle-aged, grave personage of the so thoroughly trained military kind (which was evident in his strongly uniform, planed back, stiff neck, and throat: he looked like a wolf that couldn't turn to either side). He rose. Stopping the conversation (as before), he benevolently took a step, as if to a child—getting up from the desk and going to where I stood, as if he wanted to cheer me up and lighten my mood.

In so doing, he laid a hand on my shoulder in a paternal fashion. Again, he measured me from top to bottom—my size, my shape—and not at all as one measures a child. After this examination, I noticed, it seemed for a while that no words would come to him—as if he were stuck and something far more important than words lodged in his gullet.

But he soon composed himself, and—understanding how great my love for you was just by the fact that I, so young and inexperienced, had undertaken the weighty mission of appearing before such highly decorated eyes, presuming to obtain anything at all—he—apparently wishing to exploit my inexperience and keeping his hand on my shoulder—gave me a look in the eye. And half in jest—but more in earnest (like a businessman)—he began to negotiate:

"And what will Miss Flora—as she is called—pay for this favor?"

I must confess to you, *tate*—that I was not unversed in the "rules," as they say. I must confess that—when the hand I did not wish for at all touched my shoulder—I felt like a woman, and I also realized that with such knowledge much can sometimes be obtained. . . .

I was not young and unskilled when I was put to the test of choosing between myself and you—that is, between myself *or* you, my only beloved until this point—when I extended a hand to make sure the slightest speck of indecency wouldn't fall upon me or touch you. Then, I saw myself standing before a choice that—understand me, *tate*—even the purest bearing wouldn't have been able to reject: that my tongue should lean slightly from its delicate, modest balance. . . . In so doing—for the first time in my life, it seems—I acted coquettishly, with a woman's art and feigned shame. Certainly, I observed, it made an impression on that man and forced him to believe that as much as I had offered with a look from beneath my lowered lashes just now, I would later—when he had fulfilled my request—grant him.

My look succeeded. I saw how the man, before whom I now stood—I, a young, inexperienced, and unprotected girl—began to melt like a piece of wax when he saw me and sensed the readiness he could expect later on.

Pardon me, *tate*—you, and all pious spirits, should pardon me. . . . But I swear my woman's game didn't last more than a moment. I soon caught myself, and, then and there, I accepted my punishment. Ashamed, for want of protection, and in order not to permit anything further—I glanced at your present, your ring on my hand, to remind myself from whom I had received it, and what I had been told when you gave it to me.

I held the ring before my eyes a little longer—apparently that pleased the man even more. I don't know if it was my hand with the ring, my bearing, or my expression of sincere and honest shame. He melted even more.

His mouth full of something other than words, he spoke: "You shall receive what you desire, Fräulein."

But he also didn't forget who he was or the position he held. He demanded unconditionally that I persuade you and obtain your return to the post you had abandoned. Mainly for that reason had permission been granted to visit you in prison—an exception otherwise allowed for no one.

Again, he didn't forget to remind me of the promise he believed to have received: that I, in a "proper" manner, would repay the debt I owed. . . .

He even went so far in his kindly inclination to bow to me. He wished to kiss the hand with the ring (which I still held before my eyes but, naturally, didn't extend to him).

In a seemingly childish way (but not at all without an adult's understanding), I saw how to get what was necessary from him—a pass for the prison guard, so that I would be permitted to see you, and everything else. . . . Then I went out. I don't know whether I formally took leave or not, but I somehow felt that man accompany me with a kind of gaze behind my back, which I hope will never follow me again.

✦

Dear *tate*. On the same day the prison gates and doors opened before me, when the guard saw who had written the authorization—then, we were brought together. And I saw you. But the little bit of joy I had in seeing you again—even if it was in the setting of a prison—was immediately destroyed when you abruptly—before asking *what*, before asking *who*—put the question to me:

"*How* did you get in here? Who granted you permission?"

"The *Gebietskommissar*," I responded.

"Him? How did you get to him?"

"I'm coming from him."

"You? From *him*?"

"Yes."

I saw the abundant darkness, which you brought with you from the cell, compounded by an even greater darkness when you heard my words. . . . You were silent for a time; then you spoke briefly, not entering upon any explanations.

"Don't do that anymore. . . . This is no place for you." Some unspoken suspicion wouldn't vanish from your face—and the warning it contained, directed toward me, wouldn't disappear from your lips.

"No," you said again after a little, "you can expect nothing good from that."

"But . . . *tate*"—have I done you wrong? You, whom it will soon be difficult to recognize—because neither the suit in which you went away is yours anymore, nor the shoes—you have no shoes, and you stand there alone—already three-quarters condemned, just before the passing of life. . . .

"Dear *tate*"—have I done you wrong? I had nothing to say, only a lament to make.

I saw that talking with you about taking back your decision was pointless. I saw you were resolved. Fully aware of what you had taken on, you were incapable of changing your word now. And, to tell the truth—if they had put the choice before me—I wouldn't have advised you to take your decision back, either.

"Dear *tate*," I cried, receiving no comfort from you and expecting no assurance of better prospects. I knew you yourself were not sure—and if you were, you were sure of the opposite: that there were no prospects, and you saw yourself here with me, possibly, for the last time.

You held your head turned and wouldn't look at me—locked in my arms, holding my head at your breast. You could do nothing more than that: embrace me, not let go of me, say nothing, as if tears blocking the words had made you mute.

You made an enormous effort, I saw, when you moved me back a little and freed yourself from my embrace, because then—already, soon, before saying good-bye—you still wanted to tell me something.

"Child," you said, "Don't worry about me. Maybe some opportunity will arise, and maybe not. At any rate, I've already lived my life. But you—not yet. See what you can do about getting out of here and making it where I directed you. It's the only way out."

Then the guard arrived and said that visiting time was over. And then I grabbed hold of you again—for the last time—as if to be swallowed up and, dead or alive, remain with you.

Soon they tore you from me and separated us, and. . . . It was already for good, because after that night—some knew earlier, but I found out . . . later—you had no tomorrow. You didn't wait for others to finish you off. Instead, you did it yourself. And you did it both for your own sake and for mine (lest I again feel tempted to change your fate in a manner you didn't wish).

That night (it was later determined), you took something, and that something was surely the substance which, leaving home, you had removed from the drawer. And when it seemed to you that the effect of what you had swallowed wasn't fast enough, you took something else you had brought along and cut yourself. . . .

At daybreak, when they were waking the prisoners, a neighbor who slept with you on a bunk felt he was lying in a puddle. . . . He got mad at his neighbors—at the neighbor on one side and you on the other—with whom, under such "conditions," unpleasantness could occur (from the cold, unfortunate closeness, etc. . . .). But when he took a look at you in the darkness of dawn and saw the paleness staring from your face, he immediately understood what had happened. Knowing you to be a doctor; knowing, also, that you hadn't spoken once with the others about this way out; and knowing, especially, that you had seen me, your one and only, the day before—and you had returned even more defeated (because something, they said, had been added to your woes besides what all condemned men fear . . .). Then, everything became clear. Then, already, you were no more. . . .

"May the Great Name be exalted and sanctified," they say, I guess, for the dead.

✦

Day. . . . Month. . . . Year. . . .

As soon as you were no more, I lost my privileges as your child—the child of a respected officeholder. They put me out of the home where we had lived and into the thirty-two square foot area that had been declared the rule for ghetto inhabitants. I found myself in a house—not a house, just a hole, a grave, where the walls cried, the ceiling stood at your head, and the sun, even in broad daylight, was a rare guest. I was with many other "lucky" ones like myself, who found themselves stuffed in a cage. Plus—as if to guarantee the overcrowding—there was, in addition, an older, lonesome Jew by the name of Hershel Shuster. He deserves a few words because, looking at him, one can get a bit of an idea how we appeared in the mirror we had so lovingly been granted.

The whole day, he was occupied by the labors of a workshop where boots were made for the front. He worked quietly, with masterly perfection, conscientiously—and even too conscientiously. . . .

"Hershel, why so dutiful? Why so much attention? God forbid one of *them* should remain without shoes—or even a foot! Does it matter? Would it, God forbid, weigh hard on your head?" He didn't answer—as if he couldn't hear. He continued his work, holding himself distant and not even lifting his head to see who was asking.

No one asked anymore. Everyone knew who he was—that he was devoted to work the whole day long. And when he came home at night, he was beside himself—he was . . . the Messiah. Then, he studied the role he had taken on. Reading the tiny letters, he could be a great scholar. . . . He said he saw himself as a rider on a poor donkey headed toward Jerusalem. Then, he took a step (as much as the narrow space in the room permitted) to perform a salutation and greet himself—once, twice, three times, and many more. He imagined people crowding to welcome him. He also saw himself—just as it is written in the book of Daniel—descending from heavenly clouds. He hid away, covered his head, and, trembling in delight, beheld his majestic appearance, his mouth agape. . . . Another time, he saw himself among lepers, beggars, and dissolute women at the gates of Rome. He is a leper himself, busy with his wounds, undoing and redoing bandages. No face as unfortunate as his can seen, no one in worse condition. He falls to the ground, his legs bent beneath him. In a quietly wailing voice, he begs, in the foreign Latin tongue, from all who enter and exit the city.

Yes, he is right, Hershel, about the role of Messiah. Seeing what is happening out there, no madman could assume a lesser role than his—nor should it be possible to do so.

✦

Dear *tate,* I know you are not here. But I know, too, that as you should not *not* be here, therefore when you hear what I will soon tell you, you will make a start—out of fear, out of shame, out of bitterness, and out of fatherly, human worry.

A little while ago, I was struck.

"Who?"

The tall dolt, the supervisor of the work column where I am stationed: the man with the black mustache—hard like the pincers of a beetle. He is old enough to be considered unfit for the front but fit enough to supervise us, a column of workwomen. He keeps an eye on us and doesn't let us get lazy or stand idle; he demands the work quota from us—and also more, if he wants. He has the power—he is authorized—to do that, and for this purpose he has been given not just a whip but also a gun (to use on the spot, whenever he feels the need or desire). Although he is pretty old and the joints in his knees have been broken by gout, he has, as mentioned, the whip and the gun—and, moreover, a pretty little bag of filthy words he lets loose at every opportunity (and nonopportunity), such as *Blutjude* and *Jude, verrecke.** When he lets one of them fly, he heats up and it feels good to loose a second, a third, and so on, without stopping. Apparently—besides the fact that higher-standing authorities have given him the right to act this

---

*These German terms of abuse mean "Bloodjew" (referring to usury and alleged practices of host desecration) and "Croak [die], Jew."

way—he has also claimed the right for himself. Now, he has the chance to unload his anger for one insult—a mistake of nature he has carried since birth, which he had in youth and still today (which, evidently, he must endure in silence). That is: his crooked, bent legs; the hollow between them amounts to what, in his language, they call O legs.

It wouldn't be tolerable, were it not for two weaknesses he possesses—thanks to which one can more or less take a break from him. First: "his beer." He gulps it down every day, and always at the expense of those he is watching over, who must, from their "excessive" salary, pay for it. Otherwise, everybody knows they "get a thrashing"—that is, they are beaten. When he gets what he wants, it makes him much softer, more relaxed. . . . And the second thing, which follows from the first, is that he leers at the women when he's drunk and intones his sweetly nostalgic song (which he brought along from his dearly beloved hometown).

> In Hanover, on the Lein',
> The girls' legs look fine,
> (and so on).

Grinning, he takes a look at his own legs—and, afterward, at the legs of the woman who happens to be near; then he tells her she should do him the favor, right there, of. . . .

I don't know if he was in a "bad mood" that day (at a certain time), because the workwomen hadn't taken care of his thirst. Maybe it was another reason. But on that day, he had a cruel heart and watched me with ill intent—to see whether I was doing my work well or not. And suddenly he started to grab me, scream at me, and strike me—which he deliberately didn't do with the whip but his hands.

Not so much pain, as shame, seized me. Less pain than misery left from earlier—before I was struck—stirred within me and grabbed my throat.

I stopped my work, not considering that this gave the supervisor the right to strike me more and treat me even worse (with no fear that he would have to answer for his deed before higher parties—quite the opposite: harsh as his actions might be, he, for his part, could count on approval). Not considering that, I stopped my work until—off to the side, away from my friends (who looked on)—I hid between bales of fabric and started crying. . . .

That was the first time—it seems—after I had lost you, *tate*. I was so petrified, looking at what was happening around me and where I had wound up. I cried for my youth, remembering in whose care it had been. I cried that I had been born under such an unlucky star, not knowing why. . . .

I stood there for a long time. And when I had cried myself out, I returned to work, not exchanging a single word with my kinswomen—locked up inside myself the whole time.

Later—when the supervisor had evidently gotten his beer, settled down drunk, and achieved a good-natured, Hanoverian mood—I don't know why, but today of all days, after turning his cruel heart upon me and striking me—now of all times, he picked me as the one who pleased him and at whose legs he would leer (as was his way).

And still more: this time he was so far gone in his terrible dissipation that he even extended a hand—wanting to touch the rounded, womanly shapes onto which he, when in that state, turned his ugly gaze with open impudence.

Then I gave him such a talking-to about his hand that it flew back—behind his back, and to his backside, apparently. And, behold, a wonder: he didn't feel insulted by my words of refusal (for which he should have attacked me with all his rage); on the contrary: as if he were dealing with an equal, he transformed his anger into a friendly joke. On his lips smiling pardon appeared—like a father's for a dearly beloved child who, after playing, is even dearer to him.

That's what he did. The women, however, saw the vehemence with which I cast back the supervisor's hand. They didn't know where my boldness had come from, but they knew what an action like that could entail at another time, in a nondrunken state (or even a drunken one). Quietly, so he wouldn't hear, they began to rebuke me:

How was this possible, what had I done? And why make such a scene—which might cost so much to me and everyone else—whomever the shadow of my anger touched?

Then I let loose on them:

They should be ashamed. . . . The disgrace of our situation is, after all, worse than the situation itself—and whoever doesn't realize it should eat from the same bowl as a pig.

"Just look at her," some threw back, "what's gotten into her? What makes you better than others?" And is there any other option? Others consider themselves lucky if the swine are even willing to join them.

May they choke on it. . . .

A word for a word, and it came to a loud, hateful exchange.

"Maybe you think," some said, trying to justify their weakness and willing to compromise with the inevitable, "maybe you think you can go it alone and do better."

"Of course," I said, not accepting their solution. "It's the opposite of what you say.

"Take them," I snapped, "take them, who rescue on the sly—who do what they can—who adapt and keep their eyes open—or at least one of them."

"Have you tried?" they asked, hinting at something awful. . . . And they reminded me of the certainty of defeat, with results that were grievous not just for direct participants but also for anyone upon whom the merest suspicion fell of having the slightest connection with them.

They were right, my kinswomen: many cases like that had already occurred, which all ghetto inhabitants knew and couldn't *not* know. That terrified most of the populace and was the reason people created illusions for themselves—maybe they would manage to wriggle out from what others couldn't escape. Some didn't wait for that and took care of things for themselves, out of hollow desperation, choosing one form of death instead of another and saying that—whether one put up a fight, or didn't—they were condemned anyway, and why cling to earlier ways of life? You won't change the situation. . . .

"Childishness," they said. There's no hope, and at any rate that kind of thing doesn't work for everyone—only for some, and it succeeds one time out of a hundred. And even if it does, those whose life is cheap to them should do it—those who don't care whether it happens sooner or later. . . .

"Better sooner than later," I said out of inner conviction that I was right—after experiencing a day when I had been struck and, afterward, touched in such a disgraceful manner.

At the end of the day, weeping seized me again. I couldn't contain it, and I went back to where I had been—behind the fabric bales—remembering my fallen state and the degradation of those around me, whose feeling of protest was already extinguished. I kept crying and remembered the testament that you, *tate*, left me when you went away, which indicated that I could expect help where one's hand reached easily—where it was necessary only to turn one's face to feel the breath of hope blowing. . . .

I don't know how long I stayed alone, among the bales. Only at dusk, when the sign was given to gather and go home, I emerged. I was no longer crying; rather, it seemed to me that my eyes were made of glass: I looked at the others from off to the side—and they, too, looked at me, it seems—as if my gazes stung them.

The whole time we walked back I was silent and offered no word of excuse. From the place far behind the city where our women's detail worked until we entered the town—I faced only one way. I was looking to where I expected good, not knowing how it would appear.

✦

That day, dear *tate,* was a concluding one in my life. I don't know whether your respected name helped me—or whether the occurrence with the supervisor reached the proper ears and my actions were well received. One way or the other: those who rescue by stealth evidently noticed and cast an eye upon me—and not without favor.

I could swear that from then on, I somehow sensed someone was on my trail—someone passing who watched me attentively. And when they approached me, they steered in my direction and looked—not at my beauty, surely, but rather with a certain other interest.

Later—walking through the ghetto on a rest day—I struck upon a party. The encounter—as soon as we met face-to-face—I immediately noticed was no coincidence; rather, he had foreseen the time and place in advance. He knew he would encounter me precisely there and then.

It was a little to the side of the busier streets. Coming toward me, this person made a quick start—as if, just now, he had nearly passed and failed to notice me. But now that he had seen me after all, he spoke:

"Good that we happened to meet with you. . . ."

In the word "we," it did not sound like he was referring to himself but rather as if he spoke in the name of some kind of group that had authorized him to say this.

It intrigued me, but I also got a little scared—seeing myself eye to eye with a stranger. However, I controlled myself, and, as a woman before whom someone unknown stands with a definite purpose—to get to know me—I acted with restraint.

I didn't allow myself to reply too easily or quickly, and I asked a question:

"And who is 'we'?"

"Don't be afraid, Miss Flora. No one wishes you ill, and my people are no bears. . . . We know you, and we know about you. You are considered someone to be trusted."

"Yes, but who else is this 'we'?"

"It's people you probably haven't ever heard about but who, we believe, you would like to know. You just might want to join them. Be so good and go to such and such a place this evening. Then it will all become much clearer to you."

And there the man I had encountered gave me a remote address in a still more remote dwelling somewhere in a distant ghetto alley (which was, it turned out later, not at all easy to find). And as soon as he had given it to me, he vanished without even a "be well"—as if, just now, a moment ago, he hadn't wanted a thing from me, hadn't stepped aside, and hadn't said what he had said. Hurriedly, he started to stride off in the direction he had come from. But he soon caught himself, turned back, and spoke again:

"If they ask you when you arrive, 'Who are you here to see?' answer: 'Rosin.'* I trust you understand and will remember everything."

It seemed mysterious and almost as if it had been written in a detective novel, yet I felt a hidden pull toward the man who had taken me aside and confided all this to me. I decided that it was meant seriously and not in vain, because the man him-

*This password may refer to David Rosin (1823–94), a Jewish theologian and educator from Silesia. Since Der Nister makes other references to famous women of the eighteenth and nineteenth centuries, it is worth mentioning that "Rosina" is the name of a beautiful and clever character of opera; in Rossini's *Barber of Seville* (1816), she tricks her guardian by substituting a laundry list for an incriminating love letter—an action resembling (in reverse) events that occur later in Der Nister's story.

self looked as if frivolous matters were not his business—like someone you could rely on.

That was Berl Bender. (It wasn't his real name but one he had assumed.) He looked to be a tradesman—a shoemaker or smith—someone who bears the marks of the profession underneath the skin, even after washing many times. . . . But for all that, he was not a tradesman—he was an intellectual. True, an average one, but one who acted in a hearty, blessed way—one in whom all newly arisen ideas converge as if in the air (my youthful intuition told me). These are the people who tear into the old, stagnant world in order to make space, and still more space, for the new reality. For this, they are ready to give up everything, even their last breath.

The "Born One," they called him in his milieu—not adding the word "revolutionary" because it was understood. He was continuing his prewartime, Polish-underground practice, for which the Poland of that time had imprisoned him. The state just didn't like it, and for the sake of not letting such parties multiply, it maintained a great apparatus of well-hidden agents who had the task of catching people like him and "detaining" them where necessary. (The less important and dangerous ones in smaller prisons and the more important and dangerous ones in places such as Kashubia—where he, Berl Bender, had had the honorable distinction of residing a long while.)

He was already well over thirty, yet he showed no sign of slowing down (which occurs with age and makes people more settled in their ways). No, he was still fully active and mobile— and not only in his habitual, hasty stride: when necessary, one sensed, he was capable of a wholly youthful gait (when, for example, he had to escape the grip of undesired, enemy hands).

He was strong boned and had black, shoe-polish eyes; on right-angled shoulders sat his head with high temples of black hair. Moreover, he was graced with the following two qualities:

he was delicately disposed and dedicated (to a fault) to people who shared his schooling and sensibility; also, he displayed a fiery animus toward those who opposed them (and especially the enemies with whom he had most recently come to blows—the brutal foreign conquerors).

Incidentally, *tate,* you knew about him, too. I later learned that when you still held your "position" and the authorities, unconditionally and without justification, demanded that the Jewish Council discover and hand over parties involved in the resistance (whose activities were increasing more and more in the region)—it was he (according to reliable reports the authorities had received) who had secretly remained in safety right there with us in the ghetto. . . . Then, under constraint, you assented—on the face of things. You even allowed a substantial reward to be announced—a bounty for whoever helped to locate him and put him in the proper hands. Then—because you did not, in fact, wish to cooperate—you and like-minded members of the Jewish Council devised a way for him not to be tracked down or held in constant terror. You produced his passport, covered in blood, which you said had been found at the burial of bodies after a certain *Aktion*—a sign, that is, that he was no more and should be forgotten.

That is one thing. And still another, *tate,* by the way: if I were not so young, and he, Berl, not of his age; if I were not so unfamiliar with what he is so experienced in—I confess to you that he, it seems, might be the one with whom I, your daughter, could fall in love, for the first time.

✦

The same evening, after many questions, I found the address he had given me. I entered a little room in a distant house squeezed between walls and buildings that stared through weakly illuminated, evening windows.

I saw before me a few youths and girls—summoned there, it seems, by the same man who called me. But they were already more comfortable and familiar with one another because, evidently, they had already visited the apartment more than once. They acted in a friendly manner, one communicating with the other by a half word, not saying anything (except by looks). And right after I came in, the man who had invited me also showed up. A little meeting began, and I realized I was being drawn into a circle that had the task of all such groups: on the one hand, to cause damage to whatever area of work members were employed in (which deserve it fully); and, on the other, to help out, as much as possible, those parties who alone will help in turn. . . . That means: the underground rescuers (with whom, one way or the other, communication had been established). As great as the danger was of having anything to do with them, contact and cooperation already existed. They received what they needed from the ghetto—things like clothing, linen, guns, and so on. And on the other hand—from time to time—they reached into the ghetto and brought over, into the areas of forest resistance, more people ready to fight.

Here, the man who had invited me to the secret meeting place presented me to the others, and he vouched that I was someone to be trusted. He is still my protector. . . . Soon afterward, when all the questions that had been posed or come up were settled quietly, decisively, and in a business-like manner, he—at the end of the meeting—called me aside and asked:

"Well?" Did I object to his invitation?

"No," I said—not just for the sake of appearances but out of the intense inner conviction that what was being planned was necessary—the only direction to take and the only way that was even possible in our grievous situation.

"And do you also know what the work brings with it—that is, that there is also an enemy inside?" he asked again.

"I know, and I am ready for anything," I responded, already feeling a breath of fortunate joy—as much as I could possibly imagine. . . .

Then the man started to interrogate me: where I work, what I do—with whom—and whether I was able to contribute anything. (This, I had heard, was asked of everyone.)

"I don't know," I said. "I'll see. I'll take a look."

"We'll see, too." He inquired if my workplace was opportune for something to be carried out, or if another position should be found, with better possibilities.

Everyone dispersed. I went away, borne slightly aloft, cheered that I had been admitted. I saw it as a first crack of light—I could begin what I had desired and been drawn to until now but hadn't known how to pursue.

From then on, from that evening, from the time of the secret meeting with my newly acquired friends (brothers and sisters of a shared destiny)—the soul of your daughter, dear *tate*, began its work. My mind moved in a certain direction—toward inventiveness and the desire to distinguish myself on terrain where I wouldn't have been able to get the slightest footing until now (not even having the slightest idea that it exists . . .).

✦

A few days afterward, my friends from the work column saw me do something that didn't match my angry preaching and moralizing from a little while back when, with such vehemence, I cast off the hand of the supervisor after receiving his blows. In one day, my kinswomen could see that I took to crawling before him—as if I wanted, in some cheap way, for him to find me charming, to sell myself dishonorably. . . .

I found him in a good mood and cheerful state after guzzling "his beer." By chance, I caught his eye, and he chose me as the one who pleased him and started to look at his own legs and then mine—insolently and in his drunken, Hanoverian manner. Then, leading him off to the side as one does with someone very close, I started to present a little razzle-dazzle which called forth their suspicion and ill will.

It was like this: The women looked at one another knowingly, and I could swear that their vengeful words of pleasure at my shame reached my ears (accompanied by glances to where, in a not-at-all-worthy way, I had withdrawn with the supervisor). "Look at her," they said. "She—who is so righteous and upright—who just now attacked us for a few accommodating words. Now she has gone over to more than words—to the deeds that have apparently become her taste. . . ."

My friends were right to reproach me. I had demanded strict virtue from them in their dealings with the conquerors, saying that those who hold the whip over us shouldn't be permitted to touch us, even with their eyes.

Not knowing what was happening, they were right to condemn my present behavior. Meanwhile, however, I intended something different. All that, on my part, was just an act so I could establish a relationship with someone who was no less repulsive to me than to them—and no less now than then. I did so just to obtain something useful for the holiest of purposes I had set before myself.

My new friends, after all, needed all kinds of supplies—and especially guns, which I meant to get from the supervisor in whatever quantity I could.

Maybe it was childishly risky, but it occurred to me that it was possible, and I also didn't fool myself. . . . Except for displaying a little yieldingness, I gave him nothing—nothing at all—except well-disposed, silly words, in order, ultimately, to obtain what I needed by ruse—and not in small amounts (indeed, even more than he could provide).

Once, twice, I played the brotherly-sisterly game with him— to my disgust, and to his crooked-legged delight. Seeing how he fell for my presence—soon, certain of success, I managed the boldness to speak:

"Herr Kwinkenkwas, may I be permitted to approach you with a request?" I thereby made a turn with a falsely charming expression—all sweet rock candy. . . .

"*Ach,* what—what did you say there? 'Herr Kwinkenkwas'?" He choked in laughter that I—apparently making a mistake— had pronounced his family name incorrectly, because no one called him Kwinkenkwas, only Herr Futerfas.* "For you"—for me, that is—he was prepared to "pass through fire and water," he offered mildly. With Fräulein Flora he was even ready— "just a little"—to forget his Frau in Hanover. In return—as his only reward and recompense—he received the permission to look at me in his lovesick way.

Yes, but what did my request entail? he asked.

This: as he knew, all *Juden*—both men and women—had been condemned by his people to be "butchered"—that is, to perish. She, Flora, would like—when her turn had come—to do it herself and be spared being put to death by those who acted hastily, in the vast din of crowds driven together for an *Aktion.*

It sat upon Herr Kwinkenkwas's mind. . . . As if sober and quietly ruminating what had just been suggested—then agreeing and recognizing my right (to which everyone is entitled in such matters)—he asked one question:

Was there in fact something else? If I wanted to do it myself—was anyone stopping me? And he pointed out that the German soldiers didn't do a bad job. . . .

"Please understand, Herr Supervisor, you need something to do it with—a gun. . . ." And he shouldn't think she thought she would obtain it from him—God forbid!—for free. She was ready to pay with whatever she could—whatever lay in her pos-

*Probably a joke substituting the name of a Hasidic rabbi for the name of the German supervisor. Menachem Mendel Futerfas (1906–95) is famous for having organized clandestine Jewish schools while incarcerated in Siberia.

session: the best clothes she still had after everything had been taken from her people—those she had managed to keep. Also, a little bit of jewelry was left, which the Frau of Herr Supervisor, in Hanover, would gladly receive as a present.

"*So,*" said the drunken supervisor, tasting a deal. He weighed the ways and means, one against the other, the profitability of the proposal. (Of course, he set aside the little bit of danger that might result for him when he obtained what he wanted.)

"*So,*" he said, not speaking further. You could see how it tasted to him—his greedy, hungry little fish was already half at the worm on my hook, enchanted beyond the possibility of turning back; in the end, he would be caught.

And it happened like that. On a day soon thereafter, Herr Supervisor—now not in a drunken state but sober—set aside a time to call me over with a wave the others wouldn't notice. Melting, he passed me a little thing of a gun—a small revolver of some kind. He received, in exchange, from me, payment in the form of a feminine article (which stayed hidden on his person for a long time). He turned it expertly in his hands and judged it with his eyes, seeking to figure out how big a hit it would be with his wife in Hanover.

He persuaded himself that he evidently hadn't been wrong, and he left contented. And for that, from then on—from the first time I traded with him—I held the key to the supervisor in my hand, so I could approach him more boldly, if necessary— once, yet again, and many more times—without fear that he would cast me back, much less hand me over.

Unbeknownst to himself, he had entered upon a forbidden transaction, which, if it became known, would have consequences no less dangerous for him than for me—for in speaking to him I had drawn him into a partnership.

Another time, I saw that a sister desired the same thing I had obtained. Again, of course, it wasn't for free: if he wanted to, there was money (and if not, feminine articles).

Oh, God, oh, dear *tate*! As difficult as the game was—as impure as I felt trading with him, altering myself, and receiving anything from *his* hand in *mine*—all that was redeemed by the contentment that shone from the eyes of my friends in the cell each time—after great dread at my smuggling objects through the ghetto gates, where they search everyone— I got through, after all. Everyone's eyes, looking at the result, would light up in a little holiday. . . . It was, after all, no small matter: guns (without which a resistance fighter is no resistance fighter—just a nonentity, without arms and suited for nothing . . .).

I smuggled out as much as possible—it occurred almost without risk of being discovered or handed over, on account of my partnership with Herr Kwinkenkwas, which served as a guarantee that, in any case, the first half of the operation—up to my arrival at the ghetto gates—went safely.

But in the end, even that well ran dry. Whether Mr. Supervisor was called away from his office for other reasons, or whether his person aroused suspicion, I don't know. Then, our people found it necessary to take me away from my workplace and set me up at another location, where I did what I could in the new environment (assisting others, in order to be helped myself, later on).

Because indeed: some had already—with the help of those in the forests—been brought out through the fences surrounding the ghetto; others, meanwhile, waited in line (that the same might happen for them should an opportune moment present itself).

And I, too, stood in line. I was still being tested and under the supervision of our cell's leader. He kept me, I noticed, in his sight, and from time to time I sensed from our short, secret encounters—and from his familiar tone—that he did not consider me the worst: his trust in me as a devoted operative had turned out to be justified. . . . I, too, am in line.

✦

Day. . . . Month. . . . Year. . . .

Dear *tate*. And now to part from you, it seems. The decisive hour, when I must go over from the known into the unknown—into the forest, where I will experience something recorded in no book—for which nothing offers preparation. A shame, a shame. . . . Bless me, *tate*.

This is what happened most recently. One evening, upon my arrival at our far-removed and secretly occupied location, Berl Bender called me aside and spoke to me—when everyone left, I should remain with him for a little while: he had something to discuss.

Alone with him, I realized it had been decided to send me over with a group of ghetto comrades—but not in the ordinary manner, not as usual: I would have a mission on the way. . . .

"Something serious—very serious," Berl Bender acknowledged as he entrusted it to me.

The matter was like this. . . .

A traitor had insinuated himself among the leaders of the ghetto underground and outside, too. At first, it seems, he had won their confidence by secretly creating wonders—creeping, with all kinds of forbidden material, his way through—and out from under—the various enemy agents and avoiding all damage to our cause. Everything necessary, he executed well— blinding the eyes of his own people, so that trust in him would climb without stopping and make it unthinkable that suspicion should, at any point, fall upon him. Indeed, for the sake of his traitorous purposes, he obtained great advantages at first—setting up a printing press, arranging radio relays, and bringing over everything necessary to those who awaited it impatiently. He even smuggled over, and evidently with great expertise, whole groups of ghetto inhabitants (youths as well as older people).

It occurred to no one, even when a failure had taken place, to put the so very loyal and so very capable man under a lens— to examine him and try to find traitorous bacteria. That's how it was for everyone—except one person, Berl Bender. From the first time he met him at a gathering, he had taken a dislike to him, not knowing why—or, rather: knowing exactly why. An unusual, deeply personal sense of political practice (which comes from having completed many years of underground schooling) immediately told him they were dealing with a bird decorated with the feathers of others. . . .

This individual was still a young man—under thirty but somehow already full, with extra flesh and fat in the neck and chest. He had an unclear, hazy gaze and also a large, split lower lip with a thirsty, white scar in the middle. He acted free and open, yet he gave the impression that he was somehow "playing around the back"—the opposite of everyone else.

When Berl Bender saw that bird there, he immediately felt that this individual in particular—notwithstanding all his accomplishments—deserved to be put under a magnifying glass now and then, to be examined for the expected germs.

Immediately, he tried to discuss the case with closely trusted comrades. But since everyone was openly enthusiastic about how the man had solved the most difficult tasks he had been assigned, none of the comrades would hear any talk of doubt. Berl found himself cut off by everyone in every way—so that things remained as they were, and, worse still, people suspected him of wanting to eliminate a faithful man of action because of—God forbid—his own disloyalty.

When, later, a capture occurred, everyone was inspected . . . except for that man; no one even looked his way, certain there was nothing to see. The same thing happened a second time. Finally, when such a fearful disaster struck the whole underground structure that everyone was shaken and thought we would all be rounded up right there, down to the last man—

then, at last, people started to doubt him, too. And as soon as the first little thread was found, the whole traitorous knot was unraveled: they detected a trail that made it clear that everything was from his hand, of his making. . . . But for reasons of caution, they pretended not to know, so that the individual wouldn't see that he was no longer able to continue his two-faced game and wouldn't—all of a sudden and with a single stroke of the hand—betray absolutely everybody and liquidate the underground altogether. Therefore, it was resolved to eliminate him. . . . Only, in order for him not to find out about the decision, everyone pretended to know nothing and continued to maintain apparently friendly relations with him. Indeed, they ultimately charged him with an important mission, which they were sure he would accept, since he was interested in staying what he had been until now—that is, traitorously masked (so he would have the opportunity for further misdeeds by creating more advantages for those who paid him well).

It was decided—again with his help and under his leadership—to bring a group of comrades over where they were needed, just as had already occurred more than once with his aid, and not without success.

Two objectives were to be achieved at once: to bring our comrades—those who could stay there no longer—out and away from the enemy; and, at the same time, to lead off the party himself and put him in the hands of those who would do what was fitting: render him harmless.

As mentioned, it was after a great calamity—when a whole group of highly capable and experienced members of the underground had fallen into the hands of those who had long wanted to slake their thirst and make examples of them (proof of the end waiting for people who didn't value the price on their heads).

Among them, among the men and women—there was someone, still a young girl, whose eyes always shone wondrously beneath her high, white, innocent brow. She always wore her hair in braids around her head, like a crown. I knew her, too, and I never could believe that someone like her had any connection at all with what she really did—and in what way. . . .

Looking innocent—like a child—she became a master at carrying out—through the most heavily guarded places—whatever was necessary. She made the right impression on those who, according to their office, were not supposed to let anyone through without inspection; they had before them a toothsome morsel who wasn't worth looking over (alas!)—what could a girl like that know about playing false?

But she did. Therefore, they took special revenge on her—be it those who worked at interrogation and the tortures it involved (in which she now, once again, would delight them), or the executioners afterward, who either thought up the punishment on their own—or maybe they didn't have the imagination and received instructions how to perform their business from a higher and more refined source. . . .

She was strung up half naked, without the upper part of her clothing. To her two long braids, which were thrown over her breasts, they tied dead rats as decoration and for shame. . . . It was just like what, in a similar case—I read in our history—the forefathers of today's executioners had done in the twelfth and thirteenth centuries, in Speyer, with another Jewish daughter.[*]

Everyone was downcast and distraught, despite the fact that it seemed no cruelty could surprise anyone anymore. Especially her closest "family" members felt this way (those who worked with her and saw a reflection of themselves in her skills—those

---

[*]Jews had inhabited the German city of Speyer (Rhineland-Palatinate) since at least the eleventh century. Although they enjoyed a measure of official protection, they were the victims of intermittent persecution from 1096 (the First Crusade) until their final expulsion in the fifteenth century. Der Nister is probably referring to an incident in 1146 (Second Crusade).

who boasted of her as a prize). Berl Bender, in particular, felt this way, both because he was the first one who had warned of the danger to be expected from the traitorous individual; and because she, the underground artist, had worked under his immediate supervision and direction—she was a girl like me, a member of the cell, who had been torn from him like a piece of his own flesh.

And there, after that occurrence—which everyone in the city and ghetto knew about and which especially affected those whom the same fate awaited—then, that same evening, in the secret, distant apartment, Berl Bender stayed with me and shared the decision that had been made. He said that I, too, would be sent with the group heading out; but although I would be together with everyone else, I would need to take on a special mission.

"A serious one, a very serious one," he added, not saying what it entailed.

It consisted of accompanying that certain individual and keeping him tied up—not with a rope, of course, but by other means, so he would allow himself to be led. . . .

Indeed, resolving to render the party harmless, those in command had authorized everybody—and especially Berl Bender (who had proven so capable of recognizing and sniffing out the traitorous stink emanating from people like that)—to inform themselves of his appetites and vices, thanks to which a man like that often slips and falls, which cause him to get caught by whoever it might be.

It was determined that women were his weakness. . . . A deep-lying one: his darkened gaze and lower lip (which was dry and slightly cracked in the middle) glistened and quivered whenever he saw a face that impressed him and made him forget (to the point that he grew drunk and dizzy).

"Women?" I asked, hearing Berl out and realizing what he meant.

"Yes."

"And what is asked of me?"

Then, in response to the question, no answer came from Berl's mouth. For a few moments, he even cast his eyes down, and he fixed them at the tips of his shoes—out of shame and embarrassment, not having anything to say. And those silent moments there, *tate*—I would like to use them to say a few words in my defense.

It was, of course, not easy for him to come to me with a suggestion like this—he, whom I, the first time I mentioned him, praised so; he who, as I said—if I were not so young and he . . . not of his age—if I were not so certain that he was ready to sacrifice his life, I would have fallen in love with (and for the first time). . . . He, such a principled man—in whom I see one of those who, with great exertion and sweat, carry the first stones of a new building—one most people have no idea about, since they don't live in the possibility of future existence it offers. More still: not only are people like him the bearers of bricks; they are ready to lay themselves down to secure the foundations, and often they do just that. . . .

And there, like you—him, Berl. . . . But a proposal like that—there's nothing worse. . . .

"No." He caught himself after a somewhat longer silence, embarrassed and looking down at the tips of his shoes in shame. He meant—God forbid—nothing bad. . . . I shouldn't understand him wrong. If he had considered me a weak girl, or of less integrity—naturally, he wouldn't have assigned me this kind of mission. But since he was certain of the contrary; since, in the short time before our meeting, he had observed me and studied my character (as much as anyone could); since he had also inquired of others who knew me more closely. . . . In this way, he had gained certainty that, although the undertaking was dangerous, I would carry out what was required and encounter no harm, for the common good.

"The times"—he said, holding his head down, were, after all, as I knew, unusual ones, and full of responsibilities. Now, if one takes on business like this, one must agree to bend one's conscience a little for what, in another instance, one would rather lose a hand—or even one's head.

"But," he continued—as if speaking to himself and answering his own tortured conscience—I shouldn't be afraid. . . . I wouldn't be alone but in the company of friends (should, God forbid, that man indulge his perversity). And the whole business would consist only of lightly drawing him toward me and then not drawing him—that is, holding him at a certain distance while at the same time not pushing him away. Chiefly, I was not to leave him alone but also not let him suspect me. I should talk to him, engage with him, and make him believe what he thought was true.

"Pardon," Berl felt it necessary to say, in his embarrassed state, after this last part. Seeing that I had a grip on myself and agreed to his proposal, he started to explain the task in a more detailed manner, and to advise me how to comport myself and act on the way.

He added that, before I left, an encrypted communiqué would be given to me and sewn into my dress. It would be prepared by the underground comrades here, to be seen by those before whom I would have to present myself with *that* person (in order to unmask him and reveal his true nature).

◆

And now. Before I set out on my way, I would like to say a few words about myself. Remember, *tate:* I, still so young—who only now left the school bench behind, away from the loving gazes of my fellow pupils (who allowed themselves no pleasure beyond this); I, who just now danced free as a bird—not even realizing my womanly gift to appear beautiful and pleasing; I, *tate*—why has such punishment befallen me, like a thunderbolt—why such hateful circumstances? Not only not to serve, in the joy of partnership, the one who would choose me, and I, him—but instead, the accursed opposite: to serve as a cheap toy for disgusting individuals who touch me with their repulsive hands—first the *Gebietskommissar,* then Herr Supervisor, and now, after all that, the most loathsome one of all: the traitor, near whom I must stand, and, possibly, who knows what painful contact there might be. . . .

But enough. I'll stop—to ready myself for where I will be free of all this and able to use body, soul, and all my powers for what, it seems, I have been called for: not to provide pleasure for wretches but to work and strive that there should be less of their kind in the world.

✦

Day. . . . Month. . . . Year. . . .

Today, dear *tate,* I met with Berl Bender for the last time, together with the whole group that will depart. We assembled in that secret, distant dwelling in the remote alley, where all our gatherings have taken place. There, the coded communiqué was sewn into my dress, together with the ring, my present from you—as I requested be done. At the end, Berl Bender gave me further instructions about my role and what to do.

It was time to go. A place was determined where the members of the group would meet up individually—somewhere outside the city (after, with any luck, escaping the ghetto). This, incidentally, was no small matter. Some had to sneak through the ghetto fences, which are heavily guarded. And some even through sewers, where the danger lurks of going blind in dark passages full of water, filth, and rats (which abound there); moreover, besides the danger of not emerging where one need fear no unfortunate encounter, there is a risk of getting lost in the tunnels and coming out where capture is easy (as has already happened more than once).

We dispersed, each to his residence, where final preparations were made. I went away, too, and I reached the doorway of my present lodgings. There, my face turned to where my true home had been, which I don't want to think about now. . . . It is winter. It's a snowy, cold night out there. In the distant forests, wolves howl in thick, running packs, and others flash phosphorescent lightning glances from the forest's edge, casting fear into passing travelers and horses. . . .

Standing outside, I felt no cold. I also didn't feel that warm tears were pouring from my eyes, bravely taking leave of what had once been so dear to me, which I lost so undeservedly, without knowing why.

It dawned on me that it was late. I remembered it is not just my wish—I am also observing your will and going for you.

I turned away from my former home and entered the present one. The only work I still had was to write the last couple lines—to say good-bye and beseech you: bless me, *tate*, on my way. . . .

2

There ends Flora's record. And it is also understandable why: she went off to where there was neither room nor time to hold a pen in one's hands—just a chance for something better: a rifle.

Incidentally, it should be added in parentheses that the little bit she had written up to now—after she freed herself from her life in the forest—fell into the hands of a professional, who enjoys the right to straighten, edit, and pass things through a stylizing typewriter (so to speak . . .). Now, this same professional—on the authority of oral reports he received after making her acquaintance—will relate (in the same style she used) what happened when she went into the forest.

Now, what the professional has to report:

Wonders—great wonders—befell her when she, still so very young, had to find her way in a labyrinth that neither her parents nor grandparents had ever entered.

She must have received schooling in extraordinary subjects—ones that teach you how to deal with a traitor. Or, if she received no schooling, she was armed with the innate qualities of a hunter, who moves like a wild animal. . . . And if neither of these was the case, then certainly her feminine instincts served her (as well as awareness that she was walking on the edge of a sword, and no other way of winning the game is relevant—anything else would mean putting herself, the whole group, and even the whole underground under the blade).

As agreed, the members of the group, each on his or her own, escaped from the ghetto, surmounted obstacles, and gathered at the appointed place, from where they would make the further journey together. The traitorous party also held his word and showed up; his brow could be seen to have darkened significantly—either from ordinary, sour thoughts, or from the kind of displeasure that befalls someone who goes to do something he doesn't want to.

He took a look at the group that he, a practiced individual, was supposed to lead—half in contempt, half with indifference. Still more: he looked like someone holding a weight that is too heavy for him. . . . But when he had completed part of the way with the group, and he looked more closely and with greater attention at them—then, right away, Flora, with her long legs, caught his eye. He became another man. . . .

Soon, he saw in her only womanly charms—the kind that someone like him cannot fail to notice. He approached her, and soon a new skin seemed to cover his formerly darkened brow—another disposition, ready for a more agreeable game.

Right away, he licked his dried-out, cracked lower lip, where an obvious sheen of satisfaction had appeared. It meant two things. His sweaty brow and glistening lip were signs that that man there thought he had struck upon something he hadn't expected to find. And his interest meant something else, too: it was a sign that what he had discovered could serve as the hook that would permit him to be caught.

He wouldn't leave her alone. Lacking interest, he turned his head away from anyone approaching him about anything at all. He didn't hear what he was being asked—on the contrary, he directed his gaze and attention toward Flora—in case, that is, *she* should have a question to ask him (so he wouldn't miss anything or delay his response).

Walking together, he moved ahead with her, in front of the rest; another time, he stayed behind with her. He did all that to be able to take a single look at her face, or, alternately, to measure her body from the back, with the kind of ruler that made his eyes light up with a hungry, gluttonous glow.

He was still at a manly age: around thirty and well poised. Also, he was sufficiently experienced in dealing with women he wanted something from. (He'd gotten it from many—he had had ready access to them, and success cost him no great effort. . . .)

But here, right away, he felt something different. Initially, he even lacked the boldness to utter a single word (and of course nothing more than that—especially then and there—since his intuition told him the other party would not be responsive; this was not the place to move as rashly as elsewhere).

He therefore proceeded slowly, gradually. Chatting in a friendly way, he confided in her what he had not entrusted to others. He told her of his feats in the underground and what he thought to do in the future.

He noticed how Flora, in listening, didn't lift her eyes to look at him once—surely out of fascination or respect, as occurs when someone's speech is a marvel (and he is rewarded in a silent manner—not loudly or enthusiastically). Listening to him—it was not clear, why—she held her head down and avoided his gaze. At first, he interpreted this in his favor, calculating that it stemmed from overpowering respect and great admiration—when one does not want to give oneself away (especially when a woman—a young and inexperienced one—admires a man). And later, too, when he already believed she should be feeling freer with him, thanks to his confidences. . . . Still, she didn't open up but took everything in with her head down (even when he no longer related his accomplishments but spoke with her in more ordinary terms about everyday matters).

When he attempted, now and then, a more relaxed word or expression, or touched her with his hand—wanting, it seems, to assist her as she walked (as one normally does)—then, he noticed that she shrugged everything off and moved away, to the side—as if from someone whose touch is not only not welcome but positively repulsive. . . .

It was not right on her part—not proper behavior toward someone like that (according to the role she had taken on and what it required). At first, she was unable to stop herself. She also couldn't do so later, the evening of the same day, when he—that party (the experienced guide who had already made the journey more than once)—now brought them to a remote settlement and found everyone a resting place with another unknown individual (a farmer, who, after dinner, brought a pack of straw out and spread it on the floor, so that everyone—recently arrived and exhausted from travel—could lie down and sleep).

Then, slyly—almost without intending to do so—he arranged the group in a way that his place on the floor happened to be next to hers—next to Flora, whom he had already been keeping closer than the others, passing the day with her in familiar conversation. To his mind, this had given him reason to believe he had purchased real friendship with her—and the right to spend the night at her side.

At that point, Flora almost forgot her part entirely. Openly—without the least bit of appropriate ceremony—she went away from the place the man had assigned and requested a comrade from the group to exchange places with her, because she wasn't altogether comfortable (that is, she didn't want to be there . . .).

That certainly didn't suit the party. As dark as it was in the farmer's home (where there was only dim light), it could be seen how the party lay, rejected and insulted, on the floor—without the person he wanted next to him but the stranger with whom Flora had traded places. The expression on his brow changed again, from cheerful to dark, and his lower lip got a dry, white dot in the middle—the sign of a thirst that could not be slaked so quickly.

The same marks remained in the morning, after the night had passed. Everyone rose early to get back on the road. One could see that something weighed him down (like a meal of herring). His bad mood didn't diminish one bit over the course of the day.

Then Flora remembered her mission. She recalled the directive from Berl: not to leave the man alone with his thoughts (for who knows where they might lead . . .).

It was, after all, necessary to be afraid, lest this person (even if the chance was slim) suspect that the endgame was being played—instead of being led astray, now they were leading him off. . . .

Then, she went up to him and switched roles. Now—just as *he* had done yesterday—*she* took to cheering him with a word, an expression. She even made herself touch him, drawing him into familiar conversation and scattering his thoughts.

It worked. Ultimately, he felt encouraged—he felt yesterday's impulse to please and impress Flora (and achieve what he hadn't managed previously).

He became so haughty, thanks to her open manner, that while she stayed alone with him—once again (like yesterday), far from the others (whom they either let in front or behind them)—he, this individual, even had the nerve to suggest that maybe she should entertain the possibility of splitting entirely from the group—for his sake and hers (that is, in their common interest).

He knew about a village in the area where he had a good friend—where she could stay, in complete security, the whole time the enemy and danger remained.

He saw (he continued) that the forest and wilds inhabited by the resistance were not for her. . . . And if she was afraid that someone might suspect her of falseness or cowardice (which would cause her to be rejected by the others), he would take it upon himself to persuade whomever necessary—to explain that he took responsibility for keeping her there for information, in order to have someone on their side in the village (in case it proved needful).

Yes, he went so far as to propose that to her.

"No." Quietly and with restraint, Flora refused his offer. She acted as if she were not surprised at all. On the contrary, one might—in other, calmer times—discuss similar plans. She understood, she said, why he would like to see her alone and set apart from the rest of the group.

"That's fine," she said—but not now. Now, she was bound to those with whom, until this point, she had endured life in the ghetto; she couldn't think of herself without them.

Flora—moving between different people, in the middle of her conversation with that man—suddenly made a step forward (or a movement backward), to her comrades. In so doing, she demonstrated that no, it wasn't possible—she wouldn't be torn away from them, like one limb from another.

Then, the man's face and brow grew dark. His small, obvious failure with Flora just now—on the middle of the road where he held her in his hand (just as he held the whole group and would either lead them where he was supposed to, or to their deaths)—made him have second thoughts, about failure in general. . . .

Such people—in keeping with their deceitful reasoning—are generally distrustful and full of doubt. Therefore, they are also obliged to consider the fact that those they have been fooling also hold one end of the thread of betrayal—through which they might unravel the whole knot. Thus, it is even possible that, at the moment he was walking, thinking he had her in his grip, he had in fact been caught by her—and he was the one taking his last walk. . . . It was, after all, possible for someone like that to think that way. . . .

The season was, as mentioned, winter. This individual and the group he was leading already found themselves far from the city, in a sparsely inhabited area with few villages and barely traveled roads (due to the war, which had reduced traffic—particularly in recent times, when villages were suspected of having secrets to hide from the city—that is, from the authorities, who, for the sake of security, had consolidated their presence there).

During the winter in that region, snow always lay on the side of the road, untouched and abundant. Now, thanks to the infrequent traffic, it also blocked the roads themselves, burying them: in the early morning and at night it was extremely difficult to make out where the way stopped and started.

That gave the party leading the others with dark thoughts the excuse to go off on his own sometimes, to seek the tracks of an alternate route (because, allegedly, he wanted to be sure it went in the right direction). In a way, he was right, because it really was impossible to know for certain—but, more than that, the cause for his frequent departures was what he might soon face. . . .

Some of the people being guided remarked his distress. Those to whom it had been entrusted to know the final part this person was to play at the end of the journey turned their eyes away and pretended they really believed that he was looking for what one seeks when the way is lost. Flora, however—according to the special task assigned to her—had to be more active. As the linchpin of the operation, she was bound, in all kinds of ways, not to let him extricate himself from his entanglement.

It did not come easily to her. This and that were both required: to get closer and maintain a distance—not to let him hatch other ideas, nor to let him get too familiar. . . .

Leading the group to its destination took longer that time than otherwise. The man stumbled—a little unconsciously and a little consciously, too, holding himself in mental deliberation the whole time, unsure if he was doing the right thing (whether his masquerade as a loyal party would work, so he could continue to be what he was—someone who had other, secret business . . .).

Until, all of a sudden—unintentionally, and even to his own surprise—he and the group he was leading landed among partisan guards (who lay in secure, hidden places invisible to the undesirable eyes of strangers, always waiting for their own).

Then, they reached the forest's edge—the beginning of woods that are famous throughout the whole region—and also beyond—for abundant wildlife (animals that have lived there since time immemorial). Here, for centuries on end, the rulers and wealthy parties of the land pursued—for weeks at a time, with hunting dogs and many servants, with friends from their own country and guests from abroad—sylvan hunts for wolves, bears, and other beasts. Every time, success—the capture or killing of a prime specimen—was celebrated in royal and baronial castles with great pomp and festivities (and not just for a day but for weeks on end).

Then, when the edge of the forest had been reached, suddenly a quick, cutting whistle came from an unseen guard in a hiding place—a whistle for which everyone had been straining their ears and impatiently waiting to hear. They felt great joy that finally, after so much effort, they had achieved the goal they sought as long-awaited salvation.

Yes, everyone except for him—that individual. Registering the whistle, he made an involuntary shudder (one could see).

Soon, from the concealed and secretly kept guard post, an armed man emerged—one not dressed properly at all (half in military fashion, half as a civilian). Approaching the group and the one who presented himself as their guide, he spoke the watchword and waited for the appropriate response. The individual (who knew the password) uttered it too quietly, from pale lips. . . .

Then, from other locations, more people came out. Fraternally, they took the newly arrived deep into the woods, chatting familiarly and asking for news of the outside world.

Everyone, enlivened and as if delivered from long grief, shared whatever she or he could with those who met them and escorted them into the forest in a comradely way. Everyone, again, except for that person, who seemed to carry a lock on his mouth and something else, too—a barely perceptible fear in his eyes, which made him constantly turn in a different direction. First, he faced one way, then another; a third time, he even looked behind, as if he thought something unexpected would, all of a sudden—from where he didn't know—jump out and grab him by the collar or neck.

For him, unlike those he led, there was no reason to be happy—a contrast to what appeared on the faces of those who, just now, had been freed from such entanglements. He, on the other hand, looked like someone who had fallen into quick-sand—where the ground is sludgy and each step makes one totter and sway in uncertainty.

The way into the forest was long, until a place was reached where the hidden fighters felt at home and had even arranged something like a city of earthen houses (with horses and wagons, a bakery for bread, and even a reasonably supplied work-place for doing and repairing whatever is needed).

Then the group and its leader were brought to one of the earthen dwellings where the commander of the resistance fighters lived together with the political adviser (a man charged with the spiritual well-being of the people in the forest, so to speak).

Soon, those two emerged—coming out from the dwelling as if from a cave. The commander—a young Russian—was not yet thirty, strong and wiry in frame, with bright yellow straps crossed over his chest and back; he wore a short, winter-thick fur that reached down to his knees and boots. The second man (the political adviser) was stouter and in a greatcoat but still militarily experienced: already more than fifty, he was, it turns out, a veteran of the civil war who had returned to the same activity as before.

Soon, the commander made a turn to the person who had led the group. He requested the documents normally given along when one is sent out—papers recommending the bearer as a trusted party. He also asked for the password (which serves as a means of legitimating oneself to those one meets for the first time).

Naturally, the party had the documents, which were sewn into his clothing. He began to remove them in the presence of the whole group.

But then, when he—a little pale, now that he was standing before the commander and the political adviser—began to stammer something as if he lacked a tongue—then, suddenly and unexpectedly, out of the group that had been conducted there, a young woman stepped before him, to those who were supposed to receive the papers from his hand. This was Flora. She, too, pointed to a stitched-up place in her clothing and spoke:

"Comrade Commander, I have also brought something. . . . I have papers, too."

Hastily and with a trembling hand, she tore open the sewed-up place in her clothing, produced the communiqué that had been given to her, and—before the commander could read it—already, the individual understood he was not dealing with people on his side. They had him. It was clear that the second set of papers would refute his; he had been outmaneuvered and outfoxed, and his whole dark career until this point, his criminal good luck, had now come to an end. . . .

It is unnecessary to say how the commander and political adviser, after reading through Flora's papers, gazed at the leader person; how this party—a captive caught red-handed and unmasked—had to confront himself, and what distress seized him now that, defeated, he had nowhere to turn the eyes in his head. All that is unnecessary, because it is self-evident and only this first part need be mentioned. However, there's something else:

In the same city that Flora was from; where she had been sent out of the ghetto and into the forest with the others; in that city—which earlier, before the war, belonged to Poland, and now, afterward (along with a large part of the region), has gone over to one of our western corner republics; in that city—an old and famous one, with many centuries of history, castles, and monuments—there is also a historical museum (which, incidentally, suffered greatly from the vandalism of our contemporary Vandals and now is being reconstructed and put in order). In that museum—aside from collections that existed before (for example, excavations and discoveries of stone, bone, bronze, iron, and glass, as well as clothing, pictures, books, documents, and writings, which give an idea of hidden epochs)—there are, now, acquisitions from recent times. That is, there are materials from the war that occurred only yesterday, here in the region—records of both the open war and the secret, underground one.

Among the different items collected in that part of the museum; among leaflets, announcements, posters, brochures, letters, and journals of our people—and, likewise, those of the enemy—now, one can find the protocol of a trial: the attempts of the traitor to defend himself and the witness statements of others, for the prosecution. Also, there is the judgment and how it was executed—presented as a picture, in a pair of photographs. They were made by a photographer with little experience, taken on a poor camera, and printed on bad, low-quality paper; also, they were miserably developed.

But in one of the little pictures, one can see a bit of sylvan landscape. As small as the photograph is, one can still get an idea of the forest as a whole. It recalls forests we know of in East Africa: ancient, dark ones, where, on the towering, giant trees inherited from the ages, one sees diminutive half people, half beasts—pygmies.

On one tree, it is clear, hangs a human being in the "pose" of all hanged men. And next to the gallows tree, to the side, there stands a group of girls, one next to the other. The very first one—the first to be seen in the picture—is our friend, the long-legged Flora, dressed in a partisan's "finery." She stands at attention, in cotton pants and a short dress, with a rifle thrown over her back.

Yes, that's her all right, together with others from the group. They were brought into the forest and then saved from being handed over by the same man. Conversely, he is alone, turned from a leader into one misled—a perfect, unblemished sacrificial offering. He put himself there and received, from the appropriate hands, his due. . . .

In the picture, Flora looks up at the hanged man, and her face shows dispassion.

Yes, the commander positioned her and her friends right in front of the gallows, so they would go through a little schooling from the very beginning and learn not even to raise an eyebrow when one deals with an enemy, a traitor.

Incidentally, the commander had Flora in mind more than the others. He placed her at the very front, closest to the tree, for one reason above all: when she and the leader arrived and in his presence, at the necessary moment—quickly and with trembling hands—she tore open the hiding place in her clothing and took out the coded message; then, the commander noticed how, together with the writing, she removed something else, which she promptly put in her other hand, wishing to conceal it from others.

Later—still before the execution—he asked her what she had wanted to hide when she was in such a hurry to show him the message. "A ring," she answered.

"Whose?" he asked sternly, meaning to let her know that nothing was to be kept secret from a commander.

"Mine," she answered, "a reminder of my father."

And did she know, he asked her again, that here no one thought about fathers but only aiming, shooting, and hitting the enemy?

"Yes," she answered, she knew. But it wouldn't get in the way—on the contrary, it would help her to learn the lesson now beginning. . . .

Then the commander drew a little closer and gave her more attention than the others. His first lesson on this occasion was provided by the circumstances—a test of her courage. She had to be present at the kind of thing that, at other times, makes heartier people lose their spirit. . . .

✦

She, Flora, passed the test, and more than that. Not only did she learn her first lesson well; she also learned the others asked of her in the forest. She proved one of the most agile and capable parties for all the tasks that everyone there had to perform, whether they undertook them on private initiative or they were ordered by high command.

She excelled so much that, after just a little time, anyone who had known her not long ago, in the ghetto, wouldn't believe this was the same person. When necessary, she rode a horse like lightning; when an attack was made on foot, she did so without tiring (to say nothing of the days and nights she either slept or didn't); and, whenever it was required, she was able—not budging a limb or revealing a single movement—to spend hours in hiding (where silence and caution are especially important).

In a word: she distinguished herself so much that the commander (the young Russian—not yet thirty years old, upright and powerful, with straps crossed over his chest and back), once, in an hour of good spirits after a successful fight (with prospects of continued victory), addressed her in a brotherly mood:

"Hey, you, Flora, maiden fine. . . ." Did she know that if things were not as they were at the moment, he would introduce her to a very close friend of his, someone for a lifelong partnership . . . ?

Flora understood. And when, moreover—after these foolish words—he laid his hand on her shoulder—without explanation and dreaming romantically (a little out of character)—honorably she turned from under his hand and said nothing at all. The meaning of the movement was this:

"Right. Now is not the time, and this is no place for proposals like that. . . ."

Because in truth: it was already harvest time. Singing, soon one would reap what had grown, even though it had been sown in blood and sadness. It was the time before victory, when—very soon—reality would pass over into legend, and every single participant and contributor, more or less, would have more than enough to add—including her, Flora (who, having taken part, had plenty . . .).

She will also do so. After all, she has more to say, and not just about events until she went off into the forest. Truth be told, it was nothing more than an introduction to the basic idea of the true resistance to which she dedicated herself—and for which she had requested a blessing from her father (and not just her father, but all her ancestors—her parents' parents, all the way back to their mother Deborah, the original singer of her people's deeds).

Well, and meanwhile, until she takes up what she will write in the future (with which we will occupy ourselves later), we place a period to our narrative, adding only a few small points.

3

Yes—when, where, and under what circumstances did we become acquainted with Flora?

"Well?" Where and when. . . .

It was May 9, 1945, in Moscow.*

At a Jewish social organization that had been founded in wartime for the purpose of collecting and disseminating news about the so very infamous and sad doings of the enemy. On the evening of that ninth of May, in honor of victory, a ball took place, as occurred everywhere in our country at that time (and not just among us, but in all freedom-loving countries that stood in battle against the enemy).

*The day of official victory over the Nazis (Moscow time—it was still the eighth in Berlin, where surrender documents were signed).

Before anyone else, the members of that organization were invited, as well as others who had a connection to them. They included academics, artists, writers, and, especially, military commanders (from the rank of general down to those who, then, all of them, without exception, were bedecked with distinctions for combat—decorations and medals; there were so many that, if one wanted to add anything more, it seemed there wasn't enough room on their chests). Among the military men, there were also partisans of both sexes—half of them clothed in military fashion, the others as civilians.

There was a mobbed and excited tumult in the building—already downstairs, on the first floor, at the coat check and all the workrooms—before the crowd ascended to the conference hall on the upper level, where meetings and assemblies are held.

It buzzed like a beehive. Famous military figures, newly arrived from different fronts, who had not seen one another for a long time—now, after long separation—met again, as well as the civilians who had remained in the hinterlands, helping the war effort.

It was a holiday for everyone. And when, later, the crowd was called upstairs, where in the aforementioned hall they were greeted by long, richly bedecked tables arranged along three walls of the room in the form of a *khes;** when the crowd went in one by one, in pairs, and in groups—then, one could see, among those who came later, at the end, one more couple: a somewhat short, stocky man with black, shoe-polish eyes (a little wild and bearlike in his demeanor and gait) and, at his side, a young woman—the kind that stood out even in a large crowd.

It was Berl Bender and Flora—who, after Berl had escaped from the ghetto, found each other in the same part of the sylvan resistance. They had freed themselves much earlier

*This is the eighth letter in the Yiddish alphabet (corresponding to the *chet* in Hebrew); its shape resembles a lowercase *n* or horseshoe.

than combatants in the regular army (when the last of them traversed the region, pulling westward). Nothing further had been required of the underground resistance, and they were released from their posts and places of battle. Whoever went off homeward, was gone. Whoever had no home—such as our Berl and Flora (who had lost so much, everything)—went wherever they wanted.

They decided to go to Moscow—maybe to relations, maybe to friends—or, maybe, they just wanted to go to the city that was both a relative and a friend to them.

One might suppose that Flora happened upon family. Looking at her now, when she entered the room among the latecomers, it was clear that she was coming from a home—and, apparently, a well-to-do one. Her clothes, appearance, and grace at the ball and in the salon elicited wonder not only from the men but also from all the women present (who saw no "forest" in her eyes or connection to partisan activities).

Not only her appearance stood out but also her person itself (although external factors certainly contributed). Whether she had found her gown by chance when visiting a dress shop or looked for one like it in particular—at any rate, the material, color, and cut were similar to the one her father, as we will recall, let her sew especially for the graduation ball at school (when she, a happy child, was still under his protective wing); the same belt, made from the same white material, was tied at the back, and its two ends fell down to the hem. . . .

As soon as she came in, she attracted the crowd's attention. It came from practically everybody who saw her. People immediately began to draw near and assemble around her. Even the aesthetic snobs who remained, started, out of sheer rapture, to look for a comparison—not in our generation but at an earlier part of history.

"Behold," one of them spoke, "it's Henriette Herz from the Sturm und Drang period of Germany—the Schlegel woman, around whom a whole generation of Romantics stuck, like flies on sugar. . . ."*

"And a woman like that was a fighter," a second said, "against the German and his accursed times. . . ."

Everyone took a seat at the richly furnished tables full of delights and drink in honor of the occasion.

First, at the main table in the middle, sat the most prominent family members (so to speak) of today's celebration—the military men, whom the first toasts honored.

First, of course, one raised a glass to the leaders and organizers of international victory, then to the allied peoples themselves, and then to the armies that had fought traitorous souls. And every military man, during the few minutes given him for a speech, recounted a concise, inspiring example of his practice in battle—as well as what had been done by his associates and those under his leadership, who had proved how very courageously and boldly everyone had acted (without exception—whoever and wherever, at every assigned post, no matter what the task). No one had thought of himself or considered his own person, except insofar as he served the common cause—that the enemy, through blood-covered eyes, might see his own, final downfall even sooner.

Also, nonmilitary parties spoke. Those who had participated in the war in the hinterlands also had plenty to tell.

A word was given to Berl Bender, the director of underground resistance fighters. People listened especially attentively to him—a self-effacing hero among heroes. Without aid, without ammunition, without guns—with only practically empty hands—he had marched against an enemy armed from head

*Henriette Herz (1764–1847), famous for her beauty and intellect, hosted a literary salon in Jewish Berlin. Dorothea von Schlegel (1764–1839), her friend, was the daughter of Moses Mendelssohn (1729–86), the leading figure of the Haskalah (Jewish Enlightenment), who advocated exchanges between Jewish and Gentile communities; a novelist and translator in her own right, she married the poet and critic Friedrich Schlegel.

to toe. To hymn such valor would require a special kind of troubadour or bard. . . .

Then a toast was made to Flora, too, as someone who stood out among heroic women. She was a greater wonder still. Simply rising from her seat and moving slightly to the side, she turned to those at her table and everyone in the hall. Already, the crowd—before she had spoken a word—was ready to applaud: her stature, her bearing, and her appearance alone made it impossible to imagine that a woman like that had just emerged from the forest and the harsh realities of resistance.

She got up and, finding herself in a familiar environment (from which she had been torn away), she made a speech in her own tongue. Having been in the forest, she was not used to it anymore. Everyone hailed her in amazement, be it that they were taken by her alone, or the fact that the people's well had not run dry. They saw in her a wondrous sign, after such calamity, that we still had daughters with such looks, such poise, and such eloquence.

When, in passing, she narrated a few episodes from her resistance activities, it moved the audience so much that, without noticing, everyone rose from their seats, in order to get a better look and hear her better.

They stood with mouths agape, waiting for her to continue (with the eagerness, curiosity, and fixation of thirsty people who yearn for rain).

Then, she spoke of the ghetto, enlightening the audience— which didn't know about such things, what the word meant. She said that if it had been possible—that is, under circumstances different from those the enemy had created (which prevented Jewish heroism)—perhaps every murdered child and old man would have left an example like hers. Turning toward the women's section of the audience, she said:

"Sisters, this is an heirloom ring from my father, who died. In giving it to me, he asked, so to speak, that I provide a generation worthy for the life of our people to pass through. Let us do that." As she spoke, she placed her left hand on the ring on her right, as if betrothing herself—by herself—to the present vow.

"Yes, sister"—a few fell in, applauding her gesture.

Later—after the toasts were over and the banquet had ended—the crowd wanted to continue the revelry and spend more time in celebration. The waitstaff removed the settings—the long tables, benches, and chairs—and they made space in the hall.

Then, a musician sat down at his instrument (the kind always present where events like that are held). Soon, over the keys both his hands struck a rousing chord, and the crowd heard the invitation to dance.

There were plenty of eager parties. At first, however, the crowd restrained its desire to dance, seeing how—among all kinds of couples—a pair emerged to which they owed first honors and all their attention.

It was Berl Bender and Flora, who had been invited with her closest and most intimate associate, the person with whom she had lived through the time in the ghetto and forest (as well as the dangerous episode we have mentioned).

The crowd surrounded them. They heard how Berl, her "cavalier," spoke: "Flora—our Flora. . . ."

Then, in the Cossack manner, he made a turn around her. . . . In a non-Jewish way, he gave her a lift with his right hand, on the right side of her back, going in a trot and a circle around her. She smiled, yielded, and danced with him.

Then, he exchanged the right hand for the left. Holding the left side of her back, he performed the same as before—this time with bended knees, crouched at half his height and dancing as if seated.

She, too, did as he had done. She left him standing as if in the middle of a circle, and she danced around him at a trot (and with all the steps that point to abandon and free rein, as they say—dances best performed not in halls but on the naked earth).

Of course, the crowd applauded and gave thanks. But they saw that Berl was only a comrade, not a match—on account of his age and the fact that he was too stout for her. . . .

Therefore, later, when the music invited to a second dance, the right man appeared—a young military officer, a splendid one—a dashing man from the cavalry wearing spurs, it seems. . . .

Then, a modern dance was performed—the kind that young people are used to, which expresses their natural vigor.

Flora, laying a hand on the officer's shoulder, demonstrated such elegance with her very first step that the whole crowd stood in rows at the side, waiting for her to float by and wishing to see her more closely, closer still, before their eyes.

That was certainly something to be seen—when the rider's hand held her waist and hers . . . his shoulder, and a finger from the same hand, as she floated by, gestured toward the ring that lent her such charm (even more so, when one remembered that it recalled her father, whose memory she had honored in her address).

"Long may she live!" everyone cried out—or didn't, thinking it instead. (The older people standing to the side saw a child before them who would be no shame to parents but, quite the opposite, a jewel.)

"What a magnificent girl! . . . What a girl!" Young men looked at her with envy—and at the one with his hand on her waist, holding her so close.

The only ill, we might now add, was that, among those standing in the background, one spectator was missing: Flora's father. When he watched her at the graduation from school, he modestly withdrew into the crowd, not wanting to give her bad luck, and he blocked his own sight. A shame, a shame.

Moscow, April–May 1946

Regrowth

WE ARE TALKING, here, about two half families—a man without a wife, and a wife without a man*—who lived, with facing doors, on the same floor of a single building in a big Soviet city.

No further details about them or their activities are necessary. It is enough to say that one of them was Dr. Zemelman. He was an older, ill-tempered surgeon—the silent type, inclined to solitude; he was someone with a name in his field, both in the city and even throughout the land. That was him, on the one hand. And on the other hand, there was Mrs. Zayets—a well-known pedagogue, who worked in the People's Commissariat as a division leader. And still more. . . .

To understand the following, it should be mentioned that both individuals, already for some time now, had grown estranged from their Jewish origins and all that occurred in the thickets of their people.

Both of them had only children. Dr. Zemelman had a son, and Mrs. Zayets had a daughter. The children were even of the same age. They both attended the same school in their early years, and, afterward, they continued at a higher level. And so they grew up accustomed to each other from the time they were small; naturally, between the children, there developed

*This phrasing is a bit awkward, but it preserves the tone of the original; in Yiddish, *man* means both "man" and "husband," and *vayb* (related to the English word "wife") means "woman" as well as "wife."

familiarity. And so, too, it developed between their parents, who shared the same social standing and a position in the intelligentsia (to the extent that it was possible for extremely busy people, each of whom was absorbed, up over the neck, in his or her respective field, which swallowed them up and, as it happens, left no time for personal matters).

When the children were grown, they became much closer. They shared many things together, whether in their studies or on their days off and during vacations—which they enjoyed in a youthful fashion, sometimes just together, and sometimes with other young friends.

Whenever the parents had time, they stealthily took a look at the relationship between the adolescents, whose respective merits were evident. Mrs. Zayets's daughter pleased the elderly, grumpy surgeon, who peered over his glasses and saw that it seemed she had been made for his son. And the same was true on the other side. Mrs. Zayets looked at the boy who seemed destined for her daughter, and she felt a mother's joy that her child didn't need to look far—that her promised one had been sent to her automatically, from one door to the next, and that he was there, on the same story, in a single house, as if he had been born for her.

If things had continued in this way, sooner or later there would have occurred what happens in situations like that: a joining of both half families, whose two children would complete and unite them, to the delight and happiness of their parents.

But something else occurred. The forty-first year came, with calamity for the land, for all its inhabitants—and, among them, the two families discussed here.

Both young people, despite the fact that they were not among the first to be summoned for wartime duties, felt the call to go as volunteers, as most students did, both in the city where they lived and in other cities, everywhere and without exception.

The surgeon's son—a boy who had grown up handsome, energetic, and strong willed—did not ask his father's permission or advice. Instead, he "put him before a fact," as they say: he went off to the necessary place and was enlisted as a party healthy and fit for service. Which was the truth. The other child, Mrs. Zayets's daughter, also volunteered—either because she didn't wish to do anything different from her friend and wanted to act as he did; or, possibly, she would have done so even if he hadn't—following her own conscience and what the duties of a citizen demanded, she would have resolved to do the same thing anyway.

Their parents, of course, did not object. They were loyal citizens themselves, and they knew that now one could keep nothing to oneself—however dear—but must give it over for the common good. Yet when it came to saying good-bye, on the last day—when Dr. Zemelman's only son had to depart from his father (who, by the way, had long taken on the role of a mother, too, for she had been lost at an early age)—when it came time to say good-bye, the father, the whole time his son was packing, would turn around and look in his direction. He always, apparently, needed to be just in the adjoining room, but not the one where his son was. Finally, when they were standing each before the other, when the son extended his hand, the father could do nothing more than just lean over and give his boy a silent kiss on the forehead. He didn't say a word—because, it so happened, tears were choking him.

The same thing took place in the second, facing apartment, at Mrs. Zayets's, when she had to separate from her daughter, when the girl had to go. The daughter was forced to stroke her mother's head and brow for a long time—to comfort her—and repeat the same thing: "Mama, I'm not the only one. . . . Everybody's going. . . . And nurses don't have enemies."

Both went off. The doors of the two parties who lived across the hall from each other on the same floor—after the departure of the young people—seemed more closed than before.

The parents, in order to forget themselves, would go off to work very early and spend the whole day there—until late, late at night, when they would come back to unlock their doors. (A domestic cat, which had run away at some point from one of the buildings there, would come loiter and meow behind the door—it could do so as much as it wished, but no one called from inside or went out to see what was there.)

Already then, Dr. Zemelman was busy with the injured, who had been brought from the nearby front. From each combatant's wounds he received, so to speak, a greeting from his son. Who knew what was happening with him out there. . . . On the other side of the hall, his neighbor, Mrs. Zayets—although she was an educator—had great burdens, as occurs in wartime: one did everything one could in such diminished and not at all favorable conditions. And what she alone, Mrs. Zayets, had to do, she did more than all the others, for since her daughter had gone away, her home looked so empty to her that she would rather not have gone there at all, and, if possible, she would have spent the night at work.

It happened, soon after both young people had gone off, that all trace of them vanished completely. The mother received no news from her daughter, and the father received none from his son.

As acquaintances, as neighbors, and as people who had almost become in-laws, the parents, now and then—on a day off—would go over to the other's apartment and share—not what they had heard from their children but what they hadn't heard. . . . Quietly, they would talk things over, and, taking turns, one would comfort the other. There was no alternative: "It's still early. It will be all right," the man consoled the woman. And then, the other way around: the woman consoled the man, who listened to her and looked to the side, or down at his shoes, as if he couldn't recognize them as his own.

Since war is war, before long, it transpired that Dr. Zemelman received a brief notification from the Military Commissariat that his son had fallen—heroically and in combat, but without the least explanation. . . . Afterward, he got a detailed letter from a soldier in the division where his son had served. It told him that his son, while on a reconnaissance mission, had taken a bullet and died immediately, without suffering, and that all his fellow soldiers had buried him with military honors—that he was beloved for his boldness and comradeship in battle, and that his memory was dear to everyone.

The father read this letter over many times, and of course it comforted him. But he no longer had a son.

Around the same time, just a little later, his neighbor (who really shouldn't have been so close to him if their children were to be joined with each other) received similar news—bad news—in the same style, from the same commissariat; it informed her that her daughter, in an enemy raid on the hospital where she was working, had died at her post.

Both neighbors (their doors facing, on the same floor) declined to go to the other to console themselves. . . . What for? They even broke off their relationship, because neither had any comfort to offer the other.

As much as possible, they preserved silence and dignity, as befits people in their station. They swallowed their sorrow and did not let it show when they were at work. But when they came home and found it empty and vacant, and mainly—already without hope that it would ever come to life again with the return of those who until not at all long ago had been so dearly alive for their mama and papa—each one of the parents found no refuge from the great fear that stared out at them from every corner. . . .

Because, of course, "not there" means "not there." But when one has something and then loses it, especially children—

especially only children—it destroys most of the life of those who have lost them.

However, events soon occurred that the two aforementioned parties had not anticipated, and, for a while, they had to forget the private sorrow that oppressed them.

First, they—along with part of the populace—had to go through a temporary evacuation, when the menace of being overcome by the enemy loomed over the city. Second, just after they had returned from where they had been evacuated to—after the danger had passed—and later, after the liberation of entire regions that previously had been occupied—reports began to filter in concerning the inhuman deeds committed by the enemy against the population in general, and especially the Jews; as was known from earlier, it had been decreed that they be destroyed. Then, when both of them (who themselves hailed from those regions) began to seek information about the fate of their relatives and the rest of their families who had remained there, and when they wanted to find out whether they had been saved or not, and to know the fate of entire communities (from which they had become estranged for some time)—in light of these atrocious events, which reached them from there, they had to place their personal experiences aside and somewhat in the background.

Then, again, since the aforementioned two were not terribly busy in their professions—everyone was now at war—since they also had not grown distant in the time of the evacuation (when they had gone off to different cities in order to wait out the danger), and since they were generally not estranged after the death of their children (after which they had no reason to prolong and maintain their acquaintance)—they now took the relationship up again—not on the basis of immediate proximity but on the basis of what they shared on a higher level, which now brought them together and united them.

Thus, Dr. Zemelman—who, as mentioned, was inclined to solitude and, particularly after the death of his son, held himself secluded from all society—at one point presented himself to his neighbor, Mrs. Zayets, after all. For the whole duration of the visit, he kept his eyes on his shoes, as if he didn't know they were his own. Suddenly, while discussing other matters, he spoke to her:

"You know, Mrs. Zayets"—how dear his son was to him, although he considered himself and his son fortunate that a bullet had struck him and he had not fallen into captivity, where, as everyone knows, they would have done to him what they did to all prisoners, and especially Jews. . . .

"Yes," agreed Mrs. Zayets, understanding the reason for Dr. Zemelman's words and remembering her own daughter's death, and also the luck that she, her daughter, had had.

Incidentally, the conversation occurred when Dr. Zemelman had received other, rather significant news to share with Mrs. Zayets, news he had gotten from his former home in the territories that had just now been liberated—when, among other things, he learned about the death of his older brother, a professor, who had lived in a republican capital not far from the former border.

He was told how his brother had perished with his elderly and sickly wife, who had been unable to get out of bed; on account of her, he had remained in the city and couldn't get away.

An announcement—Dr. Zemelman learned—had been made in the city where his brother lived as soon as the enemy had arrived:

". . . On such and such day . . . at such and such time . . . , all people of Jewish descent, whether young or old, without exception, are to assemble at such and such place. From there, they will be conducted out of the city, where, from now on, they are not allowed to remain."

It was winter. All the remaining Jews saw themselves forced, without an alternative, to assemble at the location. "Otherwise," the bulletin declared, "death will strike whoever is still to be found."

Since the wife of Dr. Zemelman's brother was ill and could not bestir herself, his brother—already an elderly man himself, who had no one else for assistance—had to drag her on a sled that he had found somewhere or other.

There was a procession of thousands and more than thousands of people—people old and young, women with children in their arms, elderly men who needed to be supported, and so on.

Whoever, in the non-Jewish population, had the heart to look on at what was happening, stood in the streets and at the doors of their houses and wept.

A young, non-Jewish student—a pupil of Dr. Zemelman's brother's—happened to see how his teacher was pulling his wife on the sled, without strength, and he dashed into the crowd in order to help by assuming his teacher's burden. When they saw this, the police and gendarmes accompanying the procession duly beat the young student down.

Then, again, someone else wanted to step in and ease the brother's woe, and the opposite occurred: they pushed the sick wife off the sled and ordered the man to pick her up and put her back on it.

They were not satisfied with doing it once. They ordered it over and over—until the old woman could stand it no longer. After two or three instances of being knocked off and picked up, she gave up the ghost and, already dead, was lifted up again.

The brother, because of the pain in his heart, did not survive this. Seeing that his wife's life was already over, he suddenly made a weak gesture with his hand, fell down, and lay next to her.

Then, they ordered a younger and healthier man from among the herded Jewish mass to put them both on the sled.

"How?" the man asked. There wasn't enough room. . . . There was hardly enough for one person.

"One on top of the other!" the police joked and laughed. . . .

◆

Yes, although Dr. Zemelman had grown distant from his community for many years from not having had any interaction with it, now—when such a cloud had moved in to destroy the community—he began to feel more and more that he belonged, that he had a close connection with its devastation.

That, certainly, did not happen only with Dr. Zemelman but also with many others like him—such as, for example, his neighbor, Mrs. Zayets.

Well, and then? What kinds of consequence came about from Dr. Zemelman's return to his roots?

This:

At one point, in a free moment, he showed up at Mrs. Zayets's. In the course of discussing irrelevant matters with her, he suddenly turned and asked the following question:

How did she think to honor the memory of her daughter—whose grave, it seemed, she didn't even know the location of?

Mrs. Zayets was embarrassed and didn't know what to say.

"Well, what do you think, for example, about taking in a child to raise in her memory?"

Doctor Zemelman was talking about Mrs. Zayets, but he was also thinking about himself—about his son, whose grave was also unknown to him.

"Oh?" She had never thought of that. It certainly would be appropriate. . . . But truth be told, it would also be difficult for her to see a strange child in the place of her own. However, since Dr. Zemelman had already made the suggestion to her, she saw no reason to say no.

Truly, as difficult as it was for Mrs. Zayets to welcome the thought of a strange child replacing her own, after long deliberation—after Dr. Zemelman had given her the idea—she let him talk to her, and she almost even agreed, asking only that Dr. Zemelman give her a little time to think it over more thoroughly—until she had made up her mind entirely, and for good.

Finally, she, too, arrived at her decision, after seeing that Dr. Zemelman was also prepared to do the same—that he had not made his suggestion frivolously, but in earnest, and also, it seemed, after much reflection.

Later, during a subsequent visit by Dr. Zemelman, both of them took to working out the details: what kind of child they would choose—a boy or a girl—and how old the child should be.

They reached the conclusion that—since both of them had great demands placed on them at work, which didn't permit much activity with youngsters (who demand a lot of time and attention)—it was best to take on grown children, the kind that can look out for themselves, and it's enough just to look in on them from time to time, so they have a little bit of supervision.

They didn't explicitly discuss what kind of children they were talking about, but it was clear that they had in mind the unfortunate children of refugees, or, still more, those of parents who had died in the areas the enemy had conquered for a time.

Indeed, although Mrs. Zayets was perhaps not the kind of person inclined to think in the aforementioned way (as Dr. Zemelman was), it was also her nature to have a more compassionate relationship with those to whom her heart lay close—such as those for whom the enemy had determined the worst of fates.

They decided that soon, when they had a free day, they would go off to the appropriate institutions (where one had the responsibility of finding and taking care of children in special, shared homes that had been established for them) and announce that they, Dr. Zemelman and Mrs. Zayets, were ready to care for and privately accommodate a pair.

Dr. Zemelman wanted a boy, who would fit in better with him, a man. And Mrs. Zayets wanted a girl. Soon—after a little bit of time—their wish was granted, and they were sent what they desired. No, more than they desired: not ordinary children but children of action, children who already had a story in their lives, children who had passed through the smoke and fire—in a word: partisan children.

The lad was fourteen or fifteen years old, and he was called Moishke. He came from the White Russian forests, which in wartime had swarmed with hundreds and thousands of underground fugitives who, when the regular army had come to join them, emerged from two or three years of hunting and being hunted—like cavemen, into the light, into the open, and into open struggle. . . .

The girl was a little younger than the boy and from the Ukraine. And like the lad, she, too, had had much to go through before she fought her way through to her people. First, she had stood with a whole congregation of Jews from her shtetl—family, friends, relatives, and parents—ready to be shot down; it was only by chance that she had saved herself from being one of the dead in that pit.

The lad had spent a long time living with his parents—sturdy warriors in forest conditions that weren't gentle at all—which necessarily had toughened him and changed him from a child. Still, he preserved clear skin, a youthful mouth with white teeth, and also nostrils that fanned rosily, like a young deer's, under his high, polished brow (that of a model student).

That lad there just needed a good washing after years in the forest of not undressing or changing clothes, for all his knowledge—which he had proved able to acquire on the school bench and not only preserved in his nonschool years but even increased (if not by means of books—which, in the forest situation, were naturally wanting—then by life alone, which, as they say, teaches much more than books)—for all his knowledge to shine forth, like a diamond.

When Dr. Zemelman saw him for the first time, he took a look at him and, already that first evening, he made the effort to get to know him better. It was as if his father's heart no longer felt lost when he saw how this boy here had come to be a resident in his house and received a place under his gaze. Despite how difficult it was—when he observed the lad (who looked like a sap-filled branch that he meant to transplant onto his own yellowed family tree)—he still felt somewhat satisfied and heartened—not so much from the prospect of seeing himself blossom again in renewal but in a more general way, as one feels when one looks upon a young creature at the very height of its growth, when it is still struggling with its developed and still-undeveloped charms. . . .

Soon, Dr. Zemelman's goodly inclination extended so far that when the boy, at Dr. Zemelman's request, started to recount who he was, from where he hailed (before he joined his forest brethren and rescuers)—when the boy started, in a tongue somewhat strange to Dr. Zemelman (for the lad didn't feel entirely free to express everything he had brought with him from his extremely rich experience), Dr. Zemelman at first helped him in his embarrassment—adding a word at one point and an entire phrase at another. And afterward, when Dr. Zemelman remembered that the boy had a language of his own (which he had used at home, with his parents, and also in school, to acquire his knowledge), he spoke to him, seeing his own shortcoming:

"Moishke, speak as you like, as is comfortable to you"—because he, Dr. Zemelman, understood Moishke's language well enough.

Then, the boy's eyes lit up like those of someone from whose tongue a chain has been undone. And a stream of words rushed out, as from a word granary, so that Dr. Zemelman didn't get it at first, even though it delighted him, and even wildly so—just the sound of that strangely personal language, which had been preserved by the people from whom he had been torn; hearing this boy, now, he, quietly and within himself, felt something like a bubbling source—as if he were receiving a greeting from an old, dear home that could never be forgotten.

The same thing—only just a little different—occurred in the second home, the one facing Dr. Zemelman's. Mrs. Zayets had also gotten what she wanted—a girl.

The child had grown a little short for her years, and, as it happened, she was a little more scattered than one ought to be—this was from having survived the war, which didn't help the receptivity of her brains. . . . But it seems that she was, in turn, of very hearty stock: broadly built in her girlish shoulders, with such full cheeks—firmly kneaded, with playful dimples—that it was truly amazing how this creature—who had lived without a home, without supervision, and exposed to such dangers—had managed to preserve herself and, despite everything, emerge so sturdy.

In a word, in terms of health, she was a bit of an exception, even if, in exchange, her head and mental capacity had been affected. It is possible that she had received little from school and perhaps never even sat on a bench in one. It is also possible that whatever she had acquired, she lost again in her years of not studying. Yet on the whole, it seems, she was a little dull witted. But then again, her soul had a voice, a sheer gift from God—nothing inherited or trained—and when she opened her mouth, you immediately thought that her simple, motherly nature had something to say to you as it sang out in its authentic, unmannered way.

She composed songs herself, and also the melodies for them, according to a certain popular style:

> Oh, may dogs tear you apart!
> May you go perish just as I did. . . .

There was nothing like hearing her sing a curse song, like an ancient imprecation, when she cried about her dress, which she had received as an inheritance from her mother (with whom she had lived together for a time in the ghetto, before she went away to the slaughter trench), which a gendarme had taken away from her for his beloved. . . .

Oh, may dogs tear you apart! Her accusing voice sounded with such power, as if it couldn't come from her mouth alone, but from the mouths of everyone—all those who lived with her in the ghetto and had been condemned and robbed.

When she went in to Mrs. Zayets's, she was a little awkward, not feeling entirely free in the house—or in houses in general (to which she was no longer accustomed, having spent time in the forest). Mrs. Zayets first turned her head away, unable to look at the one who had come to take the place of her daughter. But soon she gained control of herself, became more familiar, reached out to her, and asked her about everything, everything that had happened to her—a child who had escaped the butcher's knife, without a roof over her head, with no one's compassion, upon the burning earth, under a sky that offered no help.

She, the girl, was called Elke. And, as was the case with Dr. Zemelman's Moishke, she, too, did not have proper mastery of the language in which she tried to communicate with Mrs. Zayets. She mixed it up with Ukrainian, and even a little with German (which she had heard a lot of, having been in the ghetto beneath the executioner's whip). And Mrs. Zayets also always helped Elke—as Dr. Zemelman did with Moishke—whenever she got stuck because of the deficiencies that encumbered her speech (something that often occurred with that language she brought along from her lost home and preserved like a dear keepsake, close to her body). . . .

Listening to Elke and seeing her broad shoulders, her firmly kneaded cheeks with the dimples, and her watery eyes—a sign of future motherhood—even she, Mrs. Zayets, a person estranged from her traditions, now felt attached to that often-tested and much-afflicted community, whose trials could also have been her own, if, by chance, she had happened to find herself there.

Looking at Elke, there awoke in her a great compassion for that community, and she felt guilty—like another Volkhov*—in its eyes. It had left a living testament, so to speak, in the form of Elke here, that she should preserve the little bit that remained—that its name and inheritance not be cut off.

Well, the children stayed there—the aforementioned Moishke with Dr. Zemelman, and Elke with Mrs. Zayets. Incidentally, this led the adults, who now had become parents again, back to each other—and much more closely this time, on the basis of their shared interest, because of their desire to provide even better for their charges, about whom they always conferred and asked each other: How are things going? How are things working out?

Thus, for example, Dr. Zemelman—a man who was very busy and not too skilled in matters of child rearing—often went over to Mrs. Zayets's in order to inquire about his Moishke. The latter was truly exceptional in his eyes. By the way—already on the first evening, after he had had the boy tell him everything

---

*This reference—like many others in Der Nister's writings—is cryptic. Volkhov is the name of a town and a river, as well as a military front where the Red Army failed to halt German forces advancing toward Leningrad in the early stages of World War II.

that had happened, and before going to bed, before it was necessary to part with him—Dr. Zemelman went to his room and gave him a modest kiss on the forehead, feeling both pain for him—as if he were kissing his dead son—but at the same time also somewhat content that, after his son's death, he now had someone to whom to give his fatherly love.

Yes, Moishke soon occupied his proper place at Dr. Zemelman's.

One could see how Dr. Zemelman sat, late in the evening, in his study, when his ward was already sleeping in the room that had been given him, and then rose and went, quietly, to the doorway of the room, switched on the light for a while, took a look at the sleeper, and soon turned the light off again and went out, to where he had come from, carefully making sure not to disturb him. . . .

It was also possible to see how Dr. Zemelman, whenever he had the time, also went into the room he had appointed for his ward while the boy prepared his lessons for school (which he was now attending, after years of interruption). Dr. Zemelman would bend shortsightedly over the book or notebook that the boy was studying from, and he would write something in it, but he wouldn't stay long, disturb him, interfere, or say anything—as if he were certain of what was now before him: the boy would do everything himself in a fitting and proper manner. Yes, it was enough for Dr. Zemelman just to take a look, just to provide a little bit of supervision. He came to his ward from time to time—not as one does to a child one always needs to check in on, but as one might go to a self-sufficient and wise adult.

Truly, Moishke was like that: he even set time aside to record all the events where he had been present as a witness, which he recalled down to the smallest detail—the places, the deliberations, and the participants—a remembrance for the ages. (And, by the way, even professional historians took an interest in his work, later on.)

A rare gift of memory aided him—a sharp, youthful eye, and the subtle ability to express what he meant in clear, smooth, and easily understood language. Also, besides the schoolwork, he found time to take up what his young conscience demanded of him, which he pursued with great industriousness—like a grown man—as if he were placing a tombstone over both the stolen years of his youth and all those lying, already dead, in the people's burial ground.

And then, whenever Dr. Zemelman met his ward at this work, he would pause, voice his interest, and, not leaving so fast, ask a question:

"Well, where are you now?" What had he just written down in that language that Dr. Zemelman couldn't piece together?

Moishke tended to select one episode now, and then another. Of course, it was always the kind that gave Dr. Zemelman both an exact picture of the conditions in general and the details of misfortunes endured at the hands of the enemy: in the first case, death, and then, in the second, what Moishke, his ward, had experienced in saving himself from death.

That, too—one must add in clarification—gave Dr. Zemelman plenty to think about—what he had heard, that is. Either soon, right there, his eyes would darken; or, later, Moishke (and everything related to him) appeared in different dreams and quiet nightmares, as was his way.

Then, once, he saw him with his son. The latter—in military dress and with a rifle, it seemed. And Moishke—with a pen on his ear. The first youth, it appeared, was not jealous of the second—that he had taken his place at the father's side. On the contrary: he extends his hand fraternally and expresses the wish that the other do with the pen—that is, by words—what *he* did through action.

Another time, he saw him approach with a somewhat elderly man who was wrapped up in a shawl over his eyes and, also, with his face and mouth covered—some prophet of lamentation, who appears at a place of massacre, at which he intends, it seems, to stay longer and do what a prophet must. And the ward, young Moishke, like a young servant of the holy man, carries a scroll behind him, as well as a little footstool for the other to sit on, when lamenting the calamity has tired him.

Then, he saw him a third time: together with *that* person, the one with the half-shortened, black mustache, and the appearance of a small-time criminal, whom fate has selected, however, to receive great shame—to the disgrace of the land that has produced him. In a word, he, whose name it is not worth mentioning, because, like the mouth that first spoke it. . . . He, *that one,* stands somewhere piled up high, and he looks taller than he is really built. He is clothed in the hunter's outfit of his land, with a green hat and a peacock feather; but instead of a cane, as would suit the outfit, he holds a club and a net, ready for catching game.

He stands, waits, and looks around, until a great mass of condemned people appear before him—walking mechanically and driven to a ditch. And the mere sight of those trudging causes him, one can see, wild joy. But it is not enough for him—it is too little—what the others intend to do with those who must be. . . . He wants to do it himself. . . . And he swings the club, striking someone in the group; he draws back and looks, with satisfaction, at how the man twitches, casts about, and chokes in distress. Thus he proceeds with one, to his delight, and then another.

And there, all of a sudden, Dr. Zemelman sees his ward, his Moishke, about to be struck. But suddenly he breaks away—to the extreme displeasure of the dogcatcher person, who screams to his underlings in embittered rage. "Seize him! Take him! Throw him into the net!" But Dr. Zemelman sees

Moishke laugh. . . . And then he sees how Moishke turns into Moses—as the famous medieval master shaped him out of stone (with the mighty, human-divine countenance of an ancient lawgiver, a long, flowing beard, down to his knees, and darting rays from his brow, as others have painted him, too).* And Dr. Zemelman sees how one of the rays falls upon the face of the dogcatcher, who is burned and consumed—and he must, like a Mephistophelian bat, turn his head away, bow before him, and bury himself in the ground.

That there is Moishke, who made Dr. Zemelman dream at night. And, it seems, in reality and in waking, too, Dr. Zemelman saw in him the continuation of what the dogcatcher person had wanted to wipe off the face of the earth—to erase and destroy without a trace.

That there is Moishke, the young vessel brimming with skill—to whom, if ever he encountered difficulties in learning (to which he had now returned, as mentioned, after many years of interruption), one needed only point the way with a finger; he would manage the rest by himself.

But if that's how he was, Elke, who had come to Mrs. Zayets's, could not just be pointed in the right direction with a finger. She needed a whole hand—and mainly for her studies, in which she wasn't doing well. Mrs. Zayets, in her free hours, assisted her and, as a patient pedagogue, helped her as much as possible.

There was never enough time for her. Mrs. Zayets enlisted the aid of her neighbor's ward, Moishke. He hardly knew anything about the girl. When they first met—the two of them, Moishke and Elke—just as soon as they had arrived (the one at Dr. Zemelman's and the other at Mrs. Zayets's), they got to know each other thanks to the acquaintance of their benefac-

*The "medieval" sculpture in question is possibly Michelangelo's imposing *Moses,* commissioned by Pope Julius II; though portraying a seated figure, it "stands" nearly eight feet high. "Moishke" is the diminutive form of "Moses."

tors (who lived in one house, on one floor, with one door facing the other), who now, for their sake, would pay each other visits.

Naturally, Dr. Zemelman had nothing against what was asked of his Moishke. On the contrary: when he, for the first time, saw his neighbor Mrs. Zayets's ward—who was practically the same age as his own—the girl with the broad shoulders, firmly kneaded cheeks, dimples, and a constant moisture in her eyes, he had a cheerful matchmaker's thought: it wouldn't be bad—it wouldn't do any harm—if the two of them should happen, in the course of time, to grow closer.

It was, as mentioned, just a pleasing thought, which passed in a rush, and Dr. Zemelman didn't dwell on it for long because—he quickly composed himself again—they were just children, and who knows what might still happen in time? But later, when the couple, thanks to the proximity of Dr. Zemelman and his neighbor, Mrs. Zayets, also became closer; and especially when Mrs. Zayets turned to her neighbor's ward, to Moishke, with the request that he help her charge, Elke, in her lessons, in which she had fallen behind . . . ; and when Dr. Zemelman was present while he, Moishke, prepared Elke's lessons with her and, effortlessly, taught her what she, in her dullness, did not readily understand. . . . Seeing how Moishke did this so artfully, with youthful ardor and a flowing tongue—and how she, his slow student, hung on his words with both envy and a kind of awe for someone older and more knowledgeable than herself—and, still more, with something that is characteristic of newly awakened femininity. . . . When Dr. Zemelman looked upon all that, the thought intensified in him that he wanted to see the couple more closely joined, each to the other.

Because, indeed, Dr. Zemelman already had a kind of right to do so. . . . Because, if one had looked upon the couple from the first moment of their acquaintance, one would have seen, from the very beginning, how he, Moishke, related to her, who needed his help, in a slightly reserved and distant way, as generally occurs between a youth and a girl of his age, and especially when she stands so far behind him: he treated her a little condescendingly, even a little arrogantly. From the time that Elke, who was a little younger than he was, from that very moment—as soon as she saw him—she couldn't tear her eyes away from him, as if she were stuck by the glue of envy, duty, and, as mentioned, something else (which says still more about those two).

A little later, it could be seen how Moishke, too, sought a relationship with her—not because his pupil showed much improvement or great success in the lessons she received from him. No, rather because the isolated situation in the houses where they happened to be apparently bound them together like two Robinson children whom a single wave had cast ashore on a rescuing isle after shipwreck.

Yes, that, it turns out, united them. Moreover, one could see how Elke there—broad legged and slightly misshapen in her shoulders—as soon as she was out of the Robinson Crusoe forest situation, where she had had to fight and defend her very existence, when she reached safety and was in a city and among people, where she, too, was provided with a roof, a dress, and a shirt to cover herself—immediately, she assumed the role she knew was hers, displaying the womanly aptitude of being able—and wishing—to share with others the gift of love she had been granted.

At first, she regarded Moishke as a brother, to whom one is loyal. But later, when the two had grown—and grown closer— it was possible to see, whenever Elke took a longer look at Moishke, an unctuous secretion from her eyes, as if her gaze had fallen on a small fire and been dried out. . . .

As mentioned, she hung on his every word—both because he always had more to tell her (more than she was capable of taking in) and also because even when he was silent, she still couldn't take her eyes away, out of girlish infatuation.

He, too—our Moishke—one will recall, sought her company. Later, it was possible to observe greater ease on both sides, which they expressed through their frequent visits to each other and their time spent together.

Of course, Dr. Zemelman couldn't *not* notice that. He had already sensed it a little beforehand and also, silently, supported it. . . .

More than once he came with this matter to his neighbor, Mrs. Zayets, who, like every woman with a perceptive eye, had the gift of discerning what might be blossoming between the adolescents. Mrs. Zayets, like her neighbor, Dr. Zemelman, probably also silently wanted it—again, as every woman does, when she is a faithful witness to young people's relationships, and, also, as a mother, to whom it has not been granted that she see it happen with her own child (and she contents herself to watch the one she counts as her own). On account of that and also—possibly—a hidden sense ordered her slyly and unconsciously (like her neighbor, Dr. Zemelman) to find out about both of them, like a broken branch that the trunk of the tree wants to grow back. . . .

Yes, Mrs. Zayets also, maybe, desired that.

Thus, when Dr. Zemelman had a free hour and stopped in to share his opinions with her about their wards—asking what she, as a pedagogue, thought about what they had done so far for the children, as well as what else to do and what could be improved, whether they had done something wrong—when Dr. Zemelman led a conversation about these matters, one sensed not just the interest of an individual who has taken in a stranger to bring up but also a father's interest for his own child, whom he wants to provide for as well as possible.

He even showed up at Mrs. Zayets's with slightly naive in-law questions, such as:

"Well, what do you think, Mrs. Zayets? You must know, as a woman. There might be something happening there with those two"—meaning a kind of match.

"Yes," Mrs. Zayets would say with a smile and in calm agreement, like a relative, too, for her part—out of pride. . . .

Moreover: just as Dr. Zemelman was already eager to see something built anew, newly paired for a new life—recently, he had also been more strongly inclined to participate in the new construction.

"What does that mean?"

That means that he, Dr. Zemelman, who already for some time now had known nothing of family life—first, because he was no longer young, and, second, because he had devoted himself entirely to raising his son (who had made him forget everything else that constitutes a family)—now, after the death of his son, and after he had taken in the strange child to raise, he felt not only the call to be a father awakened in him but also the responsibility of a man in charge of a household. He had a practical excuse: that, since his own dedication and supervision were not enough to raise the boy he had taken in, he would gladly see what he offered increase with the help of a partner—a woman as a mother for the boy.

It's possible that he was right: that his motive was just that and nothing further. But it's also possible that a feverish desire for reconstruction had gripped him, and, wishing to see it at work in others (people younger than he was), suddenly and rashly, he had transferred it to himself—and not just himself but everyone else, too: all the survivors among his people, whom he now wanted to do the same.

With pleasure, he now looked—it could be seen—at the young, grown-up couple (who, moreover, were finding their way to each other more and more), with a kind of borrowed paternal pride and anticipation of later on. At the same time, he also, on the sly, made parentally enamored looks over his glasses toward Mrs. Zayets, whom he thought to draw—not soon, not all at once—into the existence shared by a father and a mother, seeing how she understood him intuitively (and that she cast her eyes down to her breast when he, Dr. Zemelman, didn't say what, at the moment, he didn't yet have clear words to express).

Dr. Zemelman, thanks to his newly instilled desire, now became a more frequent visitor of Mrs. Zayets's, and he entrusted to her more and more what, until now, he had been carrying around in his solitude. Often forgetting that he has already asked the question more than once, he speaks:

"Well, what do you think, Mrs. Zayets?"—yes, it looks like it will happen. . . . He means the couple—but also himself and her, with whom he now wants to live under one roof, united in a family—she with the dowry she has brought, with Elke, and he with his Moishke. It would be much easier to raise them in this way.

Well, in that direction there, recently, he has even started to have dreams. His last dream was a silent nightmare.

He sees himself together with his neighbor, Mrs. Zayets, drawn in a sled. In the sled, his brother and his wife (on whose account the brother hadn't managed to escape the city) are lying, dead. He and Mrs. Zayets are conveyed easily, without the slightest fatigue, rapidly. . . . All of a sudden, they stop and turn back around, sensing that something living is beneath them. Then they see the brother and his wife sitting upright, contented and smiling benevolently—because, it seems, he, Dr. Zemelman, and Mrs. Zayets are conducting them easily, without the slightest effort. . . . And both of them, with half-living, half-dead mouths, speak: "Congratulations. It is good that you are here, good that you are together, and may your way be a short one. . . ." Now, they appear quiet and calm. Both hold candles in their hands. The candles shine festively. No wind, no breeze touches them; they don't flicker to either side.

A procession steps forward in rows with the solemnity of the holidays. . . . And all of a sudden, a voice is heard. It is directed to him—to Dr. Zemelman, who listens. However, he does not hear everything the voice has to say—only what, it seems, he has been permitted to hear:

"There is one thing to be mindful of: the commandment of growth and regeneration, despite all that has struck everyone—and, especially, us."

And then Dr. Zemelman wakes up, resolved to appear with clear words before Mrs. Zayets—to pronounce what, until now, he has half concealed from her. . . .

1946

Heshl Ansheles

(About an Occurrence in Present-Day, Occupied Poland)

1

Heshl Ansheles was well known among the intelligentsia of the city—among journalists, writers, and the like. They would often come to ask his expert opinion about work they had finished, and, when they planned something requiring exact knowledge they lacked, they drew on him in advance—as from a reference book, an encyclopedia.

He was very gifted. Still young, twenty-five or twenty-six years old, but so learned and well-read that he already seemed a little *too much* so. The head on his neck was somewhat bent over. His face was drawn and pale, as befits someone occupied solely with learning. The hair on his head was already pretty spare. His temples were sunken, and the skin on his hands thin and transparent—like the body of a little chick (when one blows on its downy feathers).

It should also be mentioned that a rather heavy inheritance weighed on him. First of all, there was his mother, who, while she still lay in childbirth, was befallen by muteness; suddenly, she stopped answering the well-wishing and congratulations of family members and friends who came to her bedside. She showed indifference to her child, her baby—and not like other mothers. When the child was brought to her bed for nursing, she wouldn't give it her breast. She just didn't remember. (And often, even while nursing, she forgot the infant and somehow lost herself in wild thoughts.)

The silence didn't stop after her confinement, either. On the contrary, it just intensified. It went so far that people were afraid of trusting her with the child—lest she forget herself and it fall from her hands.

Presumably, that had happened to her once. Doctors were called in, and they examined her thoroughly and talked it over a few times, consulting one with the other. And they came to the conclusion that the child should be taken away from her, because, in a condition like that, she was incapable of fulfilling her motherly duties; also, she should be placed in an appropriate hospital for recovery.

That is what happened. And no time had passed at all before her situation already worsened. She sank even deeper inside herself. She gave up eating and drinking and wouldn't permit herself to be nourished, even by force. Her end was bad. One day, when the hospital staff wasn't paying attention and looked the other way, she got hold of a sharp object—a knife or fork—and she tried to cut her throat. That time, after they saved her and the wound had healed, she grew subdued. For a while she apparently didn't want any sharp objects in her hands—or even to look at them. Then another opportune moment presented itself, and this time she put an end to herself for good: she cut deep into her throat, until death.

✦

That was his mother. His father—who, it was clear, loved her very much—took the matter so deeply to heart that he thought his own life was over, too. He went about devastated, and for a long time he wouldn't let anyone console or excuse him. . . . And when, as is the custom, matchmakers later presented themselves at the house with various proposals, not only did he not want to let them finish speaking—as soon as they said anything, he screamed at them and simply drove them off. At first, the matchmakers shrugged their shoulders, thinking it was temporary—because the grief was still fresh. But after they had tried to approach him again and again, and he, with more and more anger, loosed his curses on them, they saw that it was serious—it was not feigned or just for show. Then, they began to stay away and no longer appeared before him.

He, the father, also gave up his business. When he married, his wealthy parents had provided him with ample gifts. These, in addition to the dowry that came from the bride's family, had made it possible for him, soon after the wedding, to take up wholesale trade—with prospects for further gain (as rich people can expect after marriage). Now that misfortune had struck him, he cleared out and withdrew from all that. He became a recluse and wouldn't listen to advice from his parents, nor to what other relations recommended. He would have none of their "What, then? It happens . . ."—he was still young—"you have to let people help you out!" He devoted himself entirely to the child he had deprived of a mother. He gave up business matters and the responsibilities of being head of a household. At once, he dismissed his maid, and then a young person named Shamai, whose loyalty he had acquired; he also dismissed the nurse and attendants (one of whom had taken care of the child and the others, the house).

He liquidated his business. And with the money he earned from the liquidation, he bought, for his livelihood, a large house on a well-respected street. And his manservant, Shamai, assumed the management of the house—paying attention to its affairs, collecting rent money, performing maintenance work, and so on. Shamai was a butler, an accounts manager, and in charge of almost everything, because he had no life of his own (and also no thoughts of starting a family for himself).

That was then—the father was still young when misfortune struck. And now, at the time we're talking about, he is already older by more than a quarter century. Always in a robe and slippers, he walks around about the house. He still hasn't returned to business—nor to marriage. He still owns that great house on the well-respected street, as before. He still employs his servant, Shamai, who, naturally—just like his employer—has also become older and grown to be so much a part of him that he even wears the same clothes (whatever falls off the boss—and sometimes even new things, sewn in a cheaper material, but with the same cut). He eats together with him, goes with him to the baths; and in their free hours, they constantly play chess with each other.

The house hasn't changed a bit, either. The five-room apartment on the second floor of the building he owns is richly furnished, as before. The soft upholstery is just a little faded; the curtains, too, have lost a little of their color. But everything else is as it was. And the only thing that has changed the appearance of the home is the owner's grown son, to whom the head of the household has ceded the study, which he, the son, has fitted with bookshelves up to the ceiling. It is here that people now come to visit—people with whom neither the proprietor nor even Shamai, his servant, permit themselves to interact; they hold themselves at a distance and take pleasure in the acquaintance that Heshl, the son, has with them.

They look with pride and an air of superiority at the way the visitors always cross Heshl's doorway with respect—intending, evidently, to inform themselves and receive from him what they cannot imagine others providing. The father's chest swells when he sees how the visitors knock courteously at his son's door. And Shamai's chest swells, too—he also considers Heshl his son, a little bit. Whenever the boss, in his superior and slightly bigheaded glory, stops Shamai and expresses his pride with a few words, the servant responds: "Such good fortune, sir! It's no curse—someone that others come and seek out. . . ."

That, on the one hand, is what they feel: pride and joy. But on the other hand, it annoys them greatly when they notice that Heshl continues to remain more and more of a bachelor, with his stooped back. . . . And the pale appearance of his early youth hasn't left him with age: it hasn't gone away. On the contrary, it has grown and remains a constant presence on his face. Thus, when the father takes a furtive glance at Heshl, as he often does, he sees—with horror—the tremendous similarity between him and his mother at the time of her confinement, when a certain, sad silence befell her.

That caused a great deal of apprehension for the father and Shamai. They comforted themselves by saying that Heshl was a stay-at-home and a great scholar—it's characteristic for someone like him, and also fitting for that kind of person, to be a little weak of body and frail of health. . . . And it's tolerable, they told themselves: in time, Heshl will come into greater contact with the world, and then his health will also change to a more desirable state.

"Well, what do you think, Shamai?" the boss would turn and ask, whenever worry about his son seized him.

"Yes, sir," the servant, offering consolation, would reassure his employer. But both men preserved an unspoken and quiet melancholy—and especially the boss: a heavy stone weighed on his heart whenever he thought about his son's destiny.

That was the time when Heshl became a little sick and a doctor visited him. And when the doctor had examined him, suddenly he started to ask about the mother—what she had died from. And when he had received an answer, he cast another scrutinizing gaze at Heshl. As the father accompanied him to the door, through the entryway—once again, he stopped to ask about his son's present illness. Then the doctor spoke:

"This one now is nothing; it will pass"—the main thing was to see that the boy remained protected from shocks. "What does that mean?" the father asked; he wanted to know the exact sense of the doctor's words.

"That means: no surprises, no scares. They can make people lose themselves for a while. Afterward, it's difficult to come back."

The father thought it over. Often, he could not sleep for worry. He constantly wanted to talk to Heshl about how he—Heshl, that is—should be careful, because the doctor had warned, at this and that time, about one thing or the other. But he didn't know how to begin—or whether he, Heshl, would understand him. And Heshl himself, it seems, didn't understand. And that was certainly no good. It was a sign that he didn't know the state he was in or what was happening—what was waiting for him right at his door. Bad luck might strike unexpectedly should something arise or present itself (the kind of thing capable of bringing misfortune to people like him).

Yes, but for the present no such reasons arose. Meanwhile, Heshl's life followed its course in his father's house—as before, in the channels previously established, without a change. Thus—in addition to the father, who remained a widower, and in addition to Shamai, who remained a bachelor—when Heshl grew up, there was another man who, according to all the signs, would also stay unwed. The sole difference was that Heshl was betrothed to his study—which his father had given him to use, and which he, Heshl, had furnished with high-reaching bookshelves on all four walls, up to the ceiling. There, one could always find him reading a book—now, an old one whose pages had yellowed, which smelled of the mold that had grown with time, and now, a new one, whose pages had just been cut, with the colors of the printing still bold, and the paper fresh.

Heshl, as he grew older, would, like his father, spend entire days in his robe and slippers. At the quiet games of chess that the father often played with Shamai, a third man would appear—Heshl, standing first behind one player, and then the other; but he wouldn't intervene, and he never gave either party even a single suggestion.

It is possible that—if nothing further had occurred—he would have, in a certain way, survived his heavy inheritance, and that the potential sickness in him would have stayed dormant, because it would have no reason to wake up (like the seeds of plants, when they don't have the appropriate conditions—soil, sun, and moisture—for growth).

But suddenly something did happen. That was in 1939: war erupted, and all of us—the entire world—stood in witness.

2

Then, the fascist forces fell upon the city where Heshl Ansheles lived. Before the authorities had introduced the new order— before they drove the Jews from their homes and commanded them into appointed quarters, the ghetto—at first, they sent scouts throughout the city to locate lodgings for their military and civilian supervisors, for officers and bureaucrats, and so on. They didn't exclude Jewish residences.

When they came to Heshl's father's house on the well-respected street, a neighbor—with or without ill intent—gestured toward the owner's apartment in particular as the most comfortable and appropriate place for such people as were to be quartered there.

The dwelling of Heshl's father was to their liking. And soon, at the front door, an officer appeared, already with his baggage. (He was prepared to go wherever directed.) He left the luggage downstairs for a little, for the watchman—or others— to attend to, and he went up by himself, to the second floor, to see what had been found for him.

He found the apartment agreeable. Especially Heshl's study, where he thought to install himself. And soon he gave an order that the owners should come down with him, to help him carry the baggage up.

Of course, the maid wanted to perform the task. But the officer—the one taking up residence there—dismissed her with his hand: no, she was not permitted. "I . . ."—Shamai the butler jumped in; he stepped forward, wishing to take the place of others. "No, not you, either." The officer rejected Shamai's request and readiness to serve; he denied him permission, too. Then the head of the household himself—Heshl's father—announced that he would accompany the officer. But the latter also eliminated him (so to speak) with a wave of the hand. "No," he said, "*him.*" He indicated Heshl, who stood to the side, somewhat paler than usual—just looking at the officer's gang and not understanding why everyone else had been rejected and he alone selected for the task of carrying.

"Sir, Herr Offizier. . ."—Heshl's father turned, with entreaties, to the officer. "That is my only son. You can see, officer, sir, from the books in his study—he is a scholar"—plus, it also could be seen that he was weak of health. Why his son of all people? Why him, when all the others were ready to serve the Herr Offizier—and to do so with the greatest pleasure?

"*Ach,* a scholar?" The officer cast a glance at Heshl as if he were looking at a louse or some other speck of nothingness. "So, so"—he should get used to it. He'd grow accustomed to much worse.

"Hurry up!" he ordered Heshl, as if he were speaking to some messenger boy. And he gestured with his hand: that Heshl should go ahead, downstairs, and without complaining.

Naturally, nothing helped. After Heshl and the officer had gone out the door, all the others in the house just went after them like automatons—the father, Shamai the butler, and the maid followed—not, one saw, to be useful and help Heshl, but just because a blind force animated them and made their feet move.

Descending, the officer pointed the luggage out to Heshl. It consisted of two suitcases. One was bigger and heavier, and the second was lighter. Heshl bent over and wanted to take both of them in his hands, but then the officer gave him an order. "No!" he said. He pointed to the heavier suitcase: "That one, with your hands, and that one"—the smaller one—"with your teeth."

"What?" Heshl was already a little dazed from before. Now, when he heard these last words, he looked at the officer—not understanding what the man meant, thinking he had not heard correctly.

"Yes, Jew. . . . That one—with your teeth."

For a moment, all the parties stood as if frozen. The father soon wanted to take a step, to fall at the officer's feet and beg him to take back his command. Apparently, Shamai wanted to do the same. The maid, as well. But then the officer turned on Heshl and screamed, "Faster!" so that the others understood that no entreaties and falling to the ground would help—that anyone with eyes in his head could see what must occur (and whoever couldn't handle it should turn and look away).

Heshl alone said nothing. He looked at neither his father, nor the servant (who seemed half dead), nor the maid (who was wiping her tears with her apron). He bent down to the luggage, took the heavy suitcase in his hand, and, without a choice, neared his face to the second one. . . . For a time, you could see how his back shook, bending down and up, but soon it stopped moving. And . . . woe the years . . . a human being by the name of Heshl bent down over the luggage, and then someone else rose with the suitcase between his teeth. He was already another person, it might be said, no longer a human being—at any rate, not himself.

Whoever might then have cast a more attentive look upon Heshl would have seen how his gaze had changed. His eyes—

always of a somewhat grayish color—had now, it seemed, become entirely white, as if his mother's milk had entered into them. . . . Walking, he held the heavy suitcase in his hand and the other—the smaller one—in his teeth. A quiet funeral procession consisting of the officer and the members of the household followed him. The officer—who, it turns out, was used to such things, and also, it seems, not the kind to spend much time thinking (nor even capable of gauging the dimensions of humiliation and offense that he had given another by forcing him into such service)—the officer followed as one does a normal baggage carrier: coldly, indifferently, and as if nothing were happening. And Heshl's own people—his father, Shamai the servant, and the maid (who spent the whole time wiping her eyes with her apron)—walked behind, as people follow a dead body, when there are no words in your mouth, when the calamity is so great that you don't know whether your head is your own or if your own feet are carrying you. . . .

✦

But all that was nothing compared to what happened when they came into the house and accompanied Heshl into the study. Entering his room, Heshl remained standing with the luggage—as if he had neither the force nor the desire to release it. When the officer, without words, turned to him: "Well . . ."— that is, "put it down"—he remained standing, as he was.

Then, the maid approached him and took the heavy suitcase from his hands. The other one, which he held in his mouth, stayed there until the maid went to him again and took it away, too. But Heshl kept standing there with an open mouth, as wide as the handle of the suitcase had made him open it.

"My son!" his father cried out, seeing the frozen misfortune before his eyes and stepping toward Heshl. But soon he restrained himself, and he cast a glance at the officer. The latter already considered himself to be in full possession of the study, and he wanted to enjoy his ownership—to make himself comfortable. Here, the strangers (that is, the head of the household, his son, and the others) were a bother.

"Such misfortune!" The loyal servant also moved toward his employer's son, wishing to wake him up and bring him back to his previous condition.

"March!" yelled out the officer, but Heshl didn't budge and the officer's bark made no impression on him. He didn't carry out the command. He continued to stand there—frozen, with his mouth open—until the master of the house and his servant, sobbing, placed themselves at both sides, took him by the hand, and led him out of the study.

"Woe to his father!" Heshl's father cried out, conducting Heshl into another room, seeing that he, Heshl, stayed the same way as before, in the study: silent and standing with his mouth open.

"Heshl, what's wrong with you?" cried the servant, assisting his employer; he immediately ran off for a doctor.

He brought the physician they knew, the one who always visited the house. The latter observed and examined the patient, and a silent helplessness stole over his face, because Heshl was no longer Heshl, and the doctor had no way to comfort his family.

. . . It was over. . . . Already from that point on, Heshl didn't know what was happening around him. He didn't know that one fine day—soon after the officer had moved into his father's apartment—an order was proclaimed that they, the owners of the house, had to move out. They did so, and they wound up in a shabby lodging—somewhere in a dark, remote part of town.

Heshl also didn't know that he had kept his mouth open the whole time—and that his father and Shamai now were taking care of him as one cares for a child or a shaky old man who requires another's help. He didn't notice that they often took him out for walks in this part of town, where many others like them had come—without money, without provisions, and robbed down to their clothes. But the misfortune of his father was much greater than that of the others, and every time people saw the father or his servant taking him, Heshl, for a walk, they would stop and stare. (He, Heshl, was holding his mouth open—as if he had been born with that defect. . . .)

"Woe, the times!" They deplored him and the way he had survived—that anyone had carried another's bags like that.

"How is it, then, that . . ."

"Certainly someone like that can't endure such an indignity."

"Someone should cart them off already—to an unclean place, like dead cats or dogs, with all the other carcasses."

Heshl didn't notice how his father had recently become stooped over and broken—chased out of his home, off into the unknown, and besides all that, at his age, with a sick son.

Shamai also declined significantly. After he—along with his employer and his son—was cast out from their long-inhabited home and, like everyone, left without means, without clothes, and moreover savagely humiliated (with a special mark of shame: that certain patch that Jews, according to the law, had to wear on the sleeve, on their back, or on both). Afterward, when Shamai the servant—who was greatly attached to his master's house (as if it were his own)—saw his employer in such distress, he took it upon himself to conduct the lesser of the master's affairs, to the extent that the latter's remaining resources still permitted. He also took up looking after Heshl, when the master, tired and in his downcast state often sick, went off to bed.

Shamai also was diminished. Already he would often, like a dotard, talk to himself, not hearing what he had said. When walking with Heshl, he often addressed the latter as if he could understand. "Oy, Heshl," he would say, "what happened to you and us. . . . Merciful God really should have paid notice."

Heshl didn't understand a word. He also didn't register that some of his former acquaintances and admirers—who had also lost their homes—and who also, like Heshl and his family, had wound up here, in a remote, gloomy part of town—would come visit him and see, with great regret, how he was doing. Then, in his very presence, the visitors would speak about him and his state of health as if he were a stranger; he couldn't join them.

It didn't concern him or bother him. He remained in the same condition as right after the misfortune had struck, when he carried and brought up the luggage as a dog carries something in its teeth following its master, with an open mouth. He was like no one else here: a petrified gaze stared from his gray eyes, which now looked like those of an infant when it nurses on mother's milk.

In truth—very rarely—his gaze would change for the better and become more lucid. But soon it turned glassy and stiff—and the milky blurriness acquired such a menacing expression that one feared he was going over, there and then, from inactivity to a state of savagery in which anything was possible.

That occurred whenever, taking a walk in the quarter of town that had been declared a place of residence only for Jews, he encountered a person belonging to the foreign authorities—a military man, an officer in the same uniform, of the same color, as the one worn by the man who had played that particular game with him—after which what had happened, happened.

Whenever he encountered someone like that in that kind of uniform, he would suddenly make a start—a rapid movement, as if something had gotten into his body and now strained him greatly. He would stop and stand in the middle of his way. Every time, he looked at the man's hand, whether he was carrying something that he would soon command him to take and carry for him—and not just by hand, but with his mouth, as had happened before. . . . Then, Heshl opened his mouth a little wider.

This occurred rarely, because those military people had nothing to do there, in that isolated part of town. The place was an accursed one, and on account of being narrow, cramped, and overfilled with people, it was, also, an unclean one—so that such men—respectable military people—didn't want to come and spend their free time strolling about. But every now and then, someone like that would wander in. And he would come for one thing only, for the sake of one objective: murderousness—that is, in order to take a look at how his noble power had conducted its noble business by creating such filthy misery for those whose every right they had suspended and whom they had placed outside every law in every way.

✦

It happened once that Heshl—absorbed by his illness, accompanied by his degraded and devastated father, and in the company, also, of Shamai, who stood at his other side—suddenly struck upon a group of military men, three of them, who approached from the opposite direction.

It so happened that one of the soldiers—dressed in the same uniform as the one who, earlier, had given Heshl the honor of carrying his bags—was also carrying something now. It was nothing big—that would have been inconvenient—just something he wanted to "invite" a resident of the quarter to carry for him (as such "people" always do in places like that). No, nothing heavy, just a common, handheld suitcase.

And then, suddenly, Heshl's father, who stood at one side, as well as Shamai, who stood at the other, noticed how Heshl, all at once, made a step toward the three men who were approaching. And before Heshl's father or Shamai had managed to see what was happening, Heshl had already gone up to the man who was carrying the object in his hand—and he had bent down with his face and mouth, as if he wanted to take it away from him. . . . And when the man resisted and also grew a little frightened (seeing who he was dealing with there)—and angry that this idiot here had the nerve to stop him in the middle of the street, interrupting his stroll. . . . He was going to push him away when—suddenly, a loud scream sounded forth, as from a person whose head has been doused with hot pitch. And before the man's companions (or Heshl's father and Shamai) managed to make out what was happening, one could see Heshl rising from his bow down to the man's hand. His mouth was bloody, and inside his mouth he held something powerfully, with clenched teeth.

At that moment, Heshl's face lit up and became animated—full of special enjoyment (as if he had just emerged victorious, enormously satisfied by the action he had performed, which he hadn't thought possible).

In his teeth, Heshl held a piece of the soldier's finger, bitten off from the hand. A bit of good luck had occurred, one could see—and for the first time since misfortune had struck him. Now, with full contentment, he closed his mouth. No, he didn't close it; rather, he sealed it so that one could tell that all the riches of the world wouldn't be enough to force him to open it and release what he had there, what he had bitten off.

Immediately, the two men accompanying the injured soldier came back to their senses after this initial surprise—the suddenness of the attack and their comrade's exclamation—and they reached for their guns. The first, on one side, and the other, on the other, began to shoot at Heshl with the revolvers they had quickly drawn from their holsters. They shot him in the head, in the chest, and again in the head. And Heshl fell, like an ear of grain.

A great influx of police and representatives of the occupying forces soon gathered. They saw there an assault on one of their own. Soon, the whole district was full of the enemy—out of sympathy for the attacked party. A savage decree would fall upon everyone. . . . But for the time being, the proclamation was set aside: the authorities had plenty of time to settle that score later.

Soon, the corpse was taken off to the proper place, until a full investigation had been made. The father and Shamai were not allowed to accompany their kinsman or to say a parting word to him.

For a long time afterward, *they* did not want to hand Heshl over for burial in the Jewish cemetery, either. Finally, when his body was successfully obtained, the rites began—the ones used for all the dead: washing and preparation. . . . Only, when they reached his mouth and wanted to open it to extract what his bite had taken in—the joint of the soldier's finger—it was simply impossible. His mouth was so tightly shut that no force could tear open his jaws.

The burial society argued and disputed the matter according to religious law and custom. One side was inclined to say: we must not, it isn't right . . . with another's limb in his mouth. . . . And others—the more pious ones, precisely—pressed for the opposite: especially in this case—there, one sees, what we hold to. . . .

Presumably, he was buried like that—with the bone, which couldn't be taken out.

August 1942

Meyer Landshaft

A Fragment

(About a Second Case in the Occupied Poland of Today)

1

It was a few days after their arrival. . . . People were saying that the city commander had already informed representatives of the Jewish community that they had the responsibility to carry out commands and orders that would be issued specifically for the Jewish population.

At Meyer Landshaft's house, as in all Jewish homes, everyone was running around with their heads cut off. . . . Meyer Landshaft was a Polish-Jewish merchant—the silent type, well educated, and the son of the city's righteous people. He was, that is, a keen mind, and also a pious man; this had never prevented him—either in youth or now, when he was already over fifty—from peering into religious works by Shadal, Reb Nachman, or Krochmal (or even non-Jewish authors he knew, such as Klopstock and Schiller).* That was Meyer Landshaft—

*Schiller and Klopstock are classical German writers of the eighteenth century. The Jewish authors who are mentioned represent very different sensibilities. Nachman of Breslov (1772–1810) was a mystical thinker and the grandson of the Baal Shem Tov, the founder of Hasidism. Shadal (Samuel David Luzzatto a tall man, with a broad, blond beard and blondish eyebrows above gray eyes, which looked out between his lashes like quiet lakes surrounded by willows. That was Meyer Landshaft, whose proper attire alone commanded those in his presence to behave more quietly than they did in their homes. Every time he appeared (coming in off the street, or in from another room), the party expecting him would even rise a little, on account of his dignified presence. That same Meyer Landshaft, in all kinds of situations—even in greatly straitened circumstances (like when a child was sick or there was some other worry at home)—never permitted a change on his face; his inner conviction wouldn't allow him to doubt that a better outcome was certain, even in the worst difficulty. Now, that same Meyer Landshaft—after what the new authorities had done with the Jews of their own country (which people had read about in newspapers at some length)—and especially afterward, when they had started the war against Poland, and when people realized what had been done with the Polish Jews of the various cities and villages they had conquered and subjugated. . . . Now, since Meyer Landshaft (like many others) had not managed to leave when the enemy suddenly arrived before anyone could look around and figure out whether to stay or go. . . . Now, even Meyer Landshaft felt as if he had fallen into a trap. He started to abandon the habit he had always had of believing in the better outcome. . . .

People saw it in his grayish eyes, which looked out from between his lashes like a violent storm that has disturbed still lakes surrounded by willows. People observed it in his uneasy, clipped replies whenever they asked him something (on days he came back from town, where nobody went to do business anymore but just tried to find out what was being said and mur-

---

[1800–1865]) is known for his textual criticism of the Bible. Nachman Krochmal (1785–1840) was interested in bridging Jewish thought and contemporary German philosophy.

mured about what everyone feared so greatly). . . . Even when asked by his wife, Khane-Gitl—who always went along with him in everything, held him in the highest honor, loved him and looked to him, ready to satisfy his every desire (even anticipating his wishes in advance). Even to her questions—"What are people saying? What's the news in town?"—he would respond: "Nothing, nothing. . . . Nobody's saying anything. There isn't any news." And then he would turn away. Not looking her in the eye, he would do things about the house—the kind that people do before they move out, or before going on a journey (when one is scattered and it's uncertain what to prepare for).

Now he acted in a manner that had never been his way. Before, whenever he wasn't eating or busy with someone, people saw him with a holy book in his right hand, leaning the right side of his face forward and peering into it—a little shortsightedly—with his right eye. Now, no more. Now, no religious works crossed his mind. And whenever, from time to time, he could spare a moment from his personal worries, Meyer Landshaft (like all the Jewish inhabitants of the city at the time) would use that minute just to walk around—separate from others and speaking with no one. He walked from one wall to the other and from one corner to the next, throughout the house. Cracking his fingers when no one was looking, he whispered just one thing to himself: has God now—perish the thought!—decided to make an end of, to finish with—the Jews?

But no, he had no time for that, either. Especially—and more than anyone else—he was consumed by worries about himself and his household, over whose heads he saw a sword hanging. . . . But, then again, no one in his own family entered his thoughts—he didn't think about himself (for he was in the same situation as everyone else), nor his wife, Khane-Gitl (who had gone along with him in everything his whole life long, always ready to fulfill—and even anticipate—his every wish); he didn't think about his already wedded sons and daughters, nor his sons-in-law and daughters-in-law or their children (his grandchildren). Whenever he sought some air and an exit from the cage in which he was caught (that is, trapped by the various reports that reached his ears—one more horrible than the next)—no one entered his thoughts as often as his youngest daughter, his darling Vitl. At the school where she would soon graduate, she was known as Wanda.

2

Wanda had long, delicate fingers—a sign of distinguished, noble ancestry, and perhaps also a sign that she had been a gift to her parents late in life; she, their youngest child, came after many others. She stood out from the other children through her similarity to her father, through her quiet and refined manners. She wasn't like the other children, who were closer to their mother, Khane-Gitl (who didn't descend from such an elevated social position and who, people gossiped, had cost her simple father a pretty penny to get a man like Meyer Landshaft).

She was her father's pet—because she was the youngest daughter, and also because the father saw his own reflection in her. Even though he didn't openly display more tenderness to her than to the other children, the members of the household considered her an exception. From time to time, her father directed—if not special words—then a quietly enamored gaze, which fell gently upon her.

Understandably, the mother—and even the other children— couldn't be jealous. On the contrary: to the father's special love they added their own. They weren't jealous that the father permitted her what they hadn't been allowed: to attend a *Gymnasium*. (Incidentally, the teacher of religion, a priest, agreed that she needn't study this subject—and that she have the Sabbath off—because she worked so hard the rest of the week.)

In a word, Wanda was an exception both at home and among her friends. She always behaved with reserve and in an ethically pure manner. She was the picture of her father's ways—her father, who enjoyed respect within his family and prestige throughout the city. Among all shopkeepers, among acquaintances, people agreed that Wanda never allowed any student—a boy her age—to speak a free word, nor would she permit young men to approach her. And more: she even viewed the attractiveness of her girlish form as if ashamed, and she regretted that she hadn't been born in a shell. . . .

This girl still had a great amount of childish innocence peering from her eyes; they were somewhat distant, covered with a very slight film of dreams. Meyer Landshaft, her father, was now the first to get ideas and feel worried about her, for she faced the greatest threat—that she would catch the eye and capture the fancy of someone who was not to be desired, not at all.

During that time, her father already turned his gaze upon her very often. Whenever someone approached him with a matter of any importance at all, he, in the middle of talking, would turn away from the other party and look at her—as if he were afraid that he would lose her if she escaped his watch.

Why? Because—besides the reports that circulated about the worthy deeds the new authorities had committed wherever they had already arrived, and besides what they had already done where Meyer Landshaft lived—besides all that, which was horrible enough on its own—something else reached his ears, as well as those of other worried fathers. It was something that made them tremble: reports about houses where women were taken—girls, young ones—for the shameful pleasure of the commanders and the ordinary soldiers serving the authorities.

Soon, it was not just a rumor. People vouched with certainty that the Jewish community had already received orders that they give over a number of their women for shame. People were keeping it secret, and they didn't release any details to the general population, for they meant to intercede and get the authorities to revoke this evil decree. But it wasn't successful. And then, already, they all wandered about with their minds in ruin—including, even more than others, Meyer Landshaft. He looked so shocked that no one heard a single word from him; they just saw him cracking his knuckles quietly. . . . That is one thing. And another: in the early morning, in the evening, and during the night—had anyone listened to his words to heaven—they would have heard only one wish, precisely expressed in the words of judgment, and not of prayer.* Just as the eagle doesn't fear hunters, but only other birds of prey—it flies higher than them; it takes its children and doesn't fly underneath them, but above them, saying: it were better I were attacked than my young. In this way, too, did Meyer Landshaft think: better me than my own—that is, Wanda.

3

Feeling so utterly lost, Meyer Landshaft stopped appearing in public. He stayed at home the whole day, and in order to busy himself with anything at all, he started to do things like sharpen the knives of the house (which he otherwise did only on Fridays, in honor of the Sabbath, as was his long-established custom).

*The lexical distinction here is between *posek* and *davnen*. The first word refers to a scholar or rabbi who makes an authoritative statement on Jewish law, whereas the second means "to pray."

"What's going on?" asked Khane-Gitl—and also the older children—when they saw him, in the middle of the week, at this uncustomary pursuit.

"Nothing . . . nothing," he replied without looking anyone in the eye (as usual in recent times whenever someone approached him). And out of great respect and deference, neither Khane-Gitl nor the children pursued the matter. They understood why he was now taking up such useless matters, and also why he spared words and barely answered them.

Sitting like that and sharpening the knives, he certainly had no idea what he was doing—except perhaps it was because he did know; he had found out that in difficult times (in times similar to those now), his forefathers had been forced to be the executioners of their own children, as if they were strangers: they killed them themselves, so they wouldn't fall into the hands of others. . . . He didn't know how that had been done— how his forefathers had done this to their own sons—but he considered that sometimes the greatest lack of pity is merciful; then, one must uproot compassion and extinguish it in oneself.

He certainly shuddered at the thought. . . . But after long terror, once, as he sat at the table sharpening—suddenly, he heard a ring at the door. It certainly didn't come from anyone who belonged to the household. Instead, it was from a stranger's hand, which made a strong and extended ring—a firm, demanding sound.

Surely, it was a mail carrier bringing a telegram, in a hurry for somebody to open up quickly. Or else it was people from the authorities, demanding to be let in promptly and without further ceremony by those at whose door they rang.

Surprised by the bell, Meyer Landshaft made an unlucky start and cut his hand, and blood flowed from the wound. But he didn't notice the cut or the blood. Soon, he heard someone from the household go to open the door. And from the stillness of the door being opened and the encounter with the party—or parties—who had entered, Meyer Landshaft concluded: truly, these were no ordinary visitors who had been admitted to his house and now crossed the threshold.

In the hallway in front of the dining room where Meyer Landshaft sat, the heavy footsteps of soldiers were heard. And the quietly startled—and, it seems, terrified—encounter between the resident of the house who had opened the door and those who came in was felt in all the rooms.

Everyone emerged and assembled in the dining room. It seemed the newly arrived parties wanted to go there first, as it had no door and was visible from the hallway. They did so. All the members of the household were at home (as was always the case in those days, when the citizens were still uncertain about the authorities' disposition toward the non-Jewish population, but it was abundantly clear for the miserable Jews, who already felt three-quarters condemned).

All Meyer Landshaft's people were terrified. Exposed, they huddled in the dining room. As soon as the detachment had made its entry, everyone—both the soldiers and the family—saw how Meyer Landshaft straightened his back and, very pale, rose from his seat. Looking upon everyone gathered in the room—suddenly, a single word came forth from his mouth: "Wanda." Of all the people in his family, it was Wanda who should come and stand at his side.

4

"Hands up!" A second voice, higher than Meyer Landshaft's, was heard. It came from the mouth of an officer in the detachment. And soon after the order, a second command followed, from the same officer: "Stand in a line! Men and women separate"—no one should dare make a move. . . .

They all obeyed. Everything occurred in silence. Meyer Landshaft had the men of the household—his sons and sons-in-law—to his left. Just to his right—of all the women in the house—the one nearest to him happened to be Wanda (whom he had called earlier, when he stood to meet the soldiers). Then, after her—after Wanda—stood his wife, and after her, his daughters and daughters-in-law.

The officer, a lieutenant, first made a grave look, without speaking—to see whether things were in order, whether his command had been properly carried out, and whether anybody was moving. . . . Very well. Then he made a turn to a man (not a military one) who had entered with the soldiers. That was a supervisor of some kind—someone appointed by the community and forced by the new authorities to accompany them to all Jewish households (such as Meyer Landshaft's); he was to do what they demanded of him by performing some kind of registration (which the authorities needed).

"Count," the officer commanded the community official. But . . . no! He stopped, and—having first taken a look at the row of men, and, then, at the women—he uttered a word. His gaze had fastened with pleasure on Wanda, and he let it rest on her.

Whoever could still experience fear after the humiliating ceremony saw that the lieutenant—the leader of the military detachment—was more drunk than sober. It could be seen in his swimming, blue eyes—shining and seeming to float in grease—and also in his unsure movements, which were far from balanced.

He started to count the row on the left—the men. He pointed his finger at the chest of each one: "One, two, three. . . ." Then he reached Meyer Landshaft, who—like all the others—held his hands up in the air. The whole time, he didn't direct his eyes toward the row of men to the left but at Wanda, who stood to the right.

Before he passed on—with his finger—to the women, the lieutenant stopped for a moment in front of Meyer Landshaft. Then, he extended his counting hand to Wanda. Staring greedily, very casually, he placed his finger—on Wanda's breast—as if he were dipping it in honey and ready to take a lick.

Then, a voice sounded from Meyer Landshaft's mouth. It was stern and commanding. It came from a quiet man, who had never assumed a haughty tone with anyone (and also, it seems, had never been capable of doing so).

"Get your hands off!" A stern command came from Meyer Landshaft's mouth. Then, everyone else's hands fell in terror; they forgot the lieutenant's orders to keep them in the air.

"What?!" The lieutenant seemed not to understand who was meant by this unauthorized, menacing outburst. *He* was meant. It meant him in particular. He, the Herr Offizier, should remove his hands from what didn't belong to him—there existed something from which he must keep away.

"What?!" He made a start, took a look at Meyer Landshaft, and stepped back a little from where he had heard the voice—in order to have a better look at Meyer Landshaft there. "What did you say? What did you dare say to a German officer?"

And then he cast his sloppily drunken gaze on Meyer Landshaft and saw him standing there. His hands were raised; blood flowed from one of them and ran down his sleeve.

"Blood?!" He made a second start, as if he had seen it on his own hand—as if, just now, someone had wounded him. "Whose blood is that?" He started to look around suspiciously—throughout the room, at the people surrounding him—as if there, before he had entered, someone had been harboring evil designs against him and, while sharpening weapons, cut himself.

Indeed: he looked at the table and saw knives and a whetstone. It seemed that just before his arrival someone had been preparing and readying them for illicit use. So he thought.

"Who did that? Who—was sharpening?" the lieutenant demanded, pointing at the knives on the table.

"I was!" Meyer Landshaft replied. There was a haughty, satisfied tone in his response—apparently because the business with
the knives drew the lieutenant's attention away from staring at
the girl who had caught his eye (to whom he had reached out
his honeyed fingers with such pleasure).

It lasted a few moments, until the lieutenant realized what
had to be done. (Incidentally, it should be mentioned that
everything recounted here occurred before the authorities
had shown they would execute, with their right hand,[*] their
plans for Jews in the regions where they had arrived and now
governed. At that point, they remained within certain, apparently legal, limits—unlike now, at the time of writing, when
a lieutenant like that would waste no time on someone like
Meyer Landshaft; he would just lay him flat like that—without
a second thought—in response to the slightest word eliciting
displeasure; this would occur with any Jew at all, guilty or not,
for it had been deemed necessary to proceed with them as
with plague-bearing vermin: to exterminate them. . . .)

5

"Listen!" shouted the lieutenant to the soldiers, as soon as he
realized what had to be done. "Listen to the *Blutjude,* the one
who sharpens knives against the authorities."

"Oh, no. . . ." Suddenly, Meyer Landshaft's daughter Wanda
stepped out of the line. . . . And as if modestly recognizing that
she was not interacting with her own kind—with the students
she knew (whom she never allowed a free word, nor the slightest impropriety with regard to her person), or other women—

[*]A biblical image, otherwise applied to the actions of God.

now, at a time when danger confronted her father (who, it seems, was as dear to her as she was to him, although she didn't say it openly but kept it to herself in maidenly restraint, just as her father sealed his own lips—and merely looked . . .); modestly recognizing that her behavior was unprecedented— Wanda had never exploited her gifts—still, now, stepping before the lieutenant and wishing to save her father from the trouble that had resulted from being overly direct; suddenly—nobody knows how—she let that power shine forth— the one that is common to all women at certain times, when they need to be enchanting and obtain something by means of charm. . . .

"Oh, no, Herr Lieutenant," she said, presenting herself as an adult for the first time in her life in front of the family and servants. She readily gained speech. First, she cast her gaze downward, with her usual modesty (as she always did before an unknown man). Then, she lifted it, precisely to that stranger there. Even managing a slight smile, she spoke:

"Oh, no, Herr Lieutenant, it's a mistake. Those aren't knives against the authorities. My father isn't like that. It's kind of a custom among us for fathers to do that before the Sabbath. Now, with the trouble in the city—when there is no business to be done—he has started doing it during the week. Please look, Herr Lieutenant—they're ordinary house knives."

Thereby Wanda, with lowered eyes, smiled softly. And she again let that feminine power shine forth, with which she intended to make the man before whom she now stood—the lieutenant—forget the insult he had received from her father when the latter had told him to remove his hands (which he had allowed to do something indecent . . .). She made a step toward her father and tenderly embraced him, in order to demonstrate his innocence; she guarded it with her nearness, by placing herself in front of him—that is, in front of the incriminating knives—which, as the Herr Lieutenant could see, were for distraction, and there was no reason to waste even a single word on them.

Wanda's actions were effective. It could be seen how the lieutenant's gazes became merry—yet mixed with slight shadows—when he saw her step forward from the others, when she stood before him and made excuses for her father, and especially afterward, when she went over to him lovingly and gently pressed against him.

The drunken lieutenant relented, and things stood at a balance. After just a little while, if Wanda had, in the same act of apology, said a couple more words on behalf of her father, and if the father, Meyer Landshaft, had also remained silent and allowed her to protect him—that's all it would have taken for the lieutenant to forget his anger and take back the order to arrest Meyer Landshaft.

But that's not what happened. Because as soon as Wanda lovingly placed herself by her father, and he, the father, saw by what means she—his Wanda—wanted to win the lieutenant's goodwill and turn the man's anger away from him; when he saw how Wanda wanted to buy his freedom, he pushed her away a little. And when the lieutenant—on Wanda's guarantee and as a favor to her—almost freed her father from all suspicion and no longer thought him guilty—then, Meyer Landshaft, for no apparent reason, suddenly stepped out from the row opposite the lieutenant. Abruptly and unexpectedly, he made a nonsensical pronouncement and repeated the same words as before (when, previously, the lieutenant had turned to everyone and asked: "Who was sharpening knives?"—he, Meyer Landshaft, moved forward and declared: "I was!").

"I was!" He now repeated the same words, as if he wanted to call to attention that no one else had said it—just him, Meyer—and that he was standing behind what he had said and would not back down. He had no regret and accepted no effort from others to intercede on his behalf—not even from his dearly beloved daughter, Wanda.

"What?!" the lieutenant yelled, seeing Meyer Landshaft's defiance and looking at him as if he had just sprung up out of the earth. He couldn't believe his ears—what he had just heard from this individual, who might yet have emerged a free man from his troubles. He couldn't believe that he, without the slightest reason—it seemed to the lieutenant—was now calling those problems forth again and desired to bring them on himself. It was like someone putting a healthy, innocent head into the executioner's noose.

"Meyer!" Khane-Gitl, his wife, exclaimed in terror and shock. She saw him, her husband, acting in a senseless way for the first time in his life—declaring something that, God forbid, could bring both him and everyone else into the flames.

"What on earth is this person doing?" Involuntarily (and with fear he swallowed and concealed) the question also escaped the lips of the community supervisor. He had witnessed the entire scene and heard Meyer Landshaft's defiant words—with which, it seemed, he wanted to bury himself. The supervisor saw how that man there, Meyer, was bringing misfortune upon himself for no clear reason: after all, everything could end safely and in the best possible way (something which rarely happened in cases like this).

"What is he doing?" the community representative asked himself. Meanwhile, he turned his head away, unable to look at Meyer and his senseless action. Scoundrel, he's bringing death on himself—it's suicide. He didn't say it aloud, for he didn't comprehend what was happening within this person, who didn't understand such matters—such elementary ones, it seemed: how to behave before an official from the authorities, and especially one like this! The slightest suspicion—even if it's idiotic—could result in something serious, so one must wash oneself clean. This man wasn't responsible for himself alone. Plus, he was giving up on a chance, provided by his daughter, who then and there might have been able to save him from the grave.

That's what the community representative thought, and Meyer's wife, Khane-Gitl, too—and all the others in his family. Looking at him, they stood in shock, without a word in their mouths, not understanding why he was bringing a blow upon himself as if it were something he desired dearly.

However, Meyer Landshaft understood. He had a reason and justification for his deed: he didn't want, even for a single moment, to let the lieutenant's enamored eye fall upon Wanda, for he saw how the man looked her over from head to toe, and how his insolently hungry and impure gaze lingered with pleasure on her every limb. . . .

6

"Seize him!" the lieutenant yelled to the soldiers after Meyer Landshaft had roused his anger for a second time. In his presumption, the man had even made him forget Wanda, upon whom he had gazed so eagerly just now; if only he had been granted a courteous tip of the hat, he would have renounced all ambitions and accusations for her sake.

"Seize him!" he said harshly and decisively. He no longer contemplated Wanda but did his duty as an officer. The open enemy—that Jew there, who was sharpening knives against the authorities—had to be cleared out of the way.

"Don't do it, Herr Offizier" Khane-Gitl implored the officer. Then, the older children did so, too. And then Wanda, who spoke to the lieutenant: "Me, Herr Lieutenant—take me instead of him!"

"Seize him!" the lieutenant commanded a third time, neither listening to nor deigning to look at the people who surrounded him with their pleas.

They grabbed him, Meyer Landshaft. . . . Wanda and the other children tried to accompany him to the headquarters, to where he was taken—they stayed at his side the whole time, unwilling to leave him. They arrived at the destination—at the high, wide wall running down the street—and they approached the big double door held open by watchmen; and they stood on the sidewalk across the street for some time, waiting for him to come back out. But he didn't show up, and they gave up on seeing him a free man again. And they went off to do what people do in cases like that: find assistance, run and seek aid from the community and private parties, Jews as well as non-Jews—from whoever they thought might provide help.

✦

Foolishness. . . . A flight of fancy, it seems—a joke. But already the very fact that Meyer Landshaft had been taken to headquarters on the charge of resisting the authorities—worse, of sharpening knives in broad daylight (which a person like that normally doesn't do). . . . That alone—and the testimony of the lieutenant, who confirmed that when he encountered him, he was busy sharpening—and that when he asked him what he was doing, the other man didn't deny it but, on the contrary, insolently replied that yes, that was exactly what he was doing. All that was enough for Meyer Landshaft to be dealt with seriously and immediately put in the hands of a certain investigator, to whom he was led off—into a secretly kept room hidden in the immense, soundproof headquarters building.

The investigator was a tall, aristocratic-looking individual with hollow cheeks—the result of sinful nights and years of dissolution. But now he stood strict and imposingly quiet, with a sideways gaze—like a rooster's—and a monocle in his eye. It cannot be said that Meyer Landshaft was really tortured. Just the separate and distant room in the long, deaf corridor of the headquarters . . . ; just the silent demeanor and sideways gaze of the interrogator (who had one eye that looked like it belonged to a sick, old hawk with a bad conscience). . . . That alone was enough for Meyer Landshaft—a quiet man, an educated and pious individual, who never had had any trouble with the government or found himself in the situation of being interrogated—and especially in a way like this. That alone was enough for him to feel, from the very beginning, as if he had landed in some part of Hell. . . .

In truth, at first he tried to stay free and not be intimidated by the interrogator, for he was there alone—away from the danger that, just now, at his home, had faced his Wanda. . . . He thought little of the allegation that had been made against him, which he could easily dispel and make void. As he came before the interrogator, he gathered together all he knew—everything he had acquired from books written in the language the interrogator used with him. Both modestly and a little proudly, he thought to prove that he—the interrogator—wasn't dealing with just anyone but with a refined person versed in the works of Klopstock, Spielhagen, and Schiller. The other—the interrogator—would have to understand that mere familiarity with such matters is an adequate guarantee—assurance that no hint of any wrongdoing at all should fall upon him.

The interrogator looked at him indifferently. He let him speak his piece—as if to make him, Meyer Landshaft, believe that he accepted everything he said as valid and as proof of innocence; apparently, the lieutenant who brought him in had made a mistake in suspecting a person above suspicion.

The interrogator asked him some questions. He stared at his lips for a long time and remained silent (as if he were counting every word, until the end). This made Meyer Landshaft even think he would receive an apology then and there; that he would be allowed to leave a free man—a person who had wound up where he didn't belong, for no reason at all.

That's what he thought. Then—all at once—the interrogator rose from the bench where he had been seated. This action forced Meyer Landshaft, who sat opposite, to stand up, too—he didn't know why. At the last minute, he sensed that the other's getting up somehow was not good. Indeed. . . .

It can't be said that the interrogator observed standard practice or acted as official questioners tend to do during interrogations. Meyer Landshaft wasn't thrown into a side room where certain Gestapo people then "worked him over" (say, by ordering him to crawl on a table and sit on a chair they then knocked out from beneath, so he would break his back; he also wasn't beaten with a rubber cudgel; nor did a fist in the chin, under his teeth, force him to raise his head higher and higher, until his neck practically broke).

No, the interrogator did everything himself, with no one's assistance. Nor did he act in a crude manner. . . . Silently and without words, he simply approached Meyer and—as the latter trembled in bewilderment and terror—he took him, with both hands, by both sides of his beard. All of a sudden, he gave such a quick tug that, in his hands, the interrogator promptly held two tufts of hair. Meyer Landshaft's two cheeks had been plucked. A few bits of hair remained, like abrasions after a cut—nothing more.

"Go." The tall, aristocratic-looking official (with the look of a sick, old hawk with a bad conscience) told Meyer Landshaft. "Go—and that's what you get for the knives you say you were sharpening for your stinking Jewish Sabbath. Go. If you're needed, you will be summoned—a plucked chicken."

7

He went out. . . . But none of his family and friends—had they encountered him on the way home from headquarters—would have recognized him. He had changed between the time of arrival and when he was told to leave—both because the hair of his beard had been removed and because, with his tall stature and his silent, humiliated gait, he resembled the famous picture of a mournful knight*—that is, he looked burned out from the inside, like a chimney left standing in the ruins of a building.

When he got home, nobody asked what had happened. They could see, without asking, and right away they understood his troubled and unexpressed intention: to remain alone, isolated in his room, until the indignity had passed and the hair of his beard had grown back.

None of the servants followed him there. Only Khane-Gitl, his wife, attended to him; and for the first hours and even the first days, even she couldn't get a single word out of him when she went into his room. He remained mute. And the only thing that preserved him, gave him strength, and comforted him in his isolation was—maybe—the thought that by taking upon himself the shame he had received at the headquarters from that interrogator with the hollow cheeks, long legs, and monocle—by taking upon himself the shame of that man's hands tearing at him—he, Meyer Landshaft, had saved the honor of Wanda, his child, who had faced a far worse form of dishonor than the one he experienced.

"Thanks to God Almighty," he thought with certainty, whenever Khane-Gitl came to him and he asked about what was to be heard in the city, what people were saying, what the rumors

*Possibly *Knight, Death, and the Devil* (1513) by German artist Albrecht Dürer.

were, and . . . how is Wanda doing? That was always the last question he asked; enclosed in impoverished separation from others, he didn't want to appear before the world without his dignified beard.

But the comfort did not last long. Not for nothing had the lieutenant come to visit him with the detachment of soldiers. In many Jewish houses—and non-Jewish ones, too—they had registered the women (except for those who were nursing or pregnant). From the stop at Meyer Landshaft's house, Wanda stood registered in their little book. Just what they did when they took the women away for unheard-of degradation is a chapter unto itself, and it has no equal in any chronicle of evil known to the world. Likewise, children were torn from their homes and packed into cargo trains, with only a little barred window on one side of the roof. They were all assembled at the depot. No parents or relatives were allowed to come and say good-bye. The trains packed with captive children departed from the stations—and many tears, crying, and quiet moans escaped through the barred windows of the locked wagons. There is nothing more to say about all that, because what is known is already enough.

One must picture what happened in all the houses where the children passed over the threshold for the first time, never to return again. And if they did return, both the parties who had been taken away and those to whom they were dear might have wished that they hadn't. . . .

One must picture what happened at Meyer Landshaft's house. Everyone—Khane-Gitl, the older children, the sisters and brothers—was already resigned. Then, there was Wanda herself. And more than anyone else, there was her father, Meyer Landshaft. The whole day long, Wanda prepared for the journey. (According to the proclamation, it was necessary to bring along shoes, clothing, and a few days' food—allegedly, for work.) Throughout the house, all day long, crying and lamentation escaped first from one person, and then from another, erupting in hysterics. The whole time, Meyer Landshaft did not emerge. He also didn't come out on that day, neither at the final hour, nor even the last minute, when Wanda was already saying good-bye to everyone and a wild racket from her mother, Khane-Gitl, and brothers, sisters, and other relatives surrounded her. Even when Wanda went to her father's alcove. Among all the wailings in the house, her voice spoke behind the door: "*Tate*, open up. I want to say good-bye." Even then, Meyer Landshaft wouldn't relent. He didn't open the door and embrace Wanda. He was silent for a few minutes. Afterward, he spoke: "No, my daughter, I can't." (Not out of self-pity, of course, but because he didn't have the heart.) Standing like that behind the door, Wanda, it seems, heard a sobbing. It followed her for a long time on her way—the sobbing of a man lamenting both his own catastrophe and the collapse of an entire world.

Wanda could not endure that, and she departed. . . . In the evening, at the station, the train pulled away in a long line. In the car Wanda occupied, some others whom no one had accompanied gathered at the high window, which they could hardly reach. They said good-bye, with parting gazes, to their homes, from which they had been torn. Then, Wanda stretched her head to the window, too. . . . She thought of no one, not even her mother—whose last caresses she had felt on her blouse, when she sobbed at her breast, said good-bye, and kept her head buried there for a long time, unable to separate from her—no, not even her mother; she thought of no one but her father—who had hidden away behind the locked door and heard her entreaties—the pleas of his youngest daughter, Wanda—and he just didn't have the heart to open the door, even to come out and look at her before she went away.

1943

Rive Yosl Buntsies

(About a Third Case in the Provisionally Occupied Poland of the Past)

EVEN IN A LITTLE, antiquated, piously preserved Jewish-Polish shtetl, she was a marvel—a kind of historical relic, to be displayed in a museum.

"Who?"

Rive Yosl Buntsies, who could be seen, winter and summer, in a long dress with unhemmed skirts and an old-fashioned cloak (still from King Sobieski's times*), carrying an old cane with an ivory knob, like a bishop's, as she walked with the broad, solidly belabored stride of a high church official.

She was also never seen alone but always with a grown-up girl—an orphan, whom she had brought up and raised. She, Rive, considered it her charitable duty to give the girl away in marriage and see her wed. In her place, she would then find a new girl to raise.

*Proverbial expression denoting great antiquity. Jan III Sobieski (1629–96) was an extremely popular king of the Polish-Lithuanian Commonwealth. An able military leader, he was famous for bringing stability to the realm after the Chmielnicki Uprising (a Cossack revolt that devastated Jewish communities) and the Swedish invasion at midcentury, as well as for defeating the Turks in the Battle of Vienna (1683).

The orphan who accompanied her carried a charity box. With her, Rive traversed the city, going for the most part to the town's well-to-do and collecting for the needy; other times, she approached merchants arrived from elsewhere—the traders who showed up now and then.

The locals tended to oblige her because of the out-of-towners. To the guests from whom she wished to obtain something, she presented herself at her full height, in her unhemmed dress, and with the old cane. She didn't speak—as usually occurs when requests are made—with sugary words and feigned entreaties. Instead, she addressed them commandingly—as if it was coming to her—and she also didn't speak in respectful, formal terms to anyone, whether young or old.

"Merchant, do a righteous act for the poor."

Whoever, upon seeing her, made a donation right away, without complaint, was fine. But whoever wanted to find out who she was—whether out of curiosity or in order to determine what kind of donation would be in keeping with her station (asking, "Who are you? What do you need the money for?")—to him she would say:

"Don't ask, seller-trader. Come on, the whole town knows me, and everybody knows that I won't eat your gift up—and the poor won't, either. . . ."

Whenever somebody like that was miserly and didn't make a donation that matched how Rive had sized him up in terms of appearance and wealth, she would cast a strict, censorious gaze upon him from top to bottom and speak:

"Generous man! Compassionate man! Seller-trader . . . Open, open up God's purse, which does not belong to you. . . ."

People saw that there was no messing with a person like that. No opposition and no objections were possible. They would reach into their pockets and put a little extra in the jar. Then, Rive would nod her head in agreement and add:

"Give, give, come on—your gift won't lose you any money." After receiving what she needed, she would turn her big, manly body away (which did not rest easily on her feet but bent a little from right to left—limping a little from age). And looking at her old-fashioned cape, which was fastened with two ribbons under her chin in the front (and looked like an exotic bird's plumage below), they would accompany her to the door—either in amazement or with a little smile of respect, not knowing why they smiled or where the respect came from. . . .

That's how it went with strangers. But her own townspeople knew her well and held her in great esteem—as a kind of universal grandmother from whom all were descended. Men gave her the honor she was due, and women came to her for her blessings.

No wedding took place in town at which Rive wasn't the first to wish the couple well. Nor was there a bris at which she wasn't the godmother. And the women went to her with their questions and for various bits of advice—even more than to the rabbi.

She deserved it all. Because she was wise and the kind of person who occupied a position of influence, women came to her as to a leader, whom one must hear out and obey, whose words demand respect.

That was the role she played. You had to see her, people said, on a day of fasting and mourning, at night, when half the town's women gathered around her, under the open sky, on a field scattered with blankets. Rive sat in the middle, on a cushion, looking like an empress who had descended from her throne. With a light in her hand, she read aloud to everyone from the Yiddish Bible* about infamous catastrophes.

*This seems to be the best translation available for *Taytsh-khumesh,* which contained the Five Books of Moses; no complete version of the Bible was produced in Yiddish, although an oral tradition existed.

She had to be heard, stern Rive, reading with such expressiveness. . . . Each picture of the calamity came forth from her mouth so vividly that it seemed to have occurred only yesterday. For example: King Nebuchadnezzar driving the Jews, old and young, locked in chains, through the desert, where they were given only salty things to eat—and when they begged for drink, they received jugs filled with air—at which they clutched thirstily but still remained parched; and how, then—when they came to the river of Babylon—the captors demanded of the Levites that they hymn them and play the songs of their land on their instruments; and the captives who received these commands responded by chopping off their fingers, saying to their captors: "Well, then? How should we play? You see we have no fingers. . . ." Then, Rive would raise a hand as proof to the women gathered on the ground, in the open, before her, and they gazed upon her as if she herself were one of the Levites, her fingers missing. . . .

Likewise, one had to see her on another occasion—on Rosh Hashanah, when poetic prayers were recited—for example, the "Let Us Relate the Mighty Holiness of This Day," when the scales in Heaven are balanced: then, there is judgment of sins and merits . . . for life, or—God forbid—the opposite. . . . Then—if the heart of all the women at prayer didn't sink right there in dread at the fate soon to be declared for them, their husbands, children, and families! Afterward—when Rive had ended her prayers properly—only for herself—then she rose from her place at the "pulpit," where she had been sitting, and she assumed her full height. Supported by her cane (without which she was already unable to walk), she strode between the places where the others were sitting. Like a high commander, who has the final word and gives orders to his soldiers, who rouses their hearts before battle—before everybody's fortune is read—thus did she, Rive, speak out, that all might hear:

"Women, listen. . . . Just look around. See if the angel of death isn't among you. . . ."

Yes, the townspeople respected her. Accordingly, they gave her both honor and what she demanded when she arrived with her orphan and the little jar (which was for those without assistance, for whom she was resolved to obtain what they needed).

Whenever she had to bargain with someone, she rarely coaxed the individual. If she ever noticed that the other party was hesitating, she said:

"Just look at that. . . . What? You don't want to? Impossible! Would I give you . . . ? I wouldn't accept charity from you. . . . I have enough. . . ."

And in truth, she did—Rive. Besides the good work of raising orphans until they reached a certain age and, afterward, marrying them off with great pomp—in beautiful wedding attire, with music, with holy objects, and even with the participation of all the prominent residents of the town. . . . Besides that and besides her collections on behalf of the community's poor and her secret excursions (about which nobody else needed to know)—besides that, she performed another good work: attending, in an authentically Jewish way, to a poor man's corpse—one without children or relatives, for example, a luckless vagrant whose years had expired there in the town—someone to whom, except for her, Rive, no one would show any kindness.

Then, she was seen without her orphan—alone, with the same unhemmed dress, with her cane and cape—carrying a pair of silver, polished candlesticks of fine workmanship—broad-framed ones with elaborate ornamentation. She came to the body (which the burial society had told her about earlier). She lighted them and placed them at the man's head. Before performing the final rites, she walked around the body and mourned it in the fitting manner.

When people saw her walking with the candles, they knew there was a burial in town. At first, a group of women of different ages would join, and, afterward, men—until, finally, such a throng had assembled that, in every such case, the funeral was an even bigger affair than if the town's best-known citizen had died.

Incidentally, it should be mentioned that when the whole town gathered for a funeral, this occurred less out of respect for the dead than respect for the silver candlesticks that Rive carried festively—as something sacred and dear to her above all else.

Indeed, they were candlesticks from her father, Yosl Buntsies. Before his death, he had bequeathed them to Rive's husband—the husband of his only daughter—so that he might light them whenever he was studying (which was the only thing that concerned him, for he knew no other occupation).

Rive's husband was a plaything—an empty vessel—in keeping with the pious notions of an earlier time. In him, Yosl Buntsies regarded both *this* world and *that* one. *This* world, inasmuch as the other man was a living honor to him—and *that* one when Yosl Buntsies recalled how his lights always stood before the eyes of a man immersed in the Torah (from which he never parted his gaze or voice day or night, not even once).

Those candlesticks there—which, on account of their great importance, Yosl allowed himself to light only on Rosh Hashanah and Yom Kippur—he gave to his son-in-law to use the whole year long.

Although Yosl himself was not just anybody (no Katle-Kanye, as they say)—even though he was a man of prayer and learning—still, most of his time was consumed by another matter: business with landholders. From them he derived his abundant stocks; he supplied what they needed for their lordly use and bought, for trade, what their field and forest holdings had yielded.

He, Yosl Buntsies, was of the same height and build as his daughter, Rive: a real powerhouse. He held a solid position and had influence among the town's inhabitants and in the community. Understandably, among the landholders, his standing was rather more modest; he had to present himself to them in a more subdued manner—with less pride and self-confidence. But he felt no inferiority, no dependency. It was as if he didn't need them: if they wanted what he had, that was fine; if they didn't, that was fine, too. He never changed his word—that is, his price; he always named it, whether buying or selling, as if no other traders—no competition—even existed.

Therefore, he was esteemed an honorable man. People had great confidence in him, and they dealt with him on good faith. That is, he spoke his bit beforehand: he stood to earn such and such amount; and if the other party wasn't interested, it didn't matter: he was prepared to cede his place and concession to whomever the landholders considered more reputable. . . .

He was paid better than all the others, and the landowners did business only with him their entire lives. Whenever an old nobleman had to depart from the world, before his death, he would tell his son—the heir—that he should conduct further transactions only with Yosl, whom he, the father, had known and protected.

The confidence and goodly inclination toward him were such that he was always asked to come to the courts of the landowners for holidays, weddings, and balls. On the other hand, whenever he celebrated something, he absolutely and for the sake of the Name also had to invite them—because otherwise it would mean an insult and rejection of friendship.

Out of obligation and for appearance's sake, Yosl had to invite them. . . . He especially had to do so when he married his only daughter, Rive, to the blessed son-in-law. On that occasion, he, Yosl, went wild in his opulence—because what else would be left for him to do once he had given away his only child, his only daughter? Then, he constructed a festival tent for the whole town—for young and old, without exception. He brought in numerous bands of musicians, who played for seven or eight days, as if there were a wedding every day. A celebration like that was to be put on not only for the town but also for the greater surroundings. On that occasion, Yosl definitely had to invite his friends—the landholder customers—too. They, for their part, gladly accepted his invitation and came with all the extravagance to which being a landholder disposed them—carriages, cooks, dogs, and also young noblemen and ladies. They did so in order to bring joy to the Jewish supplier who was dear to them—to whom they wanted to show their respect.

Imagine: Yosl—besides esteem—also received plenty of worries from them, the lordly "in-laws." They brought along entire packs of wedding gifts—for example, expensive silks and fine objects in boxes. But, in return, Yosl constantly had to tear himself away from his family and check in on them—they had received a special table—to make sure they lacked nothing, were being served in the best way, and felt satisfied.

He had an especially great worry, Yosl, when it was already late, during the dinner under the canopy, when the landholders had indulged in a fair amount of alcohol. Drunk, they felt the urge to dance—and not just one with the other, lord with lord—but with the Jewish community, too. That is, they wanted to dance with the rabbi, the kosher butcher, the bridegroom, and the father-in-law himself: Yosl, the head of it all.

Yosl had to give in. He entreated the rabbi, in the interest of his own people's peace—that is, for the sake of not provoking any nobleman—to agree to give him a hand and enter the dancing round with them.

The landholders laughed—they danced with the rabbi, the kosher butcher, the bridegroom, and Yosl himself. But afterward, the rabbi, secretly, rubbed his hands—as if he had finally gotten them out from a trap. Likewise, the bridegroom didn't feel it was his day at all; instead, he felt like a lost lamb after joining his hand to a landholder's. And Yosl himself thanked God when it was over and the lordly caprice had passed, peacefully. . . .

The wedding ended, as it had to. Yosl just thanked God again that he had given his daughter to the man he wanted. He could not have sought a greater joy than that: a son-in-law—a compliant one—an honor and a crown in *this* world and one deserving of *that* one. As soon as he had procured him, Yosl started to think how to reward the husband, and he came upon the thought that it would be best if, for as long as he, Yosl, was yet to live, he saw to it that the other man, his son-in-law—the instrument of his will, the dutiful student and plaything—should, after his death, be spared the need to do what he, Yosl, had done—that is, trade with nobles, which would disturb his vocation.

In his last years, he only saved, so that what remained might continue the chain of his Torah-filled existence and shine on in a new generation.

In truth, he didn't quite reap his reward—not in life and also not after death: his daughter, Rive, had no children—whether it was because she was too big, or her husband too small, thin, and obsessed. . . . He just had the benefit of seeing how his trembling respect for the son-in-law passed over to his daughter, and he was sure she would not prevent him from going on the path that he had chosen; on the contrary, she would do everything just as he, Yosl, himself had done, so that her husband wouldn't stray.

He had someone to rely on and saw how she, his daughter Rive, watched for signs from the son-in-law's lips—waiting for his every word (which was like something holy to her)—and she also looked into his eyes, as if she wanted to anticipate his every wish before he even voiced it (like a mother who knows when it is time for her child to come and nurse). . . .

Well, when Yosl Buntsies saw that, he considered that his work in this world was done—especially when he quietly drew up the final balance and convinced himself that what he had managed to accumulate would be plenty for the son-in-law (who was no man of steel).

He didn't languish for long. For quite a while before death, he remained in possession of his senses, and, finally, when he was writing his will and thinking about the best kind of thing to leave the son-in-law in remembrance, he recalled the candlesticks that he had evidently received from a distinguished forefather or grandfather. He bequeathed them to the son-in-law, even though the community elite, who were present when he was writing his will, dictated that he should leave them to everyone—so there would be a perpetual glow on the Sabbath, when the Torah was read.

"Well, well," Yosl replied, "a little bit of the lectern is mine alone." By that he meant that his son-in-law—on whom he was also counting—would, by the glow of light in his candlesticks, make no misstep, God forbid.

He died. The town buried him as was fitting and received, with open hands, a handsome donation for all kinds of alms. A generous bequest, naturally, was also made to his daughter, Rive, to whom he gave all his possessions—a stately house and garden on a prestigious square, as well as a private prayer room, clothing, and a wholly sufficient quantity of money in cash. Of course, he also took care of his son-in-law. First, besides his daughter, Rive, he gave him a pair of women servants, who watched his every step, like those of a precious child. And, second, he gave him all the "grain" that someone like that needs—that is, means of material sustenance (without which there can be no study of the Torah). He also provided him, as mentioned, with the very finest of his possessions—the candlesticks for his Torah, which anyone who wanted to could always see burning in the evening, shining out of the windows of the house where he, Yosl's son-in-law, sat and studied. Well—the latter didn't need anything more: everything was provided for, and he had a model wife in Rive—a powerhouse who looked after him and spoiled him like a child, who quietly boasted of his delicacy and fineness (for which she was truly grateful to her father . . .). Yes, and Rive herself wanted nothing more. She kept her thoughts to herself and contented herself simply with the blessing of her husband, who took the place of a child for her (not of one, but of many, which, otherwise, she might have had). . . .

But soon she lost him, too. Whether it was because he ate too little or because he read too much, he fell into lethargy—or, maybe, it came along with him from his parents' home, from when he was still a bachelor. He didn't last long, either, and he died off, leaving Rive a young widow—one who had been provided with everything but the reason every person needs—another life besides one's own.

"Why?"

Because if another woman in her place—one also possessing youth and wealth—had wanted to mourn her husband a while, she still would have allowed others to approach and speak to her, and she would have acted as God decreed. But not Rive. Even after a long period of mourning, she permitted no matchmaker to set foot at her doorway, and she would hear nothing from them. And if, once, somebody sent over a very honorable party—one she had to hear out and couldn't drive off with disrespect—say, for instance, the rabbi of the town (whom the matchmakers had persuaded to enter the fray—both in order to do a good deed and because he would receive a portion of their fee), she, Rive, certainly lent him her ear and, the whole time, didn't contradict him. But, ultimately—when he already believed that he had managed to persuade her, and she would consent on the spot—she spoke:

"No, Rebbe, I won't do that."

"Why not?"

"I don't want to. . . ." And then Rive, for the first time, it seems, acquired her severe, pointed tone—the one that, afterward, for her whole life, remained a defining characteristic. And she allowed herself to respond to the rabbi with the same words as the wife of an ancient rabbi, about whom she had learned something in her women's books. When the famous Rabbi Yehuda HaNasi—after the death of a beloved husband—sent for the widow and told her to remarry, for him—she had replied: "No, a vessel that has served holy purposes should not be used for amusement." That meant that she, Rive, would not play such a role, either. She would not get married—even if that went, as the rabbi said, against religious law, against custom, and against what was generally desired. . . .

Seeing that she would not break her resolve, no one came to her anymore and no more matches were suggested—despite the fact that a handsome number of young men was available soon after her husband's death, and also later.

She remained a widow. Being provided with everything and having nowhere to direct her womanly-motherly disposition, she took up charitable deeds, such as raising orphans and collecting donations for alms; quietly, from time to time, she glanced furtively at the candlesticks, at which her husband had always read and spent his time in his manly studies. . . .

Those candlesticks served her both as a remembrance of what she had lost and as a guide for her everyday thoughts and activities. She used them, first, for candle lighting on the Sabbath, placing to the side—in a more ordinary location—the ones at which she, while her husband was still alive, had offered her blessings. And also, she lighted them for appropriate burial rites—that is, when she needed to perform the last honors for a corpse (especially a poor one) and place them at the dead man's head.

The whole town knew. When people saw her walking with them, there awakened in everyone respect and sympathy for her youth—which she, unable to separate from what would never return, had sacrificed.

Once, there was a young fool who, on the sly, permitted himself a thoughtless laugh at Rive, her old cane, her broad stride (like a bishop's), and, in general, her antiquated, worn-out being. But even that didn't get to her—this small bit of open deprecation. No, even young people, when they saw her, cleared the way and said "Good morning"; and when there was talk about one of her funerals—one where she appeared with the candlesticks—not one of the young people (whether willingly or unwillingly) would refuse to attend.

It was understood among the older people that Rive was Rive—a well-known party to everyone, with a family and a history that people remembered well: first, there was her father, an unimpeachably honest man, the lordly tradesman, and then her depleted husband, to whom she had been married for only a short while (and now remained in the memory given form by the candlesticks).

And then . . . Then, all of a sudden, the history of Rive Yosl Buntsies was interrupted and went over from deep-rooted, set ways to unanticipated, unimagined calamity. . . .

✦

When the followers of Hitler, during the attack on Poland, entered the town where Rive Yosl Buntsies lived, they acted as they did everywhere else with the Polish-Jewish communities. First, there were laws of exception and humiliating orders—such as, for example, the prohibition against Jews' walking on sidewalks; they must stick to side streets, and they have to wear a certain sign (which reserved them for worse than non-Jews). Afterward, there were various requisitions in the form of self-taxation, which the Jewish Council—constituted for this purpose—was required to perform with its own hands. (Initially, it seems, to meet the needs of the military when it arrived, and, later, those of the authorities now established in the town— traitorous local parties under the leadership of bureaucrats and, standing over them, at their head, the infamous SS.)

Later, the Jews were driven into the ghetto—that is, the tiny part of town designated for them. This occurred, first, so they would feel choked off, since people received only a fraction of the living area they required, and filth, uncleanliness, and all kinds of disease were the result; second, the ghetto enabled proper supervision, so it was easy to calculate what could be squeezed out of them.

Half mad and already worse than that, people arrived in the ghetto. The maw of the authorities and those loyal to them was so greedy that people hardly managed to bring anything along.

All the time—again and again—linen, bedsheets, clothes, and shoes were demanded of them, and also food: such and such amount of meat, sugar, and honey (things no one had anymore in the ghetto, except maybe to sell, at higher prices, to the surrounding Polish population for cash, gold, rings, watches, and the like). If nothing was to be found at a house, the Jewish Council demanded that it be emptied out because, otherwise—God forbid—the payment would be made through human life.

People were robbed down to the last—until even their furniture was carried out from their houses. The better part simply went to those who were stronger, the authorities. Whatever had slight value—trifling things—fell into the hands of a watchman or some petty official who had placed himself in the rulers' service, hoping to gnaw at the bones under the robbers' richly laden table. . . .

Everyone gave—whoever was taxed, rich or poor. Naturally, even a party like Rive Yosl Buntsies was no exception. On the contrary: she, who had the long-established, stately house (with its many rooms and fine garden), also wound up in the quarter that had been declared the ghetto. At first—because of her age—Rive didn't quite understand what was happening. She didn't think things like that could happen in her time, never having heard about such events from her parents. Later she felt the evil decree more than she understood it—the one that had descended on her people from a new Nebuchadnezzar (about whom she had, in truth, an old-fashioned—but still correct—idea). When she realized what it meant, at first she acted like the mistress of the house and exercised her proprietary rights: she took along more and arranged things a little better than others who had been chased out of their homes by force; she secured a little corner for herself and her orphan to live in (in keeping with what the orders permitted). Afterward, when the taxations, one after the other, exacted their toll, of course, she didn't fail to give what was to be taken from her (objects, clothing, and linen that she had kept, unused at her house for many years, since her father's time).

She offered more still: herself—that is, her presence, which was a comfort to everyone. She was like a grandmother who does what she can, all of whose spiritual possessions are devoted to children and grandchildren. In this case, the whole town needed them.

Amazingly, as soon as adversity had struck—as soon as everyone was brought together into the straits of the ghetto—then, everyone, and especially women, began to look on Rive as a communal mother, their own family member, to whom they could come and complain and pour their hearts out.

They did so, they came to her: older women, younger ones, and even just girls. With respect, they looked upon her old cane and dress, which had been left to her as a living, protective amulet; near to her, a mother of her people, one felt a little safer.

She listened when people talked about politics, when they read from the newspapers about the new Haman who had devised so much evil for the Jews. After hearing them out, she made a quiet, contented, humming sound:

"Well, well. *That* one was hanged; this one will be, too."

"Oy, Rive, but there's no end in sight."

"What do you think?" she would reply. "The gallows are high, and it will take him time to climb all the way up. . . ."

The whole time, the requisitions did not stop. The sap was being sucked out from the ghetto masses. Whenever they had obtained something once, the authorities demanded still more of the kind—as much as could be extracted without taking burial shrouds from the dead.

Nothing remained to anyone at all. Rive Yosl Buntsies had nothing, either—nothing except the two silver candlesticks that she had received from her father and husband and used to honor the bodies of the poor, the candlesticks that she—up to now, until affliction struck—lighted on the Sabbath.

Now—no more. Now, she hid them. . . . She never revealed them. Even the best hiding place seemed inadequate and unsafe—until, finally, she took them into her already overcrowded ghetto bed to preserve them from misfortune. There, she found no place for them, either, and she kept them at her side, or at her head; their hard edges bothered her, pricked her, and wouldn't let her sleep. . . .

Well, in the end—when those in power saw that there was nothing more to take from the ghetto and that it had already been sucked dry, down to the marrow—the requisitions stopped. Then started the item of our concern, the *Aktionen*. First, people heard about the slaughter of children; then, it affected older people: whoever couldn't prove they were necessary and do useful work for the occupiers.

One day, the turn came for women: older ones, middle-aged ones, younger ones—the unemployed and "useless." There was no point just letting them run around to no end. . . .

It was a Friday. . . . Even the most pious women didn't think what day it was, because the dismal tumult made everyone panic and erupt in lamentation. Some tried to save themselves by making it over to where those who had been allowed to remain were standing, but the guardians of order—the local police, others brought in from a larger city especially for the *Aktion,* and the SS (who commanded them all)—didn't permit it, and they had guns and dogs. . . .

Families were broken up—the one went here, the other there; mother and child, sister and sister, had to part, never to see each other again. The police separated one from the other—those who were already condemned and those who, for the time being, were not; those to be led away were made to form a column. Then, it happened that—at the head of the column, the very first in line—there stood Rive Yosl Buntsies, taller at the shoulders than the others. She stood there with her orphan—who had grown up with her and served at her side; even now, she remained and no separation was possible.

Nobody knows if Rive had placed herself there, or if others had done so because she was an older person; perhaps the authorities had given the order and chosen her to walk at the fore. One way or the other, it was unmistakably Rive—in all her height, with her massive body and old cane (which now she absolutely needed to support herself, because of her age). It was she who appeared in the front.

The women had received orders from the authorities to bring along small packages of food for the road (until they reached the new location, wherever they were being led). Whoever had one, had one—and whoever didn't received something from the others. Rive, too, had a little package along with her. She wouldn't let it out of her hands, not even entrusting it to her orphan (who would gladly have taken it herself).

And so—in one hand she held the old cane and in the other the bundle (which didn't look like everyone else's—it wasn't round, but longish, hard, and with a point). Rive, the head of the column, like all the women standing behind her, waited for the command to move forward.

And then the order came. Because Rive went first, and because the way was difficult for her on account of her age, the whole column had to adjust to her slow step, as did the guardians of order—the police, who accompanied the procession in front, at the side, and from behind, all had to observe Rive's pace; they couldn't hurry the group as they did on other occasions.

Since Rive stood almost a whole head higher than the rest of the column, the police, unwillingly, looked upon her as a kind of leader, someone who demanded consideration. They did so, in particular, when they saw that all the women being led regarded her as an important party—not for nothing and not by coincidence did she happen to be at the head, first in line. . . .

It's even possible that the eldest of the police, as he looked at her striding quietly, closed within herself, the cane in her hand—as if she were the overseer of a convent, a mother superior—it's even possible that he felt some kind of respect (as can happen even with the worst sort if someone else's majesty compels him).

It grew quiet, after that final farewell, which had torn everyone apart—into tears, cries, and sorrowful looks backward. . . . Everyone was exhausted, as they always are after a terrible, traumatic disaster—when time comes to a standstill. . . .

The women went row by row, one next to the other. They marched quietly, and almost without a thought in their heads—first, because of fatigue, and second, it seems, from looking, from time to time, toward the front of the column, where the high-standing, massive figure of Rive Yosl Buntsies towered. They felt almost like children in the presence of an older woman who took care of them, and they didn't need to think. . . .

They felt that way even though there was no reason for it at all—even though Rive herself, like all the others, went as a prisoner, too. Still, the crowd of women being led—without the slightest idea why—looked at her as someone to follow: if she walked, they did, too; and when she was there, it seemed that the Master of the Universe was her guide.

Certainly, they were fooling themselves, it soon turned out.

They left the city. Right away, they turned off the road where people walk and ride, and they went off to the side. There, far away, some hilly place could be seen, where the leaders of the column—the police with guns and dogs—ordered the whole group to go.

It was a late-summer day—a mild one, not hot—and the sun, leaning to the west, held watch like a pitying eye over the open fields on both sides of the women walking between them, who didn't know where they were being led or what for.

They didn't talk among themselves; no one had anything to say to anyone else. They were absorbed entirely by the scenes that had just now taken place, when everyone had to separate and part from families and all they held dear. . . .

Every now and then, one of the women would let out a panicked, hysterical scream, remembering the final embrace of a beloved soul, someone not to be forgotten. But amazingly—although all the others were not far from hysteria themselves—they would pacify the screaming individual—like older people comforting a child and as if they, themselves, wanted to be governed by a higher, more lucid intelligence.

Maybe the open field extending to both sides had an effect on them. Maybe it was the pitying eye of the sun descending in the west. Maybe it was the police at the front, in the back, and to the side, who maintained order with just a look (and who fell quiet when they came to the field—as did their dogs). Maybe it was Rive, who walked in front of them all—whose head—with the old-fashioned cloak—peered out over everyone. Maybe Rive produced the effect, for looking at her, the women stayed in their places, as she did: mute, quiet, and silent.

They had arrived at the designated spot—a place the police had, apparently, known about in advance. They directed the women to an elevated site, behind which ran a long ditch, where others were digging.

Then, the column halted. Then, everyone saw the ditch. . . . Amazingly, instead of immediately bursting forth (as one thinks would have happened) in a barely human racket to fill the skies—clamoring to God, man, fields, and the setting sun—instead of that, they stayed as they were, and as they had been before they saw the ditch. Apparently, they didn't believe that there were so few steps between life and nonexistence, and that soon there would occur what the sorrowful, pitying eye of the sun would, possibly, witness—or, possibly, not. . . .

They stayed as they were. Then, the police (wanting, it seems, to rest) relaxed the order of the group and no longer paid attention to the previously regular column—as if they were giving the masses that had been driven together their freedom and the possibility to act as they wished before what had already been decided was undertaken.

And then, there, the mass of women brought to that place felt shaken to the core, without a word in their mouths. Relieved of walking and the police's supervision, they saw—stepping out from the column—how Rive, who had stood at its head, suddenly directed her gaze toward the part of the sky where the sun shone. And when she saw where it was—that it would soon set—then, she spoke to those near her (others of her age) in her characteristic, short, clipped way:

"Women, just don't forget what day it is today. . . . It is Friday. . . ."

Thereby, she turned to the bundle she had been carrying by herself the whole time (not entrusting it even to the orphan girl, who had come along to serve her). From within, she took out the pair of silver candlesticks—the ones her father had bequeathed to her, her inheritance—the ones that she, Rive, had used all the years until now only for lighting on the Sabbath and, after prayers, for performing the final honors for the dead.

She took them out from the bundle. She also removed a pair of paraffin candles, which it seems she had saved like a precious jewel in the ghetto (where such things were no longer available and where she herself, in recent times, had only tallow to light). It seems she had been keeping them for a festive moment—possibly, for the final Friday before her death; certainly, she had anticipated it: today or tomorrow, this week or the next, it would strike. . . .

Then, she called the orphan girl and told her to hold the candlesticks, in which she had placed the candles. She also got something to light them with, having remembered to bring matches. . . . And then the whole group of women gathered together and surrounded Rive in a ring.

One saw how the tall Rive took off her coat, laid it on the earth, and smoothed it out, as if she wished to make some kind of festive address to the crowd. Then, when she looked and saw the entire column of women who had been brought on the march and now—without a single exception—formed a circle around her, she spoke briefly:

"Women, just tell me. . . ."

She lifted both hands to her eyes and stood upright for a while—not speaking and not moving—in front of the two burning candles, which flamed palely in the mild air of the summer evening, in view of the great field extending to both sides, and in view, also, of the setting sun far to the west. In a louder voice, so that all would hear, she pronounced the Sabbath blessing. . . .

Then, all the women surrounding her did likewise, and they carried their hands to their eyes. Lamentation was heard. It was quiet, at first, as if everyone were crying to herself, and then it occurred so openly, on such a universal scale, and with so much noise, that no human hearing could possibly take it all in.

Even the police did not interrupt this time. Even they and their dogs were silent as they looked on the scene. Perhaps they were just captivated by the strange religious ceremony. Or, maybe, now they, too—creatures who had once been people—felt a human pulse within themselves as they looked upon the condemned women—women who would soon go to their deaths and part with the last bit of the world that remained to them.

Whatever the reason, the police did not interrupt. Then, after the whole group of women with their hands raised in front of their eyes had wailed more and more and higher and higher—to the point that they forgot who they were—and brought forth a noise that could move even a stone. . . . Then, after Rive had finally taken her hands from her eyes and ordered the orphan girl to place, onto the earth, the candlesticks that she had held until now, standing in front of Rive. . . . Then, all of a sudden, the senior official in charge of the police—who, until now, like all his men, had unwillingly witnessed the scene (which he, in keeping with his office, certainly should not have allowed, for it was like weakness, which can be held against you as a deviation from duty)—then, the police elder got a grip on himself. As if he had recovered from cowardice and were now going over to the opposite of what had stopped him for just a minute, in a bellowing voice—pressed by the demands of his office, and as if regretting the indulgence he had shown the condemned women—he barked:

"Order!"

"March!" A second command was heard. The mass of women grew terrified. Startled by his first yell, they arranged themselves back into rows and the column from before—only now, they did so with tears that remained on their faces and unvoiced lamentations.

"In groups! Five at a time! Ten!" His orders sounded a third time. . . .

✦

"Well, then. . . . There's nothing more to say about the rest, because everybody knows. . . ." It should just be added that afterward, when what had been planned (the appointed *Aktion*) had been performed—and almost all the women who had been standing there, living and breathing, were now to remain dead, without a breath, lying on top of one another, their faces down, row on row in the ditch, arranged like frozen pieces of wood. . . . Afterward, when the ditch was covered and the earth smoothed over so that it would look "natural." . . . After the police dogs had sensed the fresh blood and run about sniffing and snorting. . . . Then, the police turned back to the place where the women had gathered earlier. And when they saw the two candlesticks with the flames still burning, one of them extinguished the lights: he relieved himself on them—whether for the sake of his personal needs or in order to share something with others—it's all the same.

Moscow, December 1945

An Acquaintance of Mine

I GOT TO KNOW HIM while still in my youth. He captivated me with his good-natured, almost-sweet smile—that of a clever person, someone who was an expert at everything. But beneath the smile, one sensed the bitterness of someone for whom things weren't going well—who wasn't meeting with success in some real purpose. It was the smile of a person who, though still young, already carried age within him—one who anticipates a not at all successful destiny, which now, later, or at one point or another he will encounter. Out of his eyes, there peered a quietly muted sadness—from seeing too much in advance, it seems; therefore, he was constantly wiping them—so that no one would notice that he was not living, but only *surviving*, and that, with every minute and passing instant, he already stood a little farther away from where he was now.

And just as he himself was a little worn-out and odd, he also dressed strangely: in a little hat with a short brim that wouldn't stay on his piled-up hair (like a carriage driver's, which never stayed combed); every time people saw him—him in his hat—it was impossible to understand how it stayed on at all and why it didn't fly off, even when there wasn't any wind outside. Moreover, people always saw him in a floppy coat, an airy-windy cape, which he wore almost the whole year through, except maybe in the winter; before the cold got too severe, he exchanged it for a heavy coat, but it, too, was of a kind that wasn't at all in keeping with fashion. With his thin, tallish build and his slightly bent back, in his big clothes (and especially when there was wind), he always looked like a ship from an earlier age—one from Columbus's times—toiling and struggling to pass the waves on the sea; that's what he looked like, with his head poking into the air, when the flaps of his cape inflated him, like sails.

He wasn't old at all yet—just twenty-five or twenty-six—when I got to know him in a former Russian county seat in the southwest—a pretty provincial one (despite its honorable administrative functions); a town with narrow, winding streets, full of orchards and gardens, with quiet boulevards for retired officials and military men strolling between the high poplars—leafy in the summer and barren in winter—with loud-screeching cranes' nests in one season and empty ones during the other.

There, we met. He was already a known personality in the very brainy Hebrew literature of the time—in which he had acquired a solid reputation the moment he set foot there. I was still a youth. He had already been invited to collaborate in the thriving publications of the day, which were edited by someone who was very famous then (it was around the fifth year). The latter was a writer and critic with a sharp pen, who had great esteem for his own person but also enjoyed respect among others. From that editor, he, my acquaintance—the first time he took the pen in hand, when he submitted his first work, although he was still so young—received a response that welcomed him very courteously. The salutation read: "The gates of *The Century* are open to you." There was more: "Your name will be counted among the collaborators featured in our journal. . . ." And I, as mentioned, was a youth who could never even have dreamed of such an exalted reception. Being associated with someone like that certainly inspired great honor and respect—to the point that my thoughts followed his alone.

My acquaintance stayed in that provincial, administrative city. He didn't go off to where his proper place of residence would have been, where his profession demanded him to be— one of the big literary centers, where men like him normally congregate. This was on account of a lone love affair, which tore at him for a long time and ended unhappily. It stamped his face with the traits of an ascetic. Externally, it made him smile good-naturedly, yet a bitter deposit sat beneath the smile. It made him capable of sincerely valuing another to the point of veneration, yet also capable of throwing a stone at what he had honored; it made him dress oddly and walk—no, not "walk"—*run*, pushing his head through the air, looking like an old-fashioned ship—still from Columbus's times—with the skirts of his coat, which everyone recognized, flapping in the wind.

He loved a rich merchant's daughter, whom he had met as her tutor, at the time when she transformed from a girl to a young woman—that is, in her sixteenth-seventeenth year. She hung on his every word, for she was touched and moved by his talent and superior knowledge. This attitude came to her, first, because he was a wise person—a teacher; second—and principally—because he was someone who exploited his superior knowledge—as if it were a gun aimed at the woman who infatuated him (one who had briefly heaved a sigh of infatuation herself).

He, being older than her, loved her youth—and she, as mentioned, his superior knowledge. Her ears were attentive to what he said, and she was so curious that she didn't see that he (the one offering her this knowledge) was neither handsome nor did he fit into her father's world, on account of his whole manner and unusual profession. At best, the bourgeois society of that time pitied someone like that—and at worst, people laughed in his face, because he was not considered a practical person or the kind who could find proper employment.

But at the time, he did look handsome to her—despite his thin and worn face, even though his hair could never be combed into order, and although he stuck his head out comically when he walked—like someone not living in *this* world (and especially not the one of her father, the rich merchant). Also, she didn't think about anything practical, because she was inexperienced and didn't know yet what the word meant.

The father and everyone else in the household—mother, brothers, sisters, and domestics—noticed right away the attraction that their polished seventeen-year-old daughter had for the worn-out, badly groomed, hunched, and oldish person—the one inflated by the wind, his pockets full of erudition. But it didn't matter, and it didn't occur to them that—apart from the girl's simple interest, besides the admiration the pupil had for her teacher—there could be anything more—something more serious.

When, finally, they did see, they started to draw her away from him. They mocked, denigrated, and ridiculed him—until they convinced themselves that it all amounted to nothing. They decided to stop things abruptly—simply to show him the door—and he was fired as a tutor.

But they weren't successful. Relations continued and the couple pursued their meetings, even though they were secretive, clandestine, and conducted with great difficulty: the family had started to look after the girl, to watch her steps more closely in order to keep her away from the man; and they saw to it that she became more interested in young people of her own kind—those of her own social standing—who, as visitors, certainly received a warmer welcome into the daughter's company at her rich father's house.

Slowly, slowly, it set in. Slowly, slowly, the enamored young girl started to sober up and withdraw from the all-consuming influence of our friend. She began to see what family members had pointed out to her, which she hadn't wanted to hear or accept. Now, she accepted it, and her estimation of him as the right type of person dwindled. He was much older and quite far removed from the generally accepted bearing, manners, and tastes she had developed—the ones she shared with those of her kind, young people of her own social class; their attitudes had become her own—an essential component of who she was, which it was now difficult for her to renounce.

She cooled off somewhat. Already, she divided her time between him, my acquaintance, and others, who captivated her not with a surplus of erudition and seriousness (which had also turned *his* head and prevented him from seeing what was going on around him, right by him, and to him); she was also drawn to matters of greater importance—like flirtation, luxury, and dressing well, in order to look prettier and more striking.

Truly, everything else still pulled her toward him. She was unable to forget her first debt of love—he was the first man to make her lower her eyes in shame, then raise them again, whenever she saw him standing or sitting before her. It is true, also, that if he, her former beloved, had not been himself—that is, the restrained, measured, and modest man that he was—if, then, she had already cooled somewhat toward him, still, he— by the simple fact that he had come closer to her than all others—might have been able, in a manly fashion, to win her over and draw her to himself forever and always. And if the parents had wanted it or not—if the merchant's household had insisted or not—the matter would have been settled, never to be reversed; possibly, in the end, they would have had to make peace with him and—once again, willingly, or not—count him as one of their own, having no alternative. . . . But he was who he was, so he let the last, decisive opportunity pass him by. And, truth be told, she—his beloved—for her part, took a dim view, too, and esteemed him somewhat less.

The cooling off continued. At that point, my acquaintance took to tormenting himself, and he would loiter, at night, under the windows of the house owned by his beloved's father. He peered in when the shutters were still open. And when they were already closed, he placed an ear to her room in order to hear, perhaps, how strange men now sat at her side—whether they were living it up and acting gaily, or, perhaps, spending their time in silence (which vexed him even more than gaiety and laughter . . .).

By this time, already, she rarely visited him—nor did she (as before) meet him at some secluded place, on a distant street. When she did, it seems that it occurred mostly out of pity. . . . And then he, my friend, also started to torment *her*—with words, with reproaches, by putting to shame everything that came from her family—the sensibilities of rich merchants—and he sought to humiliate her by proving to her that she was like all the others (from whom he, the whole time, had sought to draw her away with his lessons, thinking her aims to be much higher than theirs). This had the effect that, in his presence, she grew ashamed of her fallen status—that she was unable to lift herself to more exalted pursuits. But as soon as she parted with him, she turned back to her newly acquired tastes, which she enjoyed; and she felt much better in the company of her carefree acquaintances than in his presence—which stifled and oppressed her, like a tight corset.

It reached the point that. . . . Let it remain between us, but he—for whom, as mentioned, "the gates of *The Century* had been opened" (which remained closed to so many others, their threshold impassable). . . . He—whose every article in that journal generated great enthusiasm, aesthetic enjoyment, and commentary among readers in the provinces (and not just the provinces). . . . He who, at the same time, felt so wretched and fallen in his personal life. . . . It reached the point that, once, he even sought revenge on the self-satisfied, bourgeois house of his beloved's father (which always looked out onto the street with its big windows and a rich man's opulence). One pleasant evening—quietly, and from a hidden corner—he permitted himself to throw a rock for consolation. It broke the window panes and terrified both the owners and guests who, by chance, found themselves there; they fell into a faint of terror that their own blood had almost been shed by what had been hurled at them. . . . They couldn't find out who had done it. No suspicion could arise that he was the responsible party. Surely it was some street urchin—a hooligan, someone who was drunk. In no case could anyone imagine that the hand of someone like him had cast it. Also, no one could have imagined that, at the time, our friend had fallen into the company of a drunken monk from the local, state-sponsored monastery (which lay in a remote, out-of-the-way street, hidden among orchards). With him, the monk, he would spend entire days under a tree. For these encounters, he always brought, under his coat, what the other desired—and he, too, was partial to it. Together, they indulged in what the other craved: drink.

For a certain period, he also let himself into drunken chess games with a well-known party in the city—a strange person, indeed, by the name of Bik. The latter was of the same age and a wild mathematician. The game had obsessed him since childhood. On account of chess, he had lost a great inheritance—a house, its furnishings, and a well-maintained hops field, which had been passed along to him, an only son, after his mother's death. Alleged benefactors—in reality, swindlers—had taken it from him, and they had left him with nothing at all. . . . Afterward, this Bik got a grip on himself. He had the habit of walking around in galoshes on bare feet, whether it was summer or winter. In a single year, he completed the curriculum of a *Gymnasium*. Then, making a turn in those same galoshes, he promptly completed his university studies. This made him famous in the city as the best lesson giver, which provided for his minimal needs (because he didn't pursue money and prestige but devoted the greatest and best part of his time to playing chess).

And now, my friend met up with Bik and spent entire days with him—sometimes evenings, too, and even, occasionally, entire nights. . . . Where? In Bik's detached room, which had never been swept, where the table had never been cleared, and where, also, the hard, steel bed with the bad, thin mattress was never made.

He played so long by day, night, and in the evening before lighting the lamps (which he always forgot to do), that he started to have trouble seeing. It took him quite a while to recover from the illness, as he had practically turned blind.

Around then, he also became acquainted with me. I had just arrived—also as a teacher in the house of his beloved's father—in order to tutor the younger children, the girl's brothers and sisters. That brought us together. Perceiving in me an admirer who couldn't offer competition (because my insignificance suggested the altogether slight worth of my person), he had found a confidant through whom he would have the possibility of staying in touch with the house into which—should it prove necessary for him—he secretly, and through my mediation, would be able to pass something along—or receive a message from the other party. . . .

It was like this: he became a frequent visitor of mine. Uninvited, he just showed up whenever he felt the desire—day, evening, and often late at night—and he would sit there the whole night long.

He spoke to me about different matters, but every time, he came back to what worried him most. Between one word and the next, between one sentence and the other, he always, finally, called the name of the one who caused him such distress. He would abase himself before me—he, the kind of person to whom I had to pay attention; he was forced to lower himself to the point of even pouring out his heart to me—just a youth, barely a tutor, who stood beneath him in everything: years, understanding, and all else. Just because I—some boy, a half tutor—had the privilege of breathing the same air as the one who, to his great misfortune, was dearest and most precious to him. It was painful—the point to which he sank. . . . But on the other hand—seeing my admiration, my sympathy, and the fact that I seemed not to notice the state he was in—he conferred some distinction upon me; it also seemed that he respected me a little, and he started to consider me a brother to whom he could open himself up and bare his soul without shame.

Although he had something entirely different in mind, he became my teacher, too, over time. Maintaining a relationship with me only to use me for his mournful, hidden purposes, in the course of his conversations he would speak—for decency's sake and to conceal his aims somewhat—about other matters, about *her*, the girl in whose hands his ruinous destiny had been placed; apparently, though, he also had my interests in mind, and from time to time he voiced concerns about me and my backwardness and pointed out what, at the time, I couldn't see at all.

For the sake of self-reassurance and in order, one way or the other, to free himself from the condition of perpetual jealousy, he often took up the Greco-Roman classics—especially the philosophers. He carried them in his pocket constantly and came to me to read them. For example: Plato's *Symposium* and *Phædo*, which he especially loved. Reading aloud, he proved, first, what they had meant—their Golden Logic, so to speak. Thereby—every time he stood before these sources—he said he found himself the silently cheered observer of the silver-flowing water of a placid stream that, calm and green, coursed between trees and grass; he looked on as tranquil sages caught golden fish in blessed peace.

Yes, he taught me calm, and, from all he had learned, he emerged somewhat pacified himself. Then, at one point, he got up, and, without saying anything at all—without even a "Be well"—he went off to those urban centers where his interests had called him (which, until now, he hadn't heeded). And he remained there for as long as his patience sufficed to keep him so far away from his primary object of interest. But in the metropolis, he also often thought of me—no, not me, of course, but her, with whom I happened to be in the same city and share a house. He bade me tell him anything at all about her—however slight it might be; I, for my part, eager to be of service to him, certainly did so.

The end, as mentioned, was a bad one. He went off. Then he came back. He felt that she, his beloved, was escaping his influence more and more. In truth, it only lasted a little while—her interest in him. What she had experienced concerned someone whose name meant something in certain circles, who was very well known and respected. But, on the whole, that wasn't what had captivated her. First, none of it concerned her personally. And, second, again, because of those in her father's house. . . . They made her hesitate, warning and scaring her about what she faced if she fell in with a poor man—someone who didn't have the means to live securely, a person who was half homeless, an individual who, on the whole, was an air balloon, with no position in the society that her father and those around him deemed stable and respectable.

She still wavered. . . . Around that time, his cheeks grew hollower and hollower, his back increasingly bent, his hurriedly flying gait (in a certain long coat) always faster yet wearier, and his seemingly good-natured smile of a wise man—an expert in everything—ever more distressed.

At that time—it was the beginning of summer—he would show up rather late in the evening, with the excuse that my place, where I lived then (on an outlying street lined with orchards) was the best spot to sit, at night, in silence and listen to the song of a certain bird, which had a silver bottle in its throat—the nightingale, which, as it sang under the moon, hidden in the orchard, poured forth its song in such a smitten manner that it almost choked on its own limitless possibility for song and sweetness.

At such times, as I sat with him at the doorway outside, he looked utterly dejected, hearing the hidden orchard poet call out in the language of his own sorrowful existence, which was audible in the most distant, outlying streets, and also high up, up to the very stars, it seemed. Listening to the bird, he remembered his beloved, who was now so far away from him— no, not far—that was it: she was nearby—very near—right there, in a house within an arm's reach, not on a distant street. She enjoyed a homey roof overhead, and only the tiniest thing was missing: if only things had been a little different, if only she had had a little more love for him, then, possibly, he, too, would be like the singer, the one with the little bottle in its throat. . . .

Things were already quite bad for my friend then: it had reached the point that he would either put an end to his suffering himself—or do something worse. It went so far that once (he told me), when she, his beloved, graced him with a visit—a rushed one, made in passing (as generally had occurred in recent times), more out of habit than interest, and out of pity— and when she parted from him—again, mainly out of habit—she even gave him a kiss. He, feeling her so close and at the same time so distant, quietly gathered himself together, made a bow, and spoke: "Well, dearest one, best one, my beloved. . . ."

"What?" the girl asked back, not quite hearing. "No, no," he responded, and at the same moment a burning, covetous thought flared up within him. He made another bow to her— very close—in order, with a full mouth and all his teeth, to bite her ear off: if not him, then no one—may she spend the rest of her life with an unmarried aunt. . . .

Soon, he dragged himself away from the town, afraid of doing something that wasn't good for him and something even worse to her—feeling that the end was approaching (which, incidentally, did not take long).

Because, indeed, soon his beloved was betrothed to another. It is true that she cried, people said, over the memory that haunted her, and also because she knew how he, her erstwhile suitor, would look after he had been hit by the blow of her departure and defection. . . . But she did it, and in the end she calmed herself.

A little later, I received a letter from the city my acquaintance had gone off to, with a bitter exclamation in Hebrew meaning that God alone should help him in his calamity, which he couldn't bear.

He didn't marry and remained a bachelor. From then on— as if in mourning for the past—he wouldn't separate from the sackcloth that he had worn in that town (which he had left empty, naked, and preoccupied, like someone whose house has burned down). He wouldn't part with the hat with the short brim, which hardly sat on his coachman's hair, and also not with his long coat, the airy-windy cape.

Then, he sequestered himself in a room on a high floor, which he obtained, in keeping with the means he had at the time, from people who were not at all rich. He had, through the window, a view of the flat roof of the house adjacent to where he lived. He was always throwing bread crumbs and other leftovers to the butterflies and pigeons, which came in droves—hopping, dancing, twittering, and flapping their wings as they picked them up.

There I met up with him—later, around year ten—when I, too, had settled in the metropolis. I already had a little work, and I myself hoped to secure a place among men of letters. I looked him up, and he received me very hospitably, recommending where to go and whom to see—and generally supporting me with the advice and directions a big-city person gives to someone from the provinces.

I also kept board with him. He never left me: he ate and drank together with me, and, when I was done with my modest daytime occupations, he would spend the evening with me and ask about the town I came from, which he knew so well— so much so that he remembered every stone and every street and alley, where he, in his despair, had rambled and eaten his wounded heart out.

He also, then, between words and sentences—speaking, it seems, about entirely different matters—would finally get around to what he had still not forgotten: her. It turned out that even now, from time to time, he sent her letters (to which he never received a reply).

I satisfied his desire to remain informed about the slightest details there—what was happening, how she was doing, who the person was who had taken his place, and so on.

He was very thankful to me. In return, he offered me his loyal confidence—to be my instructor, my guide. And among all the other kinds of advice that I, who kept his company, received—pieces of advice that had an immediate bearing on my existence at the time and my sojourn in the metropolis— he gave me something else. It was the kind of thing, it seems, he considered extremely important—a useful principle for me: "Get out of here," he said, "and may the God of the provinces protect you in your innocence. This is no place for you— no place for your kind of person." He looked me over and seemed to know my character, which would be ground down and extinguished there. . . . "Here," he said, "is a fair where they trade in watery ink and cheap trinkets; here, the swollen and arrogant sit with their clumsy feet on the literary table, never rising." He brought up the example of a well-known lit-terateur: "the ingenious chiseler," as he called him—a person who was filthy in all respects—to the point of having dirt under his nails and not wiping his mouth when he ate, who went out with a haughty sideways glance, his black beak and head raised majestically—as if he didn't fly just to fences and parks, like all geese, but like a neighbor of the clouds and a big shot in the Heaven of Heavens. That is, he admitted no one of the same kind into his presence; no one could manage that with him—it was not to be obtained at any price. And when anyone called upon him without using a lofty title of world renown that reminded him to lower his hands (which possessed such honor and fame) to the depths of the scribbling horde, he, the ingenious chiseler, would say: "*Pff.* . . . Truly, he has the craftsmanship, but he also writes mediocre novels." And *he* said that—he, him, that one—who—if only, if only!—he were capable in the slightest—just a little bit—if only he had but an ounce of the other's alleged mediocrity!

Thus did my friend speak to me. From what he said and, chiefly, from his tone—how what he said had come out—it was evident that he himself was already not all there. It was evident in his cultivating the pigeons on the neighbor's roof and wanting to dissuade me from staying in the big city—certainly, this was a rationalization of his attitude toward himself—he, who, although he found himself there, had been taken out, undone, and destroyed by everything. It was evident that, with his bad luck in love, he had lost something else, too: his eagerness and the urge to secure a position and make a name for himself among the café-and-literature crowd, as everyone else wanted to do. No, not him. In that respect, he was extinguished.

In exchange, however, I noticed that he had reignited at another end. He directed his love toward a region where he was free, unrestrained, and unlimited—and without the fear that he would encounter any obstacle, resistance, or opposition from the other side, that is, from what he had *now* fallen in love with (unlike what had happened the first time). He turned to his new object of devotion with the great dedication someone like him was capable of—with the ardor that sometimes befalls people after an illness or a shipwreck when they make their way back to health and solid ground, when they savor life in the world much more than before they sank entirely, utterly, and never to emerge again. He gave himself over to the people and its awakening—according to the way that he, my friend—in his day, with his upbringing, surroundings, and intellectual perspective—understood this "awakening."

Already then, living in the metropolis and keeping board with him, I noticed a notebook on his table. On its cover he had written the title *Pro et contra*—"for and against," that is. Inside, he had collected opinions and quotations of the various enemies and friends of the people—beginning with the opponents, very old opinions, and ending with ones from our times. And, on the other hand, he collected views and quotations from apologists and defenders of the people—beginning, again, in the past, with Philo the Alexandrian, up through different Roman popes, bishops, and humanists, and ending with the most recent parties who had engaged themselves for the people and taken it under their protective wings.

Speaking to me about that kind of thing, he would often mention his former love. He looked at me with his longish, slightly bent frame, the coachman's hair (which wouldn't allow itself to be combed), the hollowed cheeks of a dark color indeed, his thin hands, the good-natured but at the same time embittered smile, and, mainly, his half-extinguished but also glowing, cloudy eyes. All that, already then, made him look a little older, like an ancient apostle who can change his life for what he believes in—even going to preach in the desert, to the rocks and trees—but who also, at the same time, casts stones in great anger.

A little later, already at home again in my provincial city— where he, my acquaintance, had indicated my place and I, following his commandment, had gone (which, by the way, I never regretted afterward)—at home again, a little bit later, I received a letter from him, from somewhere in Germany. He wrote that he was now crossing the country by wagon and on foot, going where Jewish settlements had been. He was visiting graves in

Speyer, Worms, and different Alsatian cities where, in the Middle Ages, Jews had endured hardship, slaughter, and persecution. And he thought to travel from there to Spain—to Toledo, Saragossa, Granada, and Córdoba, which he wanted to visit, to see the places where the golden cradle of our crown poets had stood, home to Yehuda haLevi, Moses Ibn Ezra, Abraham Ibn Ezra, and others.*

And there we must interrupt the narrative about my friend because. . . . Life tore us apart. In the fourteenth year, the war arrived. My friend stayed where he was, in Poland (let us now say the name), which happened to be on *that* side of the border—whereas I was on *this* side.

I never saw him again, and even in the time leading up to then, I had received very little information from him. But that didn't stop me from thinking about him from time to time; he would always swim up before my eyes and waken my interest—both as a person and as a reason to write. . . . Because, indeed—if the truth be told (and to employ our crude literary jargon)—from time to time, I also thought about "exploiting" him on certain occasions and in certain thematic contexts, adding an entirely different beginning and ending to events. I also collected much more information about him, mainly about what happened during the years we were separated (unlike now, when I feel it would be bitterly inadequate and professionally unseemly if I presumed to provide the portrait of my friend in full measure and in a fitting manner). That's how I thought, but. . . . Just as the end of my acquaintance was unexpected and premature—so are the deaths of many others unexpected and premature, who now die at the murderous hands of the baneful enemy.

*These figures lived in the eleventh and twelfth centuries. (In the nineteenth century, Jewish historians and intellectuals were especially prone to idealize medieval life under Muslim rule on the Iberian Peninsula as a "counterargument" to contemporary Christian intolerance.)

The last news that I got about my acquaintance was as follows:

A Polish-Jewish man of letters who had managed to get out of Poland after a certain amount of time under the yoke of Hitler was the first person from whom I heard at length about what the population in general, and especially the Jewish people, had endured. Then, afterward, I started to ask the writer for details about specific individuals. I inquired:

"Well, and my friend, what's he doing? How is he? Is he still alive?"

He made a wave with his hand: peace be to him. . . . He was no more—dead, that is. And, he added, he had died a strange death.

It turned out that this man of letters had also been very close to my acquaintance and among those who enjoyed his esteem; he numbered among the writers to whom my friend stood closer than the others—as, for instance, had once been the case with me, when I, in my youth, "poured water on his hands" (that is, when I served him as a pupil does a master). He, the man of letters, still young, had also taken care of him during that last period, as much as the other man—an older person who had remained a bachelor—required; moreover, he, the writer, was also there at the end, and he was able to report to me, among other things, exactly what happened and all I wanted to know.

He told me:

In his final years, the other man was already pretty far gone—because of both age and the lack of success he had met with. He still wore his out-of-fashion clothes, unable to part with them: the little hat with the short brim on his coachman's hair (which now had the hue of extinguished ashes and was also much thinner; where they had stood windswept, on both sides and over the whole of his head, there was empty baldness).

Also, he hadn't been able to part with the long coat that he wore in nearly all seasons, which made everyone—whomever he met up with—step aside and look back in amazement; kids pointed their fingers at him and even laughed in his face.

Already, people also laughed at how worn-out he seemed. They laughed about the absentminded, gloomy, milk-colored film that glazed his eyes—he looked like a rooster when it's falling asleep. This was a sign that he had let a curtain fall between himself and the outside world; it set him apart, took him off, and hid him away.

Indeed: he already had very little to do with the outside world. It was enough for him to work for himself and feed the pigeons on somebody else's roof. He just devoted a little bit of time and effort to writing (which, nevertheless, certain editors and publishers always took from him hurriedly and greedily, as something of great value, out of fear that the competition would snatch it away first). Mainly, he spent his energy on one work in particular, which captivated him to the exclusion of all else, which he didn't emerge from for years, and which consumed him and held him entirely in its service.

That was his other love—one of a wholly exalted kind, for whose sake he sucked the last marrow out of his bones, until nothing was left at all. It was a work that demanded application—that is, that he remain isolated. And when he felt the slightest spark of life, knowledge, interest, or passion, he gave it to his work—and only to it. Besides that, he saw nothing else—no sense in his bare existence and having ever come into the world. It was a work to which he gave the title: *He Was and Shall Be**—it was a kind of encomium of all that comes into being and goes away, arises, exists, and passes through material form in the uninterrupted cycle of changes and metamorphoses (which are infinite and eternal). In this work, he

---

*This title is in Hebrew (and, significantly, the only such phrase in the story).

discussed higher and loftier matters: the cosmos, nature, and culture—which meant, for him, the exalted human pursuit of cooperation and communal life—to be, individually, a part of and a partner in all that exists, comes into being, and re-generates itself. It started with the most ancient times—when man walked about naked, overgrown with fur, like a beast. It went up to our own times, when many secrets and mysteries of nature (which, earlier, had been locked away—mute, deaf, harsh, sphinxlike, and dreadful) had now been revealed and accounted for. And it ended with the remotest future, which wasn't yet accessible to any eye or lens, which one can imag-ine only dimly—in distant, faraway fog—as an airy castle built wondrously and artfully in the sky for some kind of hidden be-ings, of which we have no idea; only the noblest ears can hear the great, peaceful fanfare of a parade from there, bringing honor and the message that awaits when the time of those be-ings will have come.

My friend had already advanced far in his work; he had written whole mountains. And now, from time to time, there flashed little flames of hope in his eyes—to see it completed, emerging from the years he had spent toiling and devoting all his resources to the task. Sometimes, he rubbed his hands in joy. On other occasions, he started up from the table and paced around it for a long time, almost running around the room in happiness. But that didn't happen often, because, for now, it was still too early to rejoice. For the time being, he was still so busy, caught up, and habitually devoted to his work that—whether it occupied him at that very moment and he was sitting at his desk, feeling warmth in all his limbs as he drew the creative sap from himself, or if, as happened from time to time, he was apparently free and walking down the street or sitting in a café, surrounded by the strange buzzing of the people who had gathered there—even then, he felt so indentured to its power that he didn't notice how he sometimes whispered words, sentences, and even entire parts of the work he was pursuing (which he stopped doing when others noticed and—some with scorn, others in admiration—looked at his lips move . . .).

The company of writers knew about his work and even the title he had given it. In general, they always held him in great honor for his vast knowledge and because he stood high above all the everyday, cheap tra-la-la. But they also couldn't keep from making fun of him from time to time, seeing how he held himself distant from the "unholy crowd." Often, when they encountered him as he walked down the street or sat in a café, talking to himself, they would refer to *him* by the title of his work—*He Was and Shall Be*—meaning thereby that that's *what he was*—a bachelor—and that he would remain one: somebody you pity a little, but whom, now and then, it is permitted to joke about.

Our acquaintance didn't care about that. He didn't notice, and he didn't seek anyone out, for he was busy with both his actual craft and the many books that surrounded him—ones he had bargained for, bought, and borrowed; he packed the room full with them: on bookshelves, on the table, on the bed, and even under the bed (where they lay, some in order and others in disarray).

He—my friend—was already pretty far along. And often, now, he would raise his head and eyes to the ceiling (as a chicken does when it's drinking), because he was overfull and overloaded—and, also, a cold shiver went through his bones when he thought of what he was approaching. He was nearing those future people, the hidden creatures in the pale fog of the castle hanging in the air. (And, before the stairway and entrance of the castle, the trumpeting, golden-ringing fanfares could be heard already, whenever there was an arrival or departure.)

He was already far along, my acquaintance. Not having anyone to share his work with—because, as mentioned, he kept apart from the great majority of writers—he occasionally picked someone out and approached him, one of the more deserving in their ranks—such as, for instance, the man of letters who told me about him—a person who possessed talent himself but, still more, the ability to honor someone who stood higher than he did, on account of age and skill. And for the chosen, numbered few, he would, from time to time, open up his desk drawer, take out his work, and read something aloud to them.

To all others—as mentioned—he remained closed, separate, and distant in that certain upstairs room. He preferred it that way and never left, even when the main tenants moved. The owners already knew that every time they rented out the apartment, they had to secure the right for my friend to stay, and they gave him over to the new occupant with the walls of the dwelling—like a nail in the wall.

That's how he lived, looked, and acted—my acquaintance. He was immersed in his work for years, up over his head, hoping that—any day now—he would reach the blessed, desired shore. But then, the war of the thirty-ninth year erupted. As everyone knows, Poland suffered defeat, and, in a short period of two or three weeks, the land was ground down completely and left with its military back broken.

How the new powers treated the whole Polish population after victory is known; as for their treatment of Jewish people—there can be no doubt. . . .

It was like this: soon after their arrival where my friend lived—as in other cities and villages—before they showed their true face (which they later revealed entirely)—at the beginning of all beginnings—already then, they issued certain laws of exception taken from an old, medieval codex applying to Jews. First, it meant that infamous institution, the ghetto; all Jews were ordered to move from their houses and the areas where they previously had lived into quarters appointed especially for them. The ghetto was established, walled in, and surrounded by a barbed-wire fence. Day and night, soldiers with guns in their hands held watch (lest the slightest detail from the Middle Ages—when soldiers with halberds had guarded the gates of the ghetto—be omitted).

Then, all the other junk was drawn out from that ill-starred archive. Such as: Jews not being allowed, without permission, to leave the ghetto; Jews not being permitted, without authorization, to the food markets before the non-Jewish population had already bought up everything they needed (even if there were only crumbs, remainders, and leftovers); the prohibition against Jews' receiving medical attention—and also medicine, or even soap, which the authorities conserved and considered an excessive luxury for people like that (whom they had set apart and wanted to see degraded and dirtied, not even granting them enough water, which they distributed more and more sparingly : . .).

My friend now got a little attic room on the highest floor. Unlike before—when he had enjoyed a view of the courtyard and another roof—now it just looked onto a busy street of medium size. Now, he had nothing for the pigeons, because he was in need himself, and he had to ask for help from the Jewish community, whose means were also direly limited, for they received no support from outside and had to nourish themselves with their own resources—that is, they took from the smaller paupers to give to the bigger ones. . . .

But all that is nothing compared to the greater ill that befell him during the bombardment, when a great part of his already finished work was lost, and what remained was damaged—some of it by water, and some by flames.

That crushed him completely, and, out of a human being, he turned into someone incapable of seeing the possibility of taking up the work again and rebuilding it; he didn't feel the capacity within himself—both because his years already wouldn't permit him and also on account of the conditions that, like a dismal cloud, had descended.

Then, already, people often saw him with his head and eyes lifted to the ceiling—no longer on account of their being too full and overloaded (as before) but because he was lost and looking for sense in being there at all; he found his existence superfluous and not worth dragging his feet around for. His wornness—which had always made his eyes glaze over with a gloomy, milky film—was now more pronounced. But not like before—from believing that he already heard trumpets and the sound of joyous fanfares; instead, it was the fact that all his connections to the world had become loose and untied, and reality wasn't worth looking at.

When he looked out the window, he no longer saw how Jews were being hunted and driven, old and young, into humiliation and shame, and how—for the pleasure of official supervisors or just the enjoyment of regular soldiers—someone had the idea of driving all the people together. . . . Once a mass of ghetto inhabitants had assembled, they were ordered off the sidewalk and onto the street; and, having fulfilled this command, they were told to use their garments as brooms to sweep the dust and refuse.

Since the arrival of the new powers, he had not gone out himself, for he didn't want to encounter those who (by chance, it seems) had forgotten about him and, consequently, given him no orders. He avoided appearing in their sight and meeting up with them; he knew that every ghetto inhabitant they encountered (even at times when they were not actively persecuting people) was fair game—either they just mocked him, or, worse, they tried out the strength of their impure hands (as if throwing a stone at a dead target).

Despite his own downcast state, he was still confounded, it must be said, by what he saw when he looked through the winnow, by what he heard from the people who came to visit him (which, in truth, occurred rarely, because people avoided extra walks on the street, where they were always being stopped), and also by what he heard from the landlords where he lodged: people from different regions, of different kinds, habits, ways, and parts of the city had been herded into the ghetto; people of different upbringings, such as aristocratic Polish Jews, the lesser and greater bourgeoisie, who at first held themselves far from the Jewish masses and didn't want to resign themselves to the general fate that united everyone in woe at the filthy conditions of life that had been imposed. But, gradually, they did grow accustomed; they made their peace, and, finally, they started to gather and lament in a single voice, "What will happen? What will become of us?" cried the Polish speakers. "Woe, woe, such misfortune has been sent down upon us!" cried, on the other hand, the Yiddish-speaking Jews.

Because, indeed, reality had equaled, united, and joined them in misfortune—without distinction, exception, or any decision who was to receive better treatment and more favor from the authorities (who were already holding, over everyone's head, the judgment that would soon arrive—but which, for the time being, they kept hidden in their breast).

Our friend had already reached the point where he didn't think at all of attempting to get out of the situation there—unlike others, younger people and enterprising ones, who tore themselves free from the ghetto and thought to steal off to the eastern border and reach Soviet lands, where rescue awaited them. He didn't, because he was already old and absolutely incapable of anything like that, and, also, because it was all the same to him: nothing—nothing at all (the result of his indifference and spiritual dissolution).

He now spent whole days undressed on his bed, his eyes turned to the ceiling, not expecting that any salvation would ever come to him—not even the help of the community, which was negligent with its resources and, because of the resulting lack of means, tended to respond only with delay. Thus, he passed days on end doing nothing. He didn't wait—didn't look—for rescue, because his needs had shrunk, and, generally, he thought that help would reach him to no purpose anyway: he would only take from people who needed it more than he did, who were younger and healthier—their needs greater and therefore more justified.

He no longer thought of himself and hardly even considered the work that still remained, which fortune had stolen. He only managed to lie on the bed, waiting for someone to call him forth—a certain guest, who would come and order him out—him, the kind of old man who had lost all interest in what others still clung to and, with their last forces, tried to keep.

Once, then, he addressed his acquaintances, who stood around him as he lay in bed. "If the angel of death," he said— should come to him without any pomp and demand his due, he would gladly provide it without saying a word. On the contrary, he would offer thanks. . . . "God has given, God has taken, and may the Name be praised"—for the many kindnesses he had enjoyed in life: the shoes he had worn, the dumplings he had eaten. . . .

The situation was such that they, his friends—when they heard that speech there—didn't respond at all. They didn't interrupt him or try to dissuade him, as occurs otherwise when one hears things like that from someone, but one still has enough strength and vigor to convince the other that he is mistaken and proves to him that he is not following the right course. Now—no. They were not far from thinking that way themselves, and it even seemed that they thought he was right.

When they visited him at this time, people remarked how, somewhat too often, he would cast hidden glances at little pictures on the table, which time had faded and darkened. They also sometimes found him at the table, sitting over something covered with dust—half-water-damaged, half-burned pages. When he heard someone walking, coming to see him, he would make a start and abruptly tear himself away from what he was doing (as if he had been caught at something sinful, a forbidden activity—a reason for shame).

In general, he looked half mad, like someone settling his accounts with himself. One sensed he was waiting for something very important, as on the eve of a holiday; apparently, he was ready to receive a certain guest whom—when he met him with his wasted body lying undressed on the bed—he would welcome as a desired visitor, as one of his own. People saw that wish every time, in the middle of a conversation, he turned his head to the door with a rapt look, as if the visitor who was now most important and desirable to him would soon appear.

The chief occupants of the apartment said that when domestics entered his room—in order to assist him with whatever he needed—as they were preparing to depart, he had the appearance of having waited for someone for so long that he had grown impatient; soon, he would set out to meet him, having forgotten that every step on the street was fraught with danger (especially for someone like him, who could suffer injury from a mere encounter, from the slightest brush with the enemy). They had to remind him of that and bring him back from his resolution, which it seems he had assumed in great weariness, oblivious of the distress confronting everyone.

And here, we pass on and recount what happened next, on the street, when he encountered the authorities. As mentioned previously, it was practically a kind of salvation—that is, nothing at all compared to what they later proved capable of doing.

It happened as soon as he had left the house and made a few steps—after passing a couple of neighboring houses. Suddenly, he struck upon a gang of potentates in the form of simple soldiers, led by one who turned out to be their "elder."

It further occurred that, as soon as they had noticed his strange sackcloth, a certain hat with a short brim (which he always looked for in shops among the items in storage and merchandise that had fallen out of fashion), and also a long coat (which he had already certainly exchanged many times for a new one, although the style remained the same and now made him look like an old, exhausted, and depleted actor)—when they noticed his hollowed cheeks (more bone than skin) and his cloudy eyes (both from age and from sitting at home and not going outdoors). . . . As soon as they saw him, the whole group stopped in place, sensing that he was the kind of person who might provide the kind of entertainment that kind of company needs after a satisfying meal, on a stroll, or just because they are so inclined and want to have some fun.

Then, the "elder" approached him. Looking him hard in the face, he spoke:

"Who are you, you bat?"

"Me?" Our friend saw before whom he stood, and what the latter's demeanor was. He disregarded the man's insulting words and responded seriously—as if the question had been meant in earnest:

"I am a man of letters."

"So—a writer, that means," said the elder to everyone, presenting himself as an expert. Wishing to continue the conversation, he asked: "Are you sure you've never been a clown? Never worked in a circus?"

"No," our friend said.

"Be one *now*!"

"What does that mean?"

"That means: do tricks, do somersaults, and make some light shine out of your clown pants."

"What do you mean, officer, sir?" Our friend bent his shoulders, not understanding. "I cannot do that. I'm not the right person."

"Fast! And if you can't, someone will teach you."

"Who?"

The officer—whose anger immediately spread from his eyes onto his face and, from there, into his right hand, which reached out and approached my friend's head.

Quietly, slowly, he took him with two fingers by the right ear, and, silently—without saying a word—he started to pull him down, down—so far that my friend's head and whole body had to yield and follow behind—stuck, as if in a vise, in the iron pincers of the man's fingers.

He pulled at him for so long that he made his face touch the sidewalk, where he and his company stood. Then he spoke:

"Bow down before the national comrades."

It took little for him to do so, since the man pulling him there dragged him down to the corner of the sidewalk and forced his mouth, eyes, and even his forehead to dip into the gutter.

All that was still too little for the elder—that the other simply remain bowed, humiliated, and ashamed. To crown his indignity, he lifted up the part of the coat covering his backside and threw it over his head. Turning to his associates—to the soldiers standing there and watching the game the whole time—he spoke:

"Look, national comrades. Look and tell me: it's burning, isn't it?"

"No, it's not," they yelled, neighing like horses in their joy as they looked where directed.

"It isn't? Then it will be soon!"

And then, with a harsh and sharp kick of his boot, the leader struck my friend—not at all in a good place, and not in a decent one at all. It really did burn—and not like a little light, but like a whole lamp instead. And it didn't occur where the elder had pointed to his associates: it flashed from the eyes of our friend, which suddenly ignited and then grew very dark.

Then, he collapsed—cut down, deafened, blinded, and certainly already lacking the power to stand up on his own.

Indeed. . . . And when those men had gone away, after they had finished with their pretty little piece of work—which all the others who were present could say nothing to, nor oppose (being afraid to get involved and even to come near). . . . After the soldiers had gone off, then the people on the street lifted their acquaintance up from where he lay unconscious, and, with him in their hands, they brought him to his house, up to the top floor, and then into his room. They placed him on the bed—silent, pale, and half dead.

He lay with his eyes closed, not saying a word—neither to the domestics who had rushed in, wishing to help him, nor to his colleagues and acquaintances, who, when they learned about the event, came and gathered around his bed.

He would accept no food the first day—dismissing it with a gesture that meant it should be taken away. He also permitted no doctor to visit—again with a wave: "No, there's no need. . . ."

When, now, he did open his eyes, he didn't direct them toward the door (as he had done before) but to the window, and no one knew what drew them there.

No longer did he await the longed-for guest he used to look for. After the aforementioned event, it seems he gave up on that.

The chief tenants of the apartment said that the night before—the one before he carried out his decision—he even dragged himself out of bed and, for a long time, walked with dreaming, entranced steps—like a sleepwalker when a strange force leads him. That evening, moreover, they reported what he had "said." That night, he had been singing.

And in the morning, it happened.

I wasn't present, but I imagine it, approximately. First, he asked for linen (I gather from what subsequently happened—afterward, it remained lying there on a stool). He dressed himself in a long coat, as if he were heading off elsewhere. Then, facing his desk, he turned to two pictures lying there. He took leave of them quietly—maybe with a tear, or maybe standing frozen.

And already: then, he took his ruined work from the drawer and went to the window. He opened it and began to light individual pages, and then the whole thing; he let it fall, burning, in the air. After that, he climbed onto the window ledge and stayed there for a little while. And soon people on the street and the sidewalk opposite heard a scream. If it was heard correctly, one might possibly have heard the words *He Was and Shall Be* (which, in his state of confusion, he cried out, like a kind of "Hear, O Israel" before death). But people didn't make it out clearly—it was just a scream, like a bird that falls under a wheel and is crushed. And then, again, together with the scream, people suddenly saw, from the top floor and the high window—the window of our friend—they saw, along with some burning pages (which flew in all directions) something white descending heavily and dizzyingly fast on its wings—an object, a person, or a bird. Soon, they saw that the object was no object, the bird no bird. Instead, they saw a human being—already no longer a human being—crash on the sidewalk, the whole body now smashed to pieces. . . . The people screamed, clutched their heads, and ran around in a frenzy. Afterward, they collected themselves and gathered around the fallen one.

There my friend—already dashed to bits, broken—lay dead on the earth, in his customary attire (his long coat, which he always loved and, even in death, was unable to part with).

When the man of letters and other acquaintances learned what had happened, and—not immediately, but later on that day—they went to the place where my friend had fallen, they no longer found him there. He had already been taken away, to the fitting place, and all that remained were scattered pages that, burning, had landed in different parts—most of which others (bystanders, people on the street) had already picked up out of curiosity. There wasn't much left—only little remained, in pieces. What there had been to collect—when he came over to us, here—the man of letters brought along. He showed it to me, and I recognized my friend's handwriting. Then, I undertook the work that is hereby given to the reader. Honor his memory!

Moscow, February 1944

Der Nister and the Art of Concealment

THE ROMAN DESTRUCTION of the Second Temple in 70 C.E. robbed the Jewish people of a state. The foundation of Israel in 1948, while providing a real homeland to millions and a nominal one to many more, has not resolved the pressures of living, in the biblical phrase, "scattered among the nations."[1] From ancient to modern times, Jews have wandered and settled the world over, both resisting and adapting to the societies they have encountered. Some have grown estranged from tradition, and others have maintained the ways of their ancestors. Judaism has changed outwardly many times, however much its essence may have been preserved. Concealing one's identity—on occasion, at least—is the price of survival.

Contexts

Der Nister means "The Hidden One." Although we know the real name of the person who used this pseudonym—Pinhas Kahanovitch (1884–1950)—we do not know much about him.[2] The child who would become the man who, as a writer, would retreat into artful concealment was born into a Hasidic family in Berdichev, Ukraine. In young adulthood, he was drawn to the radical causes that shaped much of the political and intellectual culture of eastern European Jewry in the decades before and after 1900. A few words on Hasidism and secular Jewish activism will illuminate many—but not all—aspects of the stories collected in this volume.

The development and many articulations of Hasidism are highly complex, but the essential traits of the movement can be passed in quick review.[3] Externally, Hasidism responded to events including, on one end of the historical spectrum, seventeenth-century Cossack uprisings and pogroms and, on the other, the political reorganization of the European map in the late eighteenth and early nineteenth centuries. Internally, Hasidism offered a new form of spirituality and social organization to threatened Jewish communities. Emerging at the margins of the religious establishment but—initially, at least—respecting traditional authority, the movement created a new center of devotional practice focused on charismatic individuals. The first such leader was Israel ben Eliezer (1700–1760), known as the Baal Shem Tov (Master of the Good Name), or, in acronymic form, the Besht. The new model of religious experience embodied by the Baal Shem Tov appealed to those who found their spiritual needs and desire for community unfulfilled in a turbulent age. In the decades following his death, numerous Hasidic "dynasties" changed the complexion of Jewish life throughout eastern Europe. Arthur Green has described Hasidism as "a revolutionary and yet inherently conservative revival"—"a spiritual democratization of sorts" that was, at the same time, hierarchical through and through.[4]

In the nineteenth century, Jewish life in eastern Europe underwent further change as revolutionary and liberal ideas from the west took root in the seemingly immutable Russian Empire.[5] As early as 1825, in the so-called Decembrist uprising, officers of the Russian Imperial Guard refused to swear allegiance to the new czar, Nicholas I, and declared their loyalty to the principles of constitutional government. The revolt failed, but its participants became the heroes of a populist movement for reform in the 1860s and 1870s. Following the emancipation of the serfs in 1861, Russian *Narodniki*, who thought that the seeds of socialism lay in traditional, communitarian ways of life, went directly "to the people." At the same time, in the name of the human brotherhood they saw forming, Jewish intellectuals increasingly encouraged their coreligionists to cast off supposedly superannuated practices.[6] The alliance between Russian populism and Jewish attempts at modernization and assimilation was fraught. The assassination of Alexander II in 1881 was seized by the government and secret police as an opportunity to defeat the revolutionary cause as a supposed "Jewish plot."[7] In the wake of the pogroms that followed, many Jews emigrated, but there also arose many forms of Jewish political consciousness—from Zionism to communism—that contributed to the triumphs and disasters of the twentieth century.[8] These movements, like Hasidism, were projects of both innovation and preservation, looking forward and backward simultaneously in the desire for an impossible utopia.

The overriding frame of reference in *Regrowth* is the National Socialist war of aggression. The plot of every story hinges on this cataclysmic event. Significantly, however, Nazi occupation does not elicit a uniform response from characters. The brilliance of Der Nister's book shines in the wildly divergent rays of light that are emitted when the flame of the incipient Holocaust shines through the prism the author provides; this lens is in equal parts traditional and revolutionary.

The literal meaning of *Vidervuks*—"regrowth"—has clear implications for a writer who witnessed the destruction of European Jewry. The title should be understood in a religious way, in the sense of the biblical injunction to "be fruitful and multiply"—especially after the loss of so many generations in the Holocaust. However, the word has other connotations, too. Vidervuks was the name of a literary group and imprint in the 1920s. Between the wars, the Kiev daily *Komunistishe Fon* (*Communist Flag*) operated a special department by this name for publishing the works of young, revolutionary poets.[9] In the play of verbal associations Der Nister loves, the term conjures up resistance. *Vider* can mean both "again" and "against"—referring, that is, to Judaism "growing anew" (from within) or "growing in opposition" (to attacks from without). It is a fact of life for Der Nister that people adhere to political causes with ardor comparable to the feelings animating their religious convictions. The Hidden One leaves us guessing as to his characters' motivations. Do they have "this world" or "that world" in mind?

Like a reader of the Torah or a political conspirator, Der Nister is attentive to hidden correspondences. His stories spin a web of intrigue in which Hasidism, Jewish political activism, and Nazi programs of extermination are fatefully conjoined. Although the tales can be read on their own, they are interrelated. For example, the bookish Meylekh Magnus of the first story resembles the unnamed "acquaintance" in the final tale; in terms of his studiousness, he also reflects Heshl Ansheles in the fourth story and Moishke in the narrative that gives the collection its name. The young woman whose torture and execution is recorded by the heroine of "Flora" calls to mind Boris Grosbaytl's daughter in "Meylekh Magnus." "Rive Yosl Buntsies" features a strong-willed protagonist, but the luckless girls the title character takes in and raises evoke the orphan Elke in "Regrowth." Rive's anonymous husband, who has immersed himself in holy books to the point of losing all personality, mirrors images of men in other tales, who often dissolve into their learned pursuits (until it is too late). The often blurry reflections that abound in the tales point toward a secret design underlying events in our fractured world.

Aesthetics and Ethics

Early stories by Der Nister have fruitfully been examined in terms of Symbolism, the fin de siècle project that sought, by crafting formally perfect works, to efface language and thereby gesture toward an ineffable truth.[10] His later writings lend themselves to interpretation along these lines, too.[11] Yet Symbolism, its spiritual striving notwithstanding, is above all a contemplative pursuit that exalts art.[12] The tales in *Regrowth* draw on other sources of luminescence. Der Nister's love of paradox creates an enigmatic literary object whose most uncanny feature, perhaps, is its adequation to both historical fact and religious truth—even if an impasse results in either case.[13] Der Nister engineers an immersive experience for his readers, who confront the same problems of interpretation and decision as the tales' heroes. A brief discussion of "Flora" will illustrate Der Nister's artistry and the line of moral questioning his tales pursue.

On the surface, "Flora" is simple enough. When events begin, the heroine has just graduated from school and stands at the threshold of adulthood. Her father, a respected man in an unspecified "Polish-Jewish city," uneasily serves as "the fully authorized head of the Jewish Council, which later was put to such shame and so greatly maligned that its name should not be mentioned." The father's inability to help his fellow Jews prompts him, in a crisis of conscience, to resign from office, whereupon he is taken into custody by the Germans. Flora attempts to intercede on her father's behalf, but she is soon left an orphan. She suffers the indignities endured by all her coreligionists until a member of the underground recruits her to join him and his comrades-in-arms. After escaping to a partisan encampment in the woods, Flora participates in their activities until the war ends. The young woman's courage is then honored by the Soviet government.

How the story unfolds is considerably less straightforward. Contravening the common practice in Yiddish literature of presenting the narrative as if it were an oral performance, Der Nister foregrounds the written source of the tale.[14] Most of the text is made up of the heroine's diary entries. Toward the end, this stream of information ceases abruptly and an unnamed "professional" continues in the third person, "on the authority of oral reports he received after making her acquaintance." At first glance, it appears that Flora herself vouchsafes the facts presented: what does not come verbatim from her diary still connects to her directly, for the text's redactor has met her personally. But who, exactly, is this professional? We never find out. The sudden appearance of another voice besides Flora's, two thirds of the way through the text, has an unsettling quality, especially in view of the fact that it coincides with the section dealing with partisan intrigue and the transition from Nazi occupation to Soviet rule. In this light, the authenticity of Flora's preceding diary entries becomes suspect: what has been altered or omitted in what we read?

"Flora," the name of a character, is also the title of the story. This work is in turn composed of varied strands of discourse ultimately held together by an unnamed and evanescent narrative instance—the professional. (At another remove, The Hidden One—Der Nister "himself"—occupies an analogous position of mysterious presence.) Matters are further complicated inasmuch as the name "Flora" plays an indeterminate role within the tale. Since the young woman's diary entries are written in the first person, only an anonymous *I* "speaks." Is "Flora" the protagonist's true name? It could just as well be a code word meant to conceal who she really is. "Flora," which means "flower," is perhaps an honorific title conferred upon a party who has taken up arms to fight the enemy. In this case, her name signifies the bloom of youth. But even so, matters are uncertain. Does the onomastic decoration—which might be glossed as "prize of young womanhood"—mean that she has served the cause of now-victorious communism, or has she received the distinction because she embodies the enduring Jewish spirit? The possibilities are not mutually exclusive.

Whether her name is authentic or not, Flora's actions reverse the traditional values it implies, according to which women and girls are most pleasing when they grow in a domestic garden. This flower, we learn, has thorns. At the beginning, the reader encounters Flora as someone who has consigned her eloquence to a diary—a modest feminine space from which it need not sound forth again. By the end, its report is audible. As the professional informs us, the girl has come to trade her *bukh* for a *biks*—that is, a book for a gun. Her actions have spoken for her.

What is the relationship between word and deed in a world—and a text—rife with confusion? The riddling nature of the tale in general captures the dilemma the heroine confronts in particular. The story points toward what historical events might mean *sub specie aeternitatis*. It thereby transforms insult, injury, and loss into signs of potential vindication, if not redemption. The confusion depicted in "Flora" is not just aesthetic in nature but also ethical. The story places the reader before a situation full of ambiguous and deceptive appearances, and it challenges him or her to exercise what, in a philosophical idiom, is called the faculty of judgment. In other words, the reader finds himself or herself in a position not unlike the one faced by the heroine, who must allow faith and reason (which do not always act in concert) to guide her through a maze of peril and intrigue.

"Flora" begins with a formulation that is repeated again and again throughout the heroine's diary: "Day. . . . Month. . . . Year. . . ." Besides marking the passing of time, the words evoke a spectral, blank space, in which events cannot be discerned in specific dimensions or precisely located chronologically. Flora's diary entries shine forth against an immense backdrop of darkness. This darkness is history—always an unclear element but especially so in the time of National Socialism. Flora punctuates the days, months, and years with repeated addresses to her father. These cries, like everything else in her journal, verge on silence inasmuch as they occur in a private document. Furthermore, they are addressed to a man who, we soon learn, has died.

The first image we have of Flora, then, is in silhouette. Consigned almost to nonexistence, she calls mutely upon her departed father, himself now nothing more than a shade. Yet the heroine's silence is also given voice, and her father's absence becomes a virtual presence. Flora's diary calls forth her *tate* from oblivion. The (fictional) publication of the journal means that her words can be "heard" by others; her silence is thereby canceled and transformed into speech.

The change from absence to presence and the attendant transference of strength from generation to generation occur by circuitous means. Flora begins her journal—or the part presented to the reader, at any rate—with a recollection of the ball celebrating her graduation from school. In the scene she calls to mind, her father assumes a retiring position: "I saw that I had been a success with everyone who had watched me dance—and also with you—yes, you, who, as if afraid of bad luck, didn't want to look at me. . . ." When all eyes rest upon the dancing girl, her father superstitiously averts his gaze, as if to signify retreat from his daughter's life. But just after this same dance, Flora receives a token from her father. He tells her that it is "an heirloom, from my grandmother, and back to times I no longer recall. . . ." The ring, which symbolizes the mysterious rebirth of the family in succeeding generations, represents continuity, in contrast to the separation otherwise emphasized.

All events recounted in "Flora" transpire on two planes: the first is the level of everyday life in occupied eastern Europe; the second occurs in a distant yet proximate dimension and partakes of the ageless, enduring life of a family and a people. Flora continues her recollection of her father's speech: "'Thereby,' you continued, your voice sounding a little festive, 'I betroth you, so to speak, to your past. To the future, child, another man will betroth you.'" The ring the father gives his daughter signifies their parting: she is now a young woman, ready to leave his house—as we subsequently learn, for marriage to the cause of resistance and revolution.

The sequence of events is less important than the causality behind them, which is never explained. Are they chance or providence, matters of character and decision or the workings of a higher power? Der Nister conceals the identity of the tale's editor, just as he avoids representing the psychology of Flora. She is a loving daughter and a courageous individual, but otherwise we know little about her. Only at the end of the journal section does she offer a few words about herself, and these comments only heighten the mystery of her personality.

What motivates Flora, this embodiment of defiance and obedience? Her diary contains no soul-searching—at least not in the common sense. Instead, it offers an apology before an eternal judge. Flora appeals not just to her departed, earthly father but to a heavenly father as well. Events unfold against a backdrop that is not wholly of this world, where their deeper— or, if one prefers, higher—meaning truly lies.

One symbol pointing toward this hidden dimension can be seen in recurring images of hands extended to help and harm. When Flora goes to plead for her father—an occurrence that, incidentally, implies a reversal of the standard roles of parent and child—she takes a small but important item with her: "Unknowingly—even to myself—I didn't neglect to bring your present along: a little something, it seems, to serve as protection. (And also with the underlying idea that I would look good. . . .)" In strictly material terms, the ring ornaments Flora and makes her more attractive. However, the ring is also a talisman, a conduit of protection that connects Flora to her father and, through him, to preceding generations.

The German men the heroine encounters address her indecently and touch her in an unseemly fashion. The first, a severe Prussian aristocrat, speaks condescendingly to Flora "like an adult deigning to speak in language comprehensible to a child." This patronizing discourse is accompanied by a gesture of subtle aggression that parodies a father's warmth: "In so doing, he laid a hand on my shoulder." The second man—who is a drunkard, sings lewd songs, and has the habit of whipping noncompliant workers—adds an unwelcome element to the treatment he deals out to Flora:

> But on that day, he had a cruel heart and watched me
> with ill intent—to see whether I was doing my work well
> or not. And suddenly he started to grab me, scream at
> me, and strike me—which he deliberately didn't do with
> the whip but his hands.

Here, we encounter a scene resembling domestic abuse, with an inebriated father striking his child for no apparent reason; there is also an intimation of further impropriety, as Flora writes that she was "touched in . . . a disgraceful manner."

In a perverse twist wholly in keeping with the narrative's many turns, Flora's verbal counterattack produces a smile on the German's lips like "a father's for a dearly beloved child." The drunkard's coarseness presents the opposite picture of the Prussian's false solicitude, but for this reason, their actions form a symbolic unit. Moreover, Flora's tongue-lashing of the overseer brings her to the attention of the underground. The agent who approaches her is a man she admits she could have fallen in love with and married—that is, one to whom she might have "given her hand." Thus, Flora's father's words to his daughter as he places a ring on her finger at the beginning go into fulfillment, if in an unexpected way. The cycle of events reveals the promise of continuity that the father gives his daughter to be true.

The chain of familial and ancestral unity is marked by violence, and by no means is Flora only the victim of others' strong-arm tactics. As the narrative closes, the same young woman who started out as a compliant daughter has become an outlaw. While there can be little objection to her fight for survival, Flora has gone against the role that her father—to say nothing of the community and tradition he represents—foresaw for her. It is hardly proper for a young lady to say and do what Flora has said and done.

In the partisan ranks, Flora's underground contact informs her, lurks a traitor—a person held in high esteem who, unfortunately, has "turned from a leader into one misled." For the good of the group and the cause they pursue—the defeat of the Nazis and, thus, the universal benefit of Jews and righteous Gentiles—Flora seduces the individual who has already been seduced by his desire for personal gain. She delivers him, along with secret directives concealed in her clothing, to those who will kill him. This abandonment of standard ethical practice has made her participate in the death of another, who "receive[s], from the appropriate hands, his due. . . ."

The actions that Flora performs raise questions. Under other circumstances, they would elicit unequivocal condemnation. Even in a state of exception—war and genocide—they are unacceptable to inflexible minds and rigid systems of morality. The "big question" is an ethical one: what is the justification for Flora's break with the role that tradition, embodied first and foremost by her beloved father, has assigned her?

An Unwelcome Revelation?

The sole work by Der Nister that an English-speaking audience is likely to have encountered is *The Family Mashber*.[15] Ruth Wisse, in *The Modern Jewish Canon*, calls the novel "one of the masterpieces of Soviet fiction,"[16] and indeed it is. In its extant state, this unfinished magnum opus chronicles the life of a Jewish family in nineteenth-century Ukraine. Leonard Wolf, its translator, observes that the novel may be likened to Dostoevsky's *Brothers Karamazov* or Thomas Mann's *Buddenbrooks* in its use of a family's triumphs and travails to offer the portrait of an age.[17] *The Family Mashber* hardly represents life as an idyll, and Der Nister often assumes a very uncharitable stance toward the kinds of characters that other authors (e.g., the better-known Isaac Bashevis Singer) treat more generously. However, aspects of the novel may well suit a certain wistful nostalgia shared by many American readers.[18]

But on the whole, Der Nister is a willfully difficult author, contrarian and combative despite (or perhaps because of) his deep humanity. Accordingly, *Regrowth* runs counter to conventional representations of Jewish life under occupation. While Der Nister acknowledges—and stresses—the monstrousness of Nazi crimes, he refuses to write stories with a clearly delineated separation between perpetrators and victims within the affected communities. As we have seen, "Flora" offers a sympathetic portrayal of a member of the Jewish Council (the heroine's father)—in other words, the kind of figure many other writers denounce as a collaborator, pure and simple. Much of the story is told by the man's daughter, who naturally wishes to believe the best of her *tate*. However, other tales also affirm that parties in this position could, in fact, help their fellow Jews.[19] Another, equally delicate subject is Der Nister's frank acknowledgment of Jewish participation in acts of violence. Der Nister's characters are crafty and use force when necessary. Finally, and perhaps most upsetting to received ideas, is the fact that the figures in *Regrowth* are almost all represented as bearing some measure of responsibility for what happens to them and their loved ones.

Regrowth is a synoptic presentation of Jewish character types from eastern Europe in the early to mid-twentieth century. The narratives concern specific individuals in specific situations, yet their actions and the occurrences to which they respond are universal in scope. "Rive Yosl Buntsies" offers a vivid portrait of a person who already in her own time belongs to another age.

> Even in a little, antiquated, piously preserved Jewish-Polish shtetl, she was a marvel—a kind of historical relic, to be displayed in a museum.
> . . .
> She was also never seen alone but always with a grown-up girl—an orphan, whom she had brought up and raised.
> . . .
> No wedding took place in town at which Rive wasn't the first to wish the couple well. Nor was there a bris at which she wasn't the godmother.
> . . .
> Besides . . . her collections on behalf of the community's poor . . . she performed another good work: attending, in an authentically Jewish way, to a poor man's corpse—one without children or relatives, for example, a luckless vagrant whose years had expired there in the town—someone to whom, except for her, Rive, no one would show any kindness.

Rive is always there in the community, at occasions of birth, marriage, and death. She seems eternal, embodying the moral duties that bind villagers together. She gruffly demands alms for the poor and boldly confronts the wealthy when they are not forthcoming. She performs good deeds almost despite herself—because it is simply "what must be done."

Rive's righteous actions reveal the shortcomings of other members of the community. Her good works implicitly indict her fellow villagers, who have strayed from the path of true religion. Rive belongs to another age, but it is perhaps the others whose lives are out of joint.

At the same time, Der Nister suggests that the heroine's exemplary virtue can be explained in a different way—one that does not involve a conscious moral decision on her part. The prominent position that Rive occupies is also due to her father. Although he died long ago, his presence looms large.

> Yosl Buntsies [had been] of the same height and build as his daughter, Rive: a real powerhouse. He held a solid position and had influence among the town's inhabitants and in the community. Understandably, among the landholders, his standing was rather more modest; he had to present himself to them in a more subdued manner—with less pride and self-confidence. But he felt no inferiority, no dependency.

Physically, Rive is the very image of her father, and she is also like him in terms of character, for they are both strong-willed, resolute people. Without her father "behind her," Rive would not have as easy a time performing her mitzvoth. Yet she is also her father's opposite: instead of trading with Gentile landlords and accumulating personal wealth, she restricts her activities to the Jewish community and distributes money to its less-fortunate members. Is it character or destiny that makes Rive who she is?

Rive's unusual sense of duty to her fellow Jews is possibly the result of a kind of accident. When Rive was young, her father found a seemingly perfect match for his daughter, but the marriage failed to turn out as it was supposed to. The heroine's husband (who is also long dead when the story takes place) was a complete nonentity—a man so wholly given over to study that even in life he barely existed at all.

The husband, who is not even named, is a caricature of the learning prized by Jewish tradition:

> Yosl . . . thanked God again that he had given his
> daughter to the man he wanted. He could not have
> sought a greater joy than that: a son-in-law—a compliant
> one—an honor and a crown in *this* world and one
> deserving of *that* one. As soon as he had procured him,
> Yosl started to think how to reward the husband, and he
> came upon the thought that it would be best if . . . he saw
> to it that the other man, his son-in-law—the instrument
> of his will, the dutiful student and plaything—should,
> after his death, be spared the need to do what he, Yosl,
> had done—that is, trade with nobles, which would
> disturb his vocation.

Yosl Buntsies found a husband for his daughter who would "make up" for his excessive worldliness by devoting himself entirely to spiritual matters. However, the man he chose deprived his daughter of the blessings of a family and home life. He did not belong to "this world" enough.

Der Nister's presentation of the father and the husband implies that there is such a thing as excessive adherence to the rules. Rive, we are told, waited on her husband hand and foot without a single complaint. Only after his death did she become the contrary of everything she had been while still under male protection. Now, Rive dares to confront the village's most prosperous citizens as if she stood above them, and even to defy rabbinical authority. Is it possible that she might have taken things too far?

What really motivates Rive? Der Nister never tells. The story culminates in a scene that underscores the mystery by shifting the question away from the high-spirited heroine to the community to which she belongs. The German invaders arrive, and they arrange for the village's populace to be liquidated. The women are separated from the men and marched off—late on a Friday afternoon, no less. At the head of the column, towering above the others, strides Rive. She proudly bears the candlesticks her father gave to her husband for his Torah study, which, after the latter's death, she would light on the Sabbath and for burial ceremonies.

> She lifted both hands to her eyes and stood upright for a while—not speaking and not moving—in front of the two burning candles, which flamed palely in the mild air of the summer evening, in view of the great field extending to both sides, and in view, also, of the setting sun far to the west. In a louder voice, so that all would hear, she pronounced the Sabbath blessing. . . .

Certain of her righteousness, Rive marches the women off to death, and she even provides a benediction.

It is easy to read the scene simply as an outrage committed by godless invaders. However, Der Nister stresses that the defiantly compliant Rive Yosl Buntsies is easily snuffed out, like her candles (which a German soldier urinates on after the women have all been shot). The author leaves it to the reader to decide whether the sublime light of Jewish religion can shine forth again—and whether the heroine, who has led the women to their doom, acted wisely in her fatalistic contempt for the enemy.

Guarded Hope

"Rive" is fraught with the ambiguity that is the hallmark of Der Nister's view of the past, present, and future. The author draws on real-life ambivalence, which his narrative technique develops further. "Regrowth," the story that gives the collection its title, provides a pendant to "Rive" and deepens the mystery by leading to new but adjacent—and equally enigmatic—terrain. Again, Der Nister depicts an interrupted tradition. As in "Rive," an ominous break with true Judaism has occurred before the Nazis ever set foot on the soil of eastern Europe.

In contrast to the closely knit shtetl environment of "Rive," the setting of "Regrowth" is one of urban assimilation. The story features two protagonists. This doubling underscores the separation that can dominate urban existence. The main characters, despite their physical proximity, lead lives of isolation:

> We are talking, here, about two half families—a man
> without a wife, and a wife without a man—who lived,
> with facing doors, on the same floor of a single building
> in a big Soviet city. . . . One of them was Dr. Zemelman.
> He was an older, ill-tempered surgeon—the silent type,
> inclined to solitude; he was someone with a name in his
> field, both in the city and even throughout the land. . . .
> And on the other hand, there was Mrs. Zayets—a well-
> known pedagogue. . . .

Dr. Zemelman and Mrs. Zayets have long "grown estranged from their Jewish origins and all that occurred in the thickets of their people." They are professionals who are well respected by their non-Jewish, Russian countrymen and countrywomen. However, they seem to share as little with the latter as they do with their forgotten Jewish brethren.

Dr. Zemelman and Mrs. Zayets are both single parents. Der Nister does not say why—whether they are divorced, whether their respective spouses have died, or if they never even married. The fractured families underscore modern alienation, but this shared condition also represents a point that the doctor and the pedagogue have in common. Thus, the incomplete state of their households also promises to bring them together:

> Both of them had only children. Dr. Zemelman had a son, and Mrs. Zayets had a daughter. The children were even of the same age.
>
> . . .
>
> Whenever the parents had time, they stealthily took a look at the relationship between the adolescents, whose respective merits were evident. Mrs. Zayets's daughter pleased the elderly, grumpy surgeon, who peered over his glasses and saw that it seemed she had been made for his son. And the same was true on the other side. Mrs. Zayets looked at the boy who seemed destined for her daughter. . . .
> If things had continued in this way, sooner or later there would have occurred what happens in situations like that: a joining of both half families, whose two children would complete and unite them, to the delight and happiness of their parents.

Like "Rive," "Regrowth" unfolds against the backdrop of shared life and community that have been put on hold.

Instead of the promise going into fulfillment (and thereby realizing a mythical perfection), history intervenes. The Nazis, who have already invaded Poland, attack the Soviet Union. The young adults both volunteer to help in the war effort, the boy as a soldier, the girl as a nurse. They are soon killed. It seems a greater misfortune for their parents, left alone in their apartments in a big-city Soviet high-rise, cannot be imagined. Yet this tragedy is but a small part of universal catastrophe affecting the Jewish populace as a whole. The troubles of the lonely "couple" sitting apart in their facing apartments seem relatively small, if one permits oneself such an ungenerous reflection—and Der Nister does—compared to the millions of people faced with complete destruction.

The principle of symmetry commanding the fiction leads the two "orphaned" parents each to adopt a child. Is this decision the result of personal grief—the desire to fill a void—or does it follow from a nobler sense of responsibility to one's people? The tale suggests both possibilities. Moreover, the parents' actions mirror those of their children, who respond immediately to the outbreak of war by placing their lives in the service of the greater good. Inasmuch as Dr. Zemelman and Mrs. Zayets have restricted their activities to a narrow professional sphere—whereas it is the son and the daughter who try to do something in the time of universal catastrophe—the adults may be seen to follow their children's example. It is almost as if the traditional hierarchy of the family has been reversed: son and daughter show the way to mother and father.

After the deaths of their biological children, Dr. Zemelman and Mrs. Zayets resolve to take in others, which entails more than they expected.

> They decided that soon, when they had a free day,
> they would go off to the appropriate institutions . . .
> and announce that they . . . were ready to care for and
> privately accommodate a pair. . . . Dr. Zemelman wanted
> a boy, who would fit in better with him, a man. And Mrs.
> Zayets wanted a girl. Soon—after a little bit of time—
> their wish was granted. . . .

The wards of Dr. Zemelman and Mrs. Zayets have witnessed what the adults have not. Despite their tender age (the boy is "fourteen or fifteen" and the girl is "a little younger"), they have firsthand experience of what their guardians can know only indirectly: they are "not ordinary children but children of action, . . . children who [have] passed through the smoke and fire—in a word: partisan children." Again, Der Nister seemingly places youth in a position superior to age. But at the same time, the narrative does not permit any judgments. Just as no one would dare openly declare that the doctor's and the teacher's motivations are really selfish, one cannot maintain that children really know more than the intellectually distinguished adults.

The boy, who is called Moishke, possesses rare gifts:

> [He] . . . set time aside to record all the events where he had been present as a witness, which he recalled down to the smallest detail . . . a remembrance for the ages. . . . A rare gift of memory aided him—a sharp, youthful eye, and the subtle ability to express what he meant in clear, smooth, and easily understood language.

On the other hand, the girl, who is named Elke, does not show the same promise.

> [She] had grown a little short for her years, and, as it happened, she was a little more scattered than one ought to be—this was from having survived the war, which didn't help the receptivity of her brains. . . .

Once again, Der Nister deviates from the symmetry he has set up by introducing details that run counter to the regularity of his story's design. One child is providentially talented, but the other, providing a symbolic counterweight, is mentally slow. The author establishes parallels only to follow one part as it veers off on a tangent and comes to run along another axis.

Witnessing his ward's preternatural qualities, Dr. Zemelman begins having nighttime visions.

> [He dreamed he saw Moishke] together with *that* person, the one with the half-shortened, black mustache, and the appearance of a small-time criminal. . . . He stands, waits, and looks around, until a great mass of condemned people appear before him—walking mechanically and driven to a ditch. . . . He swings [a] club, striking

someone in the group; he draws back and looks, with
satisfaction, at how the man twitches, casts about, and
chokes in distress. Thus he proceeds with one, to his
delight, and then another. . . . And there, all of a sudden,
Dr. Zemelman sees his ward, his Moishke. . . . Moishke
turns into Moses—as the famous medieval master
shaped him out of stone (with the mighty, human-divine
countenance of an ancient lawgiver, a long, flowing
beard, down to his knees, and darting rays from his
brow . . .). And Dr. Zemelman sees how one of the rays
falls upon the face of the [other], who is burned and
consumed. . . .

Is this dream a psychological projection or divine revelation?
Der Nister does not reveal the answer. In a sense, it does not
matter. In either case, the boy's character and intelligence beyond his years are truly like those of the lawgiver whose name
he shares—a name synonymous with the Jewish religion.

What is the future of the Jewish people? Der Nister does
not say.

Once, [in a dream, Dr. Zemelman] saw [Moishke] with
his son. The latter—in military dress and with a rifle, it
seemed. And Moishke—with a pen on his ear. The first
youth, it appeared, was not jealous of the second. . . .
On the contrary: he extends his hand fraternally and
expresses the wish that the other do with the pen—that
is, by words—what *he* did through action.

The realism behind the dream vision is that the Book of Life
is written not just in ink but also in blood. Survival can often
be assured only through combat. However, if the written word
can be a weapon, then it is not always necessary to take up
arms literally. That is, by using the pen as a sword, one can

forgo a nonmetaphorical blade and avoid the taking of life. Writing offers hope, if only by harnessing violence.

Open Endings

Der Nister's characters, even when they stray from conventional roles and tradition, cleave to the rules they seem to reject. A higher law governs exceptions as well as norms. In this context, it is important to note the handful of data we have about the author, for it reveals a close tie between the literary dynamics of *Regrowth* and the enigmatic writer's biography. This is not to say that the stories are an immediate reflection of his personal experiences; they are, however, an integral part of his life, in which, as in his writings, fact and fiction are indissolubly fused.

The name "Der Nister" is itself part of the author's oeuvre— a creation of Pinhas Kahanovitch, who presented himself to the public under an assumed identity. He is, of course, by no means the only writer to have done so, but in his case there are reasons that connect directly with the themes and modes of characterization one finds in his tales. In 1905, Kahanovitch left his native Berdichev for Zhitomir, near Kiev. In order to escape military service, he lived under an assumed name. This move into anonymity coincided with the beginning of his literary career and adoption of the alias Der Nister. Delphine Bechtel, the author of an important study of Der Nister, observes that "in Hebrew, the word *nistar* is closely associated with the mystic interpretation of the Scriptures."[20] In kabbalistic tradition, *nistar* is the word for the concealed signification of the Torah, discernible only to the few. "According to Gershom Scholem," Bechtel continues, "the word *nistar* can also apply to a *lamed-vovnik*, one of the 36 hidden just men on whom rests the fate of the world. These unrecognized saints . . . often assume the most humble appearances as peasants, artisans, [and] beggars."[21] Der Nister's pseudonym, then, makes the author himself a part of the fictions he writes—a figure whose true purposes one may only guess at.

The simultaneously hidden and revealed presence of the author in *Regrowth* is a topic that exceeds the scope of what can be addressed here. However, it is worth noting that the stories that open and close the collection both contain strong elements of self-portraiture.

The first, "Meylekh Magnus," recounts the life of an austere writer who, as a young man, is unconditionally devoted to revolutionary causes. After two unhappy love affairs—the first with a flighty girl named Feygele ("little bird") and the second with another one named Bloymke (which means "little flower" and also hints at a fickle nature)—he withdraws from the Jewish community altogether, until a wealthy acquaintance (who cannot seem to decide between assimilation and staying true to his roots) offers financial assistance. In a reversal of fortune, Meylekh Magnus becomes a noted scholar of Yiddish and Jewish tradition. The Nazis arrive and all is lost, except for what he has written in the bunker that his wealthy friend, tellingly named Boris Grosbaytl (Boris Moneybags), has secretly had built. From enigmatic fragments, which are signed with a wide array of pseudonyms, the narrator claims to have reconstructed the story one reads. These aliases point toward the man who stands behind them, half hidden and half revealed.

The last tale in *Regrowth*, "An Acquaintance of Mine," is a variant on the theme. The story begins,

> He wasn't old at all yet—just twenty-five or twenty-six—
> when I got to know him in a former Russian county seat
> in the southwest—a pretty provincial one (despite its
> honorable administrative functions); a town with narrow,

winding streets, full of orchards and gardens, with quiet
boulevards for retired officials and military men strolling
between the high poplars—leafy in the summer and
barren in winter—with loud-screeching cranes' nests in
one season and empty ones during the other. . . . There,
we met. He was already a known personality in the very
brainy Hebrew literature of the time—in which he had
acquired a solid reputation the moment he set foot there.
I was still a youth.

The "acquaintance" is Der Nister himself. The Ukrainian landscape where he was born, the first literary efforts in Hebrew,
as well as numerous details to be gleaned from the rest of the
narrative, all match up with the biography of our author. Yet
even so, the "I" who speaks in the tale—that is, the party other
than the acquaintance—is the author, too. Here, Pinhas Kahanovitch describes how he met himself as a stranger, "The Hidden One"; the years spent in the company of this secret sharer
lead to as many questions as answers.

By virtue of its hermetic style, *Regrowth* invites the reader's active participation in discerning hidden correspondences and
layers of meaning. The present appears in light of the past, and
the past in light of the present. Ancient and modern meet in a
strange dimension where different ways of handling the troubles that beset Jews (and humanity in general) are explored.
In this conjectural realm, the stories, while remaining firmly
anchored in a twentieth-century, eastern European context,
assume a timeless, archetypal quality. Thus, they bear more
than a passing resemblance to biblical narratives, which, by
recording events in a distanced manner, call for commentary
and discussion instead of being overtly didactic.[22] Der Nister's
tales are a challenge, defying the reader to find his or her way
through a fictional universe where the proper understanding

of events and an ethical course of action lie hidden—every bit as difficult to resolve as they are in the real world.

Notes

1. For an overview, see Eli Barnavi, *A Historical Atlas of the Jewish People: From the Time of the Patriarchs to the Present* (New York: Schocken, 1994).

2. For details of personal and "cultural" biography, see Delphine Bechtel, *Der Nister's Work, 1907–1929: A Study of a Yiddish Symbolist* (New York: Lang, 1990), 1–26.

3. Jean Baumgarten, *La naissance du hassidisme: Mystique, rituel et société (XVIIe–XIXe siècle)* (Paris: Albin Michel, 2006).

4. Arthur Green, "Teachings of the Hasidic Masters," in *Back to the Sources: Reading the Classic Jewish Texts,* ed. Barry W. Holtz (New York: Summit, 1984), 362.

5. The classic study of this topic is Franco Venturi, *Roots of Revolution: A History of the Populist and Socialist Movements in Nineteenth Century Russia,* trans. Francis Haskell (New York: Grosset and Dunlap, 1952).

6. Benjamin Nathans, *Beyond the Pale: The Jewish Encounter with Late Imperial Russia* (Berkeley: University of California Press, 2002).

7. Norman Cohn, in *Warrant for Genocide: The Myth of the Jewish World Conspiracy and the Protocols of the Elders of Zion* (London: Serif, 1996), 25–65, presents a masterly overview of the political uses of antisemitism in a comparative framework.

8. Ezra Mendelsohn, *Class Struggle in the Pale: The Formative Years of the Jewish Workers' Movement in Tsarist Russia* (Cambridge: Cambridge University Press, 1970); Zvi Y. Gitelman, *A Century of Ambivalence: The Jews of Russia and the Soviet Union, 1881 to the Present* (Bloomington: Indiana University Press, 2001); on Soviet cultural policy and state promotion of Yiddish, see David Shneer, *Yiddish and the Creation of Soviet Jewish Culture, 1918–1930* (Cambridge: Cambridge University Press, 2004).

9. An overview of the literary and political tendencies in Kiev and other centers of Jewish letters can be found in Irving Howe and Eliezer Greenberg, *Ashes Out of Hope: Fiction by Soviet-Yiddish Writers* (New York: Schocken, 1978), 1–21.

10. Bechtel, *Der Nister's Work,* 34–47.

11. In a letter to his brother in 1935, Der Nister addressed the fundamental conflict he faced in Stalin's Russia: "Symbolism has no place in the Soviet Union and, as you know, I have always been a Symbolist. It is not possible for someone like myself who has struggled to perfect my . . . style of writing to turn . . . to realism" (Khone Shmeruk, *Der Nister: Hanazir v'Hadgadyo* [Jerusalem: Mosad Bialik, 1963], 12; cited in Leonard Wolf, "Translator's Introduction," *The Family Mashber* [New York: New York Review of Books, 2008]).

12. Paul Bénichou, in *Selon Mallarmé* (Paris: Gallimard, 1995), examines the exemplary Symbolist and his concerns.

13. Der Nister's "Under a Fence"—an earlier story also about a father and daughter—was sharply attacked by Soviet critics for not adhering to the conventions of socialist realism. Lippman Bodoff has highlighted the religious failure implicit in the work: "While Der Nister has redeemed his art, he has not redeemed his Jewish soul. He remains a hidden Jew, a cultural Marrano masquerading . . . like all the other artists in . . . *galut* culture and society" (*The Binding of Isaac, Religious Murders, and Kabbalah: Seeds of Jewish Extremism and Alienation?* [New York: Devora, 2005], 373).

14. This does not prevent him from often adding a quick aside, in the manner of spoken commentary, or, without warning, inserting an unidentified second voice that asks a question. For a discussion of movement between oral and written sources in Hasidic storytelling, see Dan Ben-Amos and Jerome R. Mintz, *In Praise of the Baal Shem Tov: The Earliest Collection of Legends about the Founder of Hasidism* (New York: Schocken, 1984), xxi–xxx.

15. The book first appeared in English translation in 1987.

16. Ruth R. Wisse, *The Modern Jewish Canon: A Journey Through Language and Culture* (Chicago: University of Chicago Press, 2003), 124.

17. Wolf, "Translator's Introduction," 16.

18. Der Nister, rather fancifully depicted, is a character in the recent novel by Dara Horn, *The World to Come* (New York: Norton, 2006).

19. E.g., "Meylekh Magnus."

20. Bechtel, *Der Nister's Work*, 2.

21. Ibid.

22. Among many excellent books on the subject, Robert Alter, *The Art of Biblical Narrative* (New York: Basic Books, 1983), deserves particular mention.